AND THE ANGELS SING

by
J. Madison Davis

THE PERMANENT PRESS
SAG HARBOR, NEW YORK

Copyright © 1996 by J. Madison Davis

Library of Congress Cataloging-in-Publication Data

Davis, J. Madison.
  And the angels sing / by J. Madison Davis.
    p.   cm.
  ISBN 1-877946-70-2
  1. World War, 1939–1945—Fiction. 2. Band musicians—United
States—Fiction. 3. Organized crime—United States—Fiction.
  I. Title.
PS3554.A934636A8 1996
813'.54—dc20   95-19558
                                                         CIP

first edition, 2000

Manufactured in the United States of America

THE PERMANENT PRESS
Noyac Road
Sag Harbor, NY 11963

for M.,
the better angel of my nature

My son, if sinners entice thee, consent thou not.

If they say, *Come with us! Let us lay wait for blood! Let us lurk privily for the innocent without cause! Let us swallow them up alive as the grave, and whole, as those that go down into the pit. We shall all find precious substance, we shall fill our houses with spoil! Cast in thy lot among us! Let us all have one purse!*

My son, walk not thou in the way with them. Refrain thy foot from their path. For their feet run to evil and make haste to shed blood.

Surely in vain the net is spread in the sight of any bird.

And they lay wait for their own blood; they lurk privily for their own lives.

—Proverbs

Part I
The Emerald City

The Lake Shore Limited eased into Cleveland three hours late. Carl Carlson pressed close to the glass and cupped his hands to block the reflection from inside the lounge car. Feathery snow on the adjacent tracks blew upward in the whoosh of the slow moving train, and flakes like pinches of cotton candy swirled around the rail-side lights looping, rising, diving as if the laws of gravity had been suspended. The city lights blurred green: a distant view of Dorothy's Emerald City. A Christmas tree glowed on the side of a skyscraper. It was Carl's birthday, his twenty-third, the most important of his life. Cleveland was dressed up to be his early Christmas present and his birthday cake and all he had to do was get there, dammit, get there and pick it up.

"Raise a buck," said Myron Rush. The trombonist's reflection moved sharply as he shoved another match into the center of the table across the aisle.

The train passed under a wide bridge and the Emerald City blinked off as if it never existed. Carl's mouth went dry and he checked his watch. "Come on," he muttered to himself. "Come on."

Natalie Bixby, the band's torch singer, had leaned against the door, hip jutting. Draped over the back of her neck was the fox stole given to her by Giorgio Macchianti, her current boyfriend. Georgy Mack knew a lot of ways to get rid of a husband—of anybody for that matter—so Myron, her second, would soon be pleading guilty to adultery or cruelty or whatever Natalie picked out when she got around to filing. The sax man, Lou Epstein, always said a woman like her was a waste on a guy like Myron. She needed a kneebreaker like Georgy just to keep her from biting off the fly buttons of every man in a mile. As the train rocked, the preserved and flattened fox faces on her stole swung at the ends of her breasts. The light in the foxes' glass eyes shifted suspiciously from side to side.

"Myron's bluffing again," she said. "He always bluffs. That's how we got married." The band members laughed.

"Who asked you?" said Myron, holding his cards closer to his blue vest. He glanced at Ted Clough. The big drummer had laid his cards face down and covered them with his hairy hands. When Ted performed, he loomed over his drums like King Kong, yet he was quick with the sticks and delicate as a locket painter with the brush.

Myron thrust his ferret face at Ted. "You fool enough to believe her?"

"She oughtta know ya!" yelled Buzz Bixby from the bar. Lou Epstein, guffawed—too loud, as usual—and coughed his cigarette in a high arc into the aisle. Two other band members scrambled for it on their knees, but the black bartender stepped between them and nimbly plucked the burning cigarette from under the open lid of Mack Mintner's trumpet case.

"I'll get you a fresh one, sir," said the porter.

Epstein tried to say no, but was still red-faced and coughing. He reached for his cigarette, but the porter was gone.

"We'll see what she knows!" said Myron, trying to sound authoritative, but only managing squeakiness. He was just another dead fox hanging from Natalie's bust. Carl smiled. The pelt on the left jug kind of looked like Myron. The one on the right was probably her first husband. She pushed her broad hips forward as if her tight skirt concealed a great mouth that was going to swallow every man in the cabin.

Ted shifted his cards around on the table with his thick fingertips.

"Go on, Ted," said Natalie. Her Marlene Dietrich purr was on full. "Take him. I'll front you the buck."

Ted turned his apelike head. His eyes were level with the fingers she had spread across her hip bone. He blinked and slowly raised his eyes one by one up the buttons of her jacket to her face. King Kong's pelt, thought Carl, was about to be collected. 'Twas beauty killed the beast. Ted met her eyes only for an instant, then turned toward Myron.

"Go ahead," sniffed Myron. "Give him the buck! I don't care who I get the money from."

Ted reached for the deck and quickly jammed his cards into it. "Nah," he said. "I fold."

A loud groan came from the band members. Buzz Bixby shook his head.

"Ha!" said Myron. "I bluffed him with a pair of treys!" He held up the cards. "Treys!" Most of the band had turned their backs and headed for the bar. He held them toward Carl. "Three and three."

Carl checked his watch. His big chance was slipping away. "Big pot," he said drily.

"Must be five bucks." Myron counted quickly. "Four and a quarter. Where you guys going? I clean you out?"

"So move next door to Franklin D.," said Natalie. She strode up the aisle, her eyebrows arched as if she'd accidentally found herself in some Hooverville where nobody had bathed for six months.

Myron, who didn't seem to know that Natalie had plucked his victory off the end of his long nose, shouted, "Hey, any other suckers? I'm hot tonight!" When no one answered, he shoveled his money in his pocket and scurried off to pester Mack Mintner, the only one who would put up with him. Mack was red-eyed, obviously on the reefer and awash in the muggles. "Did you see that, Mack? I took the whole pot!"

"Good job," said Mack hoarsely.

Carl ground his teeth. "This train is creeping!"

"Don't worry, kid," said Ted, brushing cigarette ash from the table. "You'll get your shot. Maybe not tonight, but some day."

"An hour ago the conductor said forty minutes." Carl leaned against the glass. "You can see the glow. The city's right there. Maybe if we just got off . . ."

"If it's snowing that bad, maybe we won't be able to get to Swing Land. What's more important, maybe nobody can get to us. Maybe there's nobody to play for."

Carl hadn't thought of that. He combed both sides of his hair with his fingers, then held his palms up and stared at the sheen the Vitalis had left on them. His life was turning into *The Jazz Singer* in reverse. His father was right in this version. There wasn't going to be any big end scene where the old man forgave his son and saw that he was a big success. The old man was already dead, and Carl wasn't going to be a success. Carl Carlson, the Carolina Crooner: what a joke!

Myron was back. "So what were you holding, Clough? Catch you with a full house? Huh?"

"Why don't you scram?" said Carl.

Ted shifted in his seat. "You had me, Myron. I was just bluffing, too."

"No kidding?" Myron scurried towards the bar to tell anyone who would listen. Mack was Myron's victim again. Lou Epstein was roaring with laughter at something risqué Natalie had said and nearly choked on his rye. Some band, thought Carl. Some band.

Ted put the playing cards back in the burled wooden tray the porter had provided. He tapped them straight with the tips of his fingers, then crossed his arms and rested hunched on his elbows.

"You threw the game," Carl suddenly said.

"Huh?"

"You knew you had him beat but you folded."

"You're nuts."

There was a pause. Natalie finished her story. "Goodness," she said languorously, "had *nothing* to do with it!"

Everyone laughed. Epstein coughed again. "We saw that one together!" said Buzz. "We sneaked in—At *our age* we sneaked in so mama wouldn't see us, and then who's in the row in front of us? Len Feldman, the oh-so-good yeshiva boy!"

"You put away the cards quick so nobody'd see," Carl said.

Ted was expressionless. "You see my cards?"

"No, I just know it."

"Maybe you ought to shut up, then."

Carl turned back to the window. "No skin off my nose, you want to throw away your money."

Epstein's voice boomed through the lounge. "Barman! Peel me a grape!"

When the eruption of laughter subsided, Carl looked back

at Ted. The big man met his eyes. "So maybe everybody deserves to win once in a while, huh, kid? You, me, any geek."

"I don't know about Myron," Carl finally said.

Ted leaned forward, placed his chin on his forearms, and closed his eyes as if napping. "I only had seventy-five cents in," he said. "It'll keep the poor bastard in the game. This is a long tour."

Carl started to say that Myron acted like he'd won a C-note, but that was exactly the point. The seventy-five cents was kind of a widow's mite, charity precious in its smallness. He also, though, couldn't see how Myron inspired charity in anyone. He had just begun to sense that the big man had done it out of dislike for Natalie when the door opened with a whoosh of cold air.

"Cleveland!" the conductor shouted. "Cleveland! Named for General Moses Cleaveland in the late seventeen hundreds. *Which,* of course, was the last time the Cleveland Indians won a World Series! Cleveland!"

"Thank God!" said Carl.

"God lives in Shaker Heights," said the conductor. "And only in the summer."

The train screeched to a halt. There was a Christmas wreath in the station window and snow rolled back from the train like tumbleweeds in a B-movie. One light passed, then another, then the train stopped. On the platform, a fat man in a heavy coat stood with his back to the wall flanked by two men bobbing on their toes to keep warm.

"Are we on?" asked Mintner.

"We'll know soon enough," said Bixby. "Better hurry up, boys."

Carl, with no instrument to wrestle out of the train, grabbed his carpetbag and was on the platform first. The fat man's companions checked both directions and casually walked up to him.

"Buzz Bixby's Caravan of Swing?"

"Yeah," said Carl.

"I'm Bixby, gentlemen!" shouted Buzz from the steps.

"We know who you are," said the tough guy on the left. "Who's Carl Carlson?"

"It's me. I'm your man."

11

The tough guy seemed unimpressed. "You come with us."
Bixby rushed past them, his hand thrust out. The tough
guys reacted as if Bixby's hand were a weapon and awkwardly
slipped on the wet boards as they rushed to each of the fat
man's shoulders.

"Are we still in business?" said Bixby, his breath steaming.

"I gotta string of cabs," growled the fat man. "When we
get there you got five minutes to get on. If you gotta change,
do it in the cabs. Which of you is the singer?"

"My sister Natalie—" said Bixby.

"That's him," the tough guys said simultaneously.

The fat man brushed Bixby aside and stuck out a wool
gloved hand. "I'm taking care of you, personal," he said. "Ernie Mussolini. What can I tell ya? It was my name before it
was his."

"I—I'm real pleased to meet you Mr. Mussolini, I—"

"C'mon," said the fat man, turning away.

The tough guys cleared a path through the humid,
crowded station. At the exit doors, the fat man paused while
one tough guy rushed ahead to check the street. A policeman
getting a shoeshine tipped his hat and said, "How are you
this evening, Mr. Musso?"

"Fine, Charley. How's the missus? You watch that boy, there.
He gets going he'll set fire to your shoes!"

The black man looked up from his brushes and smiled.
"Thank you, Mr. Mussolini."

"Look at that polish smoke! Charley, you give that boy an
extra quarter, you hear? He's got kids. Christmas is coming."

"You bet," said the cop.

The tough guy opened the door. A huge green Packard
was parked at the curb. The street glistened. Snow was still
falling, but it hadn't accumulated very much.

"Well?" growled the fat man.

Carl climbed in, nearly knocking a doughnut-shaped cushion off the seat. He set his carpetbag at his feet while Mussolini adjusted the cushion under his enormous rump. When
the door closed, the space quickly filled with the thick smell
of a spicy cologne and something medicinal—camphor, perhaps. The two tough guys slid onto the wide front seat beside

12

the driver, whose puffy ear and flattened nose pegged him as a club fighter.

"Nice car, Mr. Mussolini," said Carl.

"Some people call me Musso. The cop back there did it. It don't bother me if it's done with respect. What's in a name, ya know. I don't really want to give up my name, but some people tell me it might be more politic, if ya know what I mean. Whatta you think?"

"Me? Well, I don't know." Carl was trying to think what the man wanted to hear, like at an audition, where you sing what they go for. The fat man eyed him. "I kind of think names don't matter much. It's who you are. My real name's Carl Walthers and—"

"Carl *Maria* Walthers." The chuckle rumbled in Musso's throat like a disintegrating water pump in a Hudson.

"It's from my mother. She died six months after the birth."

Musso patted Carl's knee. "I'm sorry. Maria is a pretty name."

"Well, her name was Mary, but my father—" They were passing a hotel. He hesitated whether he should get into Carl Maria von Weber. He was talking too much.

"That's the Stouffer's. You oughtta get a meal there before you go on to Toledo."

"Buzz thought Carl Carlson was easier to remember."

"The Carolina Crooner." The chuckle rumbled again. The tough guy in the middle of the front seat glanced in the rear-view mirror.

"Maybe I should change it?"

"Naw, naw. We're gonna make it famous. You're gonna sell more records than Glenn Miller and Charlie Spivak combined." He put a heavy arm around Carl's shoulder, pulling him so close that the wet tip of his hat brim touched Carl's forehead. "You're gonna sing good tonight, right?"

"Yes, sir."

"We don't wanna disappoint the Greek, now do we?"

"No, sir."

"I mean, the Greek he likes his stable of singers from the Old Country, mostly, *capiche?* With a mick or two for variety. So he's only doing it as a favor to your man in New York, ya know what I'm saying? If the boys back there say, 'Take a look at this kike,' the Greek will take a look. But he's gotta like you, too, right? Then the sky's the limit. We got nothing against kikes."

"Naw," said one man in the front seat.

Musso lifted his arm and sat back. He readjusted his cushion and winced.

"I'm not a Jew," said Carl.

"Don't get sensitive," mumbled Musso leaning to look at a grocery.

"No. I mean I'm mostly German."

"Yeah? Well, that might be a selling point, too. Your people are on the move. England is about done. I'll mention it to the Greek." He thought for a second. "So whatta you doing with this kike Mr. Buzz Bixby, the former Mr. Benjamin Glock?"

"It's a job."

"Not like Al Jolson, huh? Dixie by way of the clipped dick?" The tough guys laughed.

"No. I'm all here. I'm from Virginia originally."

"Huh." He readjusted his cushion again. "I think this one's going flat. I can't find my asshole for the hemorrhoids. It's like somebody glued on an octopus. All the tentacles hanging down."

The boxer suddenly spoke up. "The Greek calls them asteroids. Get it? *Ass*-teroids!"

"Keep your eye on the road and shut up," said the fat man. "The Greek'll be sorry to laugh at me," he muttered.

"But we're here," said the palooka.

"I can see that, ya punching bag, so shut your yap."

The reflections of Swing Land's neon lights glistened and blinked on the cobblestones: red, blue, green, yellow. He stood beside the car, one foot on the running board, and peered up at the marquee with its flickering white border.

TONIGHT TONIGHT TONIGHT
Buzz Bixby's Cavalcade of Swing
featuring
CARL CARLSON
"The Carolina Crooner"
Natalie Bixby Ted Clough Mack Mintner

His name was at least twice the size of anyone else's. Ted and Mack wouldn't care, but Buzz and Natalie would piss jawbreakers. He pushed it out of his mind. At the door, a man with a tall girl on his arm laughed. Above the marquee a neon man in a top hat tap-danced, the cane under his arm pumping back and forth. The light washed over Carl like a damp breeze rolling ashore at Virginia Beach.

"Don't just stand there," barked Musso. "It's cold. You'll catch a frog."

Carl shook off the spell and almost immediately sensed that he was too calm. When he cooked like a volcano, he always felt fluttery. His stomach would twist until he almost doubled over. The worst cases of nerves dried him out so that his tongue clung to the roof of his mouth. When that happened it took at least two songs to loosen it and the delay had cost him plenty over the last five—no, six—years. He'd lost the big gig on Long Island and a later chance to be in a road show in Boston. Strangely, whenever he'd had the chance to sing past the problem, his voice was better than anybody's. Just when he was about to walk off stage in despair, he seemed to be listening to this strange someone who lived in his throat and had notes and purrs and volume Carl Carlson could only wish for. Was he too calm, tonight? Had he fretted out all his energy as the train crept toward Cleveland? No, he told himself. The lack of nerves was confidence. The Rubicon was awash in neon and, on the other side, Rome lay waiting. All he had to do was march in and put it in his pocket. Bing Crosby, Dick Haymes, Rudy Vallee: forget 'em. Who were they? Mokes who sang before Carl Carlson came along. He twisted his head, straightened his back, and closed the Packard's door diffidently, as if the car were already his own. He could feel himself swagger and he could feel everyone watching him swagger as he rounded the car's rear and stepped onto the curb.

"Come on," said the fat man. "The Greek is already here. I'll introduce you while the band sets up."

"They're coming in the back," said one of the tough guys.

They passed into what looked like a cast iron grape arbor with a rounded top. Between the black bars Carl saw tables covered with tiger-stripe cloths. The lanterns in the centers

15

were shaped like hollowed coconuts and cast a yellow glow on a man who leaned over to light his cigarette. Halfway down the cage-like entryway a black-haired girl with lipstick the color of blood smiled warmly as she checked coats.

"This is our star tonight, Elizabeth," said Musso, handing her his damp coat. "You make sure you let the other girls have a chance at him, hey?"

"Yes, sir," she winked.

Musso leaned toward Carl as if confiding. "A good girl." He said it loudly enough that she probably heard as she dragged his enormous coat over the counter and slipped in a hanger. "Not cheap like a lot of 'em. Shouldn't work here at all, but her pop's a cripple."

The room echoed with laughter. In front of a maroon stage curtain that stretched across the entire end of the building, a man with a big red bow tie and a purple derby was getting ready to do a handstand. He leaned over, carefully stretched out his fingers, bent at the waist, and placed his white-gloved hand on the edge of the stage between two footlights. To a drumroll, he twitched his legs slightly as if about to lift them, to the left, to the right, to the left again. All at once he stood straight up and said, "That reminds me." Rimshot. Laughter. "You heard the one about Joe Dimaggio and the gold-plated Ford? Henry Ford is sitting in his office one day trying to think of ways to sell more cars—"

The comic might have been giving a talk on philately for all Musso cared. He squeezed between tables, forcing patrons to crane from one side to another to avoid his girth. Carl wondered where a man that size could buy a tux and noticed that the elbows and tail of the jacket shined as if it had been inherited through six generations. Either it was hard to find a tux that big or Musso had been sliding down the hood of his Packard. Eventually they stepped into an alcove sheltered with potted palms. At a table at least ten feet in diameter a half dozen men and women were leaning forward to listen to their host, a genial, square-jawed man, whose slicked hair and white jacket phosphoresced in the lantern light. The fat man waited for a break in the conversation as patiently as an altar boy.

"—so I say to him, 'Are you trying to tell me that the Commies are more dangerous than Hitler?' Well, he denied it, but that is what he meant. I mean, they could be dangerous in the long run, but not in our lifetimes. It is all nationality. If Germany goes Commie: look out." His companions nodded. "If Britain goes Commie, if America goes Commie—you catch my drift. But if China goes Commie, it's still China. If Italy goes Commie, so, well, maybe the trains don't run on time . . . ."

Carl studied the man carefully. There was control in his voice and a slight clipping of the words that implied the careful rooting out of an accent. He wasn't at all like the racket boys in New York, most of whom seemed to watch George Raft movies for tips on how to be the most obvious thug on the block. He was smooth. It was easy to see why the Greek moved so powerfully around the record and movie industries. There was a big stick behind him, too, and the big stick gave most bookers a respectful attitude. His mother had been the mistress of a widower don whose own sons died young from the Sicilian form of sickle-cell anemia. "The Greek could make ya; the Greek could break ya," Georgy Mack's brother Sal had told Carl.

"And Greece!" Papanoumou crossed himself and spoke quickly, "Holy Mother of God relieve the suffering of the Greek people—"

"They're doing terrible things there, I read."

The Greek nodded. "—but half Fascist, half Commie, all Fascist, all Commie, I don't give a damn what: Greeks will never be a threat to nobody from now on. Believe me, I should know. That's why my uncle got our asses out of there. Believe me."

The Greek raised his cigarette to accept the general laughter, smiling and satisfied with his performance. He scanned the table and winked at a woman two seats over. "You know what I'm saying, don't you? You bet! Same thing goes for the Polskis, right, babe?" They all laughed again. He soaked it up for a second then looked up at Musso as if a seedy process server had tracked him down.

"So, Ernie, how's the asteroids?" The flesh of Musso's face rippled as he fought to control his anger. The Greek enjoyed having struck the nerve and stuck out his hand to Carl. "Michael Papanoumou, Carl. Good to meet you. I hear good things about you."

Carl had trouble getting around Musso to shake and bumped one of the men at the table. "I hear—sorry!—good things about you, sir."

"From Sally Mack? I bet!" His slight roll of the eyes seemed more for entertaining his guests than for sarcasm.

"Mr. Macchianti said to send his best wishes."

"I appreciate that. Sal's given me some good tips in the past. We did a deal on a cornet guy who used to play with Myron Haney. I've got no complaints about Sal."

"He speaks highly of you."

He grunted. "We're going to see what we can do for you. A better booking agent to start with. You heard of Al Lampson?" He gestured at the man Carl had bumped. "He's starting back for Hollywood next Monday. Next month he starts shooting *Hawaiian Holiday*. Sal recommended some hoofers for it. Great gals. Legs all the way up to heaven. And I mean *heaven!*" The woman on his right nearly spilled her highball. "What do you think of Carl, Al? Maybe you have a spot for him in the picture. You could make him the next Dick Powell."

"We'll see, then who knows! Maybe he's the next Fred Astaire. How's your dancing?"

"I'm ready to learn better—to do it better."

The Greek paused for effect. "I think we're embarrassing poor Carl here." They laughed. "You know what a lot of singers tell me? That Astaire is the best in the business. He puts over a song better than any of the more famous ones. True!"

"I say give Carl a screen test," a woman with a cigarette holder said wickedly. Her male companion mockingly raised his arm as if he were going to backhand her. While the rest of the table laughed, the Greek pulled Carl's lapel and spoke into his ear.

"It's all set up, buddy. Do good and there will be great press. Same thing will happen when you get to the Commodore Perry Hotel in Toledo. Same thing in Saginaw and Gary. After New Year's Eve in Chicago, you'll be about half famous. I'm making sure that Ernest Byfield of the Hotel Sherman

catches your act. After that, Bixby'll be selling your con-
tract—" he snapped his fingers "—and you'll be on to the
real thing. Some new songs. Some records. I'm talking to a
fellow at Decca next week."

"I really want to thank you, I—"

"Knock'em dead. Get the girls wet and you'll be living like
a king. Understand? You'll be the Valentino of swing."

"I'll do my best."

"Now put that poor comic out of his misery, hey?" He
winked. "Make 'em melt."

Carl's mouth went dry. "The dressing rooms?" he asked
Musso, who was still waiting, his dyspeptic expression growing even more sour. The comic had finally done his handstand, and the audience applauded wildly.

Backstage, Buzz was checking himself in a mirror, smoothing down each side of his pencil mustache and tugging his
white tux tight over his barrel-shaped torso. "Well, look who
decided to drop by, the Carolina Crooner. Something's going
on here, isn't it?"

Carl felt like a traitor. "Michael Papanoumou is in the audience, Buzz. It's a great chance for all of us. And he's got a
director with him."

"Sally Mack's pulling strings for you, you little prick. Is
that why you get top billing?"

"I had nothing to do with that."

"The manager said it was the Greek's orders. Natalie is
ticked and I don't blame her."

"Mussolini said it was because of my birthday. That's all."

"Well, Happy Birthday. We're going to do the show like
always. Why can't Georgy Mack set up Natalie to be
discovered?"

"I dunno," said Carl. "May be he's got Chicago in mind.
She could be noticed here too, you know."

"Well, I'm not changing anything for you. The show's
like always."

Like always was the reason Buzz Bixby would eternally be
small potatoes. Once, when he was about twelve, Carl had
wandered over to the college and slipped in on one of his
father's lectures. It was more of a rant, really, the old man's
glorification of Nietzsche increasing the density of the humid

19

room until Carl nearly fell asleep. He remembered the way his father had shouted *Übermensch:* "The *Übermensch* achieves *bee-cause* he has *no* guilt!" The hell with Buzz and his Like always Cavalcade of Swing. Carl wasn't going to let guilt get in his way now.

Natalie haughtily passed them. "Natalie, did you know it's Carl's birthday?" Buzz called after her. "The marquee was a present by the manager. Isn't that nice?"

Carl took a deep breath and checked the mirror. He scratched at a spot on the shoulder of his tux and tugged the wings of his black tie. He heard the comic congratulating the audience on its patience and telling them to loosen up their dancing shoes. The band would be on in two minutes. That would give Carl fifteen or so. His hands were shaking and his mouth was drier. He hunted up a rust-stained sink in the back and bent under the spigot. The water was warm and tasted almost salty.

He thought again of his father. Of how he had slipped out the kitchen door and hitchhiked west toward Richmond, then north, his old carpetbag full of lyric sheets of all the popular songs. His crazy old man! He had raged that if his son persisted in this irrational wish to be a singer, he should at least sing something worthy of the human voice. How could Carl turn his back on the music he had grown up with? By age thirteen Carl could sing on demand, in German, several arias from *The Ring of the Nibelungen, Oberon, Fidelio,* and even *Rienzi.* "It is true," his father had said with moist eyes, "that your mother wore out two Victrolas listening to Caruso." He had said it bemusedly as if he were still indulging Mary's girlish weaknesses. "But that, at least, was better than jungle music!"

Carl tried to imagine what it would have been like if his mother had survived. Would the old man have been as hard? Would she have softened her husband's stubbornness and weakened Carl's? By age fifteen Carl had spent hours in the dark wearing hard Bakelite earphones, intently listening to a crystal radio he had bought from his friend Lamon. When he had run away, his father made no attempt to get him back. Later, when he wrote the old man the address of the rooming house, Carl never mentioned he was facing his second meal-less Christmas Eve stamping his cold feet on the corner at Macy's, belting out carols for pennies. His father responded with only one letter. "Your sainted mother," it said, "curses you from her grave." That only made Carl more determined. Finally, after half a decade in cheap clubs, roadhouses, and cocktail lounges, the Greek was about to prove how much Carl had "wasted" his talent.

But the old man had cheated Carl out of the pleasure of victory. Hanging their heads, the professor's colleagues attributed it to the rumors that the college would have to reduce its staff. There had been no note by the body. After the funeral Carl searched the house for the clipping he had mailed from Atlantic City. He never found it, and was ready to believe the post office had lost it. Then he noticed black ashes in the fireplace. He was haunted by the certainty that they were all that was left of his clipping and that—never mind the staff reductions—the bastard had killed himself rather than admit to Carl he was wrong. The *Übermensch* would fall on his sword rather than surrender, wouldn't he?

Carl splashed water on his face. He had to concentrate. He heard the applause subside as the orchestra began the Cavalcade of Swing theme song, "Manhattan Moonlight." Pleasant, syrupy, and utterly safe, it was the perfect theme for Buzz Bixby. The band would soon break off and rush headlong into Mack's arrangement of "Sing, Sing, Sing." The theory was to get the crowd's juices flowing with Mack's solo and Ted's drumming. As quickly as Buzz tempoed it, it still remained a lengthy number. The second set was a lugubrious rendition of "I Can't Get Started." Buzz liked to sing this one himself, flexing the baton in front of his cummerbund. He tried to sound like Bunny Berrigan, but pushed too much of it through his nose. Fortunately, he had sense enough to let most of the number be carried by the three cornets and most people didn't really listen as it was the first chance for a romantic dance. Next Buzz moved to something quick and silly, usually "Barney Google," with the whole orchestra—no solos, no singing—a throwaway to change the mood, let people get themselves a drink. It was important the house sold a lot of drinks, or the band wouldn't be invited back.

Buzz had it all figured out, he said: Hegelian dialectic without the synthesis. Surprised that Carl understood what he was talking about when he first invoked it, he explained in detail. No synthesis made the audience hunger for more. Quick, slow, quick, slow. Silly to set up romantic. Happy to set up sad. The whole band to set up a singer or a solo. Mintner had once suggested that maybe they needed a synthesis number (whatever the hell that was) to make people feel satisfied and not jerked from side to side, but Buzz said no. Maybe for a radio show you needed a culmination, so people crawled into bed ready to sleep, but in a live show you always want them begging for more: another encore, another request. "Full people don't look for the dessert cart," he had said. Maybe he was right, maybe not. He was impressed by his own theory, so what the hell? The Cavalcade of Swing was scheduled for seventy-four appearances in six months. Buzz knew something. Maybe he just didn't know enough.

Carl searched his pockets for his handkerchief. He settled on wiping his clammy hands on the curtain. Mack was milking his solo and Buzz wasn't keeping his baton in tempo with him. Ted, however, was giving Mack his head and the musicians were cuing on the bass drum rather than the baton. Myron Rush momentarily lowered his trombone and turned around to glare up at Mintner, but he seemed more resigned than confused.

That's right, Myron, thought Carl. If you want to get along, go along.

A wet kiss drowned his ear. "If I'd known it was your birthday I'd've got you a present."

When he turned, he could smell the wintergreen on Natalie's breath. That usually meant she'd been saucing.

"So there," she said. "That was your present. Maybe I'll give you more later."

He glanced over his shoulder as if he expected Georgy Mack to be standing there with a loaded Thompson. "Friendly ain'tcha?"

"It's your birthday." She watched the band for several seconds, rolling the mint around her mouth. She was wearing her low cut gown. The Valley of the Kings lay between her breasts. A lot of pharaohs had been buried in there. "Buzz is nervous, don't ya think?"

"The Greek," said Carl, licking his lips. "He could do a lot for us."

"Well, you know what they say. If they start shooting, just keep singing." She'd probably said it in every wing she'd stood in. But what it meant to her was a mystery.

"You got any more of those mints?"

"In my dressing room," she said. "I'll get ya one."

"Forget it. They're into 'Barney Google.'" He chewed his tongue to get the moisture flowing, closed his eyes and felt his heart pounding.

"You're still starting with 'One Kiss'?"

"It's okay," said Carl.

"It's too old," she said. "You ought to say ya won't do it. Buzz needs to get with the times."

"It's okay," said Carl, a little sharply.

"He associates it with his third—or was it fourth?—wife. The one with the funny teeth. What was her name?" She squinted into the rafters as if she expected her to be on the catwalk.

With Buzz flailing his arms like a capon trying to fly, "Barney Google" tumbled over itself toward a conclusion. The song ended with a screech from the cornets as Buzz crashed his elbows into his thighs, nearly taking a fetal position.

"This is it," said Carl.

"Ya ought to wipe that lipstick off your ear," said Natalie.

He looked at her as if he didn't comprehend, then grimaced. "Jeez, dammit!" He frantically rubbed his ear until it burned. "Is it off? Is it off?"

Natalie leaned her hawklike face closer and squinted. Carl rubbed harder. A wicked smile curled around her full lips as if she were readying herself to plant another. He jerked back. "Cut it out!"

She blew him a kiss.

"And now," said Buzz, "something for the ladies: the Cavalcade of Swing's own Carolina Crooner, the Southern gentleman from Charleston, Mr. Carl Carlson."

The applause rose rapidly, as if the audience had been given an electric shock. It startled Buzz. The band members looked at each other and one of the cornetists shrugged. Carl moved out on the stage, nodded, and concentrated on not wetting himself.

Buzz eased the band into the opening bars as Carl slipped in behind the large microphone and adjusted it to his height. The audience quietened and settled in to listen. When the Greek recommended someone, Swing Land's audience listened. Were they all gangsters? Were they all forced to come? The moment was coming. When the music dropped . . .

NOW.

"Ladies and gentlemen," said Carl nervously, "a lovely tune from the musical *Redheaded Egghead.*" His voice had quavered. He closed his eyes, moved his tongue around to spread the moisture that was left, and met the first note of the verse:

> *Here we are, together once again,*
> *And you're all business: to you I'm just a friend.*
> *When will you hear the magic in the air,*
> *And allow me to show you just how much I care . . .*

He fixed his eyes on a woman to his left.

> *One kiss is all you'll need to understand*
> *One kiss is all you'll need to take my hand*
> *This longing in my heart is tearing me apart*
> *I know that under your cold, cold glance,*
> *Somewhere I'll find romance.*

> *One kiss will tell you all you need to know*
> *One kiss will tell you how I want you so*
> *This agony I feel, it makes my senses reel*
> *If you'll just question my lips, my eyes,*
> *You'll know my love can't die.*

Somewhere in the first line Carl was no longer in his body. He was listening to his voice as if it were coming out of a radio horn, yet he was aware of every movement of every muscle from the lazy droop of his eyelids to his gentle motion from left to right, meeting as many eyes as possible. He could picture women's faces he couldn't see, far in the back, and he tried to make love to them with his eyes. How many times had he sung this old song? A switch had been thrown and he no longer had to think about what he was doing. He was no longer Carl Carlson, born Carl Maria Walthers, but the singing itself. This Carl guy was just along for the ride.

"One Kiss" continued to flow around him. It was a sensation somewhat like being drunk, but not as unsteady. He had tried one of Mack's reefers once, but it wasn't like the muggles either. Time didn't lurch awkwardly from moment to moment, getting hung up and then tumbling forward. It was— yes!—dreamlike. His birthday dream. His Christmas dream. He raised his arms high over his head as the song ended and dropped his head, expecting any moment to be wakened in the Pullman of some smoky train headed for another small college's prom. He kept his eyes closed, afraid to move, terrified that any thought that he was dreaming would wake him, terrified that his terror of the dream's ending would end it.

But he didn't wake. The applause was deafening as it reverberated off the ceiling. Ted winked and Buzz Bixby glanced back and forth between Carl and the audience as if to say *what the hell is this?* Buzz made a small flick of his wrist, and Carl began to back offstage, nodding and waving, throwing thank you's against the wall of sound.

He backed into Natalie as the band moved into a rapid instrumental version of "Marie." "Well," she said coldly, "ain't you the cat's pajamas?"

He fished his mind for anything to say that made sense. "Hot crowd."

She didn't seem to hear.

"*A hot crowd!*"

She ran her pinky over her lips. Whatever he did, whatever he said, she always chose the perfect response to make him feel like he was naked at a tea party.

All his life Carl would remember the rest of the evening as being similar to the calendar scene in so many movies in which an unseen hand peels back the dates as fragmentary pictures of the intervening events overlap and blend. Natalie got scattered applause. They liked her but preferred to dance or sip their drinks while she sang. It was little different from the response the band got, though Mack's and Ted's solos stirred up some excitement. It was nothing like what Carl was getting. As the audience got drunker, a man in the front row or a shrill woman beyond the stage lights would shout out Carl's name during one of the dance numbers. "Bring back the Crooner!" "Where's the blondie boy?" Buzz stuck adamantly to his program, moving in the way he always did from fast to slow, from band to singer, even when there was an audible groan by someone when he introduced Natalie for the third time. This only made him more stubborn and Natalie more determined to win them over. She became more suggestive in each verse, moving her hips, caressing the microphone, and casting her head back as if shivering with sexual pleasure. Her normally throaty voice shifted from a purr to a moan. By the time she got to "Can't Help Lovin' That Man of Mine," and "Stormy Weather" even Buzz was avoiding looking at her. She had gone beyond seductive and, from the way she sashayed off the stage, she knew it. Except for a few men who shouted as if they were in a burlesque house, most of the audience rearranged their chairs, hailed the cigarette girls, and tried desperately not to appear embarrassed.

One of Musso's tough guys appeared backstage and waved Buzz over during a dance number. He handed him an envelope. It was the first trickle of the flood of requests, all but one for Carl, most accompanied by greenbacks. A couple of fifties and half a dozen twenties all came before midnight. Three times C-spots showed. After that, they were almost throwing money on the stage. Even a couple of the gold certificates Roosevelt had withdrawn in 1933 found their way backstage. "The Lindbergh ransom!" Carl laughed, jamming them into his pockets with all those napkins with smeared dedications. "For Julia: 'You Made Me Love You.'" "Raymond to Betsie, anniversary, 'Our Love Is Here to Stay.'" "Dedicate 'Swanee' to SNOOKUMS." Where did they get the money? Was every ex-bootlegger in Ohio in the house? Buzz had no arrangements for half the songs, but Mack remembered every song he'd ever heard and could get them started. This kind of spontaneity was hard for Buzz to deal with, but he kept smiling inanely and bobbing his baton as if the gods had suddenly blessed him with success. Buzz gamely kept his sister in the show by introducing her fourth number, but when he slid into the opening bars of her duet with Carl, "I Get No Kick from Champagne," she did not come out on stage. Carl began his segment and she still did not come out. Buzz sent Myron to find her while they carried her part with the orchestra, but he bumbled his way through the curtain and shrugged.

One song slid into another. Carl sang slow, he sang fast. When he forgot the words, he made them up and they fit perfectly, though where they came from, he had no idea. He sipped Tom Collinses between numbers and kept going. His shirt was soaked with sweat and his loosened bowtie stuck to his chest like a plaster. He had a way of sliding his hand out palm down that he had borrowed from Fred Astaire. It was a silky move, something he had decided to turn into his trademark and tonight Carl was all silk. His voice was running over the lips and breasts of every woman in the room. When they climbed into bed with their husbands and their lovers tonight, they would all be making love to Carl Carlson. They would all be picturing that silky move and feeling the quiver of his voice in their loins. Carl Carlson owned them. Carl Carlson owned the world.

And yet, when it ended, it all seemed to have happened in minutes. There were about ten staggering couples left when Buzz closed with "Manhattan Moonlight." The Greek and Musso and his men had left who knows when. The smoke was dense as ocean water. Still, Carl wanted one more song, one more drink, one more silky slide into E flat. He felt like he could go on for another week, and he didn't have any sense that it was after five until he saw the pretty hatcheck girl asleep on her chair in the corner. He hefted himself over the counter and found his coat. There was a note pinned to it. The director, Al Lampson, wanted Carl to call him collect in Hollywood next Friday. It could only mean he was getting a shot at *Hawaiian Holiday*!

He rolled up one of his twenties like a cigarette and leaned over the hatcheck girl. He slid it into the top of her dress and she said something in her sleep. Impulsively, he leaned over and kissed her on her soft ear, but she still did not wake. Her black hair smelled of cinnamon and vanilla. Musso had been right. She didn't belong in a place like this and he felt a little guilty for having stuck the money in her bosom. "Sweet dreams," he whispered.

Outside, he gave a cabby a ten to wake the girl and take her home. He was sobered by the fact he had spent thirty bucks on a girl he'd hardly spoken to. Hey, so what? The Greek was going to make him rich. Al Lampson was putting him in a movie. Time to get used to success.

Their cheap hotel was near Lake Erie and Carl paced the shore until sunup, his collar lifted against the cold. The ice was rolled up in dunes and he imagined Gary Cooper and Ray Milland in their Legionnaire uniforms marching across it. He imagined himself in a Legionnaire uniform. He thought of his poor stupid father and the "heroic" gesture of the bullet in the heart. He tried to imagine what his mother would have thought of him singing in the movies. He closed his eyes in the cold wind from Canada and saw her smiling freely, guilelessly, in the same way she smiled in the photograph which had sat on the mantle. He suddenly turned toward the lake and projected Wotan's words in the way his voice teacher had demanded. "*Loge, hör! lausche hieher!*" The echo faded. He made his silky slide with his hand and laughed. "Jungle music!" he shouted.

A deep weariness crashed in on him by the time he unlocked his hotel door. Enough light filtered through the closed blinds to make out flowery wallpaper, a tattered armchair, and a half-empty bottle of scotch on the night table. It wasn't his roommate Myron who was snoring, however. It was Natalie. She wore only her stockings, bunched loosely around her knees. She was sleeping on her side and her enormous breasts seemed to be melting into a puddle on the bed. He stepped back and checked the number on the door. There was no one in the corridor. He glanced back in. Her pale skin had taken on the color of the dawn light, except around her eyes, where it was as blue as a bruise on a corpse. Ashamed for looking, he reached down to extricate the key, rattling the door knob in the process. She stirred and the bed creaked. She cleared her throat.

"Izh that you? About damned time," she said huskily.

He checked the corridor again and stepped inside. "Where's Myron?" he asked, averting his eyes. He now saw her in the stained mirror. She had rolled onto her back. "Where's Myron?" he repeated. She answered with a sniggering noise, then died to the world.

Oh, hell. She had sent Myron to her room, but he couldn't very well ask the clerk where that was. Hotel clerks kept their iceboxes stocked by keeping the Georgy Macks of the world well-informed. Myron couldn't be trusted, either, and Natalie knew that. Maybe it amused her to get the piss kicked out of Carl. Carl was working all this out, when in the mirror there was a flash of red.

On her belly. She was covering a wound with her hand. He closed the door and looked directly at her. She was on her back, her legs spread towards him, her gaping, bushy private parts open. "Natalie?" he whispered. "Natalie!"

She stirred and flung her stained hand over her head. What he had thought was blood was writing. Smeared lipstick. "Happy Birthday," it said. A smeared arrow trailed down from the words and pointed into her crotch. For a moment, he was titillated by the idea of getting into Georgy Mack's stuff. Taking the chance was irrational, but that just added to the kick. Hell, she wouldn't even remember it.

But he was coming down off his high. The sad wallpaper, the residue of all the Tom Collinses burbling in his gut, the dissolute cast of her skin all combined into a recognition that his birthday had ended. He was drained. Time to sleep.

The lobby clerk was snoring in a chair when Carl took to the sofa in a dark alcove flanked by peeling Corinthian columns. He was out all through morning and half of the afternoon. When the numbers runner burst into the lobby with the news, when people rushed out of their rooms, even when a policeman, a Swedish grocer, several newsboys, and a dozen other people from the neighborhood crowded around the Philco that the hotel manager turned up as loud as he could, Carl slept on. He wouldn't know what had happened until Ted Clough finally found him and dragged him red-eyed and nauseated to the train station. His pounding head couldn't fathom what possible effect the news would have on him. Carl Carlson was going to be a star, right? They were waiting for him in Toledo, Saginaw, and Chicago. He'd learn some new songs, that's all. Some patriotic stuff. It might even help his career. Look what it had done for George M. Cohan. What possible difference could this business at Pearl Harbor make? They could film *Hawaiian Holiday* in southern California, couldn't they?

Part II
Orpheus in the Underworld

1.

Carl was still haunted by his reflection as they pulled away from the station in Westfield. A few miles back an Amish farmer dressed black as a crow had been perched on the bouncing seat of his cultivator moving parallel to the train, snapping his wrist to keep his massive horse churning the soft earth. A breeze lifted the brim of the old man's flat black hat and flicked his long silver beard over his shoulder. He looked like someone out of a western, wearing that hat and coat in the August sun, and doing what? Mowing? Rolling new potatoes out of the earth? Turning alfalfa back in? The bushes along the tracks blocked Carl's view of the earth itself, and the old man in his death-black clothes seemed to glide over it creating an unearthly vision, a bucolic and false image for the cover of the *Saturday Evening Post*. It was the kind of all-American image that soldiers clung to on the road outside Bône while they hid in the shade of an M-4 Sherman from a sun more merciless than Rommel's panzers. In war you needed a concocted and unchanging vision of the world at peace, an icon whose protection justified any suffering.

But then, as if a movie film had snapped, the antique farmer and his field were gone. The train had passed into a stone tunnel and Carl's face, gaunt and ghostly and very real, stared back from the glass, the sockets of his eyes sharp, his cheeks sunken, the veins of his forehead in high relief. A shiver passed through him. They had plunged into the Underworld and he was staring into the cold eyes of his own shade. Instantly, the reflection exploded in sunlight. He winced. They were passing vineyards. A fat man in a linen suit tipped his panama hat. But Carl's reflection stayed in his mind. The face of war was composed of millions of faces exactly like his own, faces whose dreams had been ravaged.

He told himself that the face in the glass was not Carl Carlson. It was the face of Corporal Carl Maria Walthers, recipient of the Purple Heart. Carl Carlson would have to wait for the army to come to its senses and discharge Corporal Walthers. It was merely a question of picking up where he had left off, of anticipating the kinds of songs people would want to hear after the damned war was over. Being a veteran wouldn't hurt. There ought to be plenty of chances to get his voice back in shape at Camp Anthony Wayne. And there'd be leave. It'd be a cinch to get back in touch with the Greek. Cleveland was only a hundred or so miles away. The Carolina Crooner wasn't dead yet. They'd tried to stop him by having a war, but it wouldn't work. The face in the glass was what might be, he told himself, not what would be.

"Young man?"

A woman in spectacles startled him. Her face was half covered with a net which emerged from under the front of her purple hat.

"Young man, would you mind if I sit?"

"No, sure. Take a load off. I mean you're welcome, ma'am."

"Have you been overseas, young man?"

"Excuse me?"

She clutched her purse closer to her stomach. "Oh, I'm sorry. I know you're not supposed to talk about it. But I am not interested in anything of military significance. My name is Myrtle Kent—Mrs. Roland Kent."

"Pleased to meet you," he said flatly. "I'm Carl Walthers."

"Carl—can I call you Carl?—I was wondering if, on some chance in your travels—wherever they were, I don't need to know—you had met a Robert Euclid Kent. Bobby is my son, you see, and he hasn't written for some time now."

"Kent?"

"Robert Euclid. The last time we heard from him he was training in Texas." She fished a photograph from her purse and leaned forward, eyes hungry.

"I don't know, ma'am. I met a lot of guys." He scanned the picture. A boy standing stiffly in a baggy suit. "Did he go by Bob, maybe?" He wasn't sure why he asked. He told himself he was stalling to remember if he had run into him.

A glow came over her. She talked about Bobby's big ears

and his way with dogs. She said his favorite books were those awful Fu Manchu stories and that he loved to eat his grandmother's cinnamon apple dumplings. The more she spoke the more her lip quivered.

Carl interrupted before she lost it. "Big ears, did you say? Like Bing Crosby."

She nodded and leaned closer.

He tapped the photo with his index finger. "I think I met a guy named Kent. Yeah. He was playing with this mongrel that had wandered up."

"That's just like him!"

"It came to me because he said something about army chow and how he missed his grandmother's dumplings."

She raised her hand to her mouth. "How was he?" she asked desperately. "Did he look well?"

Carl shrugged. "He struck me as a real man's man, if you know what I mean. I had the impression the guys respected him. You'd be proud of him."

Her eyes filled with water. He lowered his head and picked at an imaginary piece of lint on his trouser leg.

She took a deep breath, pressed her hand against her bosom, and bit her lower lip. She stared right through Carl, seeing what? Her son as a baby? Her son reciting the Twenty-third Psalm? Her son swimming naked in the local pond?

"I didn't talk to him long, ma'am, but I think that must have been him. He's a fine man."

Mrs. Kent turned towards the window and watched the trees rushing past. The train creaked as it slowed. She shifted, straightening her backbone. "You're a kind boy," she said. "But you shouldn't lie."

Carl glanced at the window as if she had seen something. For an uneasy moment he expected the ghostly reflection to be staring back. "Lie?" he said angrily. "Why should I lie? Kent! Big ears! He was playing with a dog!" The loudness of his voice had drawn the attention of a priest across the car. Carl reached for his duffel bag. "What are you looking at?" he said to the priest. "Believe what you want. Why would I lie?"

The woman continued staring through the window as they entered the town. Carl paused near the doorway and peered back at her. Why had he had gotten so angry? Anger had screwed him up with the Army and it didn't make any sense here. Was he so transparent? What kind of singer would that make him? He was showing Carl Walthers when he had needed the silky Carl Carlson. "Your boy is fine," he said fiercely. *"He'll be all right."*

The woman did not move. The priest continued to stare at Carl, who was banged against the door frame when the car lurched to a stop. "Why don't you do your job?" he snarled at the priest. When the conductor reached to help him with his duffel bag he jerked it away.

The station at North East sat at right angles to a large brick hotel. A boy was hawking the *Erie Daily Times.* A policeman sat on the hood of his car eating what looked like a chunk of wedding cake, and a veiled woman in widow's weeds was embraced by a farmer and his big-boned wife. Carl spotted an olive Chevy with a white star on the side. The driver hopped out, slipped on his cap, and hurried towards the platform.

Carl hopped down to street level. "Corporal Carl Walthers." He stuck out his hand. "You meeting me?"

The boy's fingers were wiry, but he had a strong grip. He smelled like Black Jack gum and a nasty pimple was poking through his eyebrow. "Yes, sir. Private Ansel Dahl."

"I thought I'd have to get a cab."

"You never know if they got gas. We're talking Hicksville."

"Bad town?"

"It ain't St. Louis." He reached for the duffel bag and Carl let him have it. He felt a little guilty for yanking it back from the conductor.

"Looks like America. Andy Hardy lives here, right?"

"You got that right. Pittsburgh's south, Buffalo's east, and Cleveland's west. Erie's about twenty miles west, but none of them is St. Louis, either."

"So you're from St. Louis, I take it?"

"You bet. Be there in Sportsman's Park rooting for the Browns if it wasn't for Judge Willard. They were in third place last year and should be doing better. Next to last this year."

"The Yankees are running away with it, even with the draft."

"The Browns out-hit the Yankees the other day. Pounded Spud Chandler for nine hits. Did they get a run? No. Lost four to zip. Go figure!"

"Maybe you should root for the Cardinals. Who's Judge Willard?"

"Nobody you ever want to meet, brother." He opened the back door.

"I'll ride up front. Just toss the gear on the back seat."

"The camp's not far. We only have about five hundred prisoners so far, but they're expecting to get more on Tuesday and more on Thursday. They're figuring about fifteen hundred total by early forty-four."

"And I get to have tea with every one of them," said Carl drily. "Could we stop for some smokes?"

"Sure. We'll stop on Main. You get a look-see that way."

The center of North East was only a block or two away, and the crack about Andy Hardy movies was even more fitting when they got there. A dime store, a church, a hotel called the Haynes House, the Bank of North East, a barber, and a park with a monument to those who died in the Great War. Two priests sat on a bench in the park talking excitedly. There were posters in the windows urging citizens to buy bonds and Firch's Ma-Made bread. A town workman was pounding a loose cobblestone back into place, and Carl wondered how the bastard ducked the draft. Three teenaged girls passed, whispering and sneaking peeks out of the corner of their eyes. They didn't see too many men Carl's age. He winked and they scurried away giggling, faces flushed. He could smell hamburgers cooking.

Hicksville, the private had said. Carl had never lived in a place like this. Where had he lived, really? A cheap apartment in New York, the sleepy town of Williamsburg, Pullman cars, Greyhound "Super-Coaches," chintzy hotels, barracks and tents and more barracks. He remembered the model of Henry Aldrich's home town he had seen in *Life*. The radio writers had created it so that they wouldn't get confused. Andy Hardy, Henry Aldrich, the town with a nice, anonymous geographical name: Centerville, Midwest City, North East. The town that meant America. The town worth dying for. Shucks oh golly, he thought, I could sing in the church choir. Carl Carlson, Carolina Choirboy.

As they headed south, he drew deep on his Philip Morris and gave three of them to the private, who said he'd save them for later. They were soon passing rows of grapevines and climbing an incline. A wooden guard tower was silhouetted against a fluffy white cloud. When the barbed wire fences, about eight feet high, came into view, they turned onto a gravel lane leading to a double gate.

Dahl waved and the guards opened it without a word. Inside a second fence ahead of them were two neat lines of tar-paper barracks with corrugated tin roofs. There were twenty pairs until they dropped down the roll of the hill and out of sight. Similar rows stretched to the right where several prisoners, stripped to the waist, raised the frame of a wall. "Welcome to Camp Mad Anthony," said Dahl, "the place where the elite Heinies meet."

The staff buildings were no more elegant than the prisoners', though the HQ had been covered with pine planks and painted olive drab. Their boots echoed under the wooden floor as they climbed the stoop. Inside, the staff sergeant was not at his desk, so Dahl tapped on the major's door.

"Come in," growled someone.

"Private Dahl reporting." He saluted sharply. "Corporal Walthers is here."

The major's shirt was sweaty in the armpits, his tie seemed as tight as if someone had been trying to strangle him. Beads of sweat on his mottled bald head trickled into the creases of his brow and disappeared. Behind him, flypaper dangled on each side of a framed photograph of FDR as if intended for political bunting. The major held a flyswatter. "Therewego, therewego, therewego," he mumbled to himself. With a sniff he brought down the swatter so hard that he bounced off his chair.

"Damn things," he said. "Loaded with germs." He looked up as if he hadn't noticed them enter. "You're Walthers? Don't you know to salute your superior officer?"

Oh great, thought Carl. Another lead-assed Napoleon. "We did, sir. When we entered, sir."

"Well, do it again."

"If you say so, sir." They snapped to.

"That was pretty poor, corporal."

"I apologize, sir. I have trouble lifting my elbow properly."

"That so?" His voice had a mocking tone.

"My shoulder, sir." In for an inch, in for a mile, Carl thought. "And anyway you're not covered. Sir."

The major laughed wetly. He turned toward Dahl. "See that? The draftee knows his regs." He rolled his bloodshot eyes toward Carl. "Don't quote the regs to me. You're reporting to me. Private Dahl, take the man's gear over to the noncom's hut."

"Yes, sir," said Dahl, "but, sir, the corporal is—" he hesitated "—a corporal."

"Not any more. Just got the papers." He held his flyswatter like a rich Virginian testing the spring in his riding crop. "Congratulations, Sergeant Walthers. I guess it doesn't hurt to get wounded."

"Painless, like getting decked by Joe Louis."

"I mean it doesn't hurt the career."

"This isn't my career. They can keep their stripes. Sir."

"I heard you were a smartass, but you got promoted anyway. Typical Army fuckup." He waved the flyswatter at Dahl. "Go on, didn't I tell you?"

"Yes, sir."

"And close the door," he yelled after him.

The major pulled a file toward him, uncovering a polished block of wood with black letters. "Maj. Joe 'Tex' Murnow" it said.

"*I* never got wounded," he said. "All I ever killed was bugs. I sat on my ass in the Philippines for two years in the twenties. All I did was swat mosquitoes and stomp waterbugs bigger than the Moros. You think I got anywhere near any shooting? Not even in the jack-off wars. My unit went to Vladivostok, I was reassigned. There's action in Nicaragua, I get Scofield and Manila. Now I come out of the reserves to play nursemaid to a bunch of whipped Nazis." He scanned the ceiling like a gunner searching for Messerschmidts. "They've gone to roost, damn things."

"You ought to transfer if you want combat, major."

He put down his swatter and opened a low drawer. He

tipped back a bottle of whisky and took a large mouthful. He swished it around and swallowed, holding himself absolutely still until it hit bottom, when he exhaled a long ahhhhhhh. He raised the bottle towards the picture of Roosevelt. "Thank you, Mr. President, for the Twenty-first Amendment, though I think sometimes the scotch tasted better during Prohibition. You probably don't remember, eh sergeant?"

"I tasted a bit of moonshine when I was young."

"Want some?"

Murnow watched him sip it, as if afraid he'd drink too much. Carl wiped his mouth with the back of his hand. "Not bad."

"Got it in Canada. There's a ferry goes across from Erie." The major took another large swig. Sweat rolled down his bald head. A droplet hit the file as he opened it. "So you *sprechen* the Dutch, do you?"

"*Ja wohl.*"

"Don't waste it on me. Down at Washington they got some idea we might sort out the hardboiled Nazis from the ordinary Nazis. And we'll be renting the enlisted men out to relieve the farmworker shortage. There's also talk about democracy classes. If that comes up, I guess you might end up being the professor. Anyhow, for the moment, you're just supposed to talk to them, see if you can set up any squealers. Keep them happy. If not happy, quiet."

"That's what I understood."

Murnow took another belt. "So, what's it like? Not much room to hide in the desert, I'll bet." He put his whisky down without offering Carl any more.

"I didn't see action. Heard some. Could see the flashes at night. The day before I was to go forward, a sniper got me."

"Sniper?"

"One shot."

"Is that it?"

"What do you want? Sergeant York?"

Murnow moved the top sheet of paper in the file. "So you look okay to me."

"I can't move my right arm well. The wrong way and my shoulder pops out."

"So if it's so bad why didn't they discharge you?" He moved another sheet.

"'Ours is not to reason why,' is that right?"

Murnow chuckled. "Reason has nothing to do with the Army, bud. You're a bitcher. Didn't anyone tell you draftees got no right to bitch? Bitch and they grind you up."

"I learned it."

"You tried to get out of the draft. You wrote letters. Didn't anyone tell you there's a war on?"

"I didn't start it."

Murnow's eyes widened. He laced his fingers and leaned forward. "Look, bud, when St. Crispian's Day comes, you've got to grab it, no second chances. You're pissing along in life and the moment comes. You can fight and maybe die, or you can leave and go on pissing your life away. If you live, you did a good thing. You had a destiny and fulfilled it. You'll show your grandkids your scars. If you die, hey, you'll have died well. That's better than most men get. Much better."

"Saint who?"

Murnow's face sagged. Carl was clearly hopeless. "Forget it. Go settle in."

Carl cleared his throat. "Sir?"

Murnow closed the file.

"Sir, I was wondering how soon I might get a pass."

"A pass? You just got here. Are you going to give me a lot of paperwork like every other officer you've been under?"

"There are some people I need to see in Cleveland."

"Relatives?"

He started to say yes, but that would mean concocting even more of a story. "Some business associates from before the war. I was in Cleveland when the Japs attacked."

Murnow chuckled. "This bullet you took. It was meant for General Patton, right?"

"Huh? I was in an open market, right in the middle of Oran. An old man was trying to sell me an embroidered tablecloth. Red silk."

"Are you thick as well as a pain in the ass, Walthers? How in the hell did you get promoted to sergeant? You haven't cooperated from the day they called you up. You're not ten minutes here and you want a holiday."

Carl decided to play the game. "I'm sorry, sir. It was just being back in the States. When you have a brush with death, you know, you get sentimental about people and—"

"The only brush with death I ever had was appendicitis, so I wouldn't know. You'll get a pass when *I* think you need one. Hell, do your job for a change. You're not the prisoner here." He thought about the remark for a moment and lowered his head. "Dismissed," he said. "NCO digs are up that way."

Carl saluted, and said "Yes, sir." As he opened the office door, he heard the major mumbling to himself.

"All the flotsam, dammit, all of it. I am the flotsam man, Major Sam Flot. Probably shot *himself* fer Chrissakes . . ." The cork plunked as the major pulled it out of his bottle.

2.

Carl paused on the stoop of Murnow's office, took out a cigarette, and cupped his hands as he lit it. Low clouds were rolling in and the wind was shifting direction, stirring the leaves of corn in the field to the south and exposing the silvery underside of the maples in the ravine behind the office. The American flag snapped like a whip, sagged, then billowed out in the opposite direction, thumping its rope against the tall pole. Beyond the acres of vineyards to the north, and the church spires and roofs of North East, Lake Erie stretched across the horizon. It was a pewter color with one dot of white, a boat, making for shore. The sky was splattered with infinite shades of gray, from near black to cream, as if someone had carelessly mixed the paint.

The guards on the tower leaned against the rail and looked in Carl's direction. Carl raised his cigarettes and pointed at them. The guards looked at each other, and one of them enthusiastically waved him over.

There were no steps. A twelve-foot wooden ladder slanted up to a second, then a third, which poked through a trap door in the floor. He was out of breath when he climbed out on top. The guards were still on the rail. "Welcome to Mad Wayne," said the PFC, "home of the happy Hun."

Carl brushed his hands together to clean them from the ladder rungs. "Carl Walthers. Quite a view." He stepped around the machine gun and squinted into the wind. "So," he asked, offering a cigarette, "what's it like here?"

"What's it like anywhere?" said the guard. "Hurry up and wait."

They exchanged the usual questions. Where are you from? What did you do before the war? Where can you get a drink?

Private Jones pointed out the buildings separated from the prisoners' compound by a double fence. Next to the major's office were a pair of huts, one for him and one for the two lieutenants. A longer structure next door was for the NCOs, where Carl would bunk. Then there was a cluster of three enlisted men's barracks, and a long L-shaped building with a crooked metal chimney. Whenever the wind paused, the smoke drooped from the Chinese hat chimney cover and sank groundward.

A high perimeter fence and a smaller inner one enclosed the prisoners. Groups had gathered in front of their huts, joking and chatting. Some wore Wehrmacht uniforms, most wore jackets and trousers provided by the army. Where the ground began to roll down about a dozen were stripped to the waist doing calisthenics. The prisoners on work detail had stopped building their new quarters, and were sitting with their backs to the incomplete frame, sheltered from the wind of the approaching storm. Carl wondered how wise it was to let these seasoned combat troops get their hands on hammers, saws, and nails, all potential weapons. On the other hand, where would they run to? Canada? Getting into British hands after the Blitz hardly seemed like a delightful alternative. Most of them didn't look very dangerous with the big PW on the back of their jackets and the seat of their pants.

"How's the chow?" asked Carl.

"Good," said Burgess.

"Colored cooks," added Jones. "Prisoners, everybody gets the same. The Huns are eating better than most of the people in town."

Burgess laughed. "The first time they feed new prisoners, they keep the butter off the tables because the bastards will eat it right out of the bowl with their spoons."

"They're a sorry lot," said Jones, "to want to rule the world."

"Well," said Carl, "these were the ones we caught." The fact that a sniper hit him in the marketplace of Oran without getting caught said something about at least one German soldier. The MPs had speculated it was some diehard Vichy, but Carl hadn't believed it. Maybe he simply preferred to believe that it took an *Übermensch* to put him down. Anyway, he ought to be grateful. Even if the Fritz had taken away the silky slide he used to do with his right hand, he'd gotten Carl back to the States to pick up where he left off. The war, the bullet shattering his shoulder, they had been just momentary inconveniences.

"Walthers! Hey, Walthers!" Private Dahl leaned back at the base of the tower, his hands cupped around his mouth.

"What's up?"

"Major Murnow needs you right away. Problem!"

"Coming." He took one last glance at the rolling clouds and saw they were breaking up over the lake. Shafts of sunlight turned patches of water a beautiful blue. "Check you guys later," he said.

"You bet," said Jones.

Instead of leading him to the major's office, however, Dahl started toward the prisoner compound. He spoke on the move. "Major Murnow's got what he calls an incident. He hates incidents."

The opening of the gate drew the attention of the prisoners idling in front of their huts. Some of them stood. A droopy-eyed man with his cap held in front of his body nodded. Some were roundfaced, but most were gaunt. Their ages were mixed, the youngest being in his late teens, the oldest maybe fifty. They didn't look like the supermen everyone had spoken of reverently in the tents in Morocco, though most were clean, hair combed, nails clean. Those still in their Afrika Korps uniforms were buttoned up and neat enough to take the parade ground. Carl touched his left fingers to his eyebrow as if tipping a hat. A few looked down or turned away. Most of them nodded hesitantly.

When they had passed about half a dozen rows of huts, a prisoner stepped forward. "Hey, Joe," he shouted, "*zigaretten?*"

The man who had spoken was wearing his Wehrmacht uniform. The top two buttons were missing, and crude stitching patched a tear in the sleeve. From each shoulder hung a crescent-shaped flap of cloth striped in aluminum braid.

"*Was sind diese?*" asked Carl, pointing.

"*Ich bin Klarinettist.*" The man smiled and tootled his imaginary clarinet. He was missing a front tooth. *"Wie Benny Goodman, ja?"*

"Ja," said Carl. He fumbled in his shirt pocket. There were only a couple of cigarettes left and he had smoked only three of them himself. He handed the pack to the man. "From one musician to another. *Ich bin Sänger."*

"Ja? Wie Bing Crosby."

"Besser," said Carl. "Much better!"

The German's laugh popped out in one "ha!" and he tossed back his head.

"Come on," said Dahl. "You aren't supposed to give them stuff."

The man nodded. *"Danke,* Joe. *Danke schön!"*

"The major will kill you," said Dahl, pulling Carl by the sleeve.

"Hey!" He jerked his arm away. "Don't yank me like some kid."

"You shouldn't give the prisoners nothing for free."

Ahead of them was a larger building. A GI stood on the porch with his rifle across his chest. A number of prisoners hovered close to the building as if trying to hear what was going on. The major was pacing.

"Where the hell have you been, sergeant?"

"The tower, sir."

"Well, you should have noticed this incident the Storm Troopers want to cook up!" He snapped his arm as if pulling Carl in. "And, private, keep these gawkers back."

Inside, three German officers sat stiffly at a dining table as if about to conduct a court martial. A narrow sheet of paper lay in front of the one in the middle. A gaunt American lieutenant with dark circles under his eyes faced them. They seemed to be trying to burn holes in each other by staring. "The bastards speak English," the lieutenant whispered, "or at least enough, but they won't."

"They want some kind of incident," muttered Murnow. "They demand—get that!—*demand* to see a Swiss consul."

Carl removed his cap, reversed a ladderback chair, and straddled it, draping his cap on the second rung. "Good afternoon," he said in German. "I understand you men have a complaint."

The officer in the middle was a beady-eyed, squat man with a bulldog face and a Groucho Marx mustache. The one on the left was handsome, but with freckles that made Carl wonder about his age. It seemed a strain for him to hold his rigid pose; his pinky twitched even when he tightly laced his fingers. The one on the right, in contrast, had droopy eyelids and cheeks scarred with smallpox or acne. It appeared he might flop forward on the table asleep.

"In the name of the Reich and the men of this labor camp, I demand to see a member of the Swiss legation."

"Very well. What is the reason for this request?"

"There are obvious irregularities which we wish to convey to our government through a neutral party."

"Perhaps if you told me what these irregularities are . . ."

"You are merely an enlisted man."

Carl leaned back, holding the sides of his chair as if they were the control sticks on a tank. "Listen, friend, I am the translator. That is why the War Department sent me. Let's start over and talk man to man. I am Carl Maria Walthers, and you gentlemen are?"

The officer glared nastily at the American lieutenant, then at Major Murnow.

The handsome one could not contain himself and spoke "I am Lieutenant Ulrich Messer, the third-ranking officer of this camp."

"And you?" asked Carl.

"You shall not use *du* with me!" said the mustachioed one.

"Very well," said Carl, "I shall be quite formal, but it might be helpful to know your name."

"SS-Captain Gerhardt Läufer," he snapped, "and this is Captain Albert Dorn." The sleepy man nodded.

Murnow interrupted. "What is going on?"

"Hold on," said Carl, raising his hand.

"Nothing," the gaunt lieutenant answered. "It's bullshit." SS-Captain Läufer sneered at him.

Carl went back to German. "So, what seems to be the problem?"

"We have a list of demands."

Carl smiled. "You're not in a position to make demands."

"These are in accordance with the rules of war and with

47

the Geneva Conventions. We have a right to place them before the Swiss legation."

Carl turned to Murnow. "They insist on a Swiss diplomat."

"But why, for Christ's sake?"

"They haven't said."

Murnow opened his hands and spoke directly to the Germans. "Ah, look, fellows, if there's something wrong, we can fix it. There's no need to get into all this diplomatic crap. I don't even know where the closest Swiss consul is—probably New York. The Red Cross will be coming along in a few weeks. What's the big deal?" He touched Carl on the shoulder. "Explain that to them. We can fix it."

"Put 'em on bread and water," said the lieutenant.

"You shut up, Valdez," said Murnow.

Carl explained that the major wanted to treat the officers with the respect they deserved, but that it was impossible for him to know what to do without being informed. Carl was certain that SS-Captain Läufer had understood Murnow. He had been listening to the major too closely. There was a curl of his lips under his mustache, however, as if he were amused by Murnow's plea translated into Carl's formal request.

"Very well, then," said Läufer, picking up his list. "First, we demand to be treated as officers and moved to a camp which consists of officers. This is our right."

"For crying out loud," said Murnow after hearing the translation, "they have their own quarters and their own table in the dining hall. That's all I get."

"Secondly," continued the captain, "it is obvious that an attempt has been made to separate men from their comrades in their units in order to make men lonely and possibly suicidal. There are members of the 999 *Strafbataillon* mixed with units which have distinguished themselves on the battlefield. We demand the right to separate these criminal elements from the general population and to be restored to our own military units. We also demand the right to punish those criminal elements which refuse to conform to the general rules of order."

Carl summarized the argument. Though he understood that *Strafbataillon* meant a "criminal battalion" he didn't know exactly what it was. Lt. Valdez never removed his eyes from

48

the SS-captain as he said, "They drafted all the jailbirds. They didn't have enough criminals so they gathered up some more."

"How many more of these demands are there?" asked an exasperated Murnow.

"Thirdly, the food is not suitable," said Läufer.

"They don't like the chow," repeated Carl.

"What's wrong with the food? We had roast beef yesterday. Mashed potatoes and corn. They had salami sandwiches for lunch and canned peaches. They get eggs every morning. They even had sauerkraut and knockwurst last week. What do they want? Lobster? They sure eat enough!"

"Let 'em eat their own putzes," said Valdez.

"Will you shut up?"

The Germans were enjoying Murnow's consternation. "What displeases you about the food?" Carl asked Läufer quickly.

"How can we be expected to eat what those niggers cook?"

"The major says you have all been eating like hogs."

"What choice do we have? We demand our own kitchens, our own cooks. We will not accept our men working under the command of niggers."

"The Third Reich never fed you so well."

"You know, corporal, you surprise me. Carl Maria Walthers sounds like a German name and your accent even has a twinge of Swabian, which is quite a relief after those horrible Low German speakers, these—how you call it?—Pennsylvania Dutchmen, they used on that ridiculously long and unnecessary train ride. Surely you understand that the situation is humiliating."

"You *are* prisoners," Carl said. "My father had a Negro cook. There was nothing wrong with her food."

"Perhaps for you."

"Continue," said Carl staunchly.

"Fourthly, the Geneva Conventions allow us to have symbols of our culture and of our political leaders. We wish to have a photograph of the Führer hanging here in our dining hall."

Carl's expression now turned as stony as Lt. Valdez's. "That'll be the day," he said in English.

"What now?" asked Murnow.

Carl leaned into the SS-captain's face. "Listen to me well, mister. You do not understand the situation. Thanks to your Herr Hitler I was dragged away from the only thing I ever wanted. Thanks to your Herr Hitler one of your snipers wrecked my shoulder. Understand I do not care, have never cared, what you people do at home, but I have serious doubts I ever want to see Herr Hitler's face hanging anywhere in my country."

Läufer stared directly into his eyes. His intense whisper was barely audible. "You cannot escape being a member of the German race by sailing across an ocean. Germany is in your heart."

Major Murnow placed a hand on Carl's upper arm. "What the hell is going on? Dammit, are you going to flake out like Valdez?"

Carl snatched the list off the table and spun away. "Why don't I translate the rest of them and save some time?"

"Yeah, sure," said Murnow. "We'll get back to him. Tell him that. I'll talk to the general. It's almost dinner time. We'll talk tomorrow, right?"

"Right," said Läufer in English. He smiled like the Mona Lisa.

"Fucker," muttered Valdez.

"I'll put you on report," threatened Murnow. "In my office!" He was so furious when he put on his cap he didn't notice how crookedly it sat on his head. Murnow led a miniature parade down the path between the buildings, followed by Lieutenant Valdez who ambled in his gangly way as if he were birdwatching. Carl followed and the guard scurried along behind.

When they got to the office, Murnow immediately reached into his desk drawer and lifted out his whisky. He took a deep swallow and used the bottle as a pointer. "I blame you for this, Abe. What did you do to get them riled up?"

Valdez crossed his arms. "They're just trying to maintain their position with their men."

"Demands! Do you know what will happen if we get Swiss diplomats parading around here? The word will get to Washington for sure." The major turned sideways and tilted his head almost at the same angle as the profile of FDR. All he needed was the cigarette holder. "Quiet is what this job's about. Quiet. Set up the camp, keep it quiet."

Valdez glanced at Carl. His Sad Sack face showed nothing of what he was feeling. He picked at a tooth with his fingernail. The major spun and pulled his chair closer to the desk. "This is Carl Walthers. He'll be a sergeant as soon as we get the stripes. He's fluent in German—not like you! I shouldn't have let you near the prisoners. You provoked them."

"They need a good slapping."

Murnow fumed. "What the hell else is on the paper?"

Carl took it from his shirt pocket and unfolded it. "One is officers to have their own camps. Two is reuniting military units. Three is they don't like Negroes cooking. Four, they want pictures of Hitler."

Valdez spat a burst of air.

"Let's see. There are four more. They have been threatened by certain of the guards when they have attempted to do the Hitler salute as their—as their regulations require."

Valdez spat again.

"The Geneva Conventions allow that," pleaded Murnow. "I showed you the guidelines from the War Department."

Valdez stared at his shoes.

"Go on, go on," Murnow said to Carl.

"The next is that they refuse to do slave labor and will not permit their men to do so."

"What do they mean, slave labor? They'll get paid. They're going to pick grapes. Germans know about grapes. What if they go on strike with me? My butt will be—" He took another swallow of his whisky.

"They don't want to hear any more of the radio propaganda to which they have been subjected during meals. And they want to screen the newspapers which are being brought to them because they are full of lies."

"They ought to be able to recognize a lie when they see one," said Valdez.

Carl laughed and turned the paper toward the officers. "And they want to run up their flag every morning and sing 'Deutschland über Alles.'"

Murnow gawped.

"They're humiliated by having to line up and listen to the 'Star-spangled Banner,' every morning."

"Tex," said Valdez, "they're testing you. Stuff the paper up Läufer's ass."

"We wouldn't be in this fix if you hadn't riled them!"

"They're *Nazis,* Tex. They set the world on fire. They're exterminating everybody they don't like. Me. You."

"You don't know that."

"I'm an intelligence officer, Tex. I know."

"That's not my problem. I got to keep the lid on. That's all I'm supposed to do. Then maybe I can get a command."

Valdez came to his feet. "Tex, if you give in to these bastards at all, I'll raise hell all the way to Secretary Stimson's office. That's all I have to say. I'm going to dinner before you get rid of the cooks and introduce SS cuisine." He saluted in a highly artificial manner.

"Sit down, Abe."

"Sergeant, you meet me at the mess in the morning. I'll brief you on what we're doing here."

"Aw, Abe!" said Murnow. "Don't make waves or we'll be stuck here forever."

"You've got a command, Tex. You just don't know what the fuck to do with it."

"Don't use that language with me!"

The screen door clattered as Valdez left.

"Did you see that?" said Murnow. "He disobeyed an order, didn't he? I told him to sit. I could bring him up on charges."

"Yes, sir," said Carl. "I'd rather not be a witness, if you don't mind."

Murnow sipped his whisky again. "Charges would make an incident, though, wouldn't they?"

"True."

"What am I going to do with these demands? They're right about some of these Geneva things. At least that's what I understand."

Carl, who had been holding the list of demands in his right hand, felt a throb in his shoulder. "Maybe the guy who shot me is out there," he said.

"Fortunes of war," said Murnow, rotating his chair. "You're lucky. The same guy never had a chance to shoot at me."

3.

Carl had trouble sleeping, something strange for him. He had learned to snatch sleep wherever he could get it when he was touring with Buzz Bixby's band, or when he was up most of the night singing in one of Sally Mack's clubs and then doing a society luncheon for the mobster's politicians. He'd even managed to sleep during the Atlantic crossing. They'd hit a storm and the ship bounced like a cork. His sergeant had told him that anybody who could sleep through that was born to be a combat soldier. Carl told him to drop dead and was soon doing fifty push-ups on the wind-raked and slippery deck.

But tonight was different. He didn't know what it was exactly. Maybe because the Emerald City was a hundred and twenty miles down the track and the Greek was still there somewhere, the Wizard behind the curtain, pulling strings and levers. Papanoumou wouldn't forget how Carl had wowed them a year and a half ago. He might even be able to pull a lever to get Carl discharged. The war was a bull market for peddling influence. It was just a question of getting there and locating the guy.

After Carl lay on his cot for ninety minutes or so, a mosquito hummed near his ear and Pike, the provost sergeant, began to snore. Carl swung his feet into his boots and wandered behind the barracks to the edge of the ravine. He sat on a slab of rock, lit a cigarette, and listened to the insects in the trees. The warm throb in his shoulder had returned and he swiveled his arm to quiet it. The doctors had said it might be stiff the rest of his life, though the long train ride and the dampness of the lake had likely aggravated it. "Learn to pitch southpaw," joked one doctor. It wasn't pitching he

53

wanted, though. The silky slide. That little thrill he could feel from the dames when he slid his hand out and up on a rising note. It was like brushing his fingers down a woman's back and hearing her breath flutter. The silky slide would be back, he told himself. It was just a question of time.

The wound had gotten him home. If he'd kept his mouth shut, maybe he'd be free. That was the Army way. Bitch and they break you. He was lucky he wasn't digging a foxhole in Sicily. A captain had bluntly told him he had two choices, he could translate in Alva, Oklahoma, or translate in North East, Pennsylvania. Northeast Pennsylvania would have put him near New York City and he was already turning over the prospects of chumming back up to Sally Mack. He choked when he found out that North East was the name of a town in the northwestern corner of the state, named because it was northeast of Erie. Later he saw on a map that it was near Cleveland. Hallelujah, brother! It had all the smackings of destiny: Wounded Veteran Wows Broadway, Carl Carlson Conquers Flix.

He whistled the opening bars of "One Kiss." An owl hooted. He softly began singing one of Natalie's songs, "This Is No Laughing Matter." As the last words faded into the trees, he heard a soft rumble. A stream down in the darkness. Or maybe it was nature applauding. Didn't the streams listen to Orpheus? His father had told him all the myths in the same exaggerated way in which he lectured. When Carl was very small it was wonderful. Later it seemed much too excessive. Also there was the strange connection his father tried to make between the Classical world and the future Supermen of Germany. He had always said it was Nietzsche who had shown the way to the future through the past.

"Orpheus," Carl said out loud. Maybe that was the river Styx down there. He listened for a few seconds, then lay back on the rock and began singing "Marie." Some of the words got away from him. He needed lyric sheets, as many as he could get on his lousy army pay. He also needed to hear as much radio as he could to find out what was hip these days. He had to be ready. He returned to his cot, not because he was sleepy, but because he resolved to sleep to protect his voice.

The next morning was cool and dewy. The sky shifted from rose to a blue so deep you could dip a pen in it. Valdez was a few minutes late and showed up with a leather bag. He was as droopy looking as if he too had been awake most of the night. He said little until they were inside the prisoners' compound. "Walk tall," he said as the guard closed the gate. "The Huns need to know we're not intimidated by baby-killers."

Carl straightened up and felt bone scraping against bone in his upper back.

The prisoners watched them. Some of them said *Guten Morgen*. Valdez did not answer, but Carl cautiously nodded.

"How badly were you wounded?"

"Bad enough to get me here."

"Major says you're a lousy soldier."

"He's right."

They passed a line of men waiting to wash in a bucket. "He's lousier. I suppose the ace translators get taken by O.S.S."

Carl wasn't sure what the "ace" was supposed to imply, so he didn't respond.

"These Huns could be a wealth of information and I intend to prove it."

In the early light, the Germans looked pasty and stupid, not like *Übermensch* at all. Several of them were sweeping out huts.

"I can understand most of what they say from Yiddish, but they get their noses out of joint if I use it. You talk to them, I'll listen for any useful intelligence."

"Your name doesn't sound Yiddish," Carl commented.

"Sephardic," said Valdez. "Fourteen ninety-two was a big year for us." He studied Carl to see if he understood. Carl nodded, though he didn't. He was sure Valdez knew he didn't. "I was in an orphanage with regular Yids, Ashkenazim, though."

"I knew a lot of Jews in the music business. New York was my home base."

Valdez stopped, his eyes glassy, and grabbed Carl's sleeve. "You don't have to be polite. Call us what you normally call us: Yids, kikes. It doesn't matter. Beat us. Spit on us. Shoot us. We're not going away."

Carl was stunned. A cluster of Germans nearby stopped talking and stared. "Hey," Carl finally joked, "you're crumpling the material."

"I'm proud to be vermin. The vermin of the earth are the strongest. We'll be left when the pretty boy Nazis and Japs and everybody else is dead."

"Aw, knock it off, lieutenant," said Carl weakly smiling. "Religion's a crock to me. People are people."

Valdez lowered his hand as if thinking something of such overwhelming sadness he couldn't explain. Carl took a hesitant step and the lieutenant began walking again. Carl remembered he had intended to work on Valdez to get him a weekend pass. What a brilliant idea. A regular fucking Einstein of an idea.

They approached a building near the end of one row. A German waited on the stoop, his chest puffed out. Valdez was suddenly the officious lieutenant. He read three names and prisoner numbers from a clothbound notebook he removed from his briefcase and dispatched the German to get them. Valdez circled the structure and looked under the hut. Satisfied no one was hiding, he began to explain the procedure. Inside the hut was a potbelly stove, a table, and a few chairs. Carl would chat up prisoners about where they were from, and who they were before the war, the goal being to identify the Nazi party members and the draftees, the potential informers and the Hitler worshippers. If anyone let anything slip about where he lived and the factories, bridges, and mines were in his home town, well, that was gravy.

"You know how to make coffee?" asked Valdez.

"Sort of."

"Listen to me then. It's part of your job and I don't want it messed up." He pulled a small cloth bag from his valise and lifted an enameled pot from behind the stove. Valdez explained very precisely in his characterless voice. He wanted coffee made in the European style, the most delicious the prisoner had ever tasted. It was better than truth serum, he said. Whatever fit had come over Valdez had passed. Maybe the lieutenant had taken a bullet in the head, thought Carl.

If there wasn't anything wrong with him, why else would he be here?

Valdez greeted each prisoner with a mixture of English and German. He handed them coffee with great dollops of cream as if they had been invited into someone's parlor. Carl then moved into chitchat, explaining that Americans had nothing against any of the German people personally and that they wanted to make them as comfortable as possible, given the circumstances. Were there any little complaints or inconveniences? The camp was going to put enlisted men to work in the local vineyards and farms, for which the prisoners would get eighty cents a day in scrip which they could spend at a special store in the camp. Did the prisoner have any special skills? Was there some kind of job he'd prefer? This method wasn't so much a question of getting a big secret out of a lonely man far from home, Valdez explained, but of accumulating details and seeing the pattern. That's why the game was called intelligence. You had to see the forest in the trees.

Carl pretended to be interested. A great singer needed to be an actor, too, so he might as well pretend to care. After all, most prisoners would know why they were being courted, and those that couldn't figure it out would be warned. True to form, most of them were unable to resist the coffee and cigarettes, but were evasive. One or two refused the coffee and said little more than name, rank, and serial number. Others, probably misfits, did their best to ingratiate themselves. It was soon apparent that the men who might be most helpful were the ones least likely to open up, while the ones who went on at great length couldn't be trusted. A reliable soldier wouldn't look for friends among his enemies, would he?

While waiting for the last man that afternoon, Carl raised this with Valdez, who had listened studiously and occasionally asked for clarification of what a man had said. "Even an outcast sees and hears things," said the lieutenant. "Even a liar tells you the truth if you can deduce why he's lying." They ended the day having heard about a son one corporal had never seen, about a wife another corporal was happy to be away from, and about how to crack a safe with one of the expensive time locks. None of this was going to shorten the war, but the safecracker was a sign of what kind of man the Reich was now scraping up to defend itself.

All that rich coffee upset Carl's stomach, and the corned beef hash in the mess that night did nothing to settle it. Germans served up the food watched by Sergeant Lang, a large black man with foggy spectacles. He chewed his cigar as if he were about to run wild with the cleaver he held at his waist. The Germans didn't understand, or pretended not to understand, what Americans said and often put huge scoops of squash or hash on the plate of a soldier who had asked for only a little. What you got stuck with you were required to eat. Lang stepped forward at one point and yelled at one of the Germans for handling the bread too much. The German pretended to misunderstand him until Lang quietly, smilingly, threatened to chop off his pinky.

When Carl slid onto the rough bench at the table, Murnow's aide, Sergeant O'Hurly, said that there was a big blow-up going on in Murnow's office. The quartermaster, Lt. Jack Morris, was trying to keep Valdez and the major from killing each other over Murnow's concessions to the Nazi demands. "The major has no choice on some stuff," said O'Hurly. "The dopes in Washington have told him what he's got to do. They can have their salute and they can hang pictures of the Führer in their barracks. That's orders. Tex keeps explaining he isn't giving in, but Valdez doesn't want to hear it."

"Valdez has a point," said Carl. "Those guys need to know who's boss. Who wrote those Geneva rules anyway? A kraut?"

"Yeah, but what about our guys over there?"

"You know they're treating ours worse than we're treating theirs."

"It could be worse, though," said O'Hurly. "Valdez says there's reports of whole towns including girls and kids being buried alive. It's hard to believe."

"Valdez is not an easy guy to believe," said Carl carefully.

O'Hurly glanced around. "Should have been Section Eight." He raised his palms. "You never heard it from me." He leaned conspiratorially. "Bughouse. Broke down like a tin watch."

"He's an odd bird is all I meant."

"Could happen to anybody. The stories I could tell! You see a lot of files where I am. You never know what'll break a man."

"So maybe he exaggerates. The Germans aren't the Japs. They're an enlightened people: philosophy, music, science . . ."

O'Hurly paused, his fork suspended in midair, and studied Carl for a second. "Take off their dress pants and they got gorilla hair on their butts like everybody else."

Carl scraped up another lump of hash. "None of my business. I'm just here to translate. Say, what are the chances for a weekend pass?"

"Not much until everything settles down."

"I got friends in Cleveland."

O'Hurly leaned forward. "There's pussy closer than that. I'll introduce you."

"I said friends."

"Yeah," he grinned. "I got a fifth of a friend hidden near our cabin. Smooth as milk and a kick like ethyl. Better than what Tex sucks up. I'll introduce you."

"You know plenty, don't you?"

"There are so many skeletons in the closets you can't get the doors shut." O'Hurly noticed a PFC eating alone and watching. "What are you looking at?" he barked. "Eat your fuckin' squash."

A half hour later Carl casually wandered to the camp commander's office. As O'Hurly had finished eating a piece of very sweet sheet cake, he had whispered to Carl that he and "his friend" would meet him back at the noncom barracks in about an hour and a half. Carl had a sudden thought and asked about a phone. O'Hurly said he might be able to hitch a ride into town sometime, or, if he could think of some cover story, and Murnow and Sergeant Pike weren't around, he could use the one on O'Hurly's desk.

The lowering sun raked the top of the trees. In the tower, two men, as usual, leaned on the rail and stared toward the distant lake. A corporal with a rifle slung over his shoulder paced along the fencing enclosing the prisoner compound. Inside, Germans were clustering in circles, telling jokes, gesturing, heading off together towards their latrines. It re-

minded Carl of a CCC camp he had sung in when Buzz
Bixby's Cavalcade of Swing was still Buzz Bixby's Six-Bit
Combo: a half-dozen mokes playing for not much more than
meals and change. It beat the soup kitchens, but not by much.
He carefully squeezed out the fire in his last cigarette between his forefinger and thumb. He popped it back into the
pack, and pocketed it. He quickly stepped into O'Hurly's
office and dialed the phone.

"Can I help you?" said the operator.

"I'd like to call a Mr. Michael Papanoumou in Cleveland."

"Number, please."

"This number?" He read it off the dial. "38–723."

"And his number?"

"I've lost his number. I'm just back from overseas. I'm his
brother."

"What was that name again, soldier?"

"Papanoumou, Michael." He hoped she didn't ask for the
spelling, but she did. He gamely rolled into it, but had no
idea whether he was right. "I'm not sure about that."

"You're not sure of your brother's spelling?"

"It got changed, ma'am."

"Oh. You should've took something American. I'm Mimsy,
I'll call you back."

"I'm Carl," he said.

He rocked back in the desk chair and whistled. Several
minutes passed. He picked up two pencils and drummed the
desk blotter as if he were Ted Clough ripping through "Barney Google." Whatever happened to Ted, anyway? He tried
to picture the big guy in a uniform. They probably jammed
him into a tank. Or a sub.

The phone startled him.

"Carl?"

"Yes."

"There's no Michael P-A-P-A-N-U-M-U in Cleveland."

"Maybe the spelling's mixed up a little."

"There's nothing like it. We tried Shaker Heights, Euclid,
the whole area. Anything for a hero."

"I'm no hero," said Carl. "What about Swing Land? It's a
nightclub. Have you got a number for that?"

"Swing Land closed. I used to go there."

"No kidding?" said Carl. He felt elated. "Were you there when Buzz Bixby's Cavalcade of Swing played?"

"Who?"

"They had a singer, Carl Carlson. The Carolina Crooner."

"Never heard of him."

You will, thought Carl. You will.

"I'm sorry I couldn't help you."

"Wait. Could you try to find another number?"

"Sure."

"Ernie Mussolini. Maybe he goes by Ernest Musso, now."

"Mussolini?"

"Yeah, like Hitler's pal. But don't forget to try Musso."

"Okay, Carl. I'll get back to you."

He reached for the pencils and it suddenly struck him. Swing Land was closed. What had happened? When he remembered that night, his birthday, it all seemed like it was many years ago: ten, twenty, like a vivid memory from elementary school, something you're not sure you recall correctly. And yet it was less than two years ago. The war had transfigured everything from jobs to bodies to time itself. He stood, disturbed at the notion that maybe his voice had changed, too. Or maybe he was the only thing that hadn't changed and his singing would no longer have the right appeal.

He walked away from the desk and aimlessly tried the olive drab file cabinet. It was locked. He bent over and peered out the window. A tree shifted on a breeze and a distant orange sparkle off Lake Erie was momentarily revealed, then covered by the leaves again. Mother Nature's fan dance, he thought. He cracked the door, checked that no one was coming, and paced some more. He paused at the major's door and considered raiding the man's whisky. Murnow could use a little less. But he left the door closed, went back to the chair, and pulled open the drawer of O'Hurly's desk. There were two magazines: a *Life* and a *Liberty*. Beneath them was a photo of a nearly naked girl with her back to the camera. She wore a garter, stockings, and nothing else. She had her arms on her hips and looked back over her broad shoulders with a wink. A heart had been drawn on her round, pale buttocks. Three X's were lined up across the wide part of

the heart. *Life, Liberty,* and the pursuit of happiness, thought
Carl. He noticed two files underneath. One was labeled
"VALDEZ, Abraham. 55–765–210." The other, "PIKE,
James Arnold. 41–572–402." O'Hurly should have locked
these in with the others. He'd have to watch this guy. The
room was getting dim, and Carl glanced around as if to make
certain no one else was there before opening the file on Valdez. Just as he did, the phone rang.

"Carl Papan—what's your name?"

"I'm here."

"I'm sorry, no listing for an Ernie or Ernest Mussolini or
Musso. If he has a phone the people in Ohio don't know
about it. Can I help you with anything else?"

Carl sagged and rubbed his forehead. He could try Sally
Mack or his brother Georgy, but he decided it wasn't his day.
It hadn't been his day for a long time. Maybe he'd used them
up. "That's all right, precious. I give up."

"The name's Mimsy, hero," she said sexily. "Have a nice
evening."

Carl hung up and perused the enlistment sheet on the top
of Valdez's file. Why bother? He closed it abruptly, slipped
it back under *Life, Liberty,* and the pursuit of happiness, and
crept out of the office.

Twilight tinted everything blue. None of the Germans were
outside their barracks anymore, yet he could hear a faint
voice speaking inside the compound, as if to a group, with
firm, careful pacing to his words. He couldn't make out what
was being said. Then there was the gentle roar of a large
number of men laughing.

Carl thought about meeting O'Hurly to work on his
"friend" but the files made him feel funny about the guy, so
he strolled instead to the edge of the ravine, deciding to
finish off his last cigarette. He was surprised how deep it
looked. Across, in the deepening shadows, layers of thin gray
shale were stacked like a pile of ragged sheet music. "Hello!"
he shouted, expecting an echo. Only the murmuring of the
stream answered. *"Once in love with Amy . . . ,"* he sang slowly.
Still no echo.

A path descended to his right. Steep and uneven, it curled
into the rough brush, disappeared, then became visible again

where it switched back along the face of the slope. Carl picked his way down, often grasping at a sapling or a low branch for support, his shoulder complaining when he seized a limb too firmly. He stumbled several times and was dizzied by the thought of being thrown into this miniature canyon, but he went on, even when the brush closed in with scratchy leaves. He thought of Orpheus again and he knew why he was descending into the Underworld. Why else? To sing. Getting out when it got darker would be the tricky part.

The noise of the stream got steadily louder until he found himself on a gravel plateau next to it. The canopy of trees rustled, filtering down very little of the remaining light. The looming slate wall was now almost black and the stream water had darkened to ink. His audience of shadows waited, whispered, shifted in their seats. He stepped up onto a slab of stone jutting out over the water and imagined it as his stage. Carl Carlson, the Carolina Crooner, closed his eyes, took a deep breath, and began snapping his fingers. He listened to the band's up-tempo introduction, carefully counted it out, and caught the first beat perfectly. *"Birds do it, bees do it, even educated fleas do it . . ."*

He was driving the sound forward a hundred miles an hour, totally at the mercy of the frantic pace, but never missing a word. When he hit the last phrase of the first verse he held the word *love* and modulated it into four syllables as a springboard for the Mack Mintner trumpet solo. As he stepped back, the leaves and the stream rustled their approval, and he nodded, mouthing thank you. He picked up the next verse and rushed through it in similar fashion clearly enunciating each syllable like a shot from a rifle, then letting the end burst from his lungs like a 50-mm howitzer shell. He automatically crooked his back and tried raising his arm, but the heat in his shoulder rose. He tucked in his elbows to prevent showing the audience that anything was wrong. He'd save the silky slide for some other time.

The applause roared as loud as it had at Swing Land. He cleared his throat as the imaginary band eased into the opening bars of "Someone to Watch Over Me." He was rusty, but he sang until after midnight, a dozen songs and then a dozen more, "Tea for Two," "Isn't It Romantic?", "Two Lips Like

Tulips," "You Made Me Love You," "Honeysuckle Rose," "When Shadows Fall," songs he'd known forever, songs he thought he'd forgotten. He was good, he told himself, damn good. Perhaps not quite good enough to raise someone from the Underworld, but damn close. It was the best concert that ravine had ever heard, and he'd do even better the next night.

4.

Reveille came much too early, but there wasn't a hell of a lot to do about it. Basic training pretty much put you on automatic pilot, anyway. You could get up, shave, put on your uniform, and make your bunk in less time than most people wash up. You'd do all this without thinking or feeling anything. Sometime later in the day you'd wake up and wonder how you got where you were. For all that, Carl knew that he was going to feel like Rosie the Riveter had been jackhammering his eyes, and nothing would help. He'd be knocking back coffee with the prisoners all day, so there was no sense in trying to crank his engine with that thirty-weight Army brew.

As Carl took his position among the men, Sergeant O'Hurly read down his clipboard. "Adams!"

"Raymond!"

"Ardmore!"

"Charles!"

"Berringer!"

"Eugene!"

"Birdsong!"

"Tony!"

O'Hurly looked up. "What was that?"

"Anthony, sir."

"After assembly I want fifty, private. Branden!"

"Ronald!"

"Burgess!"

"Ezekial!"

And so it went. Inside the wire, the prisoners had assembled in lines outside their barracks, many of them with their eyes closed or squinting as they faced the rising sun. A head count was being done by Sergeant Pike. The MPs by each double line of Germans shouted.

"Barracks A-3, twenty!"

"Check!"

"Barracks A-4, twenty!"

"Check!"

"Barracks A-5, eighteen!"

"Check!"

The syncopated rhythm of the voices was like the rocking of a rowboat in a slow river. You wanted to drift forever.

"Walthers!"

His own name had crept up on him. "Carl!" he finally said.

"Sing it out!" said Lieutenant Morris. The men laughed. "We expect a big effort out of you for the national anthem, right, men?"

"Yes, sir!" they shouted.

"Yes, sir," said Carl dryly. He tried to remember the words and wasn't sure. Did Morris mean Carl was to do it solo? Oh, hell. This was going to look dumb.

"Sir, all present or accounted for," Morris said to Major Murnow, who nodded and looked toward the prisoners. The man assisting Sergeant Pike was scribbling on the clipboard, holding it close to his face as if he were nearsighted. Finally, he looked up, saluted the sergeant, and said, "All prisoners present or accounted for, sir!"

"'Ten-SHUN!" shouted Morris, who spun to the flag pole and saluted. All of the men snapped to as a private began hooking the flag to the rope. The bugler raised his horn, played a few notes of the refrain of the "Star-spangled Banner," and the entire corps began to sing it. Carl could feel the men on his right and left watching him out of the corners of their eyes, but he didn't make any special effort. The words all came back effortlessly, as if written on his sleeve. School had embedded it in him, more deeply than he had known.

Half-way through the first verse, he noticed the slow motion of a horse pulling a hay wagon past the entrance. Farm girls and boys were scattered on the single layer of bales. They waved and flashed victory signs. What more could you want? Soldiers singing at dawn. The flag. Kids. A wonderful combination for a movie, just the sappy kind of thing they were always playing for the suckers these days.

A rumble, at first seeming to come from the children, gradually grew louder, disturbing Carl's reverie as the hay wagon receded towards North East. The men around him shifted their heads slightly to steal glances at the prisoner's compound. The men in the tower hurried to the big machine gun and the MPs hefted their guns to their chests.

The Germans were singing. More than five hundred voices were rolling "Deutschland über Alles" over the rolling hill and vineyards beyond like a great thunderstorm. The Americans glanced at each other and the "Star-spangled Banner" ended in a nervous, off-key mumble. Lieutenant Morris hurried up to Major Murnow and exchanged inaudible words. Murnow shrugged, looked back at the compound, and said something else to Morris. Morris seemed to be protesting, but Murnow motioned, hands down. Valdez charged up to them and was waving his hand frantically. Murnow thrust a finger at him, which Valdez leaned into, his voice carrying over the anthem. "So fire in the air! *Do something!*"

Murnow gritted his teeth and dressed the lieutenant up and down. Morris tried to calm them, but Valdez spun on his heels and walked away. The red-faced Murnow kicked at the dirt and screamed "You're on report, you son of a bitch! You're on report!"

"Fuck Tex!" said someone behind Carl and almost in unison, the enlisted men began to boo. The men in the tower picked it up and then the MPs on the compound perimeter. This only made the Germans sing louder, though some of them lowered their heads when an MP moved close and unleashed a stream of obscenity.

Murnow threw his cap on the ground in exasperation and stalked the line of troops. "Attention! Anyone not at attention will be punished. I mean it, you bastards! I mean it."

Lieutenant Morris looked around as if he knew how dangerous this had all become. The guards were getting too nervous. If someone opened fire, if a German made a grab at a gun . . . He ran for the tower and waved his arms at the machine gun.

Suddenly, then, the song ended. The Germans snapped to

attention and *"Heil Hitler!"* resonated into an eerie silence. The Americans fidgeted, but the Germans all stood still, their arms thrust skyward, their smirking visible all the way to the far barracks.

"Fuck Hitler!" said Dahl, breaking the silence.

"Shut up!" said Murnow.

"Fuck Hitler," said someone, obviously trying to keep his lips from moving.

"Who said that?"

"Fuck Hitler," said another.

"I want absolute silence," said Murnow, "and I want the men who spoke to step forward. Immediately."

Dahl immediately took a step. A short PFC did likewise. Two more men stepped forward, then five. Then three more. Soon everyone had taken a step forward but Carl. Oh, brother, he thought. He shrugged and took his step, too. The men on the tower were having a hard time keeping from laughing. A red flush rose from the major's neck to his cheeks to his forehead. It looked like his balding head would pop. He stared, panting, then spun back at the prisoners. Sergeant Pike moved closer to the gate and waited for the major's orders.

Murnow snatched his cap off the ground, took one more look at the men, and said to Morris. "I'll want a punishment report by noon." He marched for his office.

"But, sir," said Morris. "Major, sir! What—?" The lieutenant rolled his eyes and made several turns as if whatever he was supposed to do might be sneaking up on him. Finally he raised his hands toward the sky in a "Why me?" gesture and addressed O'Hurly.

"Sergeant, tell Sergeant Pike to confine the prisoners to barracks. We'll figure out what to do about breakfast later." He sighed and flicked his wrist to get O'Hurly moving. He clasped his arms behind his back and stalked along the front rank.

"Fine," he said. "Fine. You know how much paperwork is on my desk? I haven't got time for this! We're talking about the coal we're supposed to get this winter. We're talking about *your* winter gear. You want guard duty without a coat?" He shook his head in disgust. "Like a bunch of damned kids."

The prisoners were neatly moving back into their barracks. The faint sound of celebrating leaked from inside.

"Okay," said Morris, "we'll stand here until the krauts are back in. Then I want to see fifty push-ups. You get any dirt on your uniform I'll take fifty more. And nobody leaves the camp for a week except on my say-so." He shook his head again and watched the prisoners moving back into their barracks. It was a silly punishment and everyone knew it. If Murnow was angry about it later, the repercussions would fall on Morris. The quartermaster must have known that, and because he knew that, Carl could see him grow several more inches in the men's eyes. Some men instinctively did the right things in the right situations, Carl thought. Who can explain it?

Three hours passed before Valdez and Carl were in their hut interrogating prisoners. Valdez was still steaming and said he'd wring their necks until they blabbed on who organized the singing.

A rumpled man with a hairy mole on his upper lip was first. He held his hat in both hands, eyes shifting from Carl to Valdez and back. Carl stuck out his hand and spoke in German, "Good morning, I am Carl Maria Walthers and you are . . ."

"Jan Herder."

"Take a seat, Jan. This is Lieutenant Valdez."

Herder nodded.

"We have just made coffee. Would you like coffee?"

He shook his head.

"This is not that bitter coffee the mess serves. This is special and we have the best cream, very thick."

The cream made him reconsider, but he shook his head.

"Are you afraid? We are not here to hurt you. We are merely trying to find out who will be best at certain tasks. Next week we will be beginning some agricultural work. You'll be able to leave the compound and get out in the country. Have you ever done agricultural work: harvesting grapes, picking tomatoes . . . ?"

He watched Valdez slowly pour a cup of the coffee.

"Coffee?"

He shook his head.

"Well, Jan, have you been in the army long? What did you do before the war?"

"What kind of coffee is it?"

Carl didn't know how to answer that. "It's the kind families drink in the evenings after dinner when they sit together on the sofa listening to the radio." He didn't know where the homey image came from, but from the way Herder stared through the table top, Carl sensed he had struck a nerve. I could be good at this, Carl thought.

"My mother died."

Carl signaled to Valdez to get Herder coffee. "Ask him about the singing," Valdez said.

Carl's scowl was too late, Herder lifted his head, his memories broken off. "Your name is not common in Germany is it? Did your mother name you after your father?"

"There are lots of bastards in Hamburg," muttered Herder.

"If you had a father like I had, you would be happy you didn't know him."

"A boy needs someone to hate," said Herder. "I had the priests and the police. They often took my mother away and I would live in the pantry until she came back. The last time she did not come back."

"I'm sorry," said Carl.

Herder shrugged. "They tell us you drug the coffee."

"The coffee?"

"Truth serum."

Carl laughed and translated for Valdez, who didn't know the word. Valdez laughed, but like a man with something to hide, checking how his forced amusement was affecting the prisoner.

"That's nonsense," said Carl. Herder eagerly flicked his wrists for Valdez to bring the coffee.

"I like mint schnapps in my coffee."

"We can't give you that, I'm afraid."

"Pity. But truth serum, schnapps, it's all the same. I have nothing to tell you. They came to my cell one day and said I had been pardoned. I was to protect the Fatherland." He laughed. "So they sent me to Tunis! Do I look like a Berber? Could my father have been a Berber sailor? Have you ever heard of a Berber sailor?" He laughed again and sipped his coffee. "More cream." He was nothing like the man who had entered.

"So you were in prison. Politics? Are you a Red?"

"Red follows me wherever I go." He made a throat-cutting motion. Carl raised an eye at Valdez. "I would have made an excellent Brown Shirt. But you are wasting your time, they would never trust me with anything you want to know."

"We're not after military information. We know only the worst of you would betray your friends. This holding prisoners is new to us. We want to keep things quiet. Maybe appoint a few leaders."

"Don't worry about that. The Gestapo is already here."

"What do you mean?"

Herder shrugged.

"Are they who organized the singing this morning?"

"We have been told it was a spontaneous outpouring," winked Herder.

"We would like to know more. We can help men like you."

"I don't know anything."

"Maybe you do not know the value of what you know," insisted Carl. "We can protect you."

"It does not matter. I am true to my guild. I do not inform." He sipped and tapped his cup. "Perhaps more cream. It seems a bit thin."

Carl looked at him sternly, then slowly poured more cream.

Private Jan Herder, they wrote after he left, had been talkative, but coy. They noted his claim that the Gestapo was operating among the prisoners and that he had said he was a murderer freed for the *Strafbataillon*.

"Do you believe that twerp is a murderer?" asked Carl.

"We'll find out," said Valdez. "He's either bragging because he is, or he's bragging because he wants to be. You're not pressing hard enough."

"Rome wasn't built in a day."

Valdez grunted.

The next was a sergeant, tall, gruff, and missing at least three teeth. He had some kind of gum problem, but fortunately said very little and kept his breath to himself. He said the singing was a spontaneous outpouring of emotion. Carl made a note to get the guy to a dentist before he killed another prisoner by breathing in his face.

The third man, also a sergeant, was square-jawed and as stiff as if he expected to have ice picks driven under his fingernails. Alone of the three, he resisted the coffee and said only that he was "Sergeant Helmut Ansbach of Vienna." Carl talked of pastries and every other thing he could remember about the city, but the sergeant stared straight ahead, not drawn in by the banter. "Well," said Carl, "I can see you're one of the Third Reich's best soldiers. It's a shame you are stuck here with all these petty criminals from the 999."

Ansbach gave him a sharp look. "I don't know what you mean."

"You do, but let that pass. I have got to hand it to you National Socialists, you have made real soldiers out of many of those men and they respect you for it."

Ansbach watched Carl carefully. This tack was good. It confused the sergeant somewhat.

"Only men like you could have talked some of those hardened men into the singing this morning."

"It was a spontaneous outpouring of emotion."

Valdez struck the table and shouted in German. "Liar!"

The sergeant's spine went stiff as an iron bar.

"What the lieutenant means," said Carl, crossing his arms, "is that we've been told you were behind it. It takes a special leader to organize something like that."

"It was a spontaneous outpouring of emotion."

Valdez spoke very slowly in German. "Mister, we are able to make a man hurt very much."

"It was a spontaneous outpouring of emotion."

Valdez struck the table again.

"Get out of here," said Carl in English. "Beat it! *Schnell!*"

The sergeant stood sharply, defiantly cracked out his arm in the Hitler salute, about-faced, and marched out.

"What are you doing?" said Valdez. "We just started!"

Carl ran the tip of his tongue along his teeth and dug at a tiny piece of bacon that had embedded between two molars. "Well?"

"'Well' what, lieutenant? That guy can't be bullied. He might talk, but he won't if he's pushed around."

"How would you know? I'm the intelligence officer."

"Well, for an intelligence officer, you're not very smart."

"You want to lose your sergeant's stripes even before you get them sewed on? You don't know what you're dealing with!"

Carl tried pleading. "Look, I don't care about the stripes. Just listen to me. I've got a feeling for people. Before the war I had a lot of practice feeling out what an audience wanted."

"Yeah, right."

Carl stood. "Yeah, right!"

"Just because you can keep people awake with your singing doesn't mean you know anything about interrogation."

"Awake? I was way the hell down in that gorge."

"Yeah, right."

"Fine," said Carl. "You question them!" He stormed out of the hut past the guard and down the stairs of the stoop. He fished for a cigarette and realized they were all gone. "Son of a bitch!" he said and paced furiously beside the building. "Who the fuck cares?" he muttered. "Who the fuck cares?"

He was still pacing when a prisoner timidly stuck his head around the corner. "Joe, am I now to going in?"

Carl wiped the sweat from the upper part of his lip. The face was familiar. "You are the clarinettist," he said in German.

"You remember."

"You're next?"

"Private Oswald Ülsmann."

"I haven't got the list," he said in English. "Go on in. And watch for when he comes at you with the brass knuckles."

"Excuse?"

"Go in!"

"Excuse, but you have excellent voice, Joe."

Carl contemplated the dust on his shoes. "I'm a regular Lauritz Melchior. Go on inside, I'll be a minute. Have some coffee. We got plenty of fucking coffee."

"*Danke.*" Carl heard the clatter of the man's shoes as he climbed the stoop, then the slap of the screen door. He wondered where he could get some cigarettes. He took a deep breath and watched two birds circling each other, locking together in midair, and tumbling. They separated with a shriek like the attack cry of a hawk. They circled again and disappeared behind the trees on the opposite side of the ravine. He expelled the air from his lungs in a long stream and went back into the hut. If Valdez bitched about him, he'd never get leave.

On the second step up he noticed a prisoner leaning against the hut opposite. The man quickly averted his eyes and walked away. "That man over there," he asked the guard, "was he there long?"

"About half an hour. Why?"

"Nobody is in hearing distance, okay?"

"Sure."

"And make sure nobody gets under the building, either. No eavesdroppers."

The prisoner skittered around a corner. "I'd keep my back to the wall, too. These guys might find a use for your rifle."

"Where would they run to?"

"You want to chase them?"

Back inside, the clarinettist was chatting happily in his bad English with Valdez. "—I am, ah,"—he used his hands to express the thought—"pressed into the Wehrmacht. We many parades march. I am no military man."

Carl walked to the stove and poured coffee. He switched the conversation to German. "We have something very special for you. And very thick cream."

"You know how to make a man talk, eh?"

"Only if he wants to, Oswald."

The clarinettist smiled. "I must watch you, Joe. You might give me truth serum."

"I'm Carl Walthers. This is Abe Valdez."

"Good morning, Abe."

Valdez nodded.

"Who told you we might drug you?"

"I don't know. Someone. You know how it is. There is always loose talk where soldiers gather."

"What else do they say?"

"Nothing important."

"I heard there are Gestapo men in the camp."

"Of course."

"Of course?"

"The Gestapo is everywhere." He raised his bushy eyebrows. "Don't you know that?"

"You're teasing."

Oswald shrugged. He stirred his coffee with his finger and sucked off the creamy liquid.

"The song this morning was extraordinary."

"Maybe tomorrow the 'Ode to Joy.' You must bring us Bruno Walter to conduct. Perhaps you are related?"

"No."

"I auditioned for him at the Vienna State Opera. I was more suited for dance halls, but all the Jews had been dismissed."

"I'm a dance band guy myself."

"We could just hear you last night. Maybe you'll give us a recital."

"Maybe I'll get you to play for me."

"It's been months. You lose too much if you don't practice."

"True. You know how to get to Carnegie Hall?"

Oswald blinked. "It is in New York."

"No. You practice."

Oswald nodded. It lost something in the translation. "So you are from Vienna?" asked Carl.

"Not far."

"Do you know Sergeant Ansbach? He's also from Vienna."

Oswald gave a slight shudder. "He only likes one kind of music."

"What do you mean?"

"Marching music." He moved his fingers as if playing his clarinet. "Oomp-pah, oomp-pah, bah tata dah! I played it until my fingers ached. But what could I do? If you wanted to make music, you had to take a loyalty oath. I asked myself whether cooperating was worth it. I decided it was. Could I give up music? Politics means nothing to me. I could not live without my music, even if I have to play what they want."

"I understand completely," said Carl. Valdez's eyes bored into him.

"I was in Paris on holiday once. I went to all the jazz clubs. I saw Miss Josephine Baker. I shook hands with George

Gershwin—his last visit to Europe before he died. Such a woman he had with him! What marvelous music! I almost went to the American embassy for a visa. I was willing to immigrate for it. What must that music be like in New York, Chicago, St. Louis! The saxophone is the greatest invention since the pipes of Pan and I was thinking about learning it."

"You do love jazz, don't you?"

Oswald wickedly placed a finger to his lips. "Of course not, that is inferior music that dilutes the race."

"Absolutely," said Carl. "Do you have trouble with the Nazis in the camp?"

"Me? I'm a musician. That has nothing to do with politics."

"But there are men who have trouble with the Nazis."

"Some men have trouble with everybody."

"But there are Nazis in the camp who are a little too zealous, eh?"

"What they do is their concern."

Carl glanced at Valdez, who had slumped in his chair disgusted. "You're quite a dancer, besides a musician."

"Better to dance with you than with them."

Carl looked at his watch. They might be able to get one more guy in before breaking for lunch. "You can go, Oswald, but you know, if you're really thinking about immigrating, I know we could do a lot for a man who has helped us."

Oswald gulped the last of his coffee and grinned. "Why should I come to America? Don't you know the Luftwaffe has leveled New York, Boston, and Philadelphia?"

Valdez stopped doodling.

"That's what they told us last night."

"Who?"

"I didn't know him," said Oswald, "and I would never be able to recognize him again, but he was a very devoted Hitler man."

"Naturally," said Carl. "Think about it. You know where we are."

"Sure, Joe," said Oswald in English.

5.

Lieutenant Morris was not the kind of man to rescind an order, Carl judged. The quartermaster's problem managing the supplies got bigger every time more prisoners were unloaded and that happened as quickly as huts were built to house them. There were now three separate enclosed compounds of three hundred to three hundred and fifty men each, as well as a compound of a hundred officers. Morris also organized the buses that hauled prisoners to work on the farms, the food they would eat out there, and supplies for the small camp hospital. The damned Germans used soap as if trying to cause a shortage, he grumbled, and they ate butter and sugar like they were planning to break out dressed as cookies. Carl mentioned that he needed to get to town for more cigarettes to induce prisoners to talk, but Morris wouldn't discuss it. The only men who got in and out of Camp Wayne were the ones guarding the farm labor.

So Carl floated with the tempo. He bummed cigarettes and threw himself into the interrogations. He met safecrackers and career soldiers, Nazis who told him that the Luftwaffe raid on New York on July 4 had shattered the arm of the Statue of Liberty, and men from the Siebenburger who resembled the master race about as much as Warner Oland playing Charlie Chan. One broke down when he talked of how he had panicked when the Australian Ninth attacked at El Alamein. Another laughingly reported the search for General Stumme after he died of a heart attack and tumbled unnoticed from his speeding armored car. Many begged to send messages to their families. Three asked if it were possible to stay in America. Many sat stiffly and refused to say anything. One of these had obviously had a nervous breakdown. His eyes were big as canning lids and he flinched every time either Carl or Valdez made the slightest move.

Valdez took copious notes, but for what purpose it wasn't clear. On the whole, it was surprising how devout the true believers still were when it was obvious how badly things were going for them. Did they really imagine that the Americans would lavish meat, butter, and fruit on prisoners merely to break their spirits? One of the Nazis called it the Carcassonne strategy, referring to the legend of a French citadel that on the verge of starvation lifted the siege by pelting its attackers with bread. Sure, there was rationing out there, but when the buses drove out to the fields the Germans could see that people were a long way from starving.

One afternoon, as one of the true believers ranted about the Philco broadcasting nothing but lies about the Allied advances in Sicily and on the Eastern Front, Carl pictured his father in the chair. His father would have liked a chance to fight to the death. Maybe he thought he was when he put the bullet in his heart, fooling himself that he was somehow showing courage, that all his bunk mattered. In a month or two when the Allies began knocking at the doors of Germany itself, the Germans would come to their senses and toss Hitler into the same dust bin they had tossed the Kaiser. Then the politicians could go back to waiting for the next "just war."

It was a Saturday when he finally hitched a ride with Private Dahl. As they descended into North East, the sun was shining, the apple orchards and vineyards green, and the air fluttered over the jeep's windshield clean and free. On the horizon, the lake rolled over the edge of the world in delicate shades of blue. Carl felt the same exuberance as when he'd stuck out his thumb on the highway leading north from Richmond. He began to sing. "*Give me land, lots of land, under starry skies above . . .*"

"*Don't fence me in!*" joined Dahl.

"*Let me lie in the sun with the floozy that I love.*"

"*Don't fence me in!*"

They sang through it twice, making up more dirty lyrics, smiling at women sweeping their porches, Carl grasping the windshield and precariously rising off his seat for the repeating line. They ended with Dahl doing his own peculiar version of harmony just as they pulled up on Main Street next to the park. A man wearing pince-nez glasses sternly peered at them as if to say, "More drunk soldiers!" But the old woman feeding pigeons, the children playing near the war memorial, and the two priests Carl remembered sitting on the bench on his first visit to town, all smiled.

Carl slapped Dahl on the shoulder. "Hey, you're okay, buddy!"

"What are you saying?" Dahl laughed. "I stink!"

Carl counted his money. "I need a cheeseburger. You want one?"

"I got some business to take care of. If you want to wait about a half hour . . ." Dahl reached into the back and picked up a small, stained cotton sack by the drawstring.

"I'll go with you."

"That's okay. Look around. I'll meet you here at eleven." Dahl was already across Main and heading down Lake Street.

So, scram, thought Carl. He counted his money again. Enough for three packs of cigarettes, the cheeseburger, and a few steel pennies left over. He'd be broke until pay day. He could skip the cheeseburger and eat back at camp. Ah, so what? Carl crossed the street whistling and scanned the shops. "Buy Bonds!" was in the corner of every window. The intoxicating smell of bread poured out of the bakery and gray-haired farmers happily chatted as they got haircuts. In the window of a mom-and-pop grocery, a sign announced a special on Pillsbury's Wheat-Soy-Rice pancake mix and another extolled the virtues of Sunkist lemons in relieving constipation. Inside a butcher shop a woman in calico tried to convince the butcher she'd bring in her ration coupons Monday, but she positively had to have those chops. Most people paid little attention to Carl, though one elderly man, a veteran of Château-Thierry, insisted on shaking his hand.

He found himself in a five-and-dime, the wooden floors creaking as he moved along the counters, touching the spools of thread, the curling irons, the envelopes of flower seeds, and the boxes of pencils. Things were spread out because of shortages of this and that, but a peaceful calm came over him. He hadn't been in a five-and-dime since—when? The girl behind the counter—she didn't look old enough to wear a brassiere—asked him if he needed help and he said, "I'm fine." He really was. You're getting soft, Carl Walthers. A five-and-dime in Andy Hardy town! Gosh, gee, we could put on a show in Pop's barn!

"Have you got any sheet music?" he asked.

"No," she said dreamy-eyed, "but there's a music shop around the corner on Vine Street. He's got some." She leaned over a set of towels, resting her head in her hands. "Do you like music?"

"Ask me when you're a little older, and we'll make some."

She blushed, he winked, and she closed her eyes as if she were going to melt into the towels.

You still got it, said Carl as he headed in the direction she had pointed. With a mere lowering of the eyes, you can rob any cradle.

Enough instruments hung on wires from the old tin ceiling to supply the NBC Symphony. The brass needed polishing and the dings beaten out. Dust coated the three pianos and the bass viol case leaning in the corner. An old man with wild hair resembling Toscanini's dozed in a chair behind a case of harmonicas, reeds, and strings. Toscanini did not wake from the tinkling of the doorbells. Behind him was a room divider with a sign on it: INSTRUMENTS TO RENT.

"Now, remember, Timmy," said a warm voice behind the divider, "you curl the fingers. Curl. Like a snake."

"Yes, sir." The boy said sadly.

"Now let's try those scales again. Back straight. Hands out and relaxed."

Timmy was a long way from Carnegie Hall. As the thumping notes rattled the stringed instruments above, Carl made his way to the music rack. Chopin. Beethoven. Xaver Scharwenka. Edwin McDowell. None of it was in any order and most had yellowed with age. He moved down the rack past the hymns to a popular music section, but he saw nothing dated after 1932. He scanned a few of these, anyway. Some of them were from musicals he had heard of, like *Redheaded Egghead* and *Anything Goes,* but he didn't recognize the songs. No jazz. No lyric sheets.

"Very good, Timmy. One more time and I'll give you a peppermint! You'd like that, wouldn't you?"

Carl closed the door gently. When he got back to Main Street he saw Dahl trying to pick up a black-haired girl by blocking her entrance to the drug store. When a nun left the store with her enormous hat, and Dahl stepped out of the way, the girl slipped inside.

"Sweet-talking the dames, private?" said Carl.

"Who, me?"

"Let's go sit at the counter."

"My treat," said Dahl. "I just came into some dough."

"How you boys doing?" said the woman behind the counter. A picture of an airman hung over the Coca-Cola cooler behind her. It was draped in black. The shrine was flanked by signs advertising Sanida ice cream and Ma's root beer.

"Cheeseburger. Everything on it since the private's paying."

"You bribing your officer, are yeh?" chirped the woman.

"Can't hurt," said Dahl. "Same for me. And a chocolate soda."

Carl glanced over his shoulder at the girl with black hair. Young, but ripe. Very ripe.

"You're not grilling prisoners today?"

"Valdez is getting a tooth pulled."

"Maybe that's his problem!"

Carl watched himself smiling in the mirror. He was still skinny, he thought. The girl was also sneaking a look at his reflection. She turned as the druggist handed her a tin canister with a skull and crossbones on it. A sweet girl to be buying arsenic. "So," said Carl, "what's up? You got a bookie? Betting on the Browns?"

"Naw, gambling's for suckers."

"Betting on the Browns is."

"What are you going to say when there's an all St. Louis World Series, Browns and Cardinals?"

"I'd say Jesus had come down to bat clean-up."

"If he's available Luke Sewell will sign him."

"The Yankees'll get him first. Well, if it wasn't a bookie it must be a woman, but I got to tell you they usually appreciate more than half an hour."

The counter woman lowered her head, suppressing a laugh as she sliced a tomato.

"A half hour of me is too much for most women. It's like too much of a good thing."

"You got the first part of it right."

"I sell a few things, that's all—," he raised his head suddenly. "No Army stuff. I wouldn't do that."

Carl shrugged, "No skin off my—" The girl with black hair tapped him on the shoulder.

"Hey, you changed your mind," said Dahl, "but you got the wrong guy."

"No I haven't," she said sweetly, then turned to Carl. "I know you." When she lifted her white hand to brush her hair back over her ear, Carl knew she was right. But from where? New York? Atlantic City?

"Wait a minute," he said. "The name will come to me."

"Just call her gorgeous," said Dahl.

"Elizabeth," she said.

He squinted. "Elizabeth?"

"Elizabeth Way."

"Way?"

She smiled. "Beth. I was a hatcheck girl."

Carl dropped his jaw. "Well, I'll be! Swing Land!"

She nodded. "I wasn't sure it was you, with the uniform and all. You were the best I ever saw, except maybe—Aw, never mind. I'll say you were best."

"Heck, I put you to sleep."

"You didn't!"

"That's okay. It was late. Have a seat. I'll buy you a sundae or something. How about it? Miss? Bring the girl a chocolate sundae."

She slid onto the counter seat next to him. "You don't have to do that."

"I want to. Anyway, my pal Ansel Dahl is treating."

Dahl craned his neck around Carl. "For you, precious, anything. Elizabeth Way? Italian? You have such beautiful hair."

"Half-Italian. My mother was from Taranto. My grandpop's name was Waytowich, but that got changed." While she answered Dahl she never took her eyes off Carl.

"I got Vikings on my family tree," said the private. "That's why I'm good at the looting and pillaging, and the et cetera, too."

"So," interrupted Carl, "what are you doing in this burg? I heard Swing Land closed."

"I heard that, too. Mr. Musso told me that business was down. I think he just thought I didn't belong there. Maybe I wasn't good at it."

The counter woman shoved the burger plate into Carl's forearm. "Sorry."

"How could you be bad at checking hats?" said Carl. "He didn't like the idea of a nice girl working in a club."

"I miss the shows, though," said Elizabeth, "and nobody got out of line. It's worse at the factory."

"Factory?"

"Mr. Musso got me the job and arranged the boarding house and everything."

"Yeah?" The horrible thought that Musso had set her up as his mistress crossed his mind.

"It's good for my pop. He has somebody to talk to when I'm working."

"You live with your father?"

"Yeah, he's crippled, you know. He was shot in the hip when he was younger."

"It's no fun getting shot."

She lifted a spoon of ice cream to her full lips. Chocolate syrup dribbled on her white chin.

Ripe, Carl thought. *Very* ripe. He lifted his cheeseburger.

"So, what do you do at the factory?"

She playfully slapped at his shoulder. "You know I can't talk about that! 'Loose lips sink ships!' We've got a big sign over the work area. And there's others, like 'Remember Leonard Parsons' and 'Remember Lou Spognamiglia.'"

The counter woman pointed at the picture draped in black. "That's Lou right there. Army Air Corps. He enlisted the first day. Could've played for the Pirates."

"Did better," said Dahl. Everyone looked at him. "Than the Pirates, I mean. I didn't mean dying was better." He cleared his throat. "I can tell he was a good man."

"You'd be right, buster," said the woman. "I would've married the guy if he'd've wanted me. Like that!" She snapped her fingers. "So would've half the women in this town."

No soldier like a dead soldier, thought Carl. They ate quietly until the woman bent to wipe up something.

"Are you at Camp Wayne?" Beth asked. "What are the Germans like?"

"Like anybody, I guess. They're clean, pretty much, and they do good work when they go out to the farms."

"I hope you're kicking their butts," interjected the counter woman.

"They're not all Nazis," said Dahl. "Most are gunsels who got drafted and don't care one way or the other."

"We treat them pretty good," said Carl.

"Why?" asked Beth.

"The Geneva Conventions of 1929 are the rules of war. We can't force officers to work. The enlisted men can be ordered to work, but they have to get paid. In scrip only, though. Stuff like that." He thought of Valdez. "Some of it gets in the guys' craws, though."

"Like what?"

Carl chewed and swallowed. "Oh, I don't know." He told her about the singing of the German anthem. Murnow had decided that it was okay for them to do it as long as they allowed the "Star-spangled Banner" to be played first.

"They're singing their song in America?" said the counter woman.

"It doesn't hurt anything," said Carl.

"It's an insult! In Lou Spognamiglia's town!"

"Well, it's out of town," said Carl.

"I can't believe it," said Elizabeth.

"We have to think of our guys over there."

"You can bet," said the counter woman, "they aren't coddling our guys!"

He started to say that they weren't coddling at Camp Wayne, either, but didn't. After a moment of silence, the church bells began tolling eleven.

"Oh, gosh," said Beth, slipping off the stool, "Gotta run! It was so nice seeing you again, Mr. Carlson."

He swallowed a big chunk of burger and rotated towards her. "We could give you a ride."

"Maybe I'll see you in town. Maybe you could get an evening off and sing for us."

"That'd be great!"

She shook his hand. She was so soft. "Bye-bye," she said. He watched her go out the door.

"You could've got her number," said Dahl. "Charley Barnet's going to be at the Columbia Theatre on the thirtieth."

"Jesus!" said Carl. He jumped off the stool and ran after her. "Beth!" A truckload of chickens barely missed him as he jumped to the curb in front of the Haynes House and caught her arm.

"Yes?"

"Ernie Musso," he panted. "You must know how to get hold of Musso. I don't know his number and the phone company was no help. Not with Mussolini, Musso, Ernest, Ernie—"

She looked in her purse. "He doesn't use Mussolini any more. I thought I had it here, but—"

"Could you get it for me?"

"I suppose, but I'm working the late shift tonight and—" Her eyes lit up. "The Catania Social Club, on the east side. That's where he hangs out." She spelled Catania.

"Great! I could kiss you!"

She pursed her lips and stepped back. "Not on the street!" She blushed. "I mean not anywhere. In public, I mean." She stamped her foot in frustration with an "Oh!" then quickly chirped "Bye-bye, Mr. Carlson," as she walked away.

Carl almost danced back to the drug store. Dahl was paying the tab from a stack of bills about a quarter of an inch thick. "Keep the change," he said.

The counter woman gave him a wink. "Give 'em hell and come back soon," she said in a stage whisper.

Dahl smiled until his back was to her, then rolled his eyes. "Okay, sarge, let's hit the—"

Carl rushed past him and into the phone booth across the store. Dahl followed. As soon as the door closed in his face, he tapped the glass and pointed to his watch.

"I won't be long!"

Dahl said something about meeting him and held up the

list of things they were supposed to be buying. "Twenty minutes!"

Carl gave him a thumb up.

About two minutes later, the operator connected. "Catania Social Club," said a caustic voice.

"I'm calling long distance. I'm trying to reach Ernie Musso."

"Who?"

"He used to go by Ernie Mussolini. A big guy and I mean big."

The man was silent.

"We're old pals. I'm Carl Carlson, the Carolina Crooner. I sang at Swing Land before the war." About ten hours before, he thought.

The man grunted. "Carolinah Croonah?!" He started to laugh, but it made him cough. "Hang on. I'll see if anybody knows this Mussolini." Carl could barely make out his shouting. "Hey, anybody know anybody named Mussolini!" He imagined a room full of mafiosi laughing. He tapped his finger on the shelf in front of him. "Hurry up!" he muttered to himself.

"You're a singer?" said a phlegmy voice.

"Swing Land, Mr. Musso. A year and a half ago. Mr. Papanoumou was going to help me out, but after Toledo the tour got canceled and I got drafted."

"Right. The blond boy! Buzz Bixby. I don't know what I was thinking. Getting old. So, how're you doing, boy?"

"I'm a couple of hours up the road, Mr. Musso, at Camp Anthony Wayne."

"I'd heard you was overseas."

"I was wounded."

"I heard that, too, I think."

"Really?"

"We'll talk face to face."

He didn't understand what Musso was getting at. "My shoulder is stiff, but everything else is working."

"Face okay? Voice okay?"

"Oh, yeah. I can't move my arm like I should, that's all. They kept me in to translate."

"You should've called me. I might could've fixed it."

"Could you?"

"It's what a man a' honor does. Helps out."

"Listen, I saw Elizabeth Way here and I've been trying to get hold of Mr. Papanoumou. Since I'm Stateside I thought maybe I could reconnect, you know, get ready to pick up where I left off. Could you put me in contact, or give me his number?"

"Hmmm," Musso growled. "Come see me. There's things to talk about. We could help each other. The Greek isn't what-ya-say available."

"I'm trying to get a pass."

"You help us, we could see what strings could be pulled. You're a hero now. That ought to count in show business. When can you get here? I need you right away."

"I don't know."

"One hand washes the other, right?"

"Yes, sir, Mr. Mussolini. As soon as I can."

"I'm just Musso now," he snorted. "Damn him, ruined my good name. We're getting even with the bastard now, boy. He's just cooling his heels in jail until some of our people hang *him* from a lamp post. Badoglio, too. All the *fascisti*. They're all snakes. They'll be sorry they messed with us."

"You bet," said Carl.

"You get here soon."

"Yes sir!"

Carl came out of the booth with a whoop. He clenched his fists until the tightness burned in his shoulder. "Bah da-dah!" he sang out. "Bah da-de-ya-dah! In the mood, bah da-de-ya-dah!" He danced out to the sidewalk, oblivious to the stares of the shoppers. The whole town of North East was a movie set in which everyone was about to burst into song, something like the end of *San Francisco* or *Easter Parade*. He spun on one foot and faced down the street where Elizabeth had disappeared. She had looked so embarrassed when he said he could kiss her. When her lips had puckered in surprise, they had reminded him of a tiny pink rose.

"Oh, you beautiful doll!" he shouted. An old woman scurried away.

6.

Back at camp, three packed busses blocked the gate. Prisoners rubbernecked to see their new home. The number of them looked like no lunch for the guards who had to check them in. "Who're these boys?" Dahl asked.

"I-ties," the guard answered. "They brought them in early on a freight from Pittsburgh. Major Murnow is looking for you, sergeant."

"It figures," said Carl.

"I told you we took too long," said Dahl. "And don't forget those five bucks, you. I need it."

"Take it easy," said Carl. A sergeant wasn't supposed to borrow from an enlisted man, but however Dahl had gotten the money was shady in the first place. "Is Lieutenant Valdez back yet?"

"He's not due back until one."

After Dahl managed to squeeze the jeep between two of the buses, Carl found Murnow watching the Italians move along a row of tables. Their names were recorded, each was dusted with DDT, then given a chocolate bar, the PW jacket and pants, a sheet, and wool blanket.

"I hope the hell you speak wop," Murnow said.

"*Allegro, andante, largo,* and spaghetti are about it."

"Another pain in the ass problem."

Cuts down on the cocktail hour, thought Carl.

"You get the cigarettes?" He pointed at the oblong package under Carl's arm.

Carl couldn't believe it. He'd forgotten his excuse to go to town. "Yes, sir," he said.

"Now they tell me the Red Cross is bringing us a couple of boxes tomorrow. And then Morris is going to have them

88

stocked anyhow, now that the prisoners' payday is coming. They'll buy their own with the scrip. How much are they talking?"

"Not much. Most talk about being drafted and not liking it." Murnow gave him a look but Carl went on. "There are a lot of guys from the *Strafbataillon,* the 999th Light Afrika, including the 961st Afrika Rifles, the 962, and some others. There are some Eighth Panzer, 104th Panzer Grenadiers, 33rd Antitank and even three U-boat guys. The 999 men are the interesting ones. A lot of crooks: drafted right out of the poky into the desert. They're not much on Nazism but some of them are probably worse. Mack the Knife."

"Make sure everyone knows who he is. We'll keep an eye on him." The major scanned the Italians until he noticed Carl staring at him. "What?"

"I meant God knows what kind of killers, thieves, and con men we're dealing with."

"That's what I understand. Can we separate the dangerous ones from the work details? We don't want anything to happen."

"We don't know who's dangerous."

"I don't want some Fritzy Dillinger taking it on the lam."

Carl shifted the package to his left arm. "I'm not the one who thinks they ought to be picking vegetables out there."

"It's good for everybody. The War Department, the unions all agreed. Have we got any men good with Italian?"

Carl shook his head. "There's enough Italians around, though."

"Maybe we get some civilian volunteers. War effort and all that." He grinned. "The volunteer wop brigade!" He pointed to the package, "Is that mine?"

"No, Dahl's got yours." King William IV scotch.

"You know," Carl continued, "if you'd give me a weekend pass, I could get you a fluent Italian speaker in Cleveland."

"Why go so far?"

"Because I know people there."

"There's a Little Italy in Erie."

"But I don't know anybody. Whether we could trust them."

"Where is Private Dahl? Always lollygagging. I don't know why judges force punks in. They don't make good soldiers."

Murnow took several steps, then paused, studied the prisoners again, and cocked his head in their direction. "Amazing such a sorry lot can cause so much trouble."

Look who's talking, thought Carl.

He went to the prisoner compound to begin interrogating without Valdez. By the time he brewed the coffee and got the first in, the lieutenant should be back. First, though, he went to the recreation field, where prisoners not on farm work were cheering a sweaty game of soccer. He gathered from the insults being traded that a team of Bavarians was playing a team of Franconians. He waded into the men on the sidelines and asked, "Who is winning?"

"Two to two," said a prisoner with a nasty scar on his forehead. "You want to play?" The man was holding a wad of betting slips, but there were greenbacks sticking out of the pile here and there.

"Where'd you get the American dollars?" Carl asked.

He pulled it down and held it close to his hip. "GI's bet, too."

"Don't let an officer see it."

"No."

"Is Oswald Ülsmann here?"

Several men shook their heads. "Tell him I need to see him."

"Digging potatoes," said someone.

"Tell him Sergeant Walthers needs to see him."

The men were distracted by a collision between players. Carl recognized SS-captain Gerhardt Läufer playing referee. No one complained when he awarded the Bavarians a free kick.

The Americans were forbidden to give prisoners money because it could be used in escaping. He considered reporting it, but Valdez would try to get Murnow to strip search every damn prisoner and that was a lot of assholes someone would have to look up. It wasn't like the prisoners could accumulate enough money to bribe their way back to the Third Reich. Maybe if one of them turned rabbit with his stash he wouldn't go out and slit some granny's throat for her pennies. He remembered that Sergeant Pike had hung a painting of Christ over the head of his bed and said that a prisoner had painted it for him. The greenbacks were probably from things like that. People wheel and deal every chance they get. I'll give you this if you give me that. Whatever Dahl was up to on the side. One hand washes the other, as Musso had said.

A prisoner was already waiting when Carl reached the interrogation hut. His name was Ude Wieschensohn and he wasn't on the list, but he wanted desperately to talk. He needed no coffee, no urging, but launched immediately into it, reaching his hands across the table and pulling at Carl's arm until he felt discomfort in his shoulder.

"Where is the lieutenant? You must protect me. They will kill me." The wide-eyed man's bushy eyebrows twitched.

Carl pulled back. "Who? What are you talking about?"

"The *Lagergestapo*." He looked back over his shoulder as if he expected to see someone standing in the corner.

"Slow down. What camp Gestapo?"

"The Nazis."

"You're all Nazis, aren't you?"

"No!" said the man. "If they find out, they will kill me."

"Find out what?"

"About me." The man was pretty big. He ought to be able to handle himself, but the shake of his hands was almost out of control. He was pale as a cornstarch pudding.

"What can they find out?"

"My father."

"Pull yourself together!"

"My father was a trade unionist in the Socialist uprising."

"That was a long time ago."

"Later he was arrested for distributing pamphlets. They broke his skull—" he smacked his palm for emphasis "—and he lost his mind. He confessed to all sorts of things that weren't true. To having gone to school with Stalin, to raping the Czarina before shooting her, to providing the Jews with petrol for the Reichstag fire, to anything."

"Very well, he was your father. What has this to do with you?"

"I wrote to the newspapers and complained. They never printed it, but soon I was jailed, too."

"For writing a letter to the editor?"

"Of course!" He said it as if he were dealing with an idiot.

"It must have been a strong letter. I mean I know that they are strict about the press."

"Yes."

"But, Ude, that is not the point really. The point is, why do you think there is a camp Gestapo that will kill you?"

"Because I saw him!"

"Who?" Carl asked angrily.

"I don't know his name, but he was a warder in the jail I was in. He knows why I was arrested. He spit on me one day and kicked me in the leg."

"Here?"

"No, in Bremen."

Carl thought a minute. He shouldn't have started without Valdez. On the other hand, Valdez might blow the whole thing out of proportion in order to carry out his personal vendetta against the Nazis. What should he do? Valdez would overreact; Murnow wouldn't react. It wasn't Lieutenant Morris' job.

"Please, I am not a Nazi. I will never live in Germany again. They will kill me!"

Carl raised his hands to calm him. "You are getting vexed over nothing, Ude. You served your country in the military, in combat. How can your loyalty be questioned?"

"I myself have seen a hero of the Great War, a man who won an Iron Cross in the Ardennes, beaten to death on the street in Bremen."

Carl said nothing for several seconds. "Well?"

"They said he was a traitor. He was one of those who had betrayed us in 1918. A war hero!"

"Look, I've read some of the Hitler Youth get carried away, but, my God, your officers here maintain a keen discipline. No one has been attacked here."

"No one you know of."

"Who, then?"

Wieschensohn shook his head.

"If you know anything, you should tell me."

"I know what they are like. The old man was wearing his medals when they beat him. He could barely breathe because of what the gas had done to him. They put in the paper that

he had died from that. They did not mention the beating."
He pointed to a stain in the table in front of him as if there
were a picture of the incident at his fingertips. "The shinbone
tore through his trouser leg and stuck out like an ivory
knife."

Wieschensohn sat back, frozen by the image.

"There are hooligans everywhere," Carl said. "You're telling me about something that happened back in Germany. I
can only deal with what's here. Maybe there was some other
reason for the attack. All of that's got nothing to do with me."

"He was a Jew, but that doesn't matter."

"Are you a Jew?"

"No! But my father was Socialist. I am a political."

"Do they beat up politicals like they beat up Jews?"

Wieschensohn pulled his cap from his head as if he were
going to shred it. "Are you mad? Have you been listening
to me?"

"A man can change his politics, but he can't change his
race. You're not a Jew, maybe you should play along with the
Nazis for a while. Can that be so hard? In America we have
a saying, 'Who goes along, gets along.'"

"These people used machine guns to get us to attack. They
strafed their own troops to keep us from running. We were
kindling to them. This is what Rommel and his generals
think of us. Can't you understand? I can tell from the way
they are looking at me that I am a dead man."

Wieschensohn was so compelling that Carl had begun to
believe him. Almost. Machine-gunning your own men? The
Afrika Korps? This guy was probably jailed as a con man.

"You're getting carried away," said Carl. "They wouldn't
dare kill you here. If you're really afraid of them, play along.
Hang a picture of Hitler over your bed like a lot of them do.
When they sing 'Deutschland über Alles,' sing loudly."

Wieschensohn lifted his head and scrutinized him. "You
are one of them."

"Ude . . ."

"Yes, they told us. There are many of you in America. You
will soon rise against the inferior races, that is what they
told us!"

"Calm down, Ude."

He tossed his head from side to side. "Where is the lieutenant? Where is he? You were here to make me reveal myself! Where is the lieutenant? Where?" Wieschensohn stood, knocking his chair out behind him. He clutched his cap in his hand, rotating it frantically as if it were a rosary. When Carl reached out to him, he shrieked and crashed out of the hut.

By the time Carl got to the door, the private was just losing his grip on Wieschensohn's arm. The German scurried across the pathway and under the hut opposite.

"Bastard!" said the private. "Fucking door got me!" He wiped blood from his nose. "I was coming in—"

Carl handed him a handkerchief. "Tilt your head back." He now noticed that six or seven prisoners had gathered in a row along the front of a barracks hut to his left. Some of them leaned against the tar-paper wall. Others stood with their arms crossed. They were trying to appear casual, but their eyes were sparks of molten steel.

"Come back here, you fucking Nazi," Carl yelled in English. "I'll teach you to Heil Hitler in my face! Invincible Führer, my ass!" He bumped the private's shoulder with the back of his hand and said loudly, "The nerve of that guy! He says we're losing the war! Fucking Nazi!"

The spectators shifted around a bit, some turning their sides to him, others looking at each other. The private looked at the blood on Carl's handkerchief. "What are you doing, sarge, turning into Valdez?"

"Are you okay?"

"The bleeding's stopped. You want I should get the creep?"

"Naw, let him go. Where is Valdez, anyway?" He went inside, picked up the roster and looked out at the Germans. "Which one of you is Heinrich Siest? *Wer heisse Heinrich Siest?*"

Siest came forward stiffly. From his walk you could tell he was going to be more case-hardened than a ball peen hammer. Carl took his time writing up the notes on his talk with Wieschensohn and let Siest cool his heels at the table.

"So Corporal Siest—"

"SS-corporal Siest."

"SS-corporal Siest. You're a panzer man, are you? How are you liking Camp Anthony Wayne?"

"I believe it has begun to stink."

"Stink?"

"First there were niggers, now these cowardly Italians."

Carl drummed his pencil. The gods even things out: a good morning, a lousy afternoon. "You underestimate them. Those Italians surrendered as well as you did, Heinrich."

"SS-corporal Siest," he said firmly.

"And the coloreds, Heinrich, well, our Negroes will be kissing your sister back in Berlin before you will."

He could hear the sharp intake of air as Siest's nostrils flared.

Carl smiled. Valdez would have been proud of him.

He questioned five more prisoners before dinner, each time hesitating to call in the next before Valdez returned. He chatted with the guard, strolled up towards the front of the compound to see if Valdez was on his way. Only the last prisoner had anything interesting to say and that had nothing to do with military intelligence. He clammed up like a good little Nazi when he was asked anything about his activities in Africa or the officers and men of the camp. But, he had heard Carl practicing in the ravine and had a secret love for jazz. His mother had been an Expressionist artist and had often taken the boy with her to Paris. She had done many sketches of Django Reinhardt, the guitarist, and was a friend of the American painter Stuart Davis, whom Carl had never heard of.

"*Mutti*," he had said, "believed she could unify the psychological profundity of expressionism with the abstract purity of cubism. She and Stuart often argued." The prisoner stared ahead with a peaceful smile and Carl knew that his mother arguing was the prisoner's sacred memory of comfort, the quiet place to which his mind would return when lonely or sad.

Curiously, though, the only thing that had taken from his Bohemian upbringing was a taste for jazz and absinthe. At age twenty he had joined the SS and had received a number of awards for his good work. His mother had become a realist in the mid-1930s and accepted a number of commissions for large state murals. He didn't think his "little vice" of liking jazz harmed anyone and that ultimately, if the armies of National Socialism didn't triumph, the ideas would. Meantime, he was discreet about his taste in music.

At the end of the conversation, Carl asked him his favorite song, and promised to do "St. James Infirmary," if he could recall the lyrics.

"I shall be listening," said the man with a wink. Carl was sorry to see him go, especially when a stone-faced tank mechanic followed him. It was getting toward supper and this was no way to spend a Saturday evening. He tried a few questions and half-hearted gestures of friendliness, but the mechanic merely grunted or answered in monosyllables. His ideology revolved around the cam shaft. Carl decided to call it a day. He was slipping into the routine now, just as he had slipped into basic training, life aboard the Liberty ship, and singing in five towns a week. You get used to anything, like it or not.

In the mess, Sergeant Pike was shoveling in turkey, mashed potatoes, and corn as if he were afraid that this was the last of the world's supply. He was one of those guys who stirs everything together until it looks like baby food. Each time he lifted a wad to his mouth, the seams on his massive shoulders seemed ready to pop.

"I heard you had an incident," he said without greeting.

"A guy went squirrely," said Carl. "Valdez was at the dentist."

Pike tapped his neanderthal jaw. "Abscess. Had to go to St. Vincent Hospital in Erie."

The army grapevine, thought Carl. Everybody knows everything two minutes before it happens. "The prisoner was afraid the Nazis would get him."

"Those guys are a pain."

"The Nazis?" Carl found a fragment of husk in his corn and picked it out.

"No," said Pike, "the Nazis keep order. They aren't always coming up to the guards asking for transfers and stuff. It's these anti-Nazis we don't need. Ship them to special camps, I say."

"Special camps?"

"They're designating some anti-Nazi camps. I wouldn't want to work there. Troublemakers. Always agitating. Won't go along."

O'Hurly slid his tray next to Pike's and sat down. "It's the fucking Nazis we're fighting, boyo. The real hardcase storm-troopers are supposed to be shipped to Alva, Oklahoma."

Carl remembered he'd almost ended up there, wherever the hell it was. "That's punishing them," he joked.

"You wait," said Pike. "See who's easier to deal with, the Nazis or these I-ties. You can see the difference just looking at them. You'll find out when you start interrogating them."

"Don't speak the lingo."

"Lucky for you," said Pike. "You can't trust 'em."

"Aaa," said O'Hurly, "I got no bitch with wops. I grew up around a lot of them."

"Those were the ones who left. I'm talking the Old Country types."

"Aaa, bunk!" said O'Hurly. "They're Catholics. The nuns busted their knuckles. They know what's right."

"If the guy's really afraid," Carl interrupted, "maybe we should put him in solitary or something."

Pike scraped the last minuscule blobs off his plate. "He's putting on an act."

"Jesus, Mary, and Joe," interrupted O'Hurly. "Who made this turkey?"

"It's good," said Pike.

"It's Goodyear. What for we got a rubber shortage? We could make tires out of it."

"I don't think the guy was putting on an act," said Carl.

"He's a nut," said Pike.

"I yelled at him like he was a hardcase Nazi."

"That'll fool 'em," said O'Hurly sarcastically.

"Don't worry about it," said Pike. "The Nazis got discipline. They don't make trouble." He peered longingly at the food line, then checked his watch. "I better go. Saturday night movie for Heiney. Big double feature: *Wolf Man*, one of the Tarzans. We even have a newsreel and a Daffy Duck. I hope to hell it doesn't rain."

When Pike left, O'Hurly leaned toward Carl. "You headed into the ravine tonight? I got a bottle smooth as a baby's butt."

"In a couple of hours. I got to find a guy. He probably went out on the work details today."

But Oswald Ülsmann's barracks were empty and when Carl asked about him, the prisoners all played dumb. Eventually he saw him helping to hang the big sheet of canvas they were going to use for a screen. He handed him the package he had brought from town. When Oswald opened it, his eyes flicked back and forth between Carl's face and the dusty old clarinet. He seemed confused how to react. He took two sections of the clarinet and fitted them together. He placed his fingers on the keys, and hefted it.

"It'll give you something to do in the evenings."

Oswald studied the horn end. The brand name's gold lettering, "LaFayette and Company, Clarionets," had darkened and flaked.

"It isn't the best, but the reeds are in the box." Carl had expected more of a positive reaction and was getting miffed. After all, he'd borrowed the money and haggled with the old music-store owner for twenty minutes.

Oswald's eyes flashed a moment of delight, then dropped back to the instrument. "I shall see what I can do with it."

"You can play for your friends," said Carl gesturing at the sullen line of men watching. The line had different faces, but it was always there, always watching. "Maybe we can scratch up a band."

Oswald nodded. The motion of his head told Carl that he was moved more than he wanted to show. He was a guy, like Carl, who lived for his music and the lousy war had ripped him away from it. Carl touched Oswald's shoulder. He swallowed a lump in his throat, then turned to walk away.

"Hey, Joe!" Oswald called out in English. "I will play. You will sing."

"*Ja wohl,*" said Carl. "*Wir bald muzieren.* Soon! It's a promise!"

Oswald nodded and glanced at the other men.

7.

Cleveland's Union Station! Where was the shoeshine man? The cop who greeted Musso? There were other differences. At intervals along the shores of Lake Erie, he had noticed sentries with binoculars standing on wooden towers and peering out across the lake as if waiting for an invasion from Canada. In town, black curtains were tied to the sides of every window and though it was hot many people seemed to leave them shut all the time. At night, there would be no bright lights, Christmas or otherwise, and the Emerald City wouldn't glow.

When he had first come into this city, only two years ago, he had been young. Only a little older chronologically, he felt much older mentally. He'd been on a Liberty ship uncertain whether he would ever see America again. He'd been shot, and as he dropped in confusion to the urine-smelling street of Oran, it was not a spiritual sense of the meaninglessness of the material world that had overwhelmed him, it was the sure knowledge of the preciousness of waxed Chevys, cigarette smoke, and the sweet sound of a baseball meeting a catcher's mitt. Okay, so Cleveland didn't glow this time. So a ridiculous man stood behind a curtain pulling levers and creating the illusion of Great Oz. The man was still the wizard. He had the power to grant Carl the only thing he had ever wanted. The war hadn't changed that.

Murnow had given Carl until midday on Labor Day to hire a translator. Il Duce's men had been sent to Camp Wayne by mistake, said the major, and, now that Sicily had fallen, the Army needed all its translators for the battle up the peninsula. How hard could it be to hire an Italian speaker? Valdez, still mumbling from having his abscess lanced, said it was typical that no one appreciated that PW's from the Italian army might know useful things about their own country. Murnow got Morris to fiddle the books for the money to hire a civilian and for a few days they tried one from Erie. Ray, as he was called, ended up punching one of the prisoners who made fun of his Neapolitan dialect. There were plenty of other Italian speakers in Erie, of course, but Carl nagged the major until his golden three-day pass was issued.

From the station the cab took Euclid Avenue, then turned through smaller streets until it stopped in front of the Catania Social Club. Inside, when his eyes adjusted to the dim light, he saw two tables of old men playing dominoes. Ernie Musso was in the corner flanked by two bodyguards, a May/December team: one too old for the service, the other too young.

"Hey, it's the soldier!" growled Musso warmly. "Get over here, boy. You're looking good. A bit on the skinny, but good." He spoke to the room as a whole. "This is my friend Carl. Purple Heart! Got plugged in Africa. A regular Beau Geste. Bring the man something to drink. How about some *calamari*? You ever try it?"

Musso squeezed Carl's extended hand with both of his. When he settled back, the chair protested from his weight. Musso had never been this friendly. That was a good sign, wasn't it?

Musso spoke to his bodyguards. "This man has got a wonderful set of pipes."

"Thank you," said Carl.

"For somebody who's not a *paisan*." Musso laughed, rattling the phlegm in his throat.

"Thanks," said Carl.

"See that? He's a good sport. The Greek was all set to fix him up and then poof, the slanties do Pearl. Well, we're going to help the man get back. He's done his duty. We'll do good by him and he'll do good by us. Ain't that right?"

The *calamari* arrived. Carl had expected some kind of noodles. It looked like onion rings, but smelled fishy. Musso shooed his bodyguards from the table and patted the chair next to him. "Come a little closer. We got to talk."

The bodyguards positioned themselves in chairs halfway

to the domino players and faced the door. Carl sipped the
blood dark wine to be polite. He'd never acquired a taste for
the stuff.

"So, boy, how's the shoulder?"

"It's a little stiff. I think it'll loosen up eventually."

"Good. And the voice?"

"I've been practicing. There's this gorge next to Camp
Wayne. On hot nights I climb down there, maybe have a
drink, and sing. The guys can hear me. They say it's great.
It's sort of a ritual, if you know what I mean."

"Uh-huh." Musso was studying a *calamari* as he ate it.
"You're not going back tonight, are ya?"

"You want me to sing? Well, I haven't rehearsed with a
band or—"

"Did I say anything about singing? I'm talking social
occasion."

"Great! I wanted to see Mr. Papanoumou as soon as I
could."

"He isn't what-ya-say available."

"He's out in Hollywood?"

"Could be." Musso shifted, adjusting the cushion under
his rear. "But it ain't likely. I seen a newsreel once and this
girl said that Hollywood was heaven. Well, if it is, that's where
the Greek is."

Carl tried to understand.

"The Greek ain't been seen for six months. I figure he's
feeding the lake perch." Musso flicked at the dish with his
hand. "Try the *calamari*."

"He's dead?"

"Gotta be."

"Nobody knows?"

"Well, we know. We got the dead balls to prove it."

"What do you mean?"

"I mean his walnuts showed up in the mail, that's what
I mean."

"Jesus!"

"Absolutely. That's what I'm saying."

The smell of the *calamari* was suddenly sickening. Carl
thought for a moment, then asked, "So who's handling his
show business connections?"

Musso shrugged. "Brother! I tell you a man's dead and all you think about is your career."

Carl sipped the wine. "There are a lot of dead guys out there."

"Almost you."

"A man's got to take care of himself. Dead lasts a long time."

Musso sniffed. He leaned closer. "You hear what happened to your band?"

"Buzz Bixby's?"

"Who else?"

"Not much. I heard Mack Mintner was touring with the USO."

"I don't know from no Mack Mintner," said Musso. "Shut up and listen."

"Okay."

"So Natalie goes back to her boyfriend, right? Even though she gets some razzmatazz on the side with you and who knows who else, she heads back to the borough of Queens and Georgy Mack."

Carl raised his hand. "Hold it. 'Razzmatazz'? I never touched that woman."

Musso laughed, his thick neck jiggling.

"I never touched her!" insisted Carl.

"Yeah, right. Just let me finish."

"I never touched her. Who said I did?"

"Shut up. Sally Mack decided to work something out with the Greek. Sal had this idea about television. He figures once the war's over this is gonna be big, like radio. They're already broadcasting fifteen hours a week and having a tough time finding enough performers. But like when Sal recommended you to the Greek, he only knows from the clubs in New York."

Carl nervously bit into a *calamari*. It was rubbery. He chewed, trying to ignore the taste.

"So Sally sends Georgy here to us. He was coming anyway on some other matters. We got a tight treaty with Sal, that's all I can say. Anyhow, the bosses think this television thing's got possibilities and they like the idea that the Greek might be able to pull strings on both coasts. You got the movies on the right and this television thing on the left. You can cut everybody off at the pass and charge 'em a toll. So the bosses tell the Greek to do a deal with Georgy. You follow?"

"Okay."

"But Georgy's got Natalie around and, I don't know, maybe Georgy gets Natalie to influence the Greek. She's got the talent. You know what I mean. She don't care whose pole she greases."

Carl lowered his eyes. "I'm listening."

"But she falls for the Greek. He's got a way, you know."

"Natalie? She wouldn't fall for nobody. The band used to say she was like a kid with a six ounce Nehi. Drain it. Toss it."

"I'm telling you, she fell. Or seemed to. The Greek puts her up in a big apartment in town. He's out with her at least four times a week. Sometimes in threes with a girl named Harriet. Georgy Mack gets pissed, makes a big scene one night, but nobody gets hurt. Sally Mack sits on him and he apologizes. The deal's too important. Business is business. Natalie Bixby is just a champeen whore, but there's plenty of those out there."

"So what happened to the Greek?"

Musso reached into this pocket and lifted out an envelope. "They had firmed up the deal when this—" He spread the front page of the *Plain Dealer* on the table, smoothing it with his bloated hands. It was hard to read in the dim light, but the gist was that three thugs had smashed their way into "torch singer Natalie Bixby's love nest" and had beaten her and "entertainment figure and playboy Michael Papanoumou" unconscious. Harriet Maynard, "a friend of Miss Bixby's," had been struck several times before being thrown from the window. "She plummeted six stories before crashing to a loading dock." There was a photograph of staved-in crates where she landed. Three policeman posed next to them like hunters around a dead moose. Natalie had been hospitalized, said the article, but was getting stronger.

Carl folded the clipping and handed it back. "Georgy Mack was behind it?"

"Who else? Now the bosses figure that Georgy done it, that's easy, because he disappears the same day as the Greek is snatched. A day later, the Greek's jewels get delivered by the mailman. The U.S. Post Office!"

"The Macchiantis aren't subtle."

"Sally calls and claims the Greek faked the whole thing and popped his brother. That's an act. He's just covering for him. Why'd they kill Harriet and not Natalie? Maybe because they wanted Natalie to learn something. She ain't seen no other men since then and that ain't our Natalie." Musso inhaled, his nostrils wheezing, then continued. "Well, we know we ain't hiding the Greek. We can't afford no wars during the war. People get upset and they'll dangle some of us guys from lampposts, like that fucker who ruint my good name."

Carl realized he had drunk all of his wine. One of the domino players slammed his tile down hard and said something triumphant in Italian.

"What's Georgy whacking the Greek got to do with me?"

"Well, you oughtta be pissed he killed the man who would've done so much for you. But also, one hand washes the other."

"I don't get it."

"Natalie Bixby," said Musso. "You're a sexy guy. Make like old home week."

"Huh?"

"Have I gotta draw you a picture?" He whispered, his breath whistling. "Plug her with a good hunk of cannoli and make her squeal."

"Fuck her?"

"Watch your mouth. Like its gonna hurt or something."

"Hey, whoa! I have no interest in Natalie. For all I know she's got a social disease."

"So wear a raincoat."

"Maybe she doesn't want me."

"Get serious. You disappoint her last time?"

"There never was a last time, I tell you."

"Myron Rush told on you, boy. You did it right here in our town. The bombs were dropping on Pearl and you were slipping her the torpedo. Don't kid a kidder."

"I swear," said Carl. "Maybe Myron saw her in my room or leaving or God knows, but I didn't touch her. I slept in the lobby."

Musso laughed again, his phlegm gurgling. He began to cough and swallowed a whole glass of wine before the jag ended.

"I swear," said Carl.

"Well, you might as well have."

"Why?"

"How the hell you think you got shot?"

Carl blinked. "A sniper."

"A sniper!"

Carl stared.

"Georgy don't like sharing his piece. It's a matter of honor."

Carl shook his head to clear the fog. "Georgy Mack wasn't in Oran."

"He don't personally have to pull the trigger, you know."

"You're saying he got another soldier to take a shot at me?"

"I don't know nothing but this: You help us find Georgy and we'll both be better off."

Carl shook his head again. "I think I need a belt."

Musso gestured at the bar. "Bring the man a grappa." He leaned close. "You got to want to get Georgy before he gets you, am I right? And you know, there's the other thing. You help us; we help you."

Carl extended his fingers. "Wait a minute. If Georgy beat her up and killed her friend and chopped up the Greek, why would Natalie know anything about Georgy?"

"After all that trouble, Georgy will be back."

"Why? Because he's in love? Give me a break."

"Because it's a scam. The bitch set the Greek up. Her medical bills got paid by Georgy, we know this. Her apartment has been paid regular and she ain't working and she ain't hurting for money. Every month there's a deposit in her bank account."

"But why?"

"It's one of them love things."

"So why hasn't she run off to Georgy's turf? She could disappear into Queens like a cheap aspirin in the Atlantic."

"You ask too much." He sighed like a rhinoceros clearing his nose. "Okay, so there's some money involved, too. We claim Georgy's got it. Sal claims we're holding out. We've got to get this settled or there could be trouble with the treaty."

"A gang war?"

"That's all I can say. You can help us get Georgy or he'll get you. She's waiting for something. We've been watching her. She's pretty lonely by now."

"I thought you guys could make anybody talk."

"We hurt her, Georgy disappears for good. Sal never gets his dough. Or, we can never prove Sally rigged the thing. Sometimes its better to be a fox than a lion."

"So why me?"

"Get her drunk. Get her talking. Pay attention to what she says over the pillow. Find Georgy and you'll have friends in high places, Carl."

"What you're doing is using me as a decoy to draw Georgy out."

"The whole place is covered. Don't worry about it. Jimmy Doolittle couldn't get in there."

Carl stood. "This stinks, Musso."

Musso put a finger on his lips. "So the world's fragrant? Think of yourself as a spy." He pulled out a smaller envelope. "You're supposed to be an entertainer. Entertain her. Here's her address. Show up there about six. It'll be a big surprise for her."

"Forget it." Carl snatched up his cap and headed for the door.

"Georgy's still out there," Musso growled.

Carl walked furiously for several minutes. He came out near a park with an enormous building like a Greek temple. Families picnicked on the lawn around a pond. Women pushed baby carriages and children fed ducks. Ordinary life. The American dream. Have babies and slave to feed them until you die. Suckers, right? Maybe his father had been right. There was a moment in every man's life in which he could achieve greatness. There was a moment in which you chose to become either a superman or a sucker. If you settled for the conventional, you became a sucker, screwing in light bulbs at the Ford factory. If you chose to ignore all those bourgeois inhibitions that had been drummed into your head, then you were thrusting out your chest and accepting your destiny of absolute victory or absolute defeat.

Until the bullet had shattered his shoulder, Carl had

understood it only in the abstract. It all seemed like more of Professor William Walthers' ranting. Perhaps, when, on that bright summer day, his father had put the barrel of the old pistol against his heart and pulled the trigger, he thought he was spitting in the face of ordinary morality, the ultimate gesture of the *Übermensch*. Yet, the way Carl now saw it, when his father heard he was to be denied his platform in the classroom, he chose to become a sucker by letting a setback become total defeat. Or maybe the professor was smart enough to see that the classroom was another form of suckerdom. With the world at war, who could deceive himself that ranting about Nietzsche, Schopenhauer, and Plotinus could affect history more than a single, loaded M-1? Bullets changed history. Deeds, not words. Acts, not theories. History wasn't pretty. That didn't make it any easier to know what to do.

"Julia, where's the mustard?" said a man rifling a picnic basket.

"Oh, no! I left it on the sink!"

"You know I hate salami without mustard. It's a damned waste of our ration coupons!"

"The salami's still good, and you shouldn't curse."

"All I want is mustard!"

Carl's rambling thoughts turned to anger as he circled the pond. All most people wanted was mustard. The old man had capitulated. His father had faced a moment of truth and had given up, contrary to his own preachments. The cold bastard had wanted to appear tough, and that was exactly what he had achieved, an appearance. "Superman" indeed! And what did Carl want? To be a bigtime singer, or another sucker who had wanted to be a singer? He knew how close he had come to taking advantage of the insensate bitch, simply because she was there, in his bed, legs spread. How many times had he played up to some woman just to get off? Four times? Five? There was no hypocrisy with the widow of the Legionnaire in Algiers. Chocolate for sex. No pretense.

So now he was offended at banging Natalie for more than pleasure? Do you need these gangsters or not? You're a fool, Carl Walthers. Do you want to be Carl Carlson or not? Pearl Harbor was the gods' way of telling you that there are no presents for the kid who can't steal them: no Christmas, no birthday, no nothing.

He walked to the wide steps leading up to the museum portico. He watched pigeons fluttering under the columns and saw two sailors settling down on the steps. He was suddenly aware of how much in the open he was. He had the sensation of being watched. Over his right shoulder, a man in a dark hat and pin-striped suit casually watched the ducks gathering at his feet as he opened a paper sack. As he shelled peanuts, the ducks plucked up the fragments that drifted down.

Carl backed up two steps and collided with a newsboy.

"Hey, watch where you're going, soldier!" he shouted. "You want a paper? Monty's in the toe of Italy."

The man in the suit seemed to be watching him under the brim of his hat. For a moment Carl thought the man had the build and jaw of Georgy Mack, but no, the guy was too tall. Carl could circle the pond to see if he followed him. Or he could lose him in the museum. No crook would hit someone in a museum, would he? Too many guards, not enough exits. The man would simply wait outside.

What's with you? Carl asked himself. He's just some guy eating peanuts. You believe Musso? You believe Georgy Mack could get a guy to take a shot at you all the way across the ocean in Africa? They'd heard about snipers every day. Two Free French soldiers had a grenade tossed at them in a tavern. The fairy tale of Georgy's shooter was just Musso's way of making Carl go after Natalie. Musso had concocted the whole thing.

But the man with the peanuts hadn't moved. Carl headed across the lawn, trying not to look back. When he reached the street, his shirt was wet with sweat. He dared a glance while waiting for a bus to pass. The man was coming up the hill after him, not in a hurry, but steadily. Carl bolted across the street and headed up the hill towards the Catania. He stayed close to the buildings, ready to duck into a doorway. The man soon entered the side street, still following. There were enough people that Carl didn't think the guy would pull a gun. On the other hand, the market in Oran had been jammed.

When he reached the Catania Social Club, he rang the bell and looked back. The man had disappeared. The bartender opened the door without challenging him. "Musso," he said quickly.

"Mr. Musso is gone," said the bartender. Carl's eyes adjusted until he could see that the table in the corner was empty. "But he told me I should give you this."

The bartender handed Carl a matchbook. A picture of Hitler was on the outside. The striking surface was on his ass. Inside, behind the bomb-shaped matches, there was an address.

"Hey, buddy," said the bartender, "you got to watch where you're walking. I think you stepped in something."

When he lifted his shoe, the bartender was right.

8.

The pleasure-driving restrictions had been lifted last Wednesday and the traffic was fairly heavy, but Carl didn't notice anyone tailing his cab. For a moment, he suspected the cabby had been bought off and was leading him into a trap. You're losing your mind, he told himself. The guy "following" him had probably lived over one of the stores near the Catania. Maybe he was just a 4-F killing time before his appointment with some sailor's wife. If Georgy was after Carl, however, he was damn lucky North East, Pennsylvania, and Camp Anthony Wayne turned out to be far from New York City and the Macchianti family. The only question was, how far was far enough? If Musso wasn't lying, French Africa was too close.

Natalie's apartment was on the eighth floor in a posh building near Superior and Ninth. The doorman wore a bright green overcoat with more braid than a rear admiral in a musical. He sagged on his stool by the door until he was absolutely certain you were going inside, then raised himself like a bear coming out of hibernation. The lobby had a white marble floor, and a pair of gilded cupids decorated the iron bars of the elevator cage. Little Italy baroque, thought Carl. Mafia taste wows the midwest.

The cage creaked slowly upward, a staircase rising beside it. On the third floor, two pudgy boys on the landing watched their wind-up cars circle a tin gas station. On the fifth, a pale man with dark circles under his eyes and his collar slightly askew rested on a cane waiting to go down. All night poker game until four in the afternoon? Is this where he kept his tootsie? If so, she was draining more voltage than his fuses were supposed to carry. The whole building was a pocket of lethargy in the heart of a vital city, with corridors nearly silent but for the creaking elevator. When he strolled down the hard floor looking for 814, the squeaking of his shoes was so loud he thought it would bring people out of their apartments. Small brackets under each number held neatly lettered cards. "Andrews." "MacGilacuddy." "Furness." "Nicolaus." The bracket at 814 was empty. Okay, he thought, look charming. He took a deep breath and pushed the buzzer. He raised himself on his toes and whistled a made-up tune. She's not here, he thought. Good. One more push and I'm out of here. He was reaching for the button when the door suddenly opened.

A tiny, caramel-colored woman in a maid's uniform peered up at him. "Yes?" He could hear a record, Vera Lynn singing "I'll Be Seeing You."

"Is this the Bixby apartment?"

"I'm sorry, sir—"

A husky voice called out from inside. "Who is it, Precious?" A clumsy hand lifted the needle off the record with a loud *skrutch!*

Carl called past the maid. "It's me."

He pushed the door wider, despite the maid's resistance. Beyond a marble vestibule stood Natalie, still holding the phonograph arm. She wore a slinky black evening gown with wide, lacy sleeves. "So, who is it? The Salvation Army?" She feyly laughed.

The image of her lying drunk on his bed with her legs spread flashed across his mind and his ears felt hot. "It's me. Carl."

She squinted. "Carl?" Her face then widened into delighted amazement as she dropped the phono arm and covered her mouth with both hands. "Carl! You're alive!"

"You bet," he said, spreading his hands like Jolson at the end of "Swanee." She rushed forward with a funny skittering movement caused by the tightness of the dress around her thighs. Precious stepped back and Natalie clutched him against her. She kissed him on both cheeks near his ears, her fingers embedded in his upper arms like claws, her perfume strong as gelignite fumes. He flushed when he saw Precious still holding the door and watching.

She held him at arm's length and studied his face. "You look just like the kid you were, you handsome dog you."

"And you're just like always, too. Gorgeous."

"Why, aren't you the gay blade? Isn't he a doll, Precious?" Up close he saw that all her makeup did not cover the pursing lines that had formed around her full lips. And there was an indent that showed through on the ridge under her eyebrows, a boxer's scar.

"Yes'm," said Precious. Natalie slid her hands down his arms and took his fingers, pulling him into the living room. The furniture was all in white and had mahogany lion's paw legs. Her singing didn't get her this style of life.

She pushed him to sit on the divan and went back to the phono. Her rear swung like a Studebaker with bad shocks. The needle had landed somehow on the moving record and Vera Lynn was in the middle of her song. "Can you imagine this woman is so big now? I listen to it over and over and can't figure it out."

"It means a lot to people," said Carl. You've never stood on the deck watching New York harbor recede, he thought, knowing you might never see it again.

"But it's so unemotional. No kick. No sexiness. I was better than that and look where I ended up."

"It doesn't look so terrible from where I sit. Who'd you marry, a Rockefeller?"

She pulled another record from the cabinet and slapped it on the turntable as if using it to swat flies. "Who says I got married? I saved up my nest egg and here's my nest." He thought of her crotch and pretended to study the crown moldings.

"Basin Street Blues" began after a moment of hissing and popping. "That's more like it," she said. "What can I get you to drink?"

"Bromo Seltzer," he said quickly. "Musso gave me some wine that really landed hard."

"Musso? Fat pig! So that's how you found me. What you need is the hair of a stronger dog. Brandy." She reached for a mirror which opened to reveal a well-stocked liquor cabinet.

"Really, my stomach—"

"It fixes me up every time." She was already pouring. "So, you were looking for me?"

"He mentioned you were in Cleveland."

She pouted. "You didn't come all the way around the world to find me?"

"It was a coincidence. But I would have. If I'd known."

She handed him a tulip glass half full. "You sure know how to flatter a girl. Why don't you tell me it's destiny?"

"Okay. When I said 'coincidence,' I meant 'destiny.' It's the same thing, isn't it? That make you feel better?"

She settled onto the divan, leaning against the high arm as if she were going to put her legs in his lap, but she twisted at the hip, pressing the side of her knee against his. "Mmmmm. Every woman likes to hear romantic things. Haven't you learned that yet? Drink up."

He brought the glass to his lips, but only sucked in a trickle. It warmed his cheeks like the glow of a fireplace. "You never struck me as romantic." He noticed her bosom straining against the black silk. She hadn't gotten any smaller. Nipples the size of silver dollars showed through. He cupped his drink in his hand and stared into the brown liquid. "Anyhow, I didn't get that much chance to practice romance when I was singing every night."

"Just love 'em and leave 'em a two-dollar bill."

Or a chocolate bar, he thought. He felt a pang for the Legionnaire's wife. "I've never been that casual about it."

"You're a man. Casual's in your hormones."

He suppressed a sudden urge to leave by scanning the window valances.

"You know you wanted your birthday present. How do you know I kept it for you?"

"You remember that?"

She kicked at him, shoving his knee. "Son of a bitch," she smiled.

"You were loaded. I thought you'd hate me in the morning."

"Why, Mistah Ravenal," she mocked, "you are the gentleman, aren't you?"

"Yeah. The Carolina Crooner." He took a big gulp of the brandy.

"Thatta boy," she said. "Well, I forgive you. You'll get bigger, pardon the expression, and learn to take a woman's offer. You hurt my feelings."

"I'm sorry."

"You oughtta be."

He stared straight ahead, rolling the glass between his palms. Her knee felt sweaty against his.

"What are you thinking, Carl?" she teased. "You're blushing."

"It must be the brandy." He fished in his shirt pocket. "You want a smoke? I was thinking about the guys in the band. Whatever happened to them. How's Buzz?"

"The band," she said distastefully. She took one of the offered cigarettes. He struck a bomb-shaped match on Hitler's ass. When he held it up, she fixed her half-closed eyes on his mouth and guided his hands to her cigarette. After it lit, she took a deep drag and shifted her shoulders. Her nipples had hardened and puckered.

"Buzz is in Hollywood."

"Hollywood?"

"He got a crazy idea he could write patriotic songs for the movies. He's going under Benjamin Franklin Bixby. He's still Benjamin Glock to me. I've put little Natalya Glock behind me, but Bennie—" She shook her head ruefully. "Bennie's an idiot. He's always been an idiot. He's got a good soul, mind you, but he's an idiot. He called me a couple of times to get me to go out there. He says I could be in pictures. I could do the voices for actresses who can't sing, he says. Why would I want to sing without being seen? I'm not the ugliest woman on earth. Does he think Kate Smith is a knock-out? Maxene Andrews? Hell, he's just lonely. We haven't been separated since we was growing up in the tenement. Sometimes I miss him, too, but I got my apartment here. Who knows what I'd have there? Bennie always thinks he's a block away from the big time."

"Don't we all," said Carl. "So what about the other guys?"

"Who knows?"

"Ted Clough?"

"That gorilla? The Navy got him, I heard. Lou had a heart attack. Dropped dead in Grand Central."

"No kidding. How about Mack Mintner?"

She shrugged. "Someone told me he was a gun man on a bomber."

"Mack?"

"Maybe he can see straight without the reefers."

"Isn't he too old for the air corps?"

"You expect me to know? The Cavalcade of Swing was a century ago as far as I'm concerned."

She was right, he thought. It was a fantasy. People who had become nothing more than wisps of memory, names to be forgotten. The kind of people you run into on the street. You exchange a few words, swap a few beers, and try to recapture the time you spent together. The experience could never have been as good as you remembered it and you knew that, but you would still wallow in it. "It's not that long ago," he said. "Like yesterday."

"Yesterday is vapor. Today and tomorrow, that's everything."

"You sound like you've got plans."

"Mmmmm," she said, tossing back the last of her brandy.

The maid had been dusting a bust of Napoleon in the corner when she noticed the phonograph arm wandering back and forth at the end of the record. When she lifted it, Natalie waved her glass. "Precious, get me another, will you?"

"Yes'm, and would the sir like some more?"

He shook his head and then handed her the glass anyway. The brandy hadn't helped his stomach. He felt he was adrift on a raft in the Coral Sea. For a moment, he didn't care whether he ever sang again. He wanted to slap the whore and go back to his pointless interrogations. But either the brandy slowed him or somehow he knew that he would care later. Care too much. Behind every fortune is a crime, he thought. This is my crime, to find out what's behind Natalie's good fortune and feed her to Musso.

When Precious handed him his half-filled glass, he turned towards Natalie for the first time, resting his elbow on the back of the divan and crossing his legs. He glanced at her nipples—he couldn't help it—and tried to ascertain if he was getting that tingle he had felt when the Legionnaire's wife had first sidled up to him, or when the shop girl had closed her eyes and leaned back against the oak in Central Park. All he felt was moisture in his groin, as if the brandy sweat were washing away any chance for feeling.

"How's Georgy Mack?" he asked abruptly.

The maid stopped dusting momentarily, then continued as if she hadn't heard.

"Georgy?" asked Natalie, taking a second to recover. "We've been over a long time."

"Musso told me Georgy didn't like it."

"Like what?"

"When you tossed him over for the Greek."

"I didn't." She sipped her brandy. "And they say women gossip."

"He told me Georgy's goons worked you over pretty good."

She closed her eyes as if the memory of the beating might be blocked out. "Hey, I didn't know they were Georgy's. I looked real bad afterwards. But better than Harriet."

"Who was she?"

"A party girl."

Carl waited.

"She helped Michael with business. They killed her." She shrugged. Harriet might have been a cat mowed down by bus.

"And the police didn't do anything?"

"They're just monkeys: see no, hear no, speak no. They didn't want to know it was Georgy's muscle. Personally, I think that slug Musso paid them off. He likes Michael out of the way."

"Musso? Why?"

"It's always about power, isn't it? That's what the war is about, isn't it?"

Carl ran a few scenarios through his mind and came up with Musso hitting the Greek. Maybe Georgy knew he was next and took a powder until he could get Musso first. That would explain why the fat man wanted to locate Georgy. But Carl didn't buy it. If that were true, Musso wouldn't have sent Carl to find out. He'd have sent the goons and had Natalie squealing the whole deal just before she passed into the next world. If Musso had hit Georgy, Sally Mack would have had killers on the train within an hour.

"Musso doesn't operate on his own. He's got bosses."

"So? The bosses are cleaning house. I don't want to talk about it. Some guys like hurting a woman. I got hurt like I never got hurt. I thought I was dead. Do you talk about getting shot?"

"It doesn't bother me that much."

"Then it didn't hurt that much."

"Sister, you got that wrong." He was on the verge of asking her if Georgy Mack had sent the sniper but the brandy had thickened his tongue. "Say, what do you say we get some food? I keep hearing I ought to eat at the Stouffer's Hotel. Ever eat there?"

"Often enough." She stretched her leg and ran her bare toes along his shin. "But now that I've got you here, you don't think I'm going to let you leave, do you?"

"We'll go together—," he said vaguely.

"I've saved your birthday present for you. Now you can be my present. We have unfinished business . . ." She leaned forward, placed a hand on his thigh and brushed his nose with hers.

He didn't move. "Today's your birthday?"

"Could be . . ." She draped herself around his neck and pressed her lips hard against his. Over her shoulder he saw Precious polishing the dining table beyond two half-closed pocket doors. She glanced at them, reversed her cloth, and continued rubbing.

"What's the matter?" whispered Natalie. "Are you going to kiss me back or what?"

"The maid—"

"You'd rather have Precious?" she teased.

"No," he said, "I just—"

"She's part of the furnishings, soldier. Get used to the good life. I have."

She was back on his mouth and this time he dropped his arms around her shoulders and pulled her in close, tasting the brandy on her lips and tongue, getting drunker on it than the two glasses. He imagined kissing the Legionnaire's wife (something she had refused to do) and the shop girl, and the tipsy woman who had picked him up in a bar. Natalie tugged at his shirt and the starchy tail came out of his trousers like stiff paper. She moved her mouth over his ear, cheek, and neck, slurping as she tasted his skin, raking it with her teeth. Her hands fumbled at his fly and he lowered his hands to cup her ponderous breasts.

The pocket doors closed with a clunk. Precious was calmly cleaning the sash bars one by one. How often had Natalie done this before that Precious was so indifferent? One of the dumb Army training films flickered across the ceiling. "Wait," he gasped. "Wait."

She slid back, brushing his nose with her own, and took his hands by the wrist. "Come on," she said grinning. "You'll like my bedroom."

He was numbed, as if still taking morphine for his shoulder. She manacled him with her hands, pulling both wrists, backing into her bedroom door and bumping it open with her rear. A six-ounce Nehi, he thought. She drains them and throws them over her shoulder. But so what? He was using her, she was using him. She wanted it. The conventional never stood in her way.

She spun him back on the bed. He flopped like a rag doll on the feather comforter and watched her shimmy out of her black gown. Her body was pale as milk glass and the veins in her breasts were a translucent blue. At the edge of her round belly, an appendix scar pointed to her bushy pubic hair almost as the lipstick arrow had offered her a year and a half ago. "So, what do you think, little boy?" she said, lifting each overflowing breast in her hands, aiming the dark nipples at him like weapons. She swayed from side to side, still holding her breasts and humming "What'll I Do." She danced back and forth in awkward pirouettes, never taking her eyes from him.

On the last line of the song, she twisted quickly and fell on top of him, kissing his forehead, his eyes, unbuttoning his shirt and clawing at the hair on his chest. As he tugged off the sleeves of his shirt, he saw himself in an ornate, beveled mirror, his face in an emotionless, stunned expression, as if he'd only just heard of the curious death of a friend. He watched as Natalie, only the top of her head visible, yanked his olive green shorts below his knees. "Why, there you are!" she chuckled, taking his soft penis in her hand. "Stand up and say hello." No woman had ever placed her mouth on him before and he closed his eyes and desperately concentrated on feeling every tickle of her tongue. She teased it with her breasts, she purred and cajoled, she peeled the foreskin and sucked at it as if she wanted to digest it, but it hardened only briefly. When he rolled atop her it became soft.

He concentrated on the Legionnaire's wife and remembered the feel of sliding in and out of her body. He buried his face in Natalie's breasts, listened to her moans, and became even more anxious. He tried manipulating himself, rubbing himself against her incredibly wet opening, and though the sensation was exquisite, he still was only partially erect when he felt himself coming against her, emptying himself on her hair and groin. He groaned with the pleasure of it, then sighed deeply and sadly. "I'm sorry," he gasped. "I'm sorry."

"Don't stop," she murmured, taking his wet hand from his collapsed organ. She squeezed all four of his fingers into a bundle and directed them inside her, pumping it with both hands as he took her nipple in his teeth. When it became hard as a pebble, she began to call out, "ah, ah, ah" in rhythm to the thrusting of his fingers, arched her back, then expelled a long roar of air, as if emptying her body.

"It was good?" he asked.

"Goodness had nothing to do with it," she whispered, wanly smiling. "I'll peel your grape anytime, wonderful." She pulled him close and kissed him deeply on the mouth.

He rolled onto his back. Wonderful? What had been wrong? The thought of Georgy Mack coming through the door with a .45? Too much brandy? Army VD films? Her sluttishness? The suspicion that Precious listened in? His shoulder felt hot. He had moved it too much in the wrong direction. She sighed with an open mouth, like a sleeper who couldn't be awakened. He wanted to leave, but didn't want her to know he wanted to. He turned on his side and closed his eyes. What the hell had happened? Perhaps another shot of brandy . . .

When he awoke, the room was totally dark. He forgot where he was. Long fingernails trailed along the back of his thighs and up his buttocks. He turned over and Natalie's lips were on his ear and then covering his mouth. She pressed her body against him. It was much easier the second time, in the dark, in the middle of the night, the blackout curtains softly flapping in the breeze off Lake Erie. When he thrust himself into her, he imagined she could feel it in her throat.

9.

He took the late train on Sunday night, hungry, sore from Natalie's uninterrupted themes and variations on variations of variations. It was an education you couldn't get at William and Mary. If he had waited until Labor Day morning, as he had planned, they'd have had to haul him to Union Station on a stretcher. It had all occurred in a hedonistic blur, one thought randomly replacing another, as if the mind were a metamorphic pack of cards in which the queen of spades followed the two of clubs, and the jack of hearts was transforming himself into the joker. His other sexual encounters had all been quick, only one of them lasting through the night. Was this what married life was like? No wonder tired-looking husbands escaped to bars and long afternoons at the ball park. Or was this Natalie? Drain 'em and throw 'em away. When he had said he needed to get back to Camp Wayne, she pecked him on the ear, dropped back on her pillow and curled up in a fetal position. "Happy birthday, kiddo," she yawned. "Come back and see me some time."

"I'll have a pistol in my pocket," he responded, but she had already dozed off, her voluptuous flesh sagging, a sputtering candle melting down.

His mind went back and forth. He didn't know what to make of himself. He congratulated himself on giving her all she could handle, but then arrogance would slump into self-revulsion. He'd never be able to wash the smell of her off his fingers, to get the taste of her out of his mouth. He was no better than poor old Lou Epstein, who had thought his saxophone was just a device for picking up girls. Lou, at least, hadn't screwed a woman to get information. With Lou the music had been a way of getting pleasure. And what was

121

wrong with pleasure? Everyone needs his clock cleaned now and then. Carl was using pleasure to enhance his career in music and oh did he provide pleasure! He had circled back to Carl Carlson, stud bull.

Maybe bull was all there was to it. Lou had dropped dead of a heart attack, an unknown sax man who'd gotten nothing for his romps but gonorrhea. Carl wasn't going to let himself go that way.

No one else left the train with him. It was about two miles back to the camp. He bought a pack of Chesterfields, considered bumming a ride, then set out walking. Moonlight glistened on the tracks. A breeze stirred the corn leaves in the field next to the road. Crickets chirped and the gravel crunched under foot. After about a quarter of a mile, he began to whistle fragments of various songs and did not notice the rumble of the Chrysler until its headlights, half-masked by black paint, cast long shadows ahead of him. As he watched the car approach, it abruptly pulled across the shoulder. The engine shuddered to a stop and Carl uneasily watched a man get out and look across the roof.

"You Carl?"

He couldn't make out the face. He tensed. "Who wants to know?"

"I missed you at the station. You shoulda called Mr. Musso."

"Musso?"

"He wants to know what you found out."

"Found out?"

"You are Carl, aren't you?"

"I'll get back to him. Nothing much happened."

"He said you must've found out something."

"Tell him I tried. I didn't want to make her suspicious."

The man's head turned slowly as he scanned the empty road, his eyes hidden. "You want a ride?"

"I was walking."

"You do enough of that in the Army, don't you? I'm Reese. Mr. Musso said to keep an eye on you."

Carl hesitated. So now he was being watched. Georgy Mack was still out there somewhere. Reese could one of Georgy's soldiers.

"Hey, you want a ride or not?"

Carl made sure nobody was in the back seat. "Okay," he said.

"The Army marches you enough." Reese's sharp face weakly glowed from the speedometer light. "That's how I got out. Fallen arches."

"You're lucky."

The man whistled. "You're telling me. There's a lotta dough to be made. It's legal, too."

"Even more on the sly, I suppose."

"I wouldn't know about that, though, would I?"

"I guess not." Carl wanted to ask the man what his connection to Musso was, but he didn't think he'd get an answer. He saw the silhouette of the camp towers. Oh, hell! He hadn't done anything about a translator. "Say, you know anyone who speaks Italian. Somebody reliable?"

"Yeah," he laughed, "Ernie Musso. You can rely on him."

"Gee, thanks," said Carl. "I need somebody from around here. Somebody patriotic, who won't lose his temper at Fascist crap."

"It shouldn't be hard." Reese pulled into the gate and the guard leaned into the half-open window. "I got a load of nails in the trunk for Jack." The guard nodded and they moved on. "By the way," Reese said as he braked near the barracks, "Mr. Musso said you should get another leave soon, just to make sure the cat stays warm."

"It's not always easy to get away."

"No skin off my nose. Maybe yours . . . ."

Reese may have winked. Carl wasn't sure. He felt for the door handle and climbed out.

"Hey," called Reese, "take care of yourself!"

"Yeah," said Carl. Was that a threat? He'd always heard the mob was everywhere, but he'd never really felt it. Anybody could be working for them. Sergeant Pike or O'Hurly could get out of his cot, cross the barracks and kill him. Valdez could drop him in the interrogation room. Dahl. Murnow. Anyone with two feet. He had messed with Georgy's dame for real, now. "I'll be a hell of a singer, if I live," he mumbled to himself. Okay, kill me, he thought, eying the snoring Pike as he dropped off. Just let me sleep.

At reveille he snapped upright as if he hadn't missed any sleep at all, but when the chilly breeze slapped him in the face his head spun. He moved out to the parade ground and took his place beside Sergeant O'Hurly.

"'Ten*shun!*" shouted Morris and the flag rose up the pole as the men sang.

"Oh say can you see, by the dawn's early light, what so proudly we hailed at the twilight's last gleaming . . ."

Carl was lethargic in his singing, he knew, and snapped his head further back to increase his volume. There were other voices though, higher pitched voices, and he thought at first that the Nazis had decided to mock the "Star-spangled Banner" as well as sing their own anthem. When he looked towards the rows of prisoners, however, they were as confused as he, glancing at each other furtively. Some Italians wandered toward the fences, then a few Germans, barked at by their superiors.

Outside the fence were five school buses and dozens of children, from very small ones to high schoolers with fluttering adam's apples. *". . . o'er the ramparts we watched were so gallantly streaming . . ."*

Murnow knit his eyebrows in confusion. The men smiled at each other. Lt. Morris rotated his hand and said "Louder! Louder!"

"Gave proof through the night, that our flag was still there!"

All of the prisoners had now broken ranks and moved behind the barracks to the fence. Some of the smaller children cringed back into the skirts of the girls behind them, but the lines of children did not waver. A white-haired priest and the music store owner with hair like Toscanini's stood in front conducting. In the rear were as many adults as children, men in suits, women in Sunday best and a row of young men in cassocks, presumably from the seminary. The prisoners stared only at the children, their eyes hungry. Many of the children near the priest were wearing school uniforms, but there were boys in bow ties and adult style jackets. There were boys with patches on their overalls and smudges on their fingers and foreheads. There was a boy with a cowlick and boys with hair slicked down with what looked like a pound of lard. There was even one unfortunate boy in a

Lord Fauntleroy shirt and breeches. The girls ran to pink: pink ribbons, pink roses on their dresses, pink lips and cheeks and knees. There was a pair of twins in overalls like some of the boys. Each had the same tooth missing and held each other's hand not as if they feared the hundreds of men silently watching them, but as if they always did. There were girls with freckles and girls with every shading of hair that God had created. There were two Chinese girls and half a dozen black children at the far end.

As the "Star-spangled Banner" slid upward to its close, the American soldiers raised a cheer as if they were at the Polo Grounds on July 4. They broke ranks and hustled closer to the fences. Murnow turned to Morris for an explanation, but the lieutenant said, "Beats me!" The prisoners, however, continued to be silent, holding their caps, smiling sadly as some of the children smiled back.

The man who looked like Toscanini raised his hands and the children sang "America the Beautiful." Cars puttered up and farm trucks. Soon the crowd of schoolchildren and townspeople numbered about a hundred and fifty. In the middle of the second verse, half a dozen Germans moved among their men, shoving them on the shoulder, trying to get them to sing "Das Vaterland," but the men moved their lips until the commander moved on. Carl saw Läufer and thought he should note down who was trying to rouse the Germans to defeat the Children's Crusade. He recognized two others, but could not remember their names.

The song ended and some prisoners applauded. The Italians were especially excited. Some shouted encouragement. "Stuff Hitler!" yelled a tough-looking kid with a turned up nose, but the prisoners didn't seem to understand it and continued smiling. When the priest twisted the boy's ear, several of the Germans yelled threats and the old priest lowered his spectacles as if to intimidate an unruly class.

Once again the music man's arms went up and they began "God Bless America." Kate Smith singing it put a knot in anyone's throat, but the children doing so was even more emotional. Carl joined in at the top of his voice when he saw O'Hurly with tears streaming down his cheeks. The sergeant's stare meant he could be thinking of only one thing:

friends in Europe and the Pacific. Thousands of men dying in places they'd never heard of, killing other men who, at the sight of children singing, would forget any of the patriotic babble they had ever heard. By the time he reached the end of the song, Carl was choked up, too. When a couple of the men slapped him on the back, he turned away to prevent himself from crying like any other poor sucker.

The children went on. When they sang "My Country 'Tis of Thee," prisoners began to sing with them, using the words of an Austrian anthem. This angered some of the Germans, but nothing came of it. The children followed with "Yankee Doodle Dandy" from the new movie and then "Yankee Doodle" itself. A clarinet was playing along now: Oswald Ülsmann, somewhere behind the closest barracks. The singing ended with "Battle Hymn of the Republic" with the loud bass voice of Sergeant Lang and that of his cooks rumbling above the high voices of the children.

Prisoners reached out through the fences and the braver children offered hard candy. A farmer doled out chunks of watermelon. An old woman in a gingham dress offered pocket Bibles. Some of the Germans now tried to reorganize the daily singing of "Deutschland über Alles" but the ranks had broken and it faded rapidly.

Murnow walked by with Morris. "Jack, should we be letting this happen?"

"Okay, Tex," said Morris, "we'll machine-gun the kids."

"That isn't what I meant!"

Dahl grabbed Carl by the elbow. "Some show, huh? Did you see all those grown men boo-hooing like a bunch of old ladies! Cripe, they ought to take that show to Broadway."

"Let's mingle," said Carl. "Hell, it's a holiday, right?"

"Don't want to labor on Labor Day. Does it seem awful cold for Labor Day?"

The townspeople crowded near the fence. Germans and Italians were trying to make themselves understood through hand gestures and broken English. One of them reached to touch a black kid's hair and said something to a friend inside. Carl saw the counter woman from the drug store and immediately knew from the way she was talking to the seminarians that she had been behind the whole idea. He chatted with the music store man from whom he had bought Oswald's clarinet and was introduced to the piano teacher he had heard but never seen, Louis Bassett. A rubber ball of a man who resembled Oliver Hardy, he had grown a mustache in a vain attempt to cover the scar of a repaired hare-lip.

Dahl meantime rushed up to a German who was handing an SS collar patch to a runny-nosed boy. "Hey, I could get you a buck for that!" The German merely waved the boy closer, who snatched it off his fingers like a timid cat after a hunk of fish. Dahl shook his head in exasperation, then rushed off to intercept a jar of corn relish which a shapely redhead was offering to one of the Afrika Korps men. "You can't do that," he said, handing the relish behind him to the man it was originally intended for. "What's your name, sweetheart? My name's Phil. Philip Morris."

Carl laughed. He pushed further into the crowd and was stopped by a monsignor. "Is it possible, son, for us to go inside? I believe there's more than a few who need confession."

"Father, they have chaplains, but you could ask Major Murnow over there. I'm sure it'd be okay."

He saw Elizabeth Way talking to a cluster of Italian prisoners who pressed against the wire as if it might burst. She was rattling away in Italian at a hundred miles an hour. A prisoner was teasing her, but she was giving as good as she took. She waved a finger saying something that made her tormentor slap his forehead. The other men broke up, some of them collapsing to their knees.

She noticed Carl, waved bye to the prisoners, and shouted "*Arrivederci, ragazzi!*" Several men went back onto their knees, amid much laughter, clasping their hands as if praying.

"They call me *La Fanciulla da Nordest:* 'the girl from North East.'"

"Like the opera."

"You know about that? Oh, I forgot. You're a singer."

"My mother was crazy about Puccini," said Carl, "but my father?" Carl put on a mock stern face. "Wagner, Wagner, Wagner."

She laughed.

"This is like a county fair," said Carl. "It's crazy. Wonderful, but crazy. Look at them! If it wasn't for the fence, you wouldn't know there's a war."

"Mable just couldn't stand the idea of them singing their anthem in Lou's town, as she calls it. She wanted to do it a week ago, but today worked out better for rounding up the children."

"Mable is the drug store lady?"

Elizabeth nodded. Her eyes were almost violet. He thought of how he'd spent the weekend and blushed. She now blushed, too, and averted her gaze.

"You're pretty good with Italian."

"My mom was Italian. That's how Pop got his job."

"His job?"

"The one he got shot at. He's crippled from it."

"I remember, so you work at a factory."

"For the time being. I've got to get back. They gave me a couple of hours, but everybody's giving up their Labor Day for the war effort. All the unions agreed."

"Did I know your mom was Italian? I think you told me, but it didn't register. Say, I've got an idea. Would you like to help the war effort? You'd get paid."

"I'm listening."

"We've got about a hundred and a half Italians now and nobody real good with the language. Could you do that? You were handling those guys like you were born in Rome."

She looked uncertain. "Sure, I guess so. Is it full time? What would I have to do?"

"Translate. Listen to them. Just say yes."

She pitched her head to one side. "I'll try."

"Great!"

Dahl interrupted. "Whatcha doing, sarge, proposing? If you're not, mind if I do?"

"Ooh!" said Elizabeth suddenly. "Everyone's leaving!" Children clambered back into the buses. Car doors slammed. She scurried away, waving over her shoulder.

"Wait!" shouted Carl. "How can I reach you?"

"Clinton Street. Mrs. Downey's boarding house."

"By tomorrow!"

She waved again.

Dahl whistled. "She's some dame."

Carl looked at him nastily. "That's a nice girl."

"I getcha," said Dahl. "The marrying kind."

"She's just a nice kid."

"Suit yourself," said Dahl. "But she ain't nine years old, you know."

Marrying? thought Carl. Tie me down and slash my vocal cords.

After breakfast—now two hours late—Carl headed for Murnow's office to convince him to hire the girl. He was running the arguments Murnow might use through his mind—she's a girl, Italians are lechers, what if something happened to her—when he heard the major shouting inside his office. "It can't be!"

"That's what it looks like," said Pike.

"Let me see!"

"I've toted it up three times. Two."

"Son of a bitch! That damned singalong damned incident!"

The major burst out of his office with Pike behind him, turned on O'Hurly and said, "Get me the sheriff." He patted his feet. "Some damned provost sergeant you turned out to be."

"They can't have been running long, sir," said Pike sternly.

"Well, go, then! Go!" He pointed towards the outer door. Murnow noticed Carl. "Well, go on! Help him!"

"I've found an Italian translator," said Carl quietly.

Murnow already had the phone to his ear. He covered the mouthpiece. "What? I told you to help Sergeant Pike!"

Carl saluted and chased after Pike. The sergeant's long strides were chewing up great chunks of earth as he made for the prisoner compound. "An escape?" asked Carl.

"Two rabbits. We gotta make sure who they are. If you were a kraut where would you run to?"

"I don't know—to sympathizers?"

Pike stopped and grabbed a corporal by the sleeve. "Adams, get back to the barracks pronto and roust the night shift, then get me Lt. Valdez." He sent him away with a pat on the arm. "Private Jones, begin assembly. We're going to count the bastards again."

In ten minutes the prisoners were in their rows. Some

smirked, others were genuinely curious. The nervous types squinted at the sight of additional soldiers assembling below the towers. Major Murnow paced in front of them. With two riflemen at his side and his hand on his holster, Pike marched to the front of C-2. He quickly counted heads. There were twenty.

"It's just a miscount," said Carl.

Pike opened the file he had held under his arm. He flipped through the record sheets, studying the photographs in the corners. "You!" he barked. "Step forward!"

Carl repeated the order in German. A jowly man ambled to the front. Pike flipped back and forth comparing the faces in front of him to the photos. "And you! What are you two cheesebuckets doing in C-2?"

Carl substituted "*Soldaten*" for "cheesebuckets."

"We sleep here," said the jowly man. The prisoners chuckled.

"You don't belong in C-2."

"The view is better and my friend—"

Carl stepped forward. "Stop. You are just doing this to cause confusion. Where are they?"

"Who?"

"Sergeant Pike might lose his temper. A farmer out there might get overexcited and shoot your friends. You are sitting on gunpowder and playing with matches. You cannot help your friends by keeping us from finding them. They will live if we find them. God help them if the wrong civilian gets his hands on them."

The jowly man lowered his eyes.

"What'd he say?" asked Pike.

"Nothing."

"All right, then. These two are to be punished. Make that clear. The rabbits are Privates Hermann Rolsch and Peter Gast." He showed Carl the photographs. "We'll do a full roll call to make sure they're not just shuffling them around, but these guys are it."

Carl didn't recognize them. Rolsch was a common foot-soldier, according to the records, and Gast a cook. Gast had frequently worked in the camp mess. Sergeant Lang had written one word on the comment sheet: "Lazy!" Both men

130

were from the 962nd Rifles of the 999th Light Afrika division, the *Strafbataillon*. Who knew what kind of criminals they were before Hitler had drafted them?

"Sergeant?" Private Burgess saluted Pike.

"Yes?"

"Sir, one of the officers wishes to speak to Major Murnow."

"What does he want? More complaints? Did Lowell Thomas insult him by telling him he's losing the war?"

"No, sir. He says he wants to talk about the escaped men."

"It's that icicle Läufer, I suppose."

"Yes, sir."

Pike glanced back at Carl. "I'll let you have the privilege."

"Gee, thanks."

Carl followed Burgess to the officer's huts while Pike began the laborious process of re-counting the prisoners. As each barracks was confirmed to have the correct number, and each face was compared to the photos of Gast and Rolsch, its occupants were confined inside.

As expressionless as wax dummies, the officers were neatly lined up, uniforms impeccable. SS-captain Gerhardt Läufer was in the center of the front rank, flanked by Captain Albert Dorn and Lieutenant Ulrich Messer. The Ritz Brothers of the Third Reich, thought Carl.

Carl leaned his face into Läufer's, and said in English, "So, is there something wrong with your room? Shall I get the concierge?"

"I must speak to Major Murnow."

"About what?"

"As officer to officer."

"The major is busy. He isn't coming into the compound while a shakedown is in progress. If you've got something to bitch about, I'll convey it, but at the moment I don't think he much cares what you have to say."

Läufer's eyes sparked like flint on steel. "Some day," he said, "you shall be *my* prisoner."

"And the Pope will go Protestant. I'll let the major know. Come on, Burgess." He spun to leave, but Läufer spoke quietly.

"You are not understanding."

Carl came back.

131

"We wish the major to know that we did not approve this escape."

"So who asked you?" said Burgess.

The SS-captain ignored him. "As officers we regard their attempt as a breech of our code of discipline and we further insist that we shall punish the men involved."

Carl was thrown by this. He wasn't certain whether it was the nature of the request or simply another mind whirl brought on by the weekend with Natalie, but he had nothing to say.

"Our discipline will be more effective than yours," added Läufer.

"You've got to make allowances," said Carl. "We're new at running the world." He yawned, despite himself. "Is that it?"

"*Ja.*"

"I'll tell the major."

Captain Dorn suddenly spoke up. "This kind of thing comes about because of the laxity in the operation of this camp."

"Well, General Eisenhower's thinking about replacing Tex with Lieutenant Valdez. Then you won't have a *Lagergestapo.*"

The Germans glanced at each other. Carl knew he had finally said something that surprised them. He knew about their "camp Gestapo," even if he didn't know how could it operate and who were its members.

Sheriff Bowers of North East had gathered a "posse" of old men and boys. Jaws set, they pulled up in two cars and a truck near the front tower. As Carl approached, the sheriff was telling Murnow he had sent half a dozen men throughout the town warning ladies to watch for clothes stolen off the line or stolen chickens or broken-in root cellars or odd hoboes. Unfortunately, a lot of housewives and retired people were at parks and beaches for Labor Day. Bowers had also notified law enforcement in Erie, Jamestown, Ripley, Westfield, and Corry, as well as the radio stations. He'd also called the railroads to keep an eye on the freight yards. The whole area was up in arms.

"When did they break out?" asked Bowers.

"Don't know," said Pike. "It could have been any time after roll call yesterday. I'd guess at night."

"No," said Murnow, "it was during that singing incident those school kids cooked up. I can feel it."

"That'd be terrible," said Bowers. "It was a proud thing."

"They could be two miles away or fifty," said Pike. "It's hard to tell."

"Oh, they're near," said Murnow. "You can't get anyplace without money and they haven't got any."

Carl thought about the greenbacks circulating at the soccer game. "You can't expect them to buy train tickets."

"A gas rationing coupon is more valuable these days than money," the sheriff said.

Men searched the ravine, others moved into the vineyards. Carl helped a squad check several acres of orchards. They ran into three teenage boys with squirrel rifles who said they were "hunting the Huns." He hoped they didn't end up in a fire fight with another bunch of "patriots." Later the squad got lost in a patch of woods and startled a farm woman picking wild berries. Other than that, it was a stroll in the country. It was nearly dark when they loped back into Camp Wayne. Carl felt like he hadn't slept in a month.

"Hey, there you are," shouted PFC Jones from the tower. "They got them about twenty minutes ago. You're to go to interrogation."

"Can't I eat first?" He knew the answer before he asked.

Rolsch and Gast slumped in chairs at opposite ends of the table. Their shirts were off. Their chests, backs, and faces were the color of beets. Valdez, his face still swollen from his oral surgery, looked up from his clipboard. "They went to the beach," he said.

"The beach?"

"Freeport Beach."

Carl leaned over and for a moment forgot the German word for beach. *"Sie zum Strand gingen? Warum?"*

Gast smiled and explained that one of the men had said that the Americans were lying. They were not in a prison camp in Pennsylvania, they were in northern California.

"California?" asked Carl.

Rolsch explained that the man said that all the grapes was a clue, as was the long train ride. Further, the ship could have landed them anywhere, and faked that it was New York.

"Did you not see the Statue of Liberty?" asked Carl. "How could we fake that?"

"That is what I said," Gast interjected. "But then he said that we were just stupid convicts, that anyone could see that this 'Lake Erie' was no lake."

"But I have a good nose for salt water," said Rolsch, "and I knew this wasn't so. These Nazis have lied so much, they no longer see the truth."

"So you escaped to prove it is a lake?"

"No," said Gast, "I knew they were lying. But if a lake is that big, you've got to see it yourself."

"That's why they call them the Great Lakes," said Carl.

Rolsch nodded. He pressed his finger into his sunburn and watched the white spot he had made on his forearm fill with red.

10.

Pike's MPs found nothing to contradict the story of Gast and Rolsch. There was no indication the two had planned their escape. While harvesting string beans on Sunday afternoon, they argued with someone they refused to name about whether that distant water was truly a lake or the Pacific Ocean. After the guard had counted the prisoners and loaded up the truck, he turned his back to urinate in the field. On impulse Gast and Rolsch dropped to the ground and lay still until the truck pulled away. They then casually walked north, crossing east-west roads until they came out on a high bluff.

Although they had seen glimpses of the lake from their trips out to the farms, actually standing on a promontory thrusting towards Canada was astonishing. With the water rolling in, it was like standing on the bow of an earthen ship sailing north. Both later spoke of that moment in hushed tones. They climbed down to a beach, took off their PW jackets and watched the water lap into sunset orange and red. After tasting for salt, they found supper in a tomato field, and spent the night under the bank of a deep creek. They woke to a man humming "The International" as he set up a hotdog stand on the sandy beach. They quietly discussed walking back to camp, but decided to go swimming. Soon the beach was crowded and they sat among the people celebrating the holiday, watching children play, women tug on their swim caps, and rotund older men in full length bathing suits testing the water with their toes. It reminded Gast of summers he had spent as a boy in Denmark.

As the beach grew more crowded, no one seemed to pay any attention to the foreigners in their midst. Perhaps they thought Gast and Rolsch were soldiers on leave. Neither of the Germans thought about sunburn. It seemed too cool for that, nothing like the Sahara, so they sat in the sand most of the time, hiding the PW on the seats of their pants. They committed no crime other than snatching a cold frankfurter from the stand when the wind ripped the owner's picture of Stalin from the counter and sent the dictator cartwheeling across the sand. They were not caught until after another exquisite sunset, when they tried to ask the hot dog seller the direction of the camp.

Neither Gast nor Rolsch would squeal on the Nazi who had provoked the escape by insisting that Lake Erie was the Pacific, not that such a fib was really a crime. But given that a loose mouth could get you jailed in Germany, maybe they thought the man would be punished. Lieutenant Valdez carefully drew up a list of the men in that work detail, and Carl made notes to watch for them in the questioning. Murnow placed Gast and Rolsch on bread and water for fourteen days of solitary and made a speech to the assembled prisoners which Carl, on his left, translated into German, and Elizabeth, on his right in a stern new suit, translated into Italian. While the major was trying to impress upon the prisoners the pointlessness of escape, the most attention was paid when the wind gently lifted Elizabeth's skirt an inch or two. "Hitler," one of the prisoners remarked in interrogation, "never made the mistake of speaking with a pretty girl by his side."

Other than an alarmed editorial in the *North East Breeze,* several paranoid letters to the editor of the *Erie News,* and an inquiry from the War Department originating in a congressman's office, there was little reaction to "the Big Breakout" as Sergeant O'Hurly called it, and little changed. A new dance was supposed to be sweeping America, according to the publicity: "The Furlough," invented by Fred Astaire for RKO's *The Sky's the Limit.* There was more local excitement over the opening of school and an air raid demonstration at Erie Stadium on Tuesday the seventh. Full-page newspaper ads, with cartoons of planes unloading their explosives, barked, "Learn How to Protect Your Homes and Families If Enemy Bombers Should Appear Over Erie!" The prisoners took this show to be a sign that General Von Rundstedt was just over the horizon. The soldiers took it for a laugh and some went down to the city to heckle, Cpl. Ray Adams getting ejected from the stadium for his trouble. About fifteen thousand people showed up. Somehow the demonstration got out of control and an air warden, Ann Kucharski, was burned. Fortunately it was not a serious wound, but there was rumbling about an investigation of the whole debacle. "War is not a carnival!" an American Legion commander shouted at the city council.

Carl went on with his monotonous questioning of the prisoners and, in the evenings when it wasn't raining, climbing into the ravine to practice his way through the Lucky Strike Hit Parade, usually hearing Oswald's clarinet tootling out songs the German had learned from the radio or from Carl's singing. Often, in interrogations, prisoners would ask if he would sing a song that had special meaning for them. If he didn't know it, they hummed the tune and scribbled down the words. Sometimes he recognized old German or Austrian folksongs his father had sung, but not often. Sometimes Elizabeth sent him slips of paper with requests by the Italians.

A week passed, then another. Valdez and he assembled a chart of probable *Lagergestapo* from different things prisoners had said. They were certain that seven men were case-hardened Nazis and they had a dozen more they considered likely. They also listed the names of about a dozen men they considered anti-Nazis, though they suspected one of merely pretending, perhaps to find out who the traitors were. Valdez often left Carl to interrogate the Germans on his own while he sat in on Elizabeth's questioning of the Italians. Her job was not to question them in depth, but merely to process them, find out who was who, where their hometowns were, etc. Now that the Germans had attacked and overpowered the Italian army, some of the prisoners wanted to join the Allies in liberating their country. When Mussolini was rescued by Hitler and reinstalled as Fascist leader of Italy in mid-September, one of the Italians "accidentally" broke his nose and cheekbone on a frying pan in the kitchen. No one was in a mood to ferret out the truth. "That's the guy's business if he doesn't want to squeal," said Pike.

All this time, the weekend with Natalie floated in the back of Carl's mind. He told himself to call her—the gentlemanly thing to do—but he felt shame and couldn't think what he would say. I love you? This would be followed with another kind of shame. Other men seemed able to love them and leave them. She was no innocent. Why make something romantic out of a transaction? Did he want to be a star singer or not? It was all he had lived for since he stuck his thumb out for New York. The road had taken a strange turn, but why hesitate? It was just a favor for Musso: pump her, then pump her. People had done worse for less reward. As each day passed, however, it seemed less likely she would welcome his call. But then, she was no ordinary woman. If she knew where Georgy Mack was, she had a lot of nerve banging Carl. Everyone in the five boroughs knew about the temper of Sal's little brother. Maybe she was just getting even for the beating. Maybe she wouldn't want to talk to Carl because she'd gotten even. Keep this inertia, Carl told himself, and you'll be a failure all your life: no records, no movies, no nothing.

Murnow issued passes so that most of the men, in rotation, could attend the American Legion's Grape Carnival in North East, and there was a lot of trading work assignments to get the prime hours of the beauty contest. Carl came within a hair of asking Elizabeth to go with him. When he didn't, he passed up the carnival altogether. He sang in the ravine, instead, not only because it took his mind off Natalie. Most people in the camp looked forward to it and he liked pleasing them. That was show biz. He was training for his next break when it came. By the time the Allies swept through Italy to the Alps—maybe before—the Germans would dump Hitler and there'd be peace again. Do you want to be a singer or don't you? That wasn't a choice for him.

After the Grape Carnival, he also found himself thinking about Elizabeth. That black hair, those violet eyes. It wasn't that he lusted after her. It was as if her beauty reminded him or gave him a glimpse of something he had never quite understood. She was innocent, but not stupid. She was pure in some way that everyone else seemed to have lost. Angelic, maybe, was the word. He thought others felt it, too. Whenever she went into the prisoners' compound the guards watched over her as if she were porcelain, and the prisoners strangely did likewise.

Yet Elizabeth could take care of herself. She'd had her share of bad luck, and it had made her tough, but not hard. Carl hoped his mother had been like that. His father had deified her. He had called her a delicate flower, a bonechina doll, a pale swatch of thin gossamer linen. Carl, though, had no way of knowing what she was truly like. Her picture resembled Mary Pickford. But Carl hoped she had been like Elizabeth, strong and pure in a weak and dirty world. If she were, then Carl might have inherited half a chance to triumph over his own vacillations.

On the third Tuesday in September, there was enough chill that Carl's breath showed when he sang the "Star-spangled Banner" that morning. The leaves had faded to red and gold, and enough of them had dropped that prisoners were ordered to rake them. Winter clothes were to be issued to the prisoners later in the week and three huge mountains of coal had been dumped by Reese's trucks near the southwest corner of the camp. Carl was winding down the questioning of a rather jolly prisoner who had sketched various scenes of the camp with pencil.

A political prisoner before the formation of his unit, he said his arrest had been a mistake. One of his male models had left "the wrong kind" of pamphlet in his studio. He laughed and said he had come to the conclusion that the only person who could have told the Gestapo where to look was his wife—the sow! She had been angry over his nude sketches of a Swiss art student. Abruptly, the prisoner turned the doodle he had been doing of Lieutenant Valdez and Carl recognized the style of his shading. The man had done the Hitlers that hung next to many bunks in the barracks. An artist, the man philosophized, was not a prophet. He was a servant with no choice but to please the masters of his society. This, he added, was especially true of so-called avant-garde artists. They were more dependant upon the approval of their masters than anyone. "Hitler's face is very interesting," he said. "Elusive, a challenge. But the human form is endlessly metamorphic. Perhaps it says something about God's humor that Americans hang pictures of Betty Grable and our officers insist only patriotic pictures are hung. Yet we are your prisoners, eh?"

The guard rapped on the door and handed Carl a slip of paper. It said only, "Mr. Reese is waiting to see you under tower."

When he got there, Reese leaned against one of the tower supports, arms crossed, his fedora low over his face. He stuck his hands in his coat pocket and peered up at the guard in the tower.

"Let's walk."

"If you like," said Carl.

"Camp Mad Anthony Wayne," said the man. "Do you know they boiled the flesh off his bones so he could be shipped home for burial?"

"That so?"

"There was some dope what opened a restaurant down in Erie called Mad Anthony's. It lasted a couple of months in twenty-nine, then there was the Crash. Even when it was a soup kitchen nobody went there. *Especially* when it was a soup kitchen!"

"I have work to do."

"You got that right. You been avoiding me, Carl?"

"What do you mean, avoiding you?"

"I've been in and out of this camp a hundred times. I seen you look the other way."

"No. I must not have seen you."

"You couldn't not see me. I'm here almost every day. Now you may not like me, that's one thing, but being rude—Hell, if I don't sell it to you guys, my trucks bring it in: food, lumber, you name it."

"That's Jack Morris' business."

"No, buddy, that's your business. I'm saying it to remind you that it's a mistake not to do business with us."

"I've got nothing to do with supplies."

"Carl, certain people own the ball and bat. It's the only way you get to play. Mr. Musso is concerned for your future."

"Is this a threat?"

Reese laughed. "Not yet."

"Hey, I can't pop down to Cleveland every day," said Carl sharply. "I'm in the Army, you know."

"You haven't even called the lady."

Lady! thought Carl. Some lady! "How would you know? Maybe I've been calling her every night."

"Yeah? So what'd you find out?"

"Nothing."

"You ain't been calling her."

"There's a war on."

"Don't open hostilities with me. I'm just carrying the message, see? Musso's sure the lady is real anxious to see you. She's gone a long time without a man. Cards and flowers ain't gonna scratch that itch, if you catch my drift."

"I haven't got the dough to be sending petunias."

"Roses, actually. Red, for passion. White's not appropriate."

"I haven't sent her anything."

"Yeah, and Mr. Musso is tired of pinch-hitting."

Carl stopped in his tracks. "Oh, that's prime," he said. "That's A Number One."

Reese squinted into the prisoners' compound. "It's nicer than a CCC camp, ain't it?"

"Why doesn't he send her poems? Natalie's a real schoolgirl."

"Those huts'll burn a lotta coal this winter." He turned as crisply as a sentry reaching the end of his line. "So the message is, basically, if you know what's good for you, you'll fall back in those loving arms. You gotta hold up your end of the bargain." He smirked. "Yeah, hold up your end!"

"I can't get a leave all that easy."

"Well, try real hard. Musso's salt of the earth, an honorable man, but don't crank him off."

"Natalie has no reason to tell me anything."

"That's the point, Carl." He leered down at Carl's crotch. "Give her a reason."

Carl wanted to break his weasel nose.

"Oh! And one more thing, Carl, speaking of schoolgirls." He touched Carl's elbow. "Mr. Musso says you got Beth a job, and that's nice, but that's all, see?"

"Elizabeth?"

"You stay away from her."

"I've never touched the girl, mister."

"Just so it's clear. And keep an eye on her."

"I'm not her brother, mister. She's got a father, and he's not Ernie Musso."

"She's a nice girl and he wants her to stay nice."

"I see her coming in or out. We wave." He thought of how the tower guards whistled when she passed and how Dahl often managed to be around when she left at night.

"I'm just telling you." Reese pulled out a pocket watch with a gold chain nearly two feet long. "Got to get back. Two by fours coming in."

Reese pulled the brim of his hat down against the stiff breeze. He was more than just Musso's messenger. He had been trusted with too much information. The image of Natalie opening her legs raced across Carl's mind like a gasoline fire. Okay. Sure. Why not? One hand washes the other. He fumbled for a cigarette and headed back to Prisoners' Compound A.

"Carl! Carl!" Elizabeth was calling him, scurrying around the empty flower bed at the base of the flagpole. She held a coat over her shoulders with crossed arms. Good timing, thought Carl, checking if Reese was still in sight.

"There you are," she said breathlessly. Her hair fluttered in the wind and her cheeks and nose were a delicate pink. "I have a fabulous idea and I know you'll think it's fabulous, too. Even the lieutenant was polite and said I should ask the major."

The words tumbled out so rapidly she seemed half her age. It was funny how much older, even decadent, he felt near her. She was twenty going on thirteen. "So what did the major say?"

"He didn't say anything, yet, because I haven't asked him. I think the lieutenant expects him to turn me down so I decided I'd ask you and maybe you could ask him for me. Of course you've got to say yes, too." She pulled the coat tighter and raised herself on her toes. He thought he would fall into her eyes.

"Uh, yeah, so exactly what is this fabulous idea?"

"I thought we could do a show."

He laughed. "Right here in the barn! We could make our

own scenery and borrow chairs from Mickey Rooney's dad and—"

"What's so funny? There's a lot of prisoners that play instruments. I've already asked a couple. There's Ugo, he plays the ocarina, and Emilio, the violin. There are four or five piano players. There must be a bunch like that with the Germans, too. I've heard the man with the clarinet. He can really swing it sometimes."

"That's Oswald Ülsmann. He likes jazz but the Führer's boys don't approve, so he can't play it much."

"Well, this might be his chance." Her eyebrows came closer together. "You think it's a silly idea, don't you?"

"No," he said. "I was—The idea surprised me, that's all."

"When the weather turned cooler, a lot of the men were getting down, you know? This could lift their spirits, like a sing-along. We could do some of their songs and some of ours. Don't you think it would be nice? They're so lonely."

"You're right."

"They have the movies, but a lot of them don't understand enough English to follow. But music is, well, music. Don't you agree?"

"Absolutely. We just have to figure out how to approach Tex."

"Tex?"

"Major Murnow. He's called Tex, though I don't know why. Someone told me he's really from Arizona. He's a nervous Nellie. Likes things quiet—" so he can drink himself stupid, thought Carl "—so that everything's calm."

"Well, we'll tell him it will make the prisoners calmer, right? They'll feel better about the American way of life."

"That's good," said Carl. "I'll talk to him this afternoon."

"Great!"

He paused looking at the sweet curl of her lips. They seemed too delicate to be out in the wind. A kiss would bruise them.

"Yes?"

"Oh, nothing. That's a nice coat, I was thinking."

"Thank you! I got it on layaway at Sardeson's. It was twenty-two ninety-five. There was another one I was really crazy about in the College Shop of the Boston Store, but I couldn't afford it. I couldn't afford this one really, but I did."

"Well, it's nice," said Carl. Some kind of moment had passed. He wasn't sure what it was. "I'd better get back to work. You know how Valdez is."

"Will you be practicing tonight?"

"Practicing?"

"The prisoners told me how you sing in the ravine."

"The war won't last forever. I've got to keep my instrument tuned."

"Can I come with you, tonight?"

Again he paused. "It's nothing great. It's cold down there. Not enough sun to warm the rocks."

"I've got my new coat. I'll be your audience." She was up on her toes again. A strand of her silky hair blew across her cheek.

"All right. Bring a flashlight. I'll meet you at dusk behind Murnow's office. Better yet, on his porch. It's more open there."

"I'll bring a Thermos."

"Great," said Carl.

"See you later!" she hurried back toward Compound D, where half the Italians had been bunked.

Carl fished a cigarette out of his pocket. She just wanted to hear him sing. You don't mess with a girl like that. She really wasn't as young as she seemed and he ought to face that. He'd argued how mature she was in talking Murnow into hiring her. Good timing. Warned off, then here she comes, as if to test him. Dusk would be about seven. No later. What was that song? *"Gonna meet her at seven . . ."* When he entered the compound he was humming "Got a Date with an Angel." Of course it wasn't a date, he told himself, not really.

On his way to the interrogation hut, he decided to ask Oswald about the concert. Murnow was supposed to provide entertainment to keep the prisoners from getting too restless, so talking him into it wouldn't be too much of a problem, but it was hard to tell whether the German prisoners would be allowed to cooperate. The *Lagergestapo*—whoever they were—might think it was just another attempt to corrupt them, like the Negro cooks, the newspapers, and the radio.

144

They didn't have much choice but to eat the food, but there was a committee which blacked out articles considered anti-German. Some days there wasn't much left that the English speaking prisoners could read. Even a silly human interest article about the president's dog was censored. Carl guessed that "Rosenfeld's" Fala must have been one of the Elder Canines of Zion.

When Carl saw the clarinet on the floor next to one set of bunks, he knew he was in the right place. What's more, since it sat assembled and upright he knew the clarinettist must be nearby, probably in the latrine. For all the tramping these men had done through the fields of local farms, the wooden floor was clean enough for surgery. He idled in the empty barracks for several minutes, scanning the various things tacked neatly to the walls. Someone had fashioned a swastika flag out of white paper, India ink, and some kind of red stain that had faded to the color of dried blood. There was a pencil portrait of Hitler, a Reich's eagle and a few photographs from *Life*. An inch square snapshot of a woman with high mountains behind her had faded almost yellow and Carl thought it had probably been carried hundreds of miles across the African desert and back again, a kind of scapular medal sacred to an enlisted man who would believe evermore that this tiny image had protected him if not from death, from insanity.

He checked his watch and went outside. Across the path running between the rows, a group of men eyed him suspiciously. Carl nodded. One, scraping his fingernails with a twig, turned his back. I love you, too, thought Carl. "Any of you men know where Oswald is? Oswald Ülsmann?"

"Perhaps he is making fertilizer," said one, tossing his head in the direction of the latrines. Excretory humor, the German national hobby. One of them laughed weirdly, but the others found nothing funny in it.

"Tell him that Sergeant Walthers is looking for him."

Several of them nodded. The fingernail cleaner continued digging for gold.

Later that afternoon, Carl was chatting up a gawky kid named Friedrich Kopp, a Danziger who had probably signed up to impress his classmates. If there hadn't been a war, he was the type who would have ended up as gunsel for the Danzig equivalent of Ernie Musso or Sally Mack. The boy's left cheek had a crater-like depression in it, the result of a fragment of hot steel that had ripped into it near Bir Khalda in 1942. Carl sensed it would be easy to provoke this boy into saying more than he was supposed to. Friedrich needed to believe he was a believer and would try to prove it. True believers had no need to prove anything. Carl asked him what he thought of America. Friedrich cautiously said it was big, but then explained that America would be great only if it ended the mongrelization of the Aryan race. Jews had been allowed to gain positions of power and they now controlled the banks, the press, and the film industry.

Never mind the Sicilians, the First Families of Virginia, and the Boston Brahmins. "Maybe the Jews were the only people who saw the potential in motion pictures: Goldwyn, Mayer, Thalberg, Schenck. Maybe they were intelligent."

Friedrich smiled. "The party has never said that Jews weren't clever. They are masters of craftiness. But that doesn't mean they are not inferior. Rats are clever, too, you know."

Carl waited. Friedrich wouldn't stop there.

"Have you ever seen *The Eternal Jew*?" Kopp added.

"I've heard of it."

"This is a very fine film. I cannot forget the rats running along. My girlfriend could not look. The Jews have banned such motion pictures from America to prevent your being warned."

Carl nodded, though he knew it had played here and there. There was a march against it in New Jersey. "And yet, your officers have no objection to watching our movies. This week they asked for *The Wolf Man* again. Do National Socialists like horror pictures? Why again?"

"Because it shows us what happens with the mixing of the races. As in many nations, Aryan Americans have lost their discipline and self-control, and therefore, their self-respect." Friedrich's speaking had the quality of a schoolboy's lesson, as if he were reciting. "Compare the appearance of German prisoners and Italian prisoners. Our officers maintain a high level of discipline and let nothing escape their scrutiny. Infractions are justly punished, whereas the Italian is more careless. Of course, the Italians are tainted by the Mediterranean racial type, especially in the south."

The Italians were friendlier, and no more untidy than the Germans. Carl let that slip by, then leaned forward. "Race mixing? *The Wolf Man?*"

"Yes." Friedrich enjoyed this. There hadn't been many times in his life when he had been smarter than someone else.

"What race mixing?" asked Carl pleasantly.

"The main character, Larry, is Aryan, of a good English family, yes?"

"Yes."

"And he is about to inherit his birthright."

"Yes. Claude Rains is his father."

"Ah, but what happens? He is bitten by a werewolf."

Like you, thought Carl. "I don't understand."

"His blood is made filthy. Gypsy contamination."

"I never thought about that," said Carl. "But this motion picture was made by the Jews, you say."

Friedrich was delighted. "This is what is so wonderful. The truth comes out no matter how you try to hide it, that's what Lieutenant Messer says."

"Messer?" He had been in the complaint contingent that first day Carl had come to Camp Wayne. "Ah, yes. He seems an intelligent man. Do you and he talk often?"

"Not the two of us, but his lectures are very informative."

"Lectures?"

Friedrich averted his gaze for a moment, uncertain whether he had said too much, but then his enthusiasm got the best of him. "Oh, yes! Perhaps you should listen in. We are allowed to have discussions under the Geneva rules, SS-captain Läufer says, so we meet three times a week to discuss political matters. We should know the truth, not what the Jews want us to believe. And you should, too. You are a German."

"My grandfather was. My father emigrated."

"You cannot change your blood. Surely you have felt that you are part of superior stock every time you look in a mirror."

Only when I've been drinking, thought Carl. "So you have regular propaganda meetings? That's very interesting."

"I will ask if you can come."

"I never knew that about *The Wolf Man*. More coffee? A cigarette?"

Valdez would be apoplectic about the propaganda sessions. Perhaps he wouldn't tell him. Friedrich might be a good source of information if he didn't feel betrayed. What information? Jesus, he was beginning to think like Valdez. What difference did it make what these guys did in the evening? The war was over for them. They could talk all they wanted. Talk is cheap.

He couldn't get the interpretation of *The Wolf Man* out of his head. It reminded him of some of the things that his father's friend, Professor Venable, had said. Hamlet was in love with his mother and King Lear with his daughter. Satan was the hero of *Paradise Lost*. Professors were nuts, thought Carl, but they weren't the only nuts in the bowl.

While the next prisoner rattled on about his father's bakery in Stuttgart and lovingly described each step in making rye bread, strudel pastry, and several varieties of tortes, Carl thought of *The Wolf Man*. What happened to Lon Chaney, Jr.'s Larry Talbot was that an ordinary, ineffectual man discovered he had a killer inside him. Millions of men around the world had discovered that facts about themselves in the last few years and went on discovering it and, fortunately, most of them didn't like it any more than Larry Talbot. In boot camp, Carl had bayoneted burlap sacks with the rest of them, but it wasn't the same as killing a man, no matter how much you tried to imagine it. It wasn't the same as waking up with the mark of the werewolf on your palm and your bloody footprint on the window sill.

Just before supper, he returned to C-4. No Oswald. The clarinet was still there and a German said he thought he had gone to play soccer. That was a bit strange, but the day had been a strange one altogether. Not dramatic, not surreal, just off kilter. There was the talk with Reese, Elizabeth's bubbly suggestion they put on a show, and then the odd information that this harmless thriller was being used as propaganda. How had the Nazis explained *We're Not Dressing* with Bing

Crosby and Burns and Allen? They had liked *Dead End* and *Lady Scarface*, too. We ought to give them a shot at *Gone With the Wind* and *Stagecoach*. That way we could find where the "eternal Jew" was lurking in those. Maybe it's Walter Brennan. Butterfly McQueen destroyed the South and Huntz Hall the purity of our semen. Who could have guessed?

11.

He was pacing in front of Murnow's office when Elizabeth arrived in a long plaid skirt, her new coat, and a seaman's stocking cap that made her look even more like a little girl. She swung a large Thermos bottle in one hand and a paper sack in the other.

"Am I late?" she called out.

"No," he said. "I was early."

"You should have started without me."

"Gave me a chance to digest," he said, putting out his cigarette between his fingers. Army habits, he thought. Don't leave butts lying around. "It's chilly. It'll be dark in a few minutes. It'll be even colder down there."

"It might hurt your voice," she said with disappointment.

The perfect excuse to send her home. "No," he said. "I'll be fine."

"I bundled up."

"I see."

"I brought a flashlight, too."

"Good. We'll have two," he said, picking up the battery lantern on the office porch. "You'll have to watch your step."

At the edge of the ravine, she laughed, her eyes picking up the last sparkle of twilight. "Maybe we should parachute down!"

"It *is* steep," he said.

"Well, let's go! I should be home before midnight."

"Sure," said Carl. A girl like her shouldn't go into dark places with a stranger. That she might be that innocent, that trusting, made him feel uncomfortable, as if she didn't belong with a man like him.

He led her down the path's sharp switchbacks, edging sideways, the lantern in front of him, his left arm extended behind to hold her elbow. The descent was slow and as they dropped further down, the darkness irised in on all but the circle of lantern light. Trees rustled, creaking in their motion and the stream's rustling grew into the roar of a radio losing a station to static.

She stumbled into his back and dropped her paper sack. She groped as it dropped, bumping into him. He managed to keep his balance, however, turned and caught her by both shoulders. Neither fell but he could smell the wool of her stocking cap close to his face. "Oh, no," she said. "The cookies!"

"Cookies?" He swept the lantern beam over the brush.

"They'll be broken."

"If they didn't go all the way into the water."

"I had to scrimp to save that much sugar," she said. "Oh, darn!"

"Maybe we'll see them further down. Wait." When he had turned to speak to her, he had spotted the bag behind her. It hadn't rolled down, but had stopped behind her, slightly uphill.

"Oh, good! We can at least have the crumbs. They're snickerdoodle."

"Huh?"

"Snickerdoodle. Like cinnamon. Want to try one?"

"Later. Army chow, you know."

They continued downward to the slab of stone that hung a foot over the rushing water, his stage. Again he thought of Orpheus, descended into the Underworld, standing on the shores of the Styx. Eat the tiniest pomegranate seed and you are stuck in Hades forever. Did that apply to snickerdoodle? He flung light upon the shale bluff on the opposite bank. "I think that reflects my voice. That's why they can hear me in the camp."

"Wow," she said, "it's deeper than I thought. Why do you come all the way down here? Is it pretty in daylight?"

"It's nice. At first I thought I could practice in private. I didn't know the sound would carry."

"Your voice is strong."

"Thanks." He pointed to a bump in the slab. "That's a

good place to settle. You don't want to walk around in the dark. The stream's three or four feet deep in places."

He switched off the lantern and heard the Thermos scrape the stone as she sat. He could barely distinguish the shapes and shadows around him. There was a sprinkling of light on the uppermost layers of shale from someone driving in the camp. He made out Beth's shadowy outline and then her face. Like the moon, it collected scraps of light, and though he could only see the dark line of her eyebrow, it glowed. Artemis, he thought, goddess of the moon. If you see her body, hounds tear you to shreds.

"I don't know why I still come down here," he said. "Pretty stupid, huh?"

"It's nice for the raccoons."

"They don't run nightclubs."

"This *is* their nightclub," she chuckled.

He was embarrassed to start. Why? Because he wanted to be good? Or because he didn't want to be too sexy and he normally, consciously, worked on that. Her violet eyes were trying to see him. She was waiting. "Okay, then. I warm up first. They're opera exercises, believe it or not, but they open up the throat."

"Just do what you normally do. Pretend like I'm not here."

He knew he couldn't do that, but he took a deep breath and began. He turned his back and faced the shale bluff. Closing his eyes he clicked his fingers in double time. "Ah-One, ah-two, ah-three, ah-four . . ." He pictured the tables at Swing Land, the smiling customers lighting their cigarettes in the coconut lanterns, and threw himself into a rapid fire version of "Chattanooga Choo-choo." He ripped along as quickly as Buzz Bixby had tempoed "Barney Google," the song that hurried folks to get another drink and slip away to the toilet. Usually, Carl mixed a couple of double time songs among the normal ballads. They were good for enunciation and quickly snatching a note and dropping it. When he heard Elizabeth's hands clapping, however, he immediately slipped into another breakneck rendition, "I've Got Rhythm." When that ended he ripped through "Take the A Train," and "Boogie-Woogie Bugle Boy."

He paused. Despite the damp chill, sweat trickled off the

tip of his nose and into black space. Elizabeth applauded. "That was great!" she said. "I can't believe how fast you do that. Why are you doing them so fast?"

He exhaled. "It's—I don't know—practice. Is it getting too cold down here for you?"

"No," she said, "it's comfy. You must really be from Carolina."

"Virginia, really. The Carolina Crooner was just supposed to go with my stage name. C. C. the C. C.: you see?"

Her sweet giggle chittered into the trees.

"Seriously, would you like to go back? It's got to be cold sitting on that rock."

"I'm fine. If you're cold, have some coffee. Stop worrying about me. I'm ruining your practice."

"No, no. I'm perspiring like I ran a mile." Perspiring? He was getting delicate.

"Then sing me something slow. It's the dreamy songs you're best at."

"You think so?"

"Um-hmm."

"Well, okay." He knew that if it weren't so dark she would have seen him blush. Why? He searched his mind and then saw the tree canopy part just long enough to expose a blurry moon. He sang "Racing With the Moon." It took enough concentration that he relaxed and almost forgot she was there. She asked for "I Don't Want to Set the World on Fire" and then "You'll Never Know." He followed with "Embraceable You."

She sighed as she applauded. "Gosh, you're good. Have some coffee."

He heard the scrape of the Thermos. He moved forward, his hands searching the darkness, brushed her arm, then felt the heat radiating from the warm cup.

"You want a cookie? I don't think they broke very much."

He didn't really, but she had gone to the trouble. She probably blew her sugar ration for the next month. "In a minute," he said, inhaling the steam from the cup. "What kind of coffee is this?"

"Irish," she said. "But that's brandy, not whisky."

He sipped it. There was enough fuel in it to launch a B-

17. "You been nipping at this? A girl like you shouldn't be drinking this stuff."

"What do you mean 'a girl like me'? You sound like Mr. Musso. I get tired of it." He did not hear any drunkenness in her voice and the tone revealed more exasperation than anger.

"I'm sorry," he said. "It's just you're a nice girl."

"Yeah, yeah."

"It's true."

"Yeah, yeah."

He sipped the coffee and considered sitting next to her. "How long have you known Mr. Musso?"

"All my life. He and Pop used to run together. They were close. Mr. Musso's always been a help. We owe him way too much."

"You mean money?"

"Oh, no. I meant he's been such a friend."

"But, well, he's kind of a gangster, isn't he?"

"He's no Al Capone, not if he's so good to Pop."

"I don't blame you. How did your pop get shot?"

"I don't believe what they say about that."

"Your pop?"

"What people say. If he was that kind of man, busting up stores for protection money, he'd be in jail."

Carl wished the world were that simple. "What does your pop say?"

"He was at the wrong place at the wrong time." Maybe the market in Oran, thought Carl. "A Nosy Parker, aren't you?"

"I'm sorry. I guess the job carries over." He bent towards her. "Really, I am sorry. What's your favorite song? Something from the movies? I probably know it."

He saw a glint as she sipped directly from the Thermos. She shoved the cork back in, then he heard it scrape again.

"Here's the cup," he said.

She felt along his arm, then dipped as she placed the cup behind her. He felt her hands on his biceps just before they slid to his back and pulled him close. Her ear was flat against his chest as if she were listening to his heartbeat. The wool cap tickled his nose.

"Say . . ." he said.

She squeezed tighter, pinning his arms at the elbows. He placed both hands on her waist intending to shove her back, but he hesitated, on the odd thought she might be crying. He shouldn't have talked about her pop. He wanted to know what Musso could have to do with an angel like her, that's all. Now he had hurt her.

She lifted her face to his without letting go. "Aren't you going to kiss me?" she asked.

"Kiss you?"

"Yes."

He smelled the mix of coffee and brandy on her breath. Why shouldn't he? She was asking. If it wasn't him, it might be someone else. He remembered Natalie riding him: Aphrodite goddess of sex. But this was Artemis and his thoughts fluttered, pigeons dispersed by a running child. He swallowed hard. "Aw, gee, Elizabeth, you don't want to get mixed up with a guy like me. I'll be on the road two hundred days a year, I—"

"Two hundred days?" she whispered. "I just want you to kiss me."

She did not wait for an answer, lifting her lips as the moon brightened. He saw her pale face, her closed eyes, the dark Italian eyebrows, and he was entranced. His mouth dropped upon her lips like the fluff of a dandelion upon smooth water and dissolved into them. He spiralled into her warmth, sharing her breath. The water rushed by, the stone on which they stood uprooted itself and tumbled towards the center of the earth in a delicious vertigo. He had the same sensation as when the surgeon in Casablanca placed the ether mask over his face. There was no time, no space, and all that had been solid became cobwebs.

Clasped together, they reeled. He lost his footing and staggered back. Their lips separated, but she continued to cling to him, pressing his arms against his side, further disturbing his balance. Suddenly, his foot caught on an irregular edge and he fell spinning as she squeaked out a cry of surprise. He came down hard, his legs in a pool of water, his hip slapping the mud on the shore. His face plunged into slimy leaves and his shoulder protested with a hot stab.

"Jesus!" he said.

"Carl!"

He tested his shoulder. It hadn't popped out. "I'm okay," he assured her, panting. "I didn't fall far." He moved his legs. They were okay. The water splashed as he shimmied further into the leaves, touching something wet and soft. Moss, maybe?

"You're wet!"

"Just my shoes. Are you okay?"

"I scraped my knee. I'll get a flashlight."

Carl took a deep breath. "I'll tell you what, lady. You're a helluva kisser."

She appeared over the edge of the stone only eighteen inches above his muddy knees. It had felt like a twenty-foot fall.

"A helluva kisser!" he shouted and she screwed up her face, looking almost oriental as the light raked upward across her smile. He shifted onto one hand to rise when something bright caught his eye in the brush. He glanced back to tell her to point the beam there, but the laughter in his face sagged into a gape. She saw it, too, and bit her lower lip as Carl crawled back.

The bluish hand, half the size of Carl's, lay among the leaves. Carl almost laughed, thinking he had mistaken an old piece of a mannikin for a real hand. When he touched it, however, it was soft. He jerked, and looked at Elizabeth who was frozen on her hands and knees in pale, astonished fear.

He tentatively brushed away the leaves. A forearm. An upper arm. The short sleeve and shoulder of a Boy Scout uniform. Carl paused, took a deep breath and continued. A mop of red hair shone nearly gold in the bright beam of the flashlight. "Jesus!" said Carl. Elizabeth turned away.

Carl saw no sign of anything that could have killed the boy. He might have been asleep, except for his staring eyes. And he hadn't been dead long. There was no smell and the insects hadn't gotten interested in him yet, except for a long-legged fly that hovered about the bright tip of the boy's ear.

Carl brushed the insect away and looked up the side of the ravine. "Maybe he fell. He doesn't look like he suffered."

Elizabeth was panting.

"Are you okay?"

She nodded.

Carl tried to think what to do. He felt the boy's neck. Cold and utterly still. He tried the wrist. Nothing. The body had not yet begun to stiffen. He had died not long before they had climbed down.

"We've got to get help," gasped Elizabeth.

He dropped to his knees. "We can't leave him here."

He rolled the boy over and picked him up. "Light the path," he said, hefting the body onto the stone. He climbed up and again lifted the boy.

"Poor fellow," Elizabeth said, choking up.

"Do you know him?"

She shook her head. Strands of her black hair stuck in the tears on her cheeks.

"Let's go."

Carl determined he would not put the boy on the ground again. Night insects hovered and jabbed at Carl's eyes, his shoulder burned from the leaden weight, and each step up the dirt path broke more sweat to trickle coldly down his spine. His image of himself as Orpheus returned. He was climbing out of the Underworld and bringing back a body. The soul, however, was lost among so many others, another forlorn shade seized by the covetous gods of darkness, who toyed with humans with the indifferent cruelty of a bored cat.

12.

By roll call, only a few things were clear. One was that the dead boy's name was Timmy Firenzi. He left a scout meeting at just before four to walk three blocks to the music store, where he had a twice-weekly lesson with his uncle, Louis Bassett. A taciturn boy, he resisted his piano lessons and often dawdled on his way. The alleys he normally short-cut through were temporary repositories for all sorts of fascinating junk hauled out the back doors of the shops: a distracting treasure for any boy. The war had added to the fascination. In June there had been a picture of Timmy in the *North East Breeze* with a basket of odd fragments of copper and brass he had scavenged for the war effort. Sheriff Bowers showed the clipping to everyone gathered in Murnow's office as he summarized the little that was known.

At four-fifteen, Bassett left the store to look for him. Before four-thirty he was back, and finding no Timmy, left again to look for him in his car. He searched for half an hour, then had supper in his room over the store. He wasn't going to fink on the boy so he listened to Fred Waring's orchestra on the radio and was tuning in Harry James on WABC when his sister showed up. It was only then they knew something was wrong. They interrupted Sheriff Bowers' dinner, but he smiled and said, "Timmy's like any other boy. They have to lose track of time once in a while to grow up normal." He told them not to worry, he guessed, about the time Carl fell on the body.

The sheriff put on his spectacles and hunched up over the corner of Murnow's desk to write in his notebook. Murnow drummed his fingers on his blotter, no doubt desperate to seek consolation with his King William IV.

"You didn't hear anybody? See anybody? Nothing like that?"

"No," said Carl.

Beth shook her head. "The townspeople know they're not supposed to come up here."

"And you were down there to *sing?*"

"Yes."

The sheriff peered over his spectacles.

"I sang before the war. I'm getting my voice back in shape."

"He's very good," said Beth.

"And are you a singer, too?"

"She came to listen," Carl said.

"Uh-huh."

"It's the truth," said Carl.

"And you say you fell in the leaves?"

"Yes. What do you think, we killed the boy?"

Bowers shook his head. "Lord, no. Looks like natural causes. The only thing curious is why here, so far from where he was last seen. He left the Boy Scouts and evaporated. It's two and a half miles by car, maybe two as the crow flies. He most likely came up the creek from the fishing pool down below. He could have walked it, if he didn't dawdle to pitch rocks or anything. He could easily run it in the time, but it's curious. He'd need a reason. He set out for here, I figure. Got sick, maybe, and tried to climb up. You say he was buried in the leaves? He might have disappeared for months, years."

"Well, he was covered," said Carl. "I can't say how the leaves got there. Maybe if he fell he kind of slid under."

"Could be. Usually when someone falls they get a knock on the head or something, but he's not hurt at all. He could be asleep on that slab at the undertaker's."

Beth choked off a whimper.

"I'm sorry, miss," said the sheriff. "It's a sad old world sometimes. The boy's in a better place." He closed his notebook and folded his spectacles delicately. "I suppose we might have learned something from the position of the body, but it's small potatoes. There's no evidence of foul play."

"Well, then," said Murnow, "you can see there's no wrongdoing on our part."

"I shouldn't have moved the body," said Carl.

"Well, that's got nothing to do with the camp," said Murnow. His forehead was smooth. An incident had been avoided. He could celebrate with a drink.

The sheriff shook hands with the major, then Carl. "Good day, ma'am." He nodded to Beth.

"Can I speak to you a minute?" asked Carl. "Outside?"

The sheriff paused on the porch and offered Carl a peppermint. Carl noticed the busses hadn't left for the farms yet. They should have been gone two hours earlier.

"Listen, the girl, Elizabeth, she really was just listening to me sing. I go into that ravine almost every night. Can you keep her name out of things?"

The sheriff rolled his mint around in his mouth. "Look, I don't care if you found the boy when you fell into the leaves or while you were rolling around in them. I see a lot of things they don't talk about in Sunday school."

"That's what I mean, Sheriff Bowers. People will get the wrong idea."

"You married or something?"

"That isn't it," insisted Carl. "She's a good girl. You want to tar her?"

"I don't gossip, son. Did you ever think you're making too much out of this? If you keep pressing, you'll just make people sure you've got something to hide."

"I'm thinking of the girl," said Carl. He watched the sheriff roll the mint between his tongue and upper lip with the facility of a magician rolling a silver dollar over his knuckles. "Look, son, maybe you're pestering me because you had plans and they got interrupted and now you're a little ashamed—"

"But—"

"Don't be ashamed for what didn't happen. Thoughts don't hurt anybody." Carl opened his mouth but the sheriff raised his hand. "Or maybe it's like you say." He laid his meaty hand on Carl's shoulder. "There's a boy dead, that's what matters."

"It's lack of sleep," Carl apologized.

The sheriff nodded. "I'll be on my way, then."

"Sheriff?" shouted Sergeant Pike. He was crossing the open area between the flag and Murnow's cottage with long strides. "I was afraid you'd left. I'm the provost sergeant."

"I remember."

"We've got another one, I'm afraid."

Bowers thrust out his jaw. "A body?"

"A rabbit."

Bowers seemed to be trying to digest it.

"Another escaped prisoner."

"Oh hell," said Bowers. "It never rains but it pours."

"Maybe we should check the beach," said Carl.

"Very funny," said Pike.

Bowers removed his hat. "Okay, then," he said wearily, "let's go back in and you can give me the description."

"His name is Oswald Ülsmann," said Pike. "He's a private."

"Ülsmann?" asked Carl. "I bought him a clarinet. That guy?"

"Must be," said Pike. "He left it behind."

"Why would he escape?"

"He's a prisoner," barked Pike.

The Germans made no effort to conceal it this time, which made Carl wonder if this meant the escape had been authorized by the officers. When the morning count was made, Oswald was not in his barracks. When Sergeant Pike picked up the old clarinet, he noticed its bell left a delicate circle in the dust on the floor. It hadn't been moved for a day or two, though Ülsmann had been listed as present the previous morning, so unless that was a mistake—which was entirely possible—he had skipped out sometime after seven the previous morning.

Murnow's head was now in full wrinkle again. He promptly dispatched Beth to the Italian compound to see if anyone there had anything to say. Many of them hated Germans, if the number of thumbs they were biting at the Wehrmacht was any indication. She gave Carl a tiny smile, then left the cabin.

"Major," said Carl, "you ought to let Elizabeth get some sleep."

"The trail's still hot," he shouted. "She can sleep later. Those I-ties would tell anything to a girl like her. So you knew this guy?"

"I gave him a clarinet."

"So he was the tootler," said the major. "Well, get over there and grill his buddies."

"I'd say your hoosegow is getting a little sieve-like," said Bowers.

"Too much coddling," said Pike. "We shouldn't be giving them clarinets and such."

"It keeps them more content," said Carl.

Murnow stood. "What do you mean, sieve-like? There've been two attempts."

"In how many weeks?" said the sheriff.

"We'll get this bird, too," said Murnow. "There's nothing to get alarmed about. Where can he go?"

"And who might he hurt?" said the sheriff quietly. "We'll get him if we don't yap all day. Let me use your phone."

"It's the same as last time. He's got no money and probably no English. Ain't that right, Walthers?"

Carl didn't think it was time to bring up the dollars floating among the prisoners. "He's got some English, but his accent is very heavy. He's a jazz fan, also, if that's any help."

"You never can tell," said Bowers.

"We need a decision on whether to send out the workers to the vineyards," interrupted Pike.

"This is just like any other day," said Murnow. "Everything's under control."

Sheriff Bowers eyed Murnow. "Just any other day," he said. "The boy and the escape better be a coincidence, major."

"Why wouldn't it be?" said Murnow. "Don't try to make an incident out of this."

"Incidents I can handle, but coincidences make a lawman jumpy," said Bowers.

The major took out his frustrations on Carl. "Didn't I tell you to get moving?"

"Yes, sir."

As Carl passed the three busses outside the compound gates, the Germans looked down on him with self-satisfied smirks. Authorized, he thought again. Oswald had escaped and maybe they'd pooled him some money to do so. Maybe they smirked because they knew Beth had been with him. The camp grapevine was faster than the telegraph. Any suggestion of hanky-panky would particularly entertain guys who'd been locked away from women for months. Or maybe it was that Carl and Oswald had clicked some. Their interest in music had transcended birth and borders, and now Oswald had run. Did the prisoners think this particularly ironic?

Several shirtless prisoners were washing up after exercise. They dipped into basins lined up on two benches and mopped their pale chests with their shirts.

"A bit chilly, eh, men?" he called out.

"Warmer than Youth Camp in 1937," said one. His companion grinned, sharing the memory.

"Any of you men know Oswald Ülsmann?"

Most shook their heads. A heavy man with pock-marked cheeks said, "Who?"

Carl recognized him as Captain Albert Dorn. "What do you think? That we are going to punish you for knowing the man?"

The prisoners studiously continued washing, drying, or taking inventory of their feet, their fingernails, their buttons.

"He bunked in C-4. He played the clarinet. He was a happy little guy and I don't want something nasty to happen to him."

Again, no reaction.

"People out there have lost sons and husbands. They might get carried away. With us, Oswald will be safe. With them, God knows."

One of the men, Carl noticed, began washing himself for a second time. "I didn't think he was the type to escape. Did something disturb him? Did he get a letter through the Red Cross last week? Any change in the way he was acting?"

"Why would he change?" said Dorn, resting on the stoop. "A man is the same, whatever happens."

Carl moved closer to him. "People don't change?"

"Not in the blood. Swine are swine. Aryans are Aryans."

"And Nazis are Nazis. Are people born Nazis? I thought you would know." Carl's voice was loudly sarcastic. He wanted to be certain they all heard.

"Blood is destiny."

"I have German blood and I will never be a Nazi."

"Then you do not know your true nature. What you do proves who you are. You do not have to wear a swastika to be a Nazi. You will notice that I am not a member of the SS, yet I am a proud member of the party. If you stopped listening to this nigger music that comes out of every American radio, perhaps you could see your true nature."

"It must be powerful music. Is this your explanation for losing the war?"

Dorn's thick nostrils flared. "The war is not over. Perhaps you are not Aryan at all. Perhaps your mother was not altogether truthful with your father."

Carl stepped toward the seated man with a clenched fist. Dorn raised his arms to cover his face. The other prisoners closed a circle around them. "Inbreeding," Carl said through gritted teeth. "It leads to idiocy. Brains the size of a dried pea, aspirin-sized balls, and a pencil dick. That's what science tells us. Perhaps you've got *too much* Aryan in you."

Dorn had pure hatred in his bloodshot eyes, but he, like Carl, was not stupid enough to lash out.

Carl leaned into his face. "If you ever mention my mother again, you'll be looking up your own asshole. My guess is you bastards ordered Oswald to escape, and if we get any proof of it, I'm coming after you, first."

Dorn glared as Carl straightened. "Biology is very interesting," Carl said, "but off the subject. Who lives in C-4?"

A thin blond hesitantly raised his hand.

"Good," said Carl. "Put on your shirt and come with me."

"Excuse me," said another prisoner.

"Yes? Are you in C-4, too?"

"No." He hefted his jacket and glanced hesitantly at the others. "Is it true a boy was found dead?"

Carl nodded. "A heart attack or something. Only eight."

"This is very sad." The man lowered his eyes. For a moment Carl thought the man was going to weep. Carl felt a knot in his own throat. With all the killing in the world, it was nice to know that the death of a child still meant a little.

The thin blond, Pvt. Joachim Blenner, knew nothing about Oswald, had never spoken to him, had hardly noticed the man despite sleeping less than six feet from him for the past month. He had no speculations about how one would go about escaping from Camp Wayne. He had never considered escaping. Or so he said. The timidity he had shown in raising his hand to indicate he was a barracks mate of Oswald's had hidden itself behind a rampart of stone. Perhaps the walk to the interrogation hut had hardened his resolve. Blenner sat rigid in the chair, answered everything in monosyllables, and never took his eyes off the opposite wall. "Why aren't you in the SS?" Carl concluded.

"No special reason," said Blenner.

"Get out of here," said Carl.

He checked the list of occupants of C-4. Of the twenty, ten would be on agricultural work. Three would be at work in the kitchens. Two worked in the infirmary. One was lying low in some field or barn, probably wondering why he had bothered to escape. That left three, besides Blenner, who would be somewhere in the camp. Carl walked to C-4 to see if anyone was home. A soccer match was scheduled for after lunch, but the three wouldn't have anywhere to go before then.

The sky had begun blue that day, but had turned silvery, then gray. It was getting colder, too. He crossed his arms as he slipped between the barracks opposite. He kept his eyes low, trying to avoid the mud puddles, and was emerging into the next row when he heard a noise behind him. He listened. The wind whistled. He took another step, then changed his mind and quickly danced between the puddles. In a fairly dry spot, he dropped to one knee and squinted under the barracks. Beyond a support pylon, a prisoner was crawling out from the opposite side.

"Hey, you!" he yelled. "*Halt!*"

He sprinted around the hut and dropped down. The crawler reversed direction.

"Get your ass out of there!" said Carl. "*Halt! Kommen Sie hier! Schnell!*"

The prisoner stopped shimmying along the ground and looked back.

"Ude Wieschensohn," said Carl, "get out here, now!"

Wide-eyed, his face streaked with dirt, he slowly clawed his way towards Carl.

"I meant no harm," Wieschensohn pleaded in German. "I meant no harm."

Carl grabbed his forearm and dragged him into the open.

His jacket was caked with mud. "What's with you?" asked Carl.

"Please. They will punish me."

"Who?"

"You've got to take me away."

"From whom, Ude?"

"The *Lagergestapo*. They can see through you. They know what you're thinking."

"What are you doing under the huts?"

"So they can't see me! So they can't see what I am thinking!"

Carl shook him. "Control yourself. Are they after you now?"

"They are always after you. They want you to help them and then when you help them you are one of them."

"Pull yourself together. You're not making sense. Come on. I'll take you out of here. Come on." He touched Wieschensohn on the shoulder and the man cringed.

"I don't want to die," he whimpered. "My father was a Socialist, not me. I don't care for jazz. I am not a Jew."

"The U. S. Army will protect you. Come with me."

Ude blinked, uncertain whether to trust him or not. Carl tugged and Wieschensohn shuffled one step forward, then two. They moved awkwardly towards C-4, the German's wide eyes sweeping like search lights scanning for bombers. When they reached Oswald's barracks, Carl turned Ude and sat him on the steps. "You wait here," he said.

"No!"

"I'll be right inside. Don't move. You're safe."

Ude watched Carl like a terrified child as he slowly moved past and entered the barracks. Three men lounged on the bunks. One smoked a cigarette barely an inch long. Another sat on a top bunk cleaning his boots. The third scanned the *Erie Times*. About half of each page had been blacked out by the Läufer's censors. The sports page, possibly the page of least interest to the prisoners, had somehow survived uncensored.

"You read English?" he asked.

"I am learning," the prisoner answered. "Languages have never been difficult for me."

"English has its peculiarities."

The man nodded and almost smiled.

"You're SS-Corporal Mann."

He nodded.

"It surprises me that Oswald made a run."

"Who?"

"Ülsmann." Carl pointed at the empty bunk. "You know who I'm talking about."

"Oh, him. I barely knew him."

"I suppose you never heard him play."

"I'm not much for music."

"Tone-deaf, nearly blind. The war hasn't been kind to you."

"Who has it been kind to?"

Carl turned to the man on the top bunk. "You're Private Strang. Didn't we talk a few weeks ago?"

"I'm Otto Sturm."

"Sturm." Carl casually picked up the boot Sturm had been cleaning. "You shouldn't do that on your bed."

"That's what I told him," said the smoker. "If an officer sees him . . ."

"I don't see any officers. Are you going to tell on me?" Sturm raised his boot to fling it.

"I suppose you two didn't know Oswald, either," said Carl.

Sturm shook his head. The smoker drew the fire almost to his lips, exhaled, and said, "You know him on a first name basis. Why don't you tell us why he escaped? You can read his mind better than we."

"Maybe he went to the beach."

Sturm and Mann grinned. "No one will try that again!" said Mann.

"Not after what Läufer—"

"After what, Otto?" demanded Carl.

"He gave them such a tongue-lashing," said Mann quickly.

"Worse than live machine gun fire," said the smoker.

"Terrible," agreed Sturm. "A man could get bruises from such a tongue-lashing."

The prisoners grinned.

Carl crossed to Oswald's bunk. He checked under it, then opened the small locker. There were scraps of paper with musical notes on them. One seemed to be a bar of "Taking a Chance on Love." There was one of the crescent-shaped pieces of cloth, the "wing" that musicians wore on their shoulders. An "OÜ" had been written in ink on its underside near one of the hooks. There were some other papers, the clarinet bag, and an extra reed. A stubby pencil. A safety pin.

"Provost Sergeant Pike already searched his possessions," said Mann.

Carl reached into the pockets of Oswald's uniform jersey. "Who asked you?" Empty.

Carl picked up the clarinet. "He won't be needing this when he gets back." He rotated the instrument, separated the three sections, and inspected the damage to the gilt brand name. A small "OU" had been scratched into the gold flourish below. He went back into the locker for the bag. He dropped the three sections in with the extra reed. "*Auf Wiedersehen,* boys. We'll chat again sometime."

Outside, the stoop was empty. Curiously, there were also no prisoners in view, not even the oyster-eyed watchers who always leaned against nearby huts. "Ude!" he called out. "Wieschensohn!" He climbed down and looked under the building. They had all gone to the soccer field, maybe. "Ude! You lunatic! Where are you!" He peered under two more huts. Wet dirt clung to his knees and he brushed it off angrily. "I'm leaving!" he shouted in German. "Come with me or not, I'm leaving!" His pants knees looked like they might stain. "Cockeyed bastard," he muttered. As he passed further along, he could see that most of the prisoners had drifted toward the mess. That was why the rest of the compound had seemed so deserted.

He thought about trying to locate Ude at the soccer match, then decided he wouldn't be interested in men kicking around a ball. Ude needed help. They had two nurses on full-time duty and a doctor who visited from town, but the kind of doctor Ude needed wouldn't be prescribing aspirin. Carl tucked the clarinet under his arm and resigned himself to heading for Murnow's office. He warned the guards to keep an eye out for Ude Wieschensohn, "a little guy with dirt on his jacket and crazy eyes." Ude was wacky enough to get himself shot. That might provoke a nasty "incident." Surely Murnow could understand that.

He watched Sergeant Lang in the distance giving hell to

his inmate staff as he approached Murnow's office. He was about to hit the first step when an acid smell froze him. Flies swarmed at a dollop on the step and a wide patty on the ground beside it. Jesus, thought Carl, Murnow's now vomiting out his front door. That would get Tex a combat command, all right. The Charge of the Purge Brigade. O'Hurlyopened the screen door with the bottle of King William IV in his hand.

"Get in here," said O'Hurly.

"You're into Tex's scotch."

"We're all into it. So will you."

Under the sergeant's arm Carl saw Murnow at his desk, fingers spread over his head. His skin glistened and his hands flushed red. Carl was drawn forward as if by a magnet. O'Hurly pointed to the chair and handed him the bottle. "You're gonna need it."

Murnow lifted his head and wiped his cheeks with both pudgy hands. He sniffed. "Where's Valdez?"

"On the search," said Carl.

"Oh. Yeah. When he finds out—" He sagged and wiped his face. His mustache was greasy with sweat.

"What the hell's going on? Churchill surrendered?" Carl gave a weak smile.

"Shut up, sergeant," said Murnow. "The—Oh, you tell him."

"Sheriff Bowers was calling around about—well, you know. Anyhow, his wife told him to call the undertaker and he did and—" O'Hurly's hands searched for a meaningful gesture.

"The boy was murdered," said Murnow.

"Huh?"

"Timmy was murdered!" shouted O'Hurly.

Carl sat silent, knowing a heavier shoe was about to drop.

13.

Murnow massaged his temples. O'Hurly counted floor-boards.

"Murdered," asked Carl. "What are you talking about? The sheriff said there wasn't a mark on him."

"Jesus, Mary, and Joe," said O'Hurly. "The girl! Somebody's got to tell her before she hears it from someone else."

"She doesn't need to know the details," said Murnow.

"I guess not, but it's still—"

Carl stood in exasperation. "I don't understand. Will somebody—"

"Sit down," barked Murnow.

O'Hurly squeezed Carl's forearm, stared into his eyes and explained in a whisper. "The sheriff listened, turned white as a sheet, then ran outside to toss his guts. The sheriff! Of course, he knew the boy." O'Hurly glanced away, still holding Carl's forearm, gathering his strength. When he was ready, he clamped harder and continued. "The doctor saw dried blood. He thought maybe it came from, who knows, like stomach cancer or bad constipation, something like that. He still didn't think there was anything unusual."

"Blood? I didn't see any blood."

"His underpants. His guts were full of it."

"What are you saying, O'Hurly?"

The sergeant's eyes widened. "There was jism in there, too."

At first O'Hurly's words were like an unfamiliar idiom: Plattdeutsch, Prussian. Jism? The meaning landed at the bottom of his belly with a sickening thud. A hot cannonball sizzling in the mud. Carl took a deep swallow of the whisky.

O'Hurly released his arm. "Jesus, Mary, and Joe!"

"They're sending for a pathologist from Pittsburgh," said Murnow, "but the doctor's sure. The doctor thinks he found a couple of hairs. Inside."

"A man—" Nausea rose. Carl took another belt.

"Yes," said O'Hurly.

"God help us," said Murnow. Carl handed him the bottle.

O'Hurly's monotone continued. "The tissues weren't, like, strong enough. It ruptured him."

Carl closed his eyes with the horror of it.

O'Hurly spun away from the desk, then brought his fist hard against the top of a chair. "I'll kill the son of a bitch!"

"We'll get him," sighed Murnow. "Where can he run to? Everybody will be after him."

"I'll feed him his nuts!" shouted O'Hurly.

"Oswald Ülsmann did it?" asked Carl.

"Who else?" said Murnow.

He started to say Oswald never seemed like a pervert to him, but what did a pervert seem like? "How do we know?"

"Isn't it obvious?" said Murnow. "This damned place is cursed. If we don't get him quick, this will be a helluva incident." He gulped the scotch.

"You could be jumping to conclusions," said Carl.

"Oh, yeah?" said O'Hurly angrily. "In the kid's pocket, there was one of those things the kraut musicians wear." O'Hurly prodded his own shoulder.

"The musician's wings? The crescent shaped thing with stripes?"

"Yes. With little hooks to attach it."

Carl remembered he had seen one among Oswald's possessions in C-4, but Oswald had worn one on each shoulder the first time Carl had met him.

"Well, he can't get away," said Murnow. "It ain't like he can walk into a store and buy himself a suit."

Was it time to tell Murnow that the prisoners had definitely gotten a few dollars? He sat silent, stunned by all that had battered him, too numb to think. Had he befriended a child killer? An image from the movie *M* flickered across his mind: Peter Lorre scurrying through the city streets. Carl thought of the alabaster serenity of the boy when he had laid him at Murnow's door. Did Timmy even understand what was happening to him as the rape began? These were the worst to see: the dead who in their serenity mocked the terror of their dying.

Murnow rose from his chair, unable to contain himself. "I want your ass back in the compound. Find out what the fuck those Heinies know. Nobody escapes without somebody knowing it. And don't be delicate. I want to jam that fucking clarinet up his ass!" Murnow snatched up his blotter with both hands and threw it against the office wall. The flypaper swung. The picture of Roosevelt popped off its nail and crashed to the floor. Murnow kicked at it and glass skittered against the file cabinet.

"Yes, sir," said Carl.

"We're gonna get that son of a bitch."

"We will," said O'Hurly.

"You're damn right," said Murnow. He sagged back into his chair.

Carl was half-way to the interrogation hut when he thought of Elizabeth. A lead was as likely from the the Italians as the Germans, and surely both groups of prisoners would help now. He changed direction and entered the Italian compound. The pine used on her interrogation hut had been new. Beads of sap had formed on the knotholes. One large glob appeared to be a golden tear oozing from a dark eye.

Two guards leaned back in chairs flanking the door. They were eating bean soup out of mugs. "What's up, sarge?" said one.

"Nothing good," said Carl. Beth was inside wiping the bottom of her bowl with a hunk of bread. "Hi," he said quietly.

"Carl. Did you have lunch?"

"I've kind of lost my appetite."

Her violet eyes saw right through him, though they didn't see enough. They kept probing.

"I've come to tell you something."

She peered at him for another few seconds. "This is the kiss-off, right? Geez, you've hardly given me a chance."

"That isn't it."

"You could have given me a decent chance. I'm too tired to know what to say, Carl."

"What I've got to say will keep you awake."

She smiled. "You give yourself a lot of credit. Are you afraid of me? Why do I frighten you?"

"Beth, you don't frighten me. I just think you've got a crush on me and that isn't a good idea."

"I'm not a child. When are people going to start treating me like a woman?"

"Beth . . ."

"Pop, Mr. Musso—Did Mr. Musso warn you off?" She blew upward across her forehead, fluttering her bangs. "He's got no right, you know."

"Please," said Carl. "I've got to tell you something." He came closer, rotated the chair opposite her desk, and straddled the seat. "The boy we found, he didn't die naturally."

"I don't understand."

"Somebody had—what can I say?—trifled with him."

"Trifled?"

"He was molested."

"Oh, God! And then he was killed?"

"Yes. Well, the way he was molested killed him. It was too rough."

Her face was expressionless.

"Are you okay?"

"It's terrible." The shock hadn't diminished.

Carl shrugged. "They think the escaped guy did it."

"He didn't seem the type."

"You knew Oswald?"

"No, but I saw him playing. He looked happy. He played a tarantella for my guys. That's when I got the idea for the show."

Carl shook his head. "You can't tell, can you? You never know what a person is like." Her lip trembled, but she did not lose her composure. He fidgeted, then stood. "Okay. Now you know. Get what you can out of your guys and I'll go after mine. It won't hurt to let them know why we're so interested in catching Oswald. Maybe that will help."

She bit her lower lip. "Bye."

"Bye."

"Poor kid," she said as he touched the doorknob.

"Yeah."

The guards had been eavesdropping. That's what they

were supposed to do to make sure nothing happened to Beth. They tried to buttonhole Carl for more details, but he merely repeated what he had said inside and headed back to the German compounds. He yanked Sturm and Mann right out of the soccer match, infuriating SS-captain Läufer, but he offered no explanation except a glare. He dressed Mann up one side and down the other, while Sturm waited outside chilled by the sweat on him. Carl didn't think Mann would have anything to say and he was right, but he thought maybe the sound of it might intimidate Sturm. If it sank in what their barracks-mate had done, there couldn't be any question of not cooperating. Mann would hold back until he checked for orders, however, and Sturm, well, he'd polish his boots while sitting on his bunk.

Mann eventually said a German soldier couldn't do such a thing and he wouldn't be part of a lie. Ülsmann had escaped, pure and simple. "Perhaps you ought to look among your own soldiers."

Carl grabbed Mann by the front of his sweaty shirt and reared back a fist. Mann merely tilted back his head and locked his eyes on Carl's.

"Out," snarled Carl. "Before I hurt you." He had the satisfaction of seeing that the SS-corporal believed him.

He then dragged in Sturm, who had nothing significant to say, either. He said he thought Ülsmann masturbated, but who wouldn't in a place like this? Did that make him a pervert? No, Ülsmann wasn't married as far as he knew. No, he had never talked about a girl back home. No, he'd never shown any interest in men. Yes, there were some dubious fellows in the camp, and there were rumors about one particular 961st Afrika Rifles corporal's interest in the Arab boys in Bizerte, but Ülsmann did not associate with him, and anyway the rumors were probably just jokes. No one would dare be that way in the German army, or he wouldn't last very long. No, he wouldn't say what the corporal's name was. That wouldn't be fair. He hadn't escaped, had he?

Carl threatened him with solitary, but got nothing more out of him other than the name of the man who had been smoking in the lower bunk: Fritz Schauman. He sent for him, and Schauman proved tougher than either of the other two.

He laughed at the idea that Ülsmann had attacked a boy. "You had better look to your own men. We are caged night and day. Why don't you ask those gorillas who cook for you? They're not particular." Carl shoved him back and the chair crashed to the floor. Schauman sprang up as if he were going to fight, but quickly regained his composure. "You must think I am a fool," he said.

Carl tried the men he could locate from C-3, C-2, and all the nearby barracks. After two of them, the answers began to get remarkably similar. The Americans were just trying to blame it on the prisoners. A German wouldn't do such a thing. All such degenerates had been cleansed from the Third Reich. Why aren't you looking among the Italians? Why aren't you looking among the Negroes? It was curious how many insisted that Oswald had escaped and was too clever to be caught, yet they also expressed a distaste for him while insisting he couldn't have done that to a boy. When Carl asked how Oswald had escaped, one sergeant said, "Maybe he tunneled," blinked nervously and added, "Maybe he flew." It was enough to make Carl think tunneling had something to do with it, or that maybe a tunnel was planned. All that remained obvious, however, was that the grapevine had operated at lightning speed. There was little surprise on their faces when he revealed how the boy had died. Prisoners knew exactly what to say and how much.

By dinner, Carl's ears were ringing and his head pounding. He knew he ought to grab prisoners off the bus before the grapevine got to them, but he simply couldn't. When he asked whether Oswald had been found, O'Hurly told him no. When he asked whether Beth had found out anything, he was told she had conked out about three and was still sleeping in the major's quarters. One of the Italians had told her that once when a group of them were cleaning a barn, the German clarinettist had done an imitation of Rita Hayworth on her wedding night with Orson Welles. O'Hurly thought maybe it showed something about Oswald, as if soldiers didn't frequently burlesque women.

Carl ate slowly, remembering a pianist he had been paired with in a Manhattan hotel when the man's regular partner had been sick. The pianist had been married when his wife found out he was more than just a partner to his singer. He had lost custody of his children soon thereafter and moved to New York. He told Carl not to be nervous about working with him. He wouldn't do anything Carl wasn't interested in. That was what, he said, the judge never understood, because he loved his partner didn't mean he was any threat to his children. "A man who would go after a child is worse than queer," said the pianist. He wouldn't necessarily be homosexual or appear to be so. Even if Oswald had wanted to dress like Rita Hayworth, he wouldn't necessarily be interested in an eight-year-old. It could have been Oswald. It could have been Murnow. It could have been Lang or Dahl or Sheriff Bowers himself or some other man in town, couldn't it? Anyone could have done it, except Elizabeth. But Carl really couldn't imagine that you wouldn't notice something about a person who could do something like this and, in the end, he couldn't believe that Oswald Ülsmann was any more guilty of it than the sheriff.

He was finishing a drumstick when another thought also occurred to him. He had taken Oswald's clarinet, but all the other possessions remained in the barracks. The idea had been that leaving them there would point up to the prisoners that he would soon be caught. The situation now was quite different. Carl downed his coffee and hurried back to C-4.

Prisoners lounged around the steps of the barracks smoking and talking. One of them joked about a librarian he had known whose bust was enormous. He imitated her walk and the others laughed. Another leaned against a corner, his hat pulled down over his eyes, seemingly lost in his thoughts, but when Carl approached he began whistling "Lilli Marlene" as a signal. Carl paused and sang a bar of the song, his breath condensing in front of him. The whistler turned his back without acknowledging him, though there was a flash of teeth from a man with a towel over his shoulder. As he walked on, there was a particularly large group of men chatting near C-7 with the forced animation of bad actors. Carl had interrupted one of their political meetings, he thought. The Americans didn't usually go into the compounds after dinner.

In C-4, SS-corporal Mann was in his bunk reading a cheap

paperback. It was one of the special wartime editions distributed by the Red Cross. The tiny margins and small print were designed to save paper. Another man snored in the bunk at the end of the building.

"Still learning English?" asked Carl.

"American poems," said Mann. "They are difficult. I cannot find many words in my dictionary."

Carl was in no mood for it. "Maybe you need a better dictionary."

"This Riley is worst. James Whitcomb Riley."

"You change your mind? Want to tell me about Ülsmann?"

Mann sat up. "He would not touch a boy."

"How do you know?"

"That is not possible."

"How do you know?"

"You had better look among your own."

Carl was tired of hearing it. "So help us find him. As long as he is free, we'll assume he did it."

"Assume all you like." Mann stretched back on his bunk. "It is the act of an inferior race."

"Of a subhuman," said Carl.

"That is what I am saying," said Mann.

Carl fought an urge to drag Mann out of his bunk and kick his teeth in. "Has anyone touched Ülsmann's things?"

"Sergeant Pike. You."

"Anyone else?"

"No." He pretended to be absorbed in his book.

Carl opened the clarinettist's locker. He looked more closely this time. The scraps of paper with musical notes. "All or Nothing at All." "Taking a Chance on Love." Something he couldn't decipher. The opening of "White Cliffs of Dover." A small square of wrapping paper had "SOLI MIO—Italien," with notes below. He placed them on the bed along with the pencil. There was a well-worn shaving brush and a square of cloth that had been used for polishing. A comb with several missing teeth. A newspaper clipping from September 8. Orson Welles had married Rita Hayworth. In the margin was written *Ach, wie mein Herz zerbrochen wird!* "Oh, how my heart is shattered!" Carl crossed to Mann and flicked his hand against his foot. "Do you recognize this?"

"He joked he loved Rita Hayworth."

"That's not what I mean. Is that writing from a poem?"

Mann shrugged.

"Heine or somebody?"

"I don't know much poetry."

"So why are you reading American poetry?"

"To understand you better."

"Know your enemy?"

Mann shrugged again. "Maybe to understand why you refuse to see we Aryans have a common cause."

"Keep trying," said Carl. "Maybe you'll learn something."

In the locker he found another picture of Rita Hayworth from *Life* and then a snapshot of a woman in a bathing suit. She had thick legs and a round German face divided into light and dark by the shadow of the photographer. The swimming pool behind her was as packed as a sardine can. On the back it said "Greta, 1938."

"Was Ülsmann married?" Carl called out.

Mann shrugged.

You son of a bitch, thought Carl.

He put the remaining possessions on the bed and then lifted out Oswald's Wehrmacht uniform. He searched the pockets as he had before, but felt a stiffness in the big lower left pocket. There was nothing in the pocket itself. The lining had been split and hastily basted together with blue thread. He picked it open with his fingernails and found three one-dollar bills pinned inside. So, Oswald had gotten money, like many others in the prisoner compound, but why leave it when escaping? Maybe the opportunity had come suddenly and there wasn't time to return for the few dollars, the clarinet, the picture of Greta he had carried for many years. With Rolsch and Gast's run, the guard had been urinating and they rolled under the truck. It made sense as to why only Oswald skipped and not others. In a planned escape, you send out many men, so that one or two might get away in the confusion. Maybe his impression that the officers had approved the escape was wrong.

Something nagged him. The single, take it or leave it opportunity might explain a number of things. Maybe Oswald stumbled into poor Timmy as he used the ravine to make his getaway. Maybe the boy was scared and he enticed him with the musician's wing. But if you were in a hurry why would you stop to molest the boy? Why would you not make certain he was dead in the usual way: bash him on the head, strangle him? Oh, God, Carl told himself, it wasn't rational to try to think like someone who could attack a boy! Of course a molester, penned up for months, would pause for the very thing freedom meant to him. Here, little boy, I'll give you something pretty, I'll give you—

The wing! Where was the other musician's wing? Carl quickly ran his fingers through the meager possessions and reached into the dark back of the locker. Nothing.

"Who's been in this locker?" he demanded.

Mann looked at him coolly. "You. Sergeant Pike."

"Who was in here after me?"

"Today?"

"Of course I mean today."

"No one." Mann raised his book, blocking his eyes. Carl marched to him and pushed the book aside.

"Someone stole the musician's wing."

Mann smiled impudently.

"You know what I mean. From his locker. Where is it?"

Mann sat up. "I don't know anything about it."

The man who had been snoring nearby blinked at Carl as if just recalling that he was a prisoner of war.

"What about you?" Carl asked.

The man sat up. "Me?"

Carl spun angrily and picked up the corners of Ülsmann's top blanket, to form a sack. He twisted it and slung it over his shoulder like Santa Claus' bag of toys. What else had been taken out of the locker? he asked himself. One of the bastards watched as he headed for the compound gates. Probably more than one. Maybe someone stole the wing under the direct orders of the *Lagergestapo*. Or maybe it was a petty thief who missed the money pinned inside the jacket. Whatever happened, the clarinettist's things should have been secured immediately. Whatever answers they might have provided, were gone forever.

14.

At the dark NCO barracks, he made out the shadow of O'Hurly sleeping. He stuffed the makeshift sack of Ülsmann's things under his bunk and was loosening his boots when he saw a vague white shape on his pillow. He struck a match and read the note. "Mr. Reese says they're real unhappy at the container club and you should call pronto." It took him a while to decipher "container" into Catania. Okay, Musso, okay, he thought, let me get a few zees. What's wrong? I've been putting my hands too much on Elizabeth or not enough on Natalie? He was momentarily aroused remembering his weekend with her but sleep was even more pleasurable a thought.

It seemed that reveille blared almost as soon as he closed his eyes. His feet hit the cold floor and his puffy eyelids blinked at the dawn. "When the war's over, I'm taking a year off to sleep," he said to O'Hurly as he staggered to the sink.

"Reserve me a bed," said the sergeant.

The door clattered open and Sergeant Pike, dead on his feet, his helmet and coat wet, lurched in.

"Got him?" asked O'Hurly, his mouth filled with toothpowder.

"Fuck no," said the provost sergeant, sagging to his bed. "The guy's long gone. Long gone."

O'Hurly spat. "Shit. I'll be running up and down the damn grapes all day. Is it raining?"

"Cats and dogs."

"Jesus, Mary, and Joe! Maybe I should eat soap and throw up at breakfast. It worked in high school."

"If you got any brains," mumbled Pike, "do it."

O'Hurly bumped Carl's elbow, jarring his razor and nearly making Carl cut himself. "You find out anything?"

"From the prisoners?" said Carl. "Oh, sure!"

"Well, requisition some brass knucks. Get the bastards singing."

"The dogs won't hunt in the rain," yawned Pike.

"I don't think they know anything," said Carl. "I think he ran on the spur of the moment."

"I want two minutes with that creep," O'Hurly said grimly. "One will do."

"You know, it's funny—," said Carl. He was going to repeat he had the feeling Oswald couldn't do something like that. And the German reaction still troubled him, too. They wanted everyone to know he had escaped, as if they'd planned it, yet they didn't want to admit he hurt the boy. If he'd escaped on the spur of the moment, then he hadn't gotten permission. That had irritated the officers with Rolsch and Gast. It was clear both had been pummeled, probably at a midnight session, a couple of days after their release from solitary. The Germans knew something about Oswald they weren't saying. Maybe instead of wasting his time with the barracks mates, Carl should have a little heart to heart with Läufer or Dorn.

"What?"

"Nothing." He was thinking about the musician's wings but Pike interrupted him with a snore. He wiped the soap off his face. O'Hurly was already lacing his boots. "Listen," whispered Carl, squatting. "You read a lot of files, you say."

"Yeah."

"I was wondering."

"Hey, it ain't like snooping."

Carl glanced back at the sleeping Pike, still in helmet and muddy trousers. "I don't know how to ask this. We got a lot of men, you know?"

"Spit it out."

"Any chance any of them have something on their records?"

"You mean like your bitching and getting yourself in Dutch?"

"Is there anybody with anything like a sex crime?"

O'Hurly dropped his laces. "Are you shitting me?"

"It's a possibility."

"You're nuts."

Carl shrugged. "Okay, I'm nuts. Forget it."

O'Hurly grabbed his arm. "Our guys couldn't do anything like that." He considered it, then shook his head. "No way. Hey, we haven't got a boat load of Boy Scouts—" The "Boy Scouts" made Carl flinch. "You know what I mean. We got one guy who broke into a safe, another who drove for a robbery. The judge gave Dahl a choice between breaking rocks or enlisting, but so what? I don't care if it's a kraut or even some crazy farmer who ignored the off-limits signs. Just as long as it ain't one of us." O'Hurly reached for his laces. "Jesus, Mary, and Joe, don't even think about it! Jeeeezzz . . . ."

"Sorry," said Carl.

Later, he waited until Murnow had gone to mess and O'Hurly, along with Valdez and thirty other men, had headed out into the wet countryside. He slipped behind O'Hurly's desk and placed a call to the Catania, not really expecting anyone to answer that early. If he got lucky he could just leave a message. That might hold the big man for a while. The operator called back in only a few seconds. "Hold on," she said.

"Hullo?"

"Catania Social Club?"

"Yeah."

"Is Mr. Musso in?"

"Who's asking?"

"Carl Walthers. Mr. Reese said he wanted to talk to me."

"Reese, you say? Hold on."

Carl eased O'Hurly's desk drawer open as he waited. There were no personnel files inside this time. Just *Life, Liberty,* and the pursuit of happiness: O'Hurly's girlie picture.

"Is this you?"

"Mr. Musso?"

"Tell me where you are, Carl. He'll call back."

"I can't wait long."

"Quarter hour at most. Don't go nowhere."

"Fifteen minutes. The number is 38–723."

"Got it."

Carl put his feet up on the desk and listened to the steady drizzle of the rain. He idly pulled at the other drawers.

Locked. He put his hands behind his head and knew that he had dreamed last night. It irritated him he couldn't remember what it was. The file cabinet caught his eye. He put his feet down and plucked a paperclip out of the drawer. He straightened it, peeked out the front door, then began wiggling it inside the lock. He had no idea how anyone picked a lock but he unsuccessfully felt, twisted, and scratched inside the hole until the phone startled him. He leaped across the room.

"Sergeant Carl Walthers?" asked the operator.

"Yes!"

"Hold on, please."

"Carl?" said a gravelly voice.

"Mr. Musso."

"Where you been, Carl?"

"I've been stuck. There have been some goings on. One of the prisoners may have murdered a boy."

"One of the guards?"

"No. A real boy. Only eight."

"A grown man killed a kid?"

"That's what I'm saying."

Musso made a sound like spitting. "What a world! Makes me sick." He wheezed in a deep breath. "It don't help my situation, though. I only got a few days. You promised me something. I collect on promises."

"I know, Mr. Musso—"

"And don't go telling me there's a war on. There might be another war if we don't run Georgy to ground."

"I understand, but what can I do?"

"I might say the same thing when you want to perform at the clubs of our friends."

Carl had a sinking feeling. "It's the Army. What can I do?"

"I dunno, but one hand ain't washing the other so far. You had a little fun is all. Look, I ain't saying nothing much on the phone, but the War Department owes our guys. We done our bit greasing the skids for the *fascisti* in Sicily and so on. Charley Luciano might get a medal. What I'm saying is that we got influence. Maybe it's time that wound got you discharged."

Carl thought how he hardly noticed the tight movement

of his shoulder any more. "That would be great. I wouldn't be in, if I hadn't complained outside of the chain of command."

"You gotta learn it don't do ya no good to cross your higher ups. And that includes me."

"I'm not crossing you, I swear. I just can't get a leave."

"I'll have Reese talk with him."

"Why Reese?"

"Leave it to me. But something's gotta happen. The water's boiling and the fetuccine's dry."

"I apologize totally, Mr. Musso. I know I should've—"

"I mean, what would you say if you got a woman buying white clothes this time of year? She ain't getting ready for winter. She's buying linen, Carl, good linen. Low back things. Wide hats. Sounds like sun, don't it?"

"Yeah."

"And a steamer trunk. And one of them cases what keeps lipsticks and perfumes. I'd say somebody's planning a trip."

"Yes, sir."

"So what you could do would be greatly appreciated."

"I understand."

"And anything you don't do will be greatly resented, you catch my drift?"

"Absolutely. I'll work on it right away."

"That would please me. You could go a long way. Deliver the goods, Carl."

"Yes, sir."

The line clicked and Carl sat, eyes closed, listening to the hum. If Musso got angry enough, flat-nosed men with chests like oil drums would redesign your skeleton. When it came time for an example, an example would be found. Sometimes the example is left to limp around with a large scar on his face. Other times he stretches across the front page or is very conspicuous in his absence. This whole business wasn't going away. What had he been imagining stalling would accomplish? He was a pubic hair away from getting his voice box smashed with a Louisville Slugger.

He rotated the chair. Major Murnow stood before him, fists on his hips. "What the hell do you think you're doing?"

Carl placed the receiver in its cradle.

"You're calling some damned chippy while our asses are on the line?"

Carl couldn't think of anything, so he stood and saluted.

"Maybe I need to grind you back to private. You're supposed to be finding out what those krauts know."

"Yes, sir." The shit keeps flowing, thought Carl. It was tickling his earlobes. "It wasn't personal," he lied. "It deals with some business in Cleveland."

"Business?" Murnow's bald pate crinkled. "What kind of business could you have?"

Carl was flustered for a moment, then he blurted out, "I need a pass, sir. It's very important."

"A pass? You *are* out of your fucking mind. Nobody's going anywhere until your pal is hanging from the tower out there."

"He wasn't my pal, sir. I just—"

"Shut up, sergeant. Back to your post. Now! And you are absolutely forbidden to use this telephone, am I understood? Let me put it so you can understand: *'This is the army, Mr. Jones! Don't try to use the telephones.'* You know *that* song?"

"Yes, sir."

"Then sing it when you get the urge to neglect your duty. We've got an incident here—"

Carl gritted his teeth to prevent himself from feeding the telephone to Tex, the major drunk, then suddenly, like a distant light, a scam blinked. "It was an informant, major."

"Huh?"

"Corporal Ülsmann hasn't been located yet, has he?"

"No," stammered Murnow, "Sheriff Bowers says there are reports of two stolen chickens in Fredonia and a strange man in a corn field outside Meadville, but—"

"Well, I know people in Cleveland."

"So?"

"A clarinettist showed up over there last night. He had a heavy accent and claimed to be Polish."

"So how do we know he wasn't?"

"He acted suspiciously."

Murnow squinted. "He could've gotten to Cleveland, I suppose."

"Easily," said Carl, trying to figure out whether he was

painting himself into a corner. "That's why I wanted the leave."

"No," said Murnow, "we'll call Bowers and the authorities in Cleveland will run down this rumor."

"It's no rumor, major. I was in the music business. I know who to talk to. I also know Ülsmann. The guy described to me was Ülsmann all right. And won't it look better if we get him ourselves?" He asked the question slowly to let it sink in.

Murnow's brow wrinkled.

It now occurred to Carl that he might be misdirecting the hunt for a child-killer. "You shouldn't call off the hunt around here, of course, until I nail him."

"Who told you this stuff?"

"I can't say."

"You can't say? You *will* say. What have they got to hide?"

Carl hesitated, then said, "Ah, there's a lot of shady characters in the music business. They don't want to be in the public eye."

"Gangsters?"

"Sort of."

"Sort of?"

"Yes, sir."

"Why should you believe somebody like that? Why should I believe you?"

Carl put on his sternest face. It would be pathetic if he couldn't convince somebody like Murnow. "Just because a guy's into some shady stuff doesn't mean he wants a pervert running around. You ever see the movie *M*? The underworld goes after a child molester. This is just like that."

"What movie?"

"*M*. It's a German movie."

"Why would I watch a German movie?" The major smoothed his mustache and licked his lips. "Okay, but you'd better nail the son of a bitch. I'll send somebody with you."

"I'd do better alone."

"Hell, no. You get in a wrestling match and the creep gets away."

"It really isn't necessary."

"This is an order. Maybe I should go with you."

The paint was drying around the corner. How could he

186

take Murnow? "If it's a wild-goose chase, it'd look like you'd deserted your post. How about Dahl? He's a scrapper."

"I get it. You want the credit. Fine. Morris will issue you sidearms. You get that son of a bitch back and I'll buy you a bottle and recommend you for master sergeant. That's a promise. Dead or alive. I just want the incident closed."

"Thank you, sir," said Carl.

"Don't thank me. Get him."

Carl hurried to find Dahl before the major changed his mind and tried to live up to "Tex" by heading out for Deadwood. Dahl was pulling guard duty on the southeast tower. In twenty minutes, they were in a car headed for the North East station, but when they got there the train wasn't due to leave until after lunch. They walked to the drug store for a hot dog, but settled for egg sandwiches because Mable had run out of meat. She was in a foul mood and asked why, after cornering all the meat for themselves and their prisoners, "youse Army guys have to come eat my eggs, too?"

Everyone in town was edgy: the stationmaster, the paperboy, even the priest who sat at the lunch counter with them. Though the papers had been discreet, the word on Timmy Firenzi's death had gotten around. The town, which had once seemed so safe and quiet, had now been tainted. The serpent was in the garden and someone had to be blamed for releasing it. It was unpleasant to wait inside, but it was still drizzling. They nursed their coffee and shared the paper.

Dahl's St. Louis Browns were doing better in the American League, but the Yankees had the pennant again. There were reports from Italy that the Germans were committing atrocities against Italian civilians and the troops that had resisted the reinstatement of Mussolini. A large contingent of the Italian fleet had joined the Allies. Carl hoped Murnow had enough sense to keep his Italians as separate from the Germans as possible or they'd soon be limping through another "incident." He skipped Westbrook Pegler's pontificating and scanned *Little Annie Rooney, Katzenjammer Kids, L'il Abner,* and *The Nebbs.* None seemed funny.

"I'll meet you at the station," Dahl said, rising.

"Where are you going?"

"I can do a little business."

"Sit down," said Carl.

"I'll be right—"

"Sit," Carl insisted. The priest was chatting with Mable about Lou Spognamiglia's high school days. Carl leaned close to Dahl and whispered. "No bullshit, Ansel. What are you into? I go to town with you twice and you're off doing something."

"It ain't important, sarge."

"Ansel . . ."

Dahl looked irritated. "Maybe we could work together. Souvenirs. The prisoners have patches and medals and stuff. A lot of folks will pay a few bucks to get them. You can get top dollar for an Iron Cross."

"So you get them from the prisoners and sell them?"

"Sure. What's the harm? It's not big money. A lot of guys get the things and send them home. It makes up a little for not being in the action. But I know a guy in town who'll buy almost anything I sell. He collects. Maybe he retails, too."

"Who is he?"

"Aw, now, that's a trade secret."

"Look, Dahl," said Carl, "if the major finds out that this is how the prisoners have been getting greenbacks, you're going to be in for it."

Dahl spread his hands and leaned back. He assumed a punk's expression of incredulous innocence, a pose that would only convince a mother. "Hey, plenty of guys slip them a buck now and then. What are they going to do with it? Buy a ticket home?"

"Suppose this guy we're chasing used your money to get himself down the road?"

"Shit, sarge, he got maybe a buck and a quarter from me. He had a few good things, but nothing great."

"Keep your voice down," said Carl. "Did you steal the musician's wing out of his locker?"

"Wings?"

Carl drew a crescent on the countertop with his finger. "Shaped like this. Braid. Stripes like this."

"Oh, those. I sold about a half dozen of those. There were two different colors. Most were red. One was white with alu-

minum braid. Red's artillery. White's infantry. We caught a
lot of artillery fife and drummers in our bunch. These wing
things don't get much, though. Anything with a swastika
goes bigger."

"Did you take the white one out of his locker?"

"No."

"I'm not trying to get you into trouble."

"I said no, didn't I?"

"Let me see what you've got there."

"Sarge . . ."

"Let me see."

Dahl handed him a small canvas sack, the kind store-
keepers took to the bank for change. Inside were various
patches. Eagles resting on swastikas. Death's-head collar
patches. An Afrika Korps cuff-title in green with aluminum
threads. A German Red Cross armband from the town of
Darmstadt. SS lightning patches. Enamel pins with swastikas.
Four Italian pins with various symbols. There were no musician's wings.

"A good haul," Carl remarked.

"We used to get more. Their officers don't want them to
sell their stuff, but they can always 'lose' them, or claim an
American stole them."

"What about the Italians?"

"They almost threw the Fascist stuff at us—most of them,
anyway. There's one guy who still parades around with his
jaw stuck out doing Jack Oakey in *The Great Dictator*."

Carl smiled. The memory of Chaplin juggling the globe
always made him smile. "I can't believe you can sell this stuff."
He stuffed it back in the bag.

"You get what you can. Kids really go for it."

Carl's eyes met Dahl's and he knew they were both thinking
about the musician's wing in Timmy's pocket. Dahl lifted his
eyebrow to say, "Sorry I mentioned it."

"Okay," said Carl, "meet me at the station. I have a little
business of my own."

"Elizabeth's still at the camp," said Dahl.

"Mind your own business," said Carl. "But if a musician's
wing with a white background turns up, I want to know."

The sheriff's office was only two blocks away. Bowers had

his feet propped up on the desk eating a cucumber, skin and all, as if it were an apple. "Help you?"

"I'm Carl Walthers, from the camp."

"I remember."

"I was wondering if you'd mind if I took a look at the musician's wing."

"The what?"

"The thing they found in Timmy's pocket. A Wehrmacht musician would wear it on his shoulder."

"Oh, that. What have you got in mind?"

"Nothing important. Different kinds of colors mean different things."

"Yeah?" The sheriff put his feet down. "Is it going to tell us where the maniac ran to?" Bowers' eyes had dark circles under them. "You ought've been here to tell the mother and the uncle what happened. Emma fell apart. Bassett and me had to carry her to my car." He shook his head, standing and crossing to a safe in the corner. "You turn your back, now."

Carl could hear the clicking of the dial. He watched a woman outside pushing a baby carriage. "Buy Bonds!" had been stitched into its sun shade.

"Shoot!" said Bowers. "Messed up." The dial ratcheted in a full circle again. "It never used to matter what was in here. Only had real evidence twice before. Mostly lost and found junk." Bowers emptied a wooden box on his desk: the socks, stained with humus, the dull white underpants with a small pink stain overlapping a darker brown one, the Boy Scout shirt, the neckerchief. Every item looked tiny, as if the presence of death had shrunk them. "They want to bury him in his uniform. I've got to ask the State Police if that's okay. They might take this stuff this afternoon."

"It's good I thought of this, now," said Carl. He hesitated to touch the items.

Bowers pinched the shirt between his fingers and revealed the musician's wing under it. "There it is."

Carl gingerly picked it up. Seven parallel gray braids were stitched over a white background. Another gray braid ran across them on the curved bottom. It looked like what Ülsmann had been wearing when Carl had first met him and was a match for the one in his locker. But that didn't mean it was his. Carl turned it over.

"The maniac went up in a puff of smoke," said Bowers. "Every report we've gotten is bunk. After the State Police leave, I'm meeting some people in Westfield and visit the Amish. They could be sheltering him out of misguided charity. They speak German and maybe don't know who he is. It's a long shot, but, hell, I have to do something. Even my coffee tastes bad."

Carl examined the backing material. Between two of the hooks that attached the wing to a uniform he found what he did not expect to find: in black ink, the tiny initials "OU." Ülsmann had marked the clarinet and his other wing. If it hadn't been on this one, Carl would have been reasonably certain the jolly clarinettist hadn't killed the boy. Carl dropped the wing on the desk.

"So?" asked Bowers.

"It's no damned help," said Carl, heading for the door. "Good luck with the Amish."

The sheriff hmmphed and dropped back into his chair. He stared out his front window as if the rain would never go away. "Nothing's no damned help," he said.

15.

In Cleveland, Carl told Dahl he would make his inquiries alone, so as not to draw attention. He then gave Dahl five bucks and told him to entertain himself, maybe catch a meaningless (to everyone but Ansel) end-of-season game between the Browns and the Indians. After all, the Browns had won sixty-six games, had caught Boston and were two rungs out of the cellar. Knowing no other way to get in touch with him, Carl would leave a message at the desk of the Stouffer's hotel. "Check tomorrow morning. If anything turns up we'll grab him around lunch."

Dahl's eyes lit up at the surprise leave Carl was giving him, but protested slightly. Even he wanted to get his hands on the child killer. One way or the other, Oswald didn't stand a chance. As Carl rocked gently in the street car headed for Natalie's, Carl recognized it wasn't simply the fact that he had profoundly misread the clarinettist that bothered him. There were enough cuckoos in the music business, that's for sure. He was also bothered that it was so obvious that Ülsmann had murdered the boy. With the world so full of shadings of gray, it was hard to comprehend pure black when you saw it. His inclination when he heard someone describing Hitler's evil was to try to think of something that might be said in the Führer's favor. This trait was probably the affliction of growing up in a philosophy professor's house. You always imagined more than two sides to every coin, even though coins aren't made that way.

And yet, it also disturbed him that he wanted to believe Ülsmann might be innocent. Why? Because Oswald had a picture of a woman in his locker? Did this picture of Greta mean he had normal sexual desires? The Düsseldorf Ripper of the 1930s seemed, by all accounts, to be a harmless, boring, happily married man. Carl reached for the bell cord. What the hell was the difference? He wasn't responsible for Ülsmann any more than he was responsible for his father's suicide. He never would have guessed his posturing, blowhard father would have killed himself. Why should he have known what crime Ülsmann was capable of? He stepped onto the sidewalk at Superior and Ninth. To hell with it. It was time to take care of Number One.

The door bell rang several seconds before Precious answered. "Well, the Carolina Crooner," she said. "'Bout time you was back."

"You remember me."

"Your flowers come twice a week. So nice to see flowers that don't go with a funeral." She gestured towards the divan. "Miss Bixby is napping. Let me fetch her for you."

"That's all right. I'll surprise her."

"I don't know—"

He put his hands on her shoulders and spun her. "It's okay. Go peel a grape or something. Or bring me a bourbon and branch. That's a girl!"

Precious gave in and backed away.

He slipped off his shoes and crept up to Natalie's bedroom door. He twisted the ornate knob tensely, heard the click, and stuck his head in. Natalie lay on her back, a velvet mask fringed with lace covering her eyes. The afternoon light raked her pink silk nightgown and revealed every curve of her wide breasts, abdomen, and thighs. Her skin, showing only at the top of her feet, her arms, and above her collar bones, was porcelain pale as always, so pale that the red polish on her toes and nails made her look artificial, dead, like something cheap you'd win at a carnival for knocking over a pyramid of weighted bottles. When she stirred, he felt butterflies.

He crept across the room and knelt. He slowly and gently leaned over her foot. Holding it under the arch, he pressed brief kisses from the bend of the ankle down to her big toe. "Mmmmmm," she moaned, then said something he didn't understand. He wetly tasted each toe and then caught the baby in his teeth. She jerked upright and ripped the sleep mask from her face.

"You!" she shouted, pulling her foot away.

He laughed.

"What are you doing here?"

He had envisioned embraces, mad passion, a whirling into bed without words, but she was as angry as surprised. "Who were you expecting? Georgy Mack?"

She turned her legs into a sitting position. The mask had pressed an outline around her eyes. He moved to her on his knees and caressed the silk covering on her thighs. She looked tired. Drink or late nights or worry was getting to her. Her youth was bleeding out of her much too soon. "Don't you know to knock?" she sniffed.

"I wanted to surprise you."

"You shouldn't do that. I could have been talking in my sleep."

"And what would you say?"

"It doesn't matter. You should give a girl warning."

He slid his hands upward. She grabbed them before they reached her waist. He twisted his wrists and laced his fingers through hers. "I didn't mean to startle you."

"It's just I was dreaming."

"About whom? It sounded sexy."

"That's none of your business, kid."

He grinned. "Tell me."

"No."

"Tell me." He squeezed her fingers.

"Hey!" She struggled half-heartedly. A dull throb rose in his shoulder, but then she relaxed. Her eyes had a vague look, as if she were not quite awake, and she showed no pleasure in wrestling. "If you must know, about the night Harriet died."

"When you were beaten?" He loosened his grip without letting go.

She nodded.

"I'm sorry. You didn't seem to be having a nightmare."

"It wasn't a nightmare. It was before."

"Before the goons?"

She tried to pull away. He wouldn't let her. "Yes."

"Before Georgy broke in?"

"Georgy had a key."

The thought that Giorgio Macchianti could stroll in at any time didn't exactly increase the limited sexiness of the moment. "I heard Georgy's footing the bill for this palace."

"Yeah? Well, you heard wrong. What are you? Boston Blackie? Or are you just here working for Musso?"

Carl smiled. "I'm curious. You're a suspicious piece of work."

"Haven't you noticed? It's a nasty world."

"You got to take care of yourself or who will?"

"You got it." She tossed her head and looked him in the eye. "Let me go."

"No," he said.

"I got to pee."

"First tell me if Georgy tried to get me killed."

"You?" Her eyes tightened. "Georgy?"

"Yes."

"Are you kidding me? Let me go."

He squeezed tighter, probably hurting her, but she didn't resist. "There's a rumor it wasn't a sniper. It makes sense. Why pick off some shit-ass corporal? You sent Myron out of my room. I figure he told Georgy."

"You're nuts. Georgy would've made ya suffer. And he would have done the work himself. Now let me go." She twisted and the gold chain around her neck swung. A cross which had hidden behind the cup of her nightgown dropped into her open cleavage.

"Kiss me first."

"Stop playing games."

"Kiss me and I will."

She shrugged. She moved forward as if merely giving him a quick peck, but when their lips touched, she softened. Her mouth opened and their tongues probed deeply as he tasted her, pushing her back on the bed. When their lips separated, he was atop her, his left hip crushed into her crotch, his straining erection rubbing her thigh. She clutched his ears and lifted his head. "Listen, loverboy, I'll wet the bed."

"Maybe I don't care."

"You *are* nuts." She shoved him and he rolled onto his back, staring at the ceiling. She slipped into her bathroom and only halfway closed the door. He lay with his arms spread, every nerve vibrating, and listened to her urine tinkling into the water. Rolling his head, he looked at himself in the dresser mirror. He imagined if he unbuttoned his fly, his cock would pop up like a jack-in-the-box. He laughed and watched himself laughing. On the dresser was a large crystal bottle of perfume, big enough to be a whisky decanter. Behind a tray with a silver-backed hair brush tangled with Natalie's hair was a small gold painting of a madonna. It hadn't been there before. Something about it startled him, but he wasn't sure what.

She came out of the bathroom smoothing her nightgown over her hips. She raised one arm and leaned theatrically against the doorway. He figured she had gotten the pose from a Mae West movie, but she neither smiled nor tried to look sexy. It was more as if she depended upon the lintel to keep her standing.

"What time is it?" she asked.

"What difference does it make?"

"I'm trying to get at least eight hours a day."

"Then come back to bed."

"Buddy," she grinned, "beauty rest is the furthest thing from your mind."

He perused her body from head to foot. The triangular shadow of her pubic hair teased him through the silk. "Bingo."

She shrugged. "Not now. I'm singing tonight."

He raised himself on his elbows. "No kidding?"

"USO. Gonna sing for the troops."

"That's great. What's the band?"

"Army Air is all I know."

"Glenn Miller? How'd you get the job?"

She circled the bed to the dresser. "It's not Miller himself. They called me, okay? I gotta be there at six-thirty."

"Plenty of time," he said. "Come back to bed."

"I gotta save my energy." She bent to get a closer look at herself in the mirror. She pulled down a lower eyelid and inspected it. She stuck out her tongue.

"It never stopped you before."

"How would you know?"

"Half the time we could hear it over the sound of the train whistle." Her night gown had clung in the crack of her ass. He thought of hiking up the gown and mounting her from behind.

"Well, I've changed. Need to settle down." She picked up a pair of tweezers and plucked a hair from her eyebrow. "Just because you're been wasting a fortune on roses doesn't mean I'm obligated."

He was tempted to tell her Musso bought them. "What's up, Natalie? You get religion or something?"

"What do you mean?" She was startled.

"Something's up. You're wearing a cross. You've got a Virgin Mary on your dresser." He gestured toward the little picture and fixed his eye on it again. What was it about that thing? "I'll bet Bennie would love that."

"Hey, Jesus was a Jew, wasn't he?" She flung down her tweezers. "Who says I can't wear a cross or whatever I damn well please?"

"It's fine with me. I'm just curious."

"Because I turned you down?" She hiked up her gown, revealing her pubis. "Okay," she said, "fuck me then and stop pestering me. But don't expect me to help."

He was stunned by her anger.

"You think I'm some piece of meat?" she continued. "Some kike who's pining away for your cornpone dick? Well?"

"Take it easy," he said. She dropped her hem and sat. She looked for the tweezers, then in frustration argued with his image in the mirror.

"You think I don't want a normal life? Maybe I want to be married. Have kids. Sleep with the same man every night."

"Where did all this come from?" he said sharply.

"What's it to you?"

"I thought there was something between us." It came out so fast he hadn't thought about it. It astonished him as much as it seemed to astonish her. She faced him. He looked away, feeling guilty for saying what amounted to no more than a line, something any woman might like to hear. He was playing Musso's game by instinct. One hand washed the other.

"Carl," she said quietly, "you're such a kid. But you're thinking with your balls. Like most men."

He flopped onto his back and sighed. The strain of "thinking" ached in his balls.

"Come with me," she said. "I'll get you in the show."

"You could do that?"

"Sure. We'll be winging it anyhow. You can take some of the pressure off."

"I'd like to," he said dubiously.

"And later, I'll make it up to you."

He sat up. "You're hard to figure. Isn't that against your new religion?"

"It was against my old one, too. Not that I ever practiced much of it." She reached for her brush. "Anyhow, I ain't married yet."

He thought about what songs it would be best to sing as she made herself up: curling iron, lipstick, eyebrow pencil, powder. Above the neck, she ended up looking like an older version of Maxene or Laverne Andrews, he wasn't sure which.

Precious brought cheese sandwiches at five. While Natalie dressed in her bathroom, he nibbled his sandwich and wandered to the dresser. He could see in the mirror she had not closed the bathroom door, so he decided not to open any drawers. He picked up the madonna. It was about four inches by six, in a brass frame. The picture was in an old-fashioned style. The image was very flat and the infant Jesus was overflowing fat and out of proportion to his mother. There was a lot of gold leaf in the image and some kind of medieval writing overlapped by the frame. Had he seen this before? He stared into Mary's face trying to make out what it was that made him feel she was telling him something. Maybe her head was held in a position similar to one of the pictures of his own mother which his father had lined up on the mantle. Those pictures would have been staring down at his father when he pulled the trigger.

Maybe the image was simply a reproduction of something famous, maybe one of the Emperor Justinian's mosaics in Ravenna. His father had once taken him to a travelogue at William and Mary with hand-tinted lantern slides. But this image in his hand wasn't a reproduction of any kind of mosaic. Justinian. Something about him. Or his wife Theodora. He set it back down. It was like trying to remember who pitched the called homer to Babe Ruth and knowing you knew but still couldn't form the name.

He propped up the picture and finished his sandwich. Natalie hummed as she dressed. She had left her big wardrobe open. He saw boxes of new shoes in the bottom and two hat boxes on the shelf. When he eased the dresses aside, he could see several white linen outfits. Summer stuff, like Musso said. With the war on, it would be hard to get to anywhere but Mexico. Georgy Mack might know how to get on a freighter, though. A smuggler could get them to Cuba and all points south. "When my baby smiles at me," Carl quietly sang to himself, "I go to Ri-o, de Janeiro."

Carl was surprised by the old Duesenberg that picked them up in front of the building. It probably sucked up its monthly ration of gas while the chauffeur opened the door. He was even more surprised by the temple-like home they rolled up the driveway towards thirty minutes later. The Doric columns on the portico were too large for a man's arms to circle and tall enough to embarrass Zeus, Apollo, and Hera with their ostentation. "This is some National Guard armory," he said.

"Who said anything about an armory?" said Natalie.

The owner, a Margaret Dumont sort, held her rolling chin high. Mrs. Ponder seemed to want to touch people only with her jeweled fan, but she was gamely trying out all the friendliness her pedigree would allow. Carl was wondering what a gang of lonely soldiers would do to the marble floors, the Hepplewhite furniture, and the astrakhan carpets, when the woman led them through the foyer, into a drawing room the size of an aircraft hangar, and opened the French doors to a broad patio.

"This shall be your stage, Miss Bixby," she effused. "There is more than enough room for the band. The canopy has been drawn in case of rain and the lawn is almost entirely tented." Chinese lanterns were strung between the tent posts over tables of finger foods, and dozens of bottles of liquor. A wooden dance floor had been placed on the grass just below the patio.

"Nice," Natalie said. "The boys will really be impressed."

"Officers," she said to Carl, "are *persona non grata!* I am determined that the fighting men shall enjoy themselves *sans* inhibition."

"They'll appreciate that," said Carl.

"I believe they should have something up on their generals, don't you?"

"You're a great patriot, Mrs. Ponder," said Natalie.

She tapped Natalie on the shoulder with the fan as if knighting her. "I've had a lifetime of meaningless parties. As Mrs. Roosevelt said before the war, how can anyone do anything purely social in times like these? This, perhaps, will provide some modicum of pleasure to those who truly deserve it. One must do what one can. Let the jitterbugging be unconfined!" She flourished the fan and chortled at her own wit.

A portrait of a man with a handlebar mustache loomed over the marble fireplace. He was no doubt the robber baron who had amassed the heap of gold upon which Mrs. Ponder rested her substantial derrière. Jitterbugging would not have amused him. Nothing would have amused him, in this life or the next.

Mrs. Ponder fluttered off to check on some crisis in the kitchen. Carl and Natalie wandered out onto the patio. Drums had already been set up and a trumpet rested bell down on a round table. "I didn't know you moved in high society," said Carl.

"We're strictly the hired help."

"How'd this woman find you?"

Beyond the dance floor, they heard talking. "Must be the band," said Natalie. "Let's meet them."

At ground level, they could see the tent was big enough for three circus rings and a parade of elephants. "Holy mackerel!" whistled Carl.

A wizened butler handed slices of cake to five men in air corps uniforms. Something one of the soldiers said brought a very slight nod out of him.

"Hey, look," said Natalie, "it's Mack!" She hurried across the dance floor. Carl heard her but the name did not register. The thin man in his crisp uniform, his hair cropped close, delicately spread a narrow sandwich as if he expected to find metal shavings inside. It wasn't until Natalie threw herself on him and he awkwardly embraced her with the tiny plate balanced behind her back, that his gaunt face assumed the perpetually bewildered expression that Carl recognized as Mack Mintner's.

"Natalya, baby," Mack finally said. She pulled him to her, kissing each cheek like a French general giving a medal. She then planted a loud sloppy kiss on his mouth, provoking a wolf whistle from one of Mack's companions and smiles all around, even from the butler. The red lipstick slashed across his mouth like a gory lightning bolt.

"You look so good!" said Natalie, holding him at arm's length. "You look fabulous!"

"Thankya, baby," said Mack shyly. Maybe she had slept with him, too, Carl thought, back in the touring days. Mack put down his tiny plate and slid away from her. "Carl," he said, "Mr. Carolina. How goes it?"

"Good to be back in the States."

"You've done a tour?"

"Not much of one."

They exchanged terse histories, while Natalie clutched each man's upper arm. Mack would be joining Glenn Miller's air corps band in two months. Natalie interrupted with the news about her brother. Bennie was working at Republic, writing cowboy songs. Mack glanced at Carl and they both broke up, picturing Buzz Bixby dressed like Paul Whiteman and leading a band through some yippy-kai-yai-yay. "What's so funny?" Natalie asked. Carl asked Mack about other guys in the Bixby band. Len Seltzer, one of the cornet players, had won a Silver Star in the Aleutians. Ted Clough was a swabbie. Lou Epstein had dropped dead—Natalie and Mack couldn't agree whether it was in Grand Central or Pennsylvania Station. Mack brought up the name Myron Rush hesitantly, but said he'd heard the little weasel had taken a defense job in Connecticut to duck the draft.

"How would I know?" Natalie retorted. "He's nothing to me."

"Miss Bixby," interrupted one of the band members. "Can we check with you on a couple of songs? We've only got half an hour."

"Go ahead," said Mack. "I'll catch up."

Mack looked much older. His eyelids drooped and wrinkles spread from the corners of his eyes like cracks in glazing. Everything was sliding away. The Buzz Bixby Cavalcade of Swing was as fragmented a relic as a red-figure vase, with pieces of it scattered around the globe and some of it lost forever. But it wasn't only the loss of that sorry group that saddened Carl. It was the loss of that time. That moment when he was—what? Innocent? Young? He was still young by all but the standards of a child, but he no longer felt young. Perhaps he was nostalgic for his naiveté. It had never occurred to him in those days that anything could interrupt his career. Circumstances were things you overcame. A father who resisted your singing, lean years singing for tips, connecting with the people who could launch you: these were all bumps in the road. But if you gritted your teeth and kept moving, you got past the bumps. The road went on. He had to keep believing this, though it became harder every day. His uneasiness was that he now suspected that some things were not meant to be. Everything was no longer possible.

"So," said Carl, "the lip's been good to you. Glenn Miller!"

"I've been playing Stage Door Canteens: New York, Philly, wherever. Last night here in Cleveland. Tomorrow we head west. It's better than dogfacing."

"Take it from a dogface!"

Mack offered Carl a napkin of petits-fours. "So how's it with you?"

Carl explained he was translating. He said he should have been discharged after the wound, but he'd made the mistake of insisting. Mack chuckled. If you didn't know how the Army worked, the Army would be certain to educate you.

"The war won't last forever," Mack said.

"I'm working on my connections," Carl said bluntly. "Connections are everything."

Mack slightly raised an eyebrow. Was he insulted? Did Mack think he hadn't used any connections to get hooked up with Glenn Miller? Somebody put a word in. Mack could do that for Carl, couldn't he? Mack anticipated his question. "Music's luck. Right place, right time. It's too bad you haven't got an instrument. There's always a spot for a good sax and licorice man."

202

Carl thought of Oswald Ülsmann, the licorice man he was supposed to be hunting. Maybe he'd better leave a message for Dahl.

One of the quintet members tapped Carl on the shoulder. "I'm Red," the man said, offering his hand. "Natalie tells me you sing."

"You bet," said Carl.

"A helluva singer," said Mack.

"Well, come on up and let's figure what we can do."

"Great," said Carl. If Mack wouldn't do anything for him, maybe Red or one of the others would.

As they discussed possible songs for Carl—"Under Your Window," "We've Got a Job to Do," and "Johnny Get Your Gun Again"—soldiers filled the tent from the rear and attacked the food and drink like mosquitoes buzzing a nudist convention. The busloads of girls were late, so the band played a few instrumentals such as "Moonglow," "String of Pearls," and "Pennsylvania 6–5000," with which the soldiers loudly shouted the refrain. Red then sang a novelty medley that included "Goodbye Mama, I'm Off to Yokohama," "The Betty Grable Polka," and "It's Taps for the Japs." During the applause, Mack leaned to Carl and Natalie while evacuating his trumpet. "What do we do if the girls don't show? Red's Korn Kobbler routine ain't gonna keep 'em happy forever."

"Keep playing!" they shouted simultaneously.

Red counted out the beat and they moved into "I'll be Seeing You." Mack was in good form, Carl thought. The sax man was adequate and Red moved easily over the drum skins, maybe even better than Ted Clough, now somewhere out in the ocean causing a battleship to list. The quintet was smooth, but they lacked a certain edge. They weren't pushing. On the other hand, they were still waiting for the party to begin. Midway through the song the first girls arrived. They were whirled out onto the dance floor as soon as they stuck their heads into the tent. There were a lot of GIs for a few bobby soxers, many of whom didn't look old enough to be in high school, let alone to fend off a soldier, but by the end of "In the Mood," you couldn't see the dance floor for the saddle oxfords and polished Army shoes.

Carl whispered to Natalie, "Why are there so many soldiers in Cleveland? Are we invading Canada?"

"There's soldiers everywhere," she said, annoyed to have her thoughts interrupted.

There were, thought Carl. And when the war ended, a lot of them would be dead, but the rest of them, millions of them, would want to be entertained. He was giving himself a pep talk, he realized. Why? He hadn't sung in public with a real band for what? A year? Eighteen months? Could it be that long? Yet he felt no butterflies. He had been more nervous singing for Elizabeth. To really cook, you needed to be on edge. There was too much on his mind. He needed that mindless roll in the hay Natalie had promised. He needed the uncomplicated life of travelling from town to town, singing college mixers, hotels, and nightclubs. He needed to forget about being successful, and whether some prisoner killed a boy, and whether Musso was angry, and whether trying to ferret out Natalie's plans with Georgy Mack was a cheesy thing to do, and whether he would hurt Elizabeth. What he needed most was to glide into the seat of a twelve-cylinder song and let it carry him away. He had felt that in Cleveland in 1941, but he knew he would not feel it tonight.

16.

Natalie's madonna stared at him. He wanted to turn the Virgin away, but since she had already watched them—or at least heard them—from one a.m. to two, it didn't seem too important whether she saw the resulting human wreckage with its a tangle of legs, arms, and tortured sheets with the malt smell of sex. Why couldn't he hear what the Mary was trying to say? It wasn't the obvious. Not something like, "Straighten out your life," "Stop catting around," or "Do your bit!" Something factual. Something he couldn't remember.

Natalie's white rear was as voluptuous as a fifth century Aphrodite's. Maybe primal association was what had cost Papanoumou his life, an irresistable mythological resonance that made him fool enough to steal Georgy Mack's woman. It was Ares banging the wife of Hephaistos all over again, and Hephaistos had netted him, just as in The Odyssey. Ah, this is what growing up with a professor gets you! What did the ancient gods have to do with it? Natalie as goddess? She was less classical than dissolute. An odalisque by Delacroix, not Ingres. Goethe had once said that Classicism was health, while Romanticism was disease. Natalie fit the latter. The very pleasure in fucking her was that it was nothing more than fucking, and yet it was absolutely not one pomegranate seed less than fucking, either.

But why would Georgy Mack, who had killed Papanoumou in order to keep Natalie, ignore her banging Carl? Because she didn't love him? That meant nothing to a heavy like Georgy. Could Georgy not know? If Musso could spy on the apartment building, so could he. If Georgy tried at all he would know. It didn't take the deductive powers of Philo Vance. Just a five-spot slipped to the door man. Psst, who went in? When did he come out?

Carl remembered Dahl. Oh shit. He wrapped himself in a blanket which had been tossed to the floor during the gyrations. He crept out of the room and gently closed the door. He tiptoed around the ornate bar, clutching the blanket at his waist, and spotted the telephone next to the pocket doors of the dining room. Precious startled him when he was halfway across the opening.

"Mornin'," she said.

He ran his fingers through his hair. "Good morning."

"Would you and Miss Bixby be expecting breakfast soon?"

"Breakfast? In an hour? Would that be okay?"

"That's what I get paid for," she said. She was feigning indifference but the wry lilt of her voice betrayed her amusement. He had suction marks on his left shoulder and his collar bone. He had never felt so naked.

"Well, sir?" she said. "What would you like?"

"Th-the usual," he smiled weakly. "Whatever Miss Bixby likes."

"Well, she ain't much for breakfast."

"Then whatever Mr. Mack has. That's what I'll have."

"Seems like you already had it."

Carl's ears went hot.

"But he ain't ever had breakfast here."

"Never?"

"No, sir."

She had to be lying. Somehow Natalie was seeing him. They were partners. They had killed the Greek. *Somebody* was paying for the apartment. "Look, you can level with me, Precious. It could be nasty if the two of us were surprised by him."

"Pretty nasty, already, I'd say. But Mr. Mack never ate here. He ain't ever been here, as far as I know."

"But she's going to marry him, isn't she? She's turning Christian, right?"

"Well, Catholic," said Precious. "I don't know nothing about that Catholic stuff."

"Nor I, really," said Carl. He imagined how this conversation was going to play later when Precious repeated every word to Natalie. "I was curious," he smiled. "I don't want things to get messed up for her. He's never come here? That's keeping the bride and groom separated a long time, eh?"

Precious shrugged. "Men done visited, jes' friends in the music business, but no Mr. Mack."

Visited. Army VD films flicked on the wallpaper. "Mind if I make a phone call?"

"You go ahead," she said. "But answer me one thing, soldier boy."

"If I can."

"What the hell you want for breakfast?"

Carl laughed. He hoped Precious did not get pitched from a window like Harriet Whatzername. He left a message at the Stouffer's that the trail had gone cold and Dahl should meet him at the station for the two p.m. train. The desk clerk said Dahl had called three times and left word he was staying at the Y.

When Carl returned to the bedroom, Natalie was stirring. He hopped on the bed beside her. "Hey, baby."

"You out there messing with Precious, loverboy?"

"I was using the phone."

"Sure."

"Well, what if I was?"

"It wouldn't be polite," she said.

"Believe me. I got nothing left."

"Good," she smiled.

"Goodness had nothing to do with it."

She stretched languidly. "You were good last night."

"Any time."

She hit him with a pillow. "I mean singing."

"Yeah? I didn't feel with-it."

"You were more relaxed. Your voice is more mature. You've got more control. Smooth, but strong, like a good whisky."

"I felt distant."

"Can't take a compliment? You were a heartbreaker."

"Better than a kneebreaker," he said. "Where's Georgy Mack?"

She slumped back on the bed. "What do you care?"

"He killed one guy you were sleeping with, and he may have taken a shot at me."

"You and me are nothing permanent. Just old pals. Veterans of the musical wars. Don't worry about Georgy."

"Hey, I'm fooling around with his woman."

"You ain't fooling. Anyhow Musso's guys are watching."

"What makes you think that?"

"He wants Georgy. You think I don't know a goon when I see one? You're being a pain, Carl." Her voice was sharp enough that he knew to lay off.

"Hey, you were good last night, too. You oughtta be an Andrews sister: Maxene, Patty, Laverne, and Natalie." He knew she wanted to hear that, true or not.

"You bet your ass."

She had changed her act from a lethargic rendition of Marlene Dietrich to a hepped-up Andrews Sister. When she sang "Boogie-Woogie Bugle Boy," she bent at the waist and shook her shoulders. Her tits jiggled like dice in a velvet cup. Soldiers whistled wildly and one of them had to be clubbed by the MPs. Mrs. Ponder had watched the whole spectacle with eyebrows halfway up her forehead. She seemed to have expected her very public gesture on behalf of the fighting men to come off like a tea party. The tea she served, though, was gulped, not sipped, and the liquor bill must have been staggering, never mind the broken china.

"You know, Mack is all set up with Glenn Miller once the war is over. He's got it made. Maybe you ought to stay in touch with him." Carl said it despite his seeing that what Natalie had always done was assume someone else's role. She was a mimic and would never be a star. She couldn't write songs or interpret new ones. If she had a comic talent, maybe the imitations could have been used. Buzz had been right to offer her a chance to do voices off-camera in the movies. It would have fit her. Her real talent was on the sheets. Yessir . . .

He slid his hand up her thigh and into her bushy pubic hair, tugging at the tufts with his thumb and forefinger.

"Mmmmm," she murmured. "Don't pull it out. Just the gray ones."

"You don't have gray ones."

"Why don't you take a good look?"

"I could do that," he said matter-of-factly.

"You never let a girl sleep, do you?" Her hand searched

for his growing cock and squeezed tightly. "Is that a pistol you're carrying?"

"No, I'm just glad to see you."

They kissed deeply as his fingers kneaded the flesh on each side of her opening.

Their lips smacked as he abruptly pulled away. "Just a minute."

"Wha—?"

He rolled off the bed and crossed to the madonna. He turned the picture around, saw that she was still watching in the reflection of the mirror, then placed her face down.

"Get your hands off that!" Natalie shrieked.

The reaction befuddled him. "You don't want baby Jesus and his mother watching, do you?"

"You don't touch that. Put it back."

"When we're finished. It bugs me."

"No!"

"But—"

"Why should you feel guilty?" she shouted. "I'm the one who's supposed to feel guilty!" Her feet slapped against the floor and pattered toward the bathroom, her butt jiggling with each footfall. She spun, the centripetal force dragging her breast against the molding. "Put it back!" she shouted, and slammed the door.

"Natalie!" he said desperately. He started after her, banging his shin on the corner of the bed. He hopped twice, then limped to rattle the knob. "Natalie?"

He heard nothing. One moment he was about to slip a finger into her, and the next . . . This is idiotic, he thought. He softly tapped. He pressed his ear against the door. Weeping? Water running? He saw himself in the dressing mirror, looking stupid, as all naked men do. His penis, now at half-mast, was a punctuation mark emphasizing stupidity. "Damn!" He swung his fist so hard, his shoulder stung. He returned to the dresser. Mary had a strange archaic smile. He snatched her up and cocked his arm to throw her against the bathroom door. Instead he took a deep breath, set her down, and looked for his olive green boxer shorts.

He dressed as quickly as if a brigadier general had appeared on a surprise inspection. On his way out, he paused by the door to say he was leaving. He heard the bath faucet. His hand hovered over the glossy white wood, poised to knock, then silently dropped. An hour later, he was reading a paper in the Cleveland station when Private Dahl found him.

"So," said Dahl, "where's the Fritz?"

"A wild-goose chase," said Carl grimly. "A total SNAFU."

"I wouldn't call it that," said the private. He brought out a roll of bills.

"Put that in your pocket! What'd you do? Rob a bank?"

"A little of this, a little of that. But especially a guy who thought he knew Montana Red Dog. Don't ever go after a boy who went straight from mama's milk to Montana Red Dog."

"Gambling's not my form of masochism," said Carl.

"Huh?"

"So how much?"

"The wad's mostly ones. Some Jeffersons. Two or three Abes."

"I get your point."

"I see you had yourself a good time, too."

"Says who?"

"Says the *Plain Dealer*."

"What?"

Dahl grabbed the paper. He flipped several pages then pressed a finger to an article in the lower corner. "There."

"'PONDER SPONSORS GI PARTY,'" read Carl. "Oh shit."

A passing policeman tapped Carl's foot with his baton. "Watch your language in here, son."

"Sorry, officer."

The cop pointed at the high ceiling with his stick. "Echoes."

"Yes, sir."

The cop wandered off and was soon talking to a Negro in a zoot suit.

"All I need is for Murnow to see this," said Carl.

"Why should he? You think I'll tell him? I owe you. I hope somebody escapes every week." He paused. "Not that I hope a kid gets hurt."

"Yeah. Jesus, they had to mention me as a 'special guest!' Used to be I'd want press like this."

"So what can the major say? You were looking for the clarinet guy."

"In Mrs. Ponder's punch bowl?"

Dahl shrugged. Carl checked the big clock. They still had twenty minutes to wait. He scrutinized the article again.

"You should've invited me to that party," said Dahl. "Naa, I'm fixed. Beats selling Nazi trinkets."

"Damn, did they have to—" Someone tapped Carl's foot again. "Sorry, officer, I—" But it wasn't the cop. Two heavies in overcoats and fedoras loomed over him. There was no mistaking their occupations.

"Hey, the game was straight," protested Dahl.

"Beat it," said the larger man.

Dahl looked confused. "I'll meet you on the platform."

"Okay," said Carl.

"You *will* be there, won't you?"

"Beat it!" said the man.

Dahl backed away, positioning himself to watch from the opposite side of a shoeshine stand.

"You shoulda called our mutual friend." The implied threat in the man's gravelly voice sounded as if he were born with it.

"I didn't find out anything."

"You're not holding up your part of the bargain."

"She won't talk about Georgy Mack. She's bought tropical clothes."

"We know all that."

"She's gotten religion, I think," added Carl. "And she's planning on getting married."

"So we heard, but she never goes to Mass. What does that tell ya?"

"Nothing," said Carl.

"Exactly. Did she talk to anybody at the rich broad's?"

"Lots of people," said Carl. "Maybe she used the phone. How would I know?"

The man grabbed Carl's shirt. "You're supposed to know."

"Hey, what can I tell you? I've tried. She's weird. She doesn't say anything. Maybe she's about to make her move. Other than that, I've got no idea. If she's planning to get married, why's she dragging me to bed? How would I know? She's not a person for pillow talk. She doesn't talk in her sleep. What more can I do? I can't search her rooms."

"Don't bother with that. What we need to know is in her head."

Carl pushed the man's hand away. "I've tried."

"Well," said the man almost to himself, "I can make anybody talk, but Musso says lay off."

"Maybe he loves her," chirped the other. He had a silly voice for such an enormous body.

"Look," said Carl, "I'm acting entirely in good faith. He's got to understand that. What is all this about, really? There must be other ways of finding Georgy Mack. Tell me the truth: I'm a decoy, right? I've been set up to bring him out of hiding."

The man obscenely touched Carl's knee. "Time's running out. You'll be wanting to come back to Cleveland real soon, now."

"Aw, look, guys—"

"Real soon," he insisted.

"Yes, sir," said Carl, saluting him.

They left as quickly as they had come. Carl dropped his head into his hands. Why the hell couldn't Musso just beat her until she talked? It wasn't like these people favored subtlety. Why did Natalie stay in Cleveland? Georgy Mack could protect her, make her invisible on his brother's turf in New York. None of this made any sense. Why would Natalie accept a beating from Georgy? Why would she watch her friend Harriet pitched out of the window and her boyfriend dragged away, and then convert to marry the man who did it? Fear? Carl remembered what it was like as he lay bleeding in the street in Oran. He understood how Natalie could be motivated by pure fear—oh, yes, he did understand that—but it didn't help him make sense of the whole situation. Hell, I'm just a singer, he thought. What do I know?

Dahl crept slowly towards him, one eye cocked for the goons. "So," he said, "what was all that?"

"They wanted to congratulate me," Carl said dryly.

"Man, was I relieved!"

"If you were gambling with those guys," said Carl, "you wouldn't have made it to the station. The Montana Red Dog would have chewed your leg off."

212

"Suicide kings," said Dahl.

Carl didn't ask what he meant. Carl had been gambling with those guys ever since he'd agreed to do Musso a favor. It had all seemed simple: Get laid and get famous.

"They're announcing our train," said Dahl.

17.

Carl dozed fitfully for most of the ride back. He tried to fantasize singing to a packed hall as he had done at Swing Land, 1941, and at Saratoga Springs New Year's 1940, but all of the complications buzzed around him like a mosquito. What bothered him most was that the singing at Mrs. Ponder's hadn't felt really great. The quintet was good, the crowd was spirited, and some of the soldiers got jealous of the amorous sighs he'd gotten from the girls when he sang "Our Love is Here to Stay." He was the only thing wrong—not his singing, everyone had praised it. The kick wasn't in it. Like a drug he'd become accustomed to, the effect wasn't as dramatic. He juggled various explanations. He was more mature. He had overrehearsed in the ravine. The discovery of Timmy's body had shaken him. Maybe he was losing interest in the whole business. That would be a fine howdedo! He'd never thought of doing anything else. How could he bring himself to screw in bolts on twenty Fords a day? It was as meaningless as his father's pontificating on *l'amour antique* to sleepy freshmen.

They hiked up to Main for a carton of cigarettes for each of them—both purchased by the flush Dahl—then hitched a ride in a vegetable truck labelled Reese & Son Carting and Hauling. PFC Burgess was guarding the front gate. "You find him?"

"Does it look like it?" snapped Carl.

"Valdez found how he got out."

"He sprouted wings," said Dahl.

"Very funny," said Burgess. "He tunneled."

"Tunneled?" Strange wrinkles appeared every time Carl blinked. When he reached Murnow's office, O'Hurly proudly showed the compact infantry shovel the Germans had used. It was rusty and had been hidden under one of the barracks stoops. "We figure they stole it from the mess. They use some of them to shovel potatoes, bury garbage, stuff like that."

"So where's the tunnel?" Carl asked.

"We haven't found it yet."

Carl tilted his head to one side.

"It's a matter of time," insisted O'Hurly.

"Does it make sense to dig a tunnel to let one man escape?"

"Maybe it collapsed."

"One guy gets through and it collapses behind him?"

"Why not?" O'Hurly raised the shovel. "What's this?"

"It's a rusty shovel. It isn't a tunnel."

"Well, to hell with you," said O'Hurly. "We've already let it out to the papers. We sent a report to Washington. That makes it official. There was a tunnel."

"I don't argue with the Army anymore."

"You're in enough trouble."

Carl rolled his eyes. So Murnow had read the *Plain Dealer*. It would be harder to get away from Camp Wayne, now, than to tunnel to Cleveland. "I'll be in the barracks."

"No, the major said you was to wait. I'll get him." O'Hurly locked his drawers and snatched his cap off the tree stand. Carl slumped into the chair opposite Murnow's desk and crossed his arms. FDR looked happy in his glassless frame with his flypaper bunting. He was the only one in a hundred miles who was. *He* had nothing to fear but fear itself.

Murnow hurried in about five minutes later. "What are you doing in my office? You don't enter my office until ordered."

Carl snapped out of the chair and saluted. "Yes, sir," he said with a sarcastic twist in his lip. "I understood Sergeant O'Hurly to say—"

"Never mind," said Murnow. He plopped with such force his chair slid back against the wall. A drop of red sauce had dried at the end of his mustache. "He shouldn't have left you alone."

"Why not? What'd I do now?"

"First things first. Sit. Was there any sign of the son of a bitch in Cleveland?"

Carl toyed with saying yes. It might help justify his actions.

On the other hand, it might send the police, FBI, and what all in the wrong direction.

"Well?"

Suppose Oswald *was* the killer? "None at all," he answered. "There was a Polish guy," he lied. "Acted suspicious. He was just a nut case looking for a job, but it took a long time to run him down." He added another flourish to cover the show at Mrs. Ponder's. "He told one guy he was going to a USO thing, so I went over there and hung out. He didn't come. The next morning I found him, though."

Murnow scrutinized him.

"He did resemble Ülsmann," said Carl.

"Too bad. Good work," said Murnow. "I was hoping it would work. It's getting bad. Louis Bassett, the mother, and about a dozen citizens showed up with a congressman demanding justice. They act like I did it. Like I should shoot a couple of krauts to satisfy them."

Good work? The praise confused Carl.

"But you're not off the hook," said Murnow. "You fooled with the evidence, Walthers."

"I didn't fool with anything."

"Don't argue with me! I'm the commanding officer here," he slapped his desk. "Why did you do that?"

"Sir, I don't know what you're talking about."

"You cleaned out the pervert's possessions."

"Ülsmann's?"

"You took everything. Why?"

"Because it was totally unsecured, major. The prisoners could contaminate the evidence."

"And did you think it was more secure under your bunk?"

"I don't think Pike or O'Hurly have any reason to fiddle the evidence."

"And what about you?"

"Me?" Carl shot up out of his chair as if a railroad spike had popped up through the seat.

"Sit down. Maybe your friendship with this clarinet player was a little too much. Maybe you felt sorry for him. That's what one FBI agent said."

"I found the body, Tex," Carl shouted. "You think I could

look at a dead kid and protect who did it? Not even my mother!"

"Sit down!" said Murnow. "You found the body, yes. And you disturbed the scene by moving it. And then you trot off with the sicko's possessions. That looks funny, don't you think?"

"No," said Carl.

The inevitable came. Murnow dipped below his desk and came out with a new bottle of whiskey: Three Feathers this time. King William IV was long dead. "You're just lucky," he said, "we found all the stuff under your cot."

"It wasn't like I was hiding it, was it?"

Murnow took a swallow. He shoved the cork back in and lowered the bottle into his drawer, slamming it shut. "You take anything?"

"No."

"Did you see the bills pinned in the lining of his jacket?"

"Yes."

"Where do you think he got those?"

"How would I know? Look, if I gave them to him, he would have taken them to escape, right? If I gave them to him, I would have taken them rather than let you find them, right?"

"But you hid everything."

"Under my cot? Where everyone can see it?"

Murnow blinked, as if the whisky had just thumped to the bottom of his stomach. His forehead beaded with sweat.

"Listen," said Carl, "I don't think Ülsmann killed that boy. I can't believe it. There was a picture of a girl in his locker and Rita Hayworth pictures. Does this sound like a creep who rapes Boy Scouts?"

"Look," said Murnow, "I know how it is. You think some fellow's a friend and—"

"That isn't it, major. Ülsmann wasn't the kind of guy to escape. He was happy waiting it out. He liked jazz. After the war, he wanted to stay."

"An anti-Nazi can be crazy, too. In fact, most of them don't seem very well-adjusted."

"It wasn't political with him, major. He liked jazz."

"That's 'jungle music' to the SS."

Carl lowered his head in exasperation. "I think somebody did fiddle with his things."

"What do you mean?"

"I looked in his locker before, major. I'm pretty sure the money wasn't there."

Murnow smiled wryly.

"Somebody put the money in there. And then, there was the musician's wing."

Murnow made another dive for his bottle.

"There was one in the locker. It was gone the second time. Somebody took it."

"Somebody took it. After the murder, you're saying."

"Yes. To make sure the one in the kid's pocket looked like his." But why? It *had* been his.

Murnow rolled his eyes as if Carl were the most pathetic idiot he had ever had the misfortune to talk with. "So?" he said loudly.

"So somebody is trying to fiddle the evidence."

Murnow took another swig and seemed to be gathering himself for an assault on a machine gun nest. "It all comes back to you, Walthers. To you." He laced his fingers. His bleary eyes had fire in them. "You tried to break into the files."

Carl didn't know how to respond. What did this have to do with Ülsmann? "Sir?"

"Don't play innocent with me! I startled you. You pretended to be on the phone."

"I *was* on the phone. Check with the telephone company."

Murnow smugly opened his desk. He plucked out an untwisted paper clip. "You left this in the lock."

"What are you talking about?"

"The file cabinet. Maybe you've crossed over. Maybe you've palled up with these krauts enough you're now helping them."

"You're nuts."

"You're a kraut, aren't you? Carl Maria Walthers. That isn't too American sounding, a guy named Maria."

"Hey, major, Murnow sounds pretty German to me, too. We could have adjoining cells. They could intern us with the California Japs." This confused Murnow enough that Carl pressed further. "O'Hurly reads the files. You can read the files. Did you ever take a look if there's anybody with an old morals charge, anything like that?"

"Why should we? The Army doesn't take people like that."

Carl stumbled. That was true. If they knew about it. "Well maybe somebody was cleared of something like that: Witnesses refused to testify. Maybe it got overlooked."

"Other than satisfying your curiosity, what do you think that would prove, sergeant?" He said Carl's title mockingly.

"You've got to admit it's possible one of our men molested the boy and its a coincidence that Ülsmann—"

It was Murnow's turn to bolt upright out of his chair. "Walthers, if you ever repeat crap like that, I'll rip your lungs out! Christ, the townspeople would go wild—! I ought to throw you in the stockade for treason! You were breaking into the files, dammit, and in order to place blame—! Jee-sus Christ!" He lifted his blotter with both hands and flung it against the wall. This time FDR's picture managed to hang on to its nail.

Murnow came around the desk, panting. "You aren't pinning this incident on one of my men." His nostrils hissed. "I'd be ruined. You come here like you're too good for us. You don't mix like a regular guy and you've got no respect for your superiors. Accusing one of us! You're confined to your barracks, you son of a bitch, until I decide what to do. That's all for now. *Dis-missed!*"

"Yes, sir," said Carl quietly.

As soon as he lay on his cot, the exhaustion of the long night with Natalie knocked him out. He dreamed he was in the ravine and each time he sang the first note of a song, the layered shale wall collapsed over him like an ocean wave. Battered, he would stagger to his feet and hear, in succession, Ernie Musso, Buzz Bixby, and Sal Macchianti shouting for him to sing. Behind him, Gerhardt Läufer, Albert Dorn, and Ulrich Messer in full German uniforms waited patiently to sing back-up. He opened his mouth and the wall crashed over him again. He tried to sing quietly and they would shout "Louder!" until he raised his voice enough that the shale crashed over him.

"Carl? Carl?"

The voice was gentle, quiet. When he opened his eyes,

219

Elizabeth was on one knee beside his cot, tugging at his sleeve. The lengthening rays of twilight tinted her dark hair with glimmers of chestnut.

"Carl, are you okay?"

He blinked the confusion out of his head. "Sure, yeah. What time is it?"

"You missed dinner."

"Oh." He moved to sit up, then stopped because she blocked his legs. "I—I'm being punished. I don't know whether I'm supposed to eat or not."

"You have to eat!"

"I'm not hungry." Her face was close enough to breathe his breath, perhaps to smell Natalie's perfume on his neck. He swung his legs the opposite direction and sat up, his back to her.

"Why are you being punished?" she asked.

"It's silly. Let's say I'm not so sure Oswald did it."

"He seemed nice to me."

He combed his hair with his fingers. "Killers often do."

She circled the bed and sat beside him. "They say he dug a tunnel."

"That's what they say."

"I don't believe it," said Elizabeth.

"You'll get in trouble, like me."

"My men told me they went to dig a well on the farm up the road. The rocks were terrible. When they heard that the Germans had dug a tunnel, Vicenza laughed and said the Germans were miracle workers. They strike stones with their Heil Hitler salutes and the earth parts for them, like Moses and Aaron. They thought it was real funny."

"Well, the Army has decided it was a tunnel, so tell your spaghetti-twisters they're wrong." He sighed and stood up. He rubbed his eyes and felt the puffiness around them.

"I wanted to see you," she said. "I waited near the mess."

"You shouldn't be in here," he said abruptly. "The barracks are off limit to civilians. Especially women."

"So you *do* think of me as a woman."

He avoided looking at her. He leaned against the window and peered out at the sun setting into the lake behind the long rows of prisoners' quarters. "A helluva woman, pardon the expression. That's why you shouldn't get mixed up with me. Does that answer your question? You better go before I get in worse trouble."

"That isn't why I came," she said.

He fumbled in his shirt pocket for his cigarettes. When he realized he had put them in his locker before he lay down, he crossed his arms and rested his shoulder against the window frame. "Put my foot in it. Seem to be doing a lot of that these days."

"What I wanted to ask was that my father was talking to the boarder down the hall and heard rumors about Timmy Firenzi. I know it was terrible because he didn't want to eat afterwards. Timmy being molested, that wouldn't kill him, would it?"

"Not usually," said Carl. "Beth, you don't want to know. It's the kind of thing that once you know it you can never go back to the way you were before."

"Are you afraid I'll change?"

"Let's just say it would take a lot of niceness out of the world."

She lowered her chin and blushed. "You're not taking me seriously. I have nightmares about finding him. He looked asleep. Maybe if I knew what killed him, they would go away."

"They might get worse." Carl considered it. She was an adult. Maybe she had a right to know. But he couldn't formulate the words. "It was internal bleeding," was all he said.

"But he didn't look hurt."

"I know," he said. "It was internal. He was roughed up in the abdomen and it filled with blood."

"Oh," she said, but he knew she still didn't quite understand. At her age, a lot of girls had two or three children. The protection everyone had always surrounded her with had made her the angel she was. He wasn't going to tear that down. He'd done enough bad things in his life. "So it was like a blow to the belly?"

"Yes," he said.

She crossed herself, and clenched her hands. "Poor Timmy," she said breathlessly.

"Are you okay?"

She bit her lip and nodded. You get used to one kind of

horror and it makes you strong enough for the next, he thought. "I don't know why my pop couldn't have just said it," she added.

"You're his daughter," said Carl. "Some things are hard to say. Now you'd better get out of here."

She moved next to him. "Oswald couldn't have hit a kid, could he? Not on purpose."

"I don't think so, but who knows?"

"'Who knows what evil lurks in the hearts of men?'" she recited.

"'The Shadow knows!'" he said dryly. The sun was bubbling down into the lake. The prisoners moved among the huts, dark silhouettes, wandering souls.

"You're thinking something," she said.

"Nothing."

"You are."

"You should get out of here before dark."

She tugged his arm. "That wasn't it."

He shrugged and noticed his shoulder was stiff. "I was thinking about a dizzy prisoner we have. I was thinking he knows something."

"Like what?"

"Like whether there was a tunnel. He hides under the buildings. If you're going to tunnel, you have to do it under a building. Or you have to get rid of the dirt and putting it under a building would be a good place. Aw, Sergeant Pike would have looked, wouldn't he?"

"It doesn't mean he'd find it," Elizabeth was tying a scarf over her hair. "What's the prisoner's name?"

"Why?"

"I'll go ask him."

"Forget it. Anyway, he doesn't speak English."

"Then I'll bring him to you."

"You can't do that!"

"I go into the Italian compound every day."

"Yeah, but—"

"What's his name?"

The overhead light came on. O'Hurly stood in the doorway. "Say," he said. "What are you doing in here?"

"She's just leaving," said Carl.

"None of my business," said O'Hurly. "If you need some time—"

"It's nothing like that!" said Carl. "The girl was asking a few questions, that's all."

"It ain't the questions that matter, it's the answers. I'll come back later."

Snapping his fingers, Carl grabbed O'Hurly's sleeve. "Cover for me."

"What?"

"I'm going into the prisoners' compound."

"At night? You're confined to barracks!"

"Just cover for me. I think I can find the tunnel."

O'Hurly squinted. "Look, buddy, you been acting funny, breaking into files and stuff. Maybe I ought to ask the major."

"He's loaded by now. What's he going to do? Fire me?"

"All right. Morris then. Or Valdez. I don't need to buy into your trouble. The major says you're trying to pin the killing on somebody in the camp. I don't like that."

"Look," Carl pleaded, "I find that tunnel it practically proves Oswald did it, right?"

"Please," said Beth. "Maybe you can come with me, sergeant. That way Carl's not leaving his barracks."

"Me? I ain't going in there at night."

"Terry, I have to," said Carl.

O'Hurly rubbed his nose, then pulled the light cord. "I came home. The light was off. I didn't notice whether you was here or not. That's all I got to say."

"You're a champ," said Carl.

"Just don't pin it on me," said O'Hurly. "And hurry up."

Carl tried to talk Beth out of going into the compound with him, but she wouldn't back off. In crossing the parade ground he spotted PFC Jones, coming off guard duty and heading for the enlisted men's quarters. He ordered him to come with them, also. Carl simply told everyone who questioned his going inside that it was "Tex's order." They picked up flashlights at the gate and were inside compound C five minutes later.

A cold fog was beginning to curl in over the tin roofs. Most of the prisoners had gone inside, but obscure figures moved in the murk like catfish trolling for scraps at the bottom of

a muddy river. The three of them had gone into a world
in which they didn't belong and walked nearly shoulder to
shoulder, eyes searching, listening to the rasping sound of
whispered German.

About forty feet from the gate, Carl's flashlight caught
three prisoners sharing a cigarette. "Come on," he said quietly. The men winced from the light but did not back off.

"*Guten abend,*" said Carl. The man in the center passed the
cigarette to the man on his left. "I know you, don't I?"

"We have talked." His features were distorted by the upward rake of the light, but Carl recalled he was one of the
SS corporals.

"Not much, though."

"The coffee was good." The man's eyes adjusted somewhat
to the light. When he made out that the figure beside Carl
was a woman, he tipped his cap.

"You know Ude Wieschensohn?"

"The lunatic?"

"He's the one."

"What do you want with him?"

"We've got a psychiatrist to talk to him," Carl said.

"A psychiatrist?"

"Yes."

"You should get him out of here. He is filthy."

A second man spoke. "He'll get pneumonia sleeping on
the ground."

The first man glanced at his companion as if he had spoken out of turn. "Wieschensohn imagines things."

"Like what?" asked Carl. The prisoners shrugged. "So
where is he?"

"Usually near C-8. I'll show you." He pointed at Beth. "Is
she a psychiatrist?"

"She's the Italian translator."

"I apologize," the man said sardonically. "I should have
recognized such a lovely girl. A bad night to be out, is it not?"

"Let's get on with it," said Carl.

"Come on," said the man. He whirled on his heels to lead
them between the barracks.

"Hold it," said Carl. "Why are you taking us off the main
track?"

"Why? Because he runs when he sees people."

Carl stepped closer to him. "C-8? Very well. You take your two men up the back side. We'll go up the main thoroughfare. If he runs, you hold him."

"He's filthy," said the man.

"It'll wash off."

"Maybe it would be better—"

"I'll hold you three personally responsible if he gets away."

The man shrugged. He and his companions disappeared into the darkness.

Carl explained what had just happened with the Germans as they walked down the path between the rows. "You shouldn't have come in here," he said to Beth. "I should have thought it out."

"They wouldn't hurt me," she said.

"It only takes one," said Jones.

As if to make the night even stranger, they heard a sharp whistle behind them. MPs with a guard dog? Someone in the tower? A German who admired Beth?

The fog had moved in thickly enough that the flashlights now formed a cone of white. The ground assumed a silvery sheen as the moisture coated everything. It was getting harder to read the numbers over the barracks doors, but when they reached C-5, it became obvious why the SS man had tried to steer them off the main path. Far too many men were gathered around the entrance and inside the barracks. Some of them blatantly faked conversations about silly subjects.

"What's up?" asked Jones.

"Ignore it," said Carl. "It's one of their political meetings." His impression was confirmed by Gerhardt Läufer's emergence. "Good evening," shouted Carl in German. "We're getting some help for Wieschensohn."

"You could have waited until morning," said Läufer.

"Why wait?" said Carl. It seemed a thousand eyes were straining through the fog to see them.

"Henke, Schoenmann, Budricz! Take some men and assist the sergeant," said Läufer.

"We have it under control," said Carl.

"I insist," said Läufer, already dissolving into the turgid fog behind them.

"I told the bastard," said Carl, "we didn't need his help."

"Pea soup," said Jones. "We might."

"Too many will spook him," said Carl.

"Let's just get him and get out of here."

At C-7, Carl called out. "Ude! Ude Wieschensohn! This is Sergeant Carl Walthers. I must speak with you." He whispered to PFC Jones and Elizabeth to spread out, but keep the other flashlights in sight. That was getting to be a tough thing to do. The fog had congealed into a dense white. Feet scurried just beyond sight. "Ude! Is that you?"

"Ude!" shouted Beth.

Feet now scurried behind them. Carl strained to see. Beth's light had disappeared. "Elizabeth! Stay close!"

"I can see you," her voice answered. Her light reappeared as a spectral glow. She had been behind the corner of one of the huts. Carl felt his way forward. He lowered his beam, then raised it slowly, the silvery sheen of a barracks wall suddenly filling his vision. He'd nearly walked into it. "Ude? We're here to help you. We want to take you out of the camp for a few days."

"Ude!" shouted Beth.

"Oodie!" Jones sounded as if he were calling a dog.

Carl stretched out his arm and leaned against the wall in front of him. Dropping to one knee, he probed the crawlspace with his light.

"Aaaa!" There was a movement in the fog beyond one of the support pillars. A dark blob rolled, bumped against the joist above, and was swallowed by the fog.

"Ude!" shouted Carl. "Wait!" He jumped to his feet and charged through the fog with one hand trailing the side of the building. If he could reach the other side before Ude crawled out . . .

He heard more scurrying. Someone fell with a thud. He heard a German cursing. Then, all at once, there was a scream. It was less a human voice, than the shriek of an animal in a fire. *"Nein! Bitte! Nein—!"* The frantic pleading was clipped off.

"Ude?" Carl strained to see, to hear. More scurrying. He

226

ran toward where he had heard the pleas and all at once, his entire field of vision was filled with light. He lost his footing and hit the ground on his back, a shock of pain exploding from his shoulder like a grenade. For a split second he was back in the street in Oran, his shoulder ripped by a sniper's bullet. Gradually, the agony subsided into mere pain. He rolled to his side holding his elbow and looked for his flashlight. Blood oozed from his smashed nose into his mouth.

"Carl?" shouted Beth. "Carl? I can't see your light."

His flashlight had tumbled under the barracks. "In the alley between eight and nine," he grunted. "I'm hurt."

He listened to the further scuffling of feet around him. Suppose they were after him? Suppose they wanted Beth? He scrambled under the building and turned off his light. "Beth! Get out of the compound!" he shouted. "Get out! Get Pike!"

"Sarge?" shouted Jones. "Sarge!"

A woman screamed. Beth! Carl lurched to get to his feet, but another explosion of pain from his shoulder knocked him flat and nearly unconscious.

When the spasm relaxed, Carl heard the sound of his own labored breathing. His nose was completely stopped. His shoulder had separated. He had no way to fight. He'd gotten Beth into more than he could handle. His stupidity! He ground his teeth in hatred of himself. He was trying to build up the courage to make a painful roll further back under the barracks when the earth crunched near his face. GI boots briefly became visible as two flashlight beams crossed. "Here," he gasped. "Here."

Jones knelt down. "Sarge? What happened?"

Beth was beside him. She patted his chest. "Oh, Carl! You fell! Thank God!"

"Somebody hit me!"

"Did you see him?"

"No." Another pain shot through him. He grimaced until it passed.

"We can't leave you here to get a stretcher," said Jones.

"I'll stay with him."

"No," said Carl. "Walk me out. I can do it. Where are the prisoners?"

"Gone," said Beth.

They shifted him into a sitting position. His legs were wet from a puddle under the edge of the building. He paused to catch his breath before trying to stand.

"Lord have mercy! Did you see who did it?" asked Jones.

"I said no, didn't I?"

"I meant Oodie," said Jones.

"He's dead," said Beth, wiping her nose on her sleeve.

"A GI bayonet's spiked him to the ground," said Jones.

"Oh, great," Carl sighed. "It isn't yours by any chance?"

"Maybe the escaped guy is back."

"Let's get the f-f—phooey out of here."

"On the count of three," said Jones. "One, two, *three!*"

Pain shot through Carl again as he rose, but it was either less severe or he was becoming numb. Beth pointed her flashlight in his face and squeezed his bloody nose with her handkerchief. "Let's go," said Carl. "It's not so bad."

They lurched into the main thoroughfare between the huts and turned towards the gate. He cradled his elbow like a newborn baby, but occasionally moved it wrong and was stopped in his tracks by another shock. The right kind of smooth motion was almost painless, but the ground always dropped or rose and he would be forced to stop. After what seemed an hour, but was probably only ten minutes, he was aware that each side of the path was lined with prisoners. Their faces were obscured by the fog, but as the flashlights played about them, Carl recognized Gerhardt Läufer standing atop a stoop, his arms clasped behind him, as indifferent to their halting march as if watching the waves roll in towards an oceanfront balcony. Some of the Germans seemed to sneer. Many others glanced at their comrades with questions in their eyes. Carl recognized Albert Dorn, smug as the Mona Lisa, and Sgt. Helmut Ansbach beside him. Many of the faces were familiar, but the names were long gone. He had talked to so many yet knew virtually nothing of their secret lives here in the compound.

"Wait," said Carl. He gingerly turned back. "Get that guy to help us."

"Huh?" said Jones.

"I want that guy to help."

Jones aimed with his flashlight. "You!" he said. "Come here."

"Not him," said Carl. "Him. Herder. Jan Herder. *Kommst du. Schnell.*"

The German looked around him. "Why me?" he asked in German.

"Because I said so," said Carl.

Herder scratched at the hairy mole on his upper lip. "Well, if you insist . . ."

"Move it," said Carl.

Within a few more minutes the gate was visible. Elizabeth ran ahead and the guards, nervous from the fog, clicked their rifle chambers before they recognized her. They called for more help.

"I go back now," said Herder.

"The hell you do," said Carl. "Jones, you drag this son of a bitch if you have to, but he stays with us."

18.

"**I** say shake down every inch of the place!" shouted Valdez.

"I can't do that in this fog," repeated Sergeant Pike. "Didn't I tell you two to shut up?" interrupted Morris. "I'm ranking officer. We'll wait."

Valdez nearly tripped as he crossed in front of Carl, who was slumped in a chair, shifting the knot on his sling into a more comfortable spot. "This is our chance to fix this situation, Jack. Tex will be out for hours."

"O'Hurly will bring him around."

"Lang's thirty-weight java could wake the dead," said Pike.

"Well, give some to the dead guy," said Morris grimly, "and ask who killed him." Morris pushed Valdez aside. "Walthers, you didn't hear anything, see anything?"

"I heard running. I saw fog. Then it was all planetarium, nothing but stars."

"No voices?"

"Nothing I could make out."

"Italian? German?"

"Nothing."

Morris looked at Beth and PFC Jones. They shook their heads. "You had no business in there."

"It was important," Beth protested.

"You could have waited."

"It's not her fault," said Carl. "Lay off. I did it because I was confined to barracks. Neither one had anything to do with it."

Pike rocked on the rear legs of his chair. "Could be one of you." The only sound was the board creaking under him. "Nobody knew what the other was doing. You couldn't see each other."

"Hey," said Jones, "I was ordered. All I wanted was to say my prayers and go to sleep."

"Carl could've been killed," said Beth. The fire in her eyes made them even more intense.

"It's just a thought," said Pike.

"And a lousy one," said Morris.

"But don't think it won't occur to the brass they send to straighten out Mad Anthony," said Pike.

"Tex will be lucky to end up peeling potatoes," said Morris.

"And what's wrong with that?" said Valdez. "This place is a SNAFU from the word go and the commanding officer's responsible. Those men out there are criminals, don't you understand? There won't be a Jew or a Pole or a Gypsy left in Europe if we don't stop them. It isn't a question of some loony getting bayoneted, or even the murder of a kid."

"Will you stop it with the atrocity stuff?" said Pike. "What's that got to do with the price of beans?"

Morris raised his hands. "Keep quiet. I don't know what is going on in Europe. It may be nasty but it's not our problem. A kid's dead. Now a prisoner's dead with a U.S. Army pig-sticker in his heart."

"Ude saw something," said Carl. "He would have told me."

"Go on," said Morris.

"He was out of his mind with fear. He was sleeping out-doors, under the buildings. He saw something."

"The tunnel," said Pike.

"There never was a tunnel. It doesn't make sense."

"Then he saw how the pervert escaped. Same thing."

"No, Pike. No."

"Holy mackerel!" said Morris suddenly. "A guard let him out!"

"What?" said Pike.

"If there was no tunnel," said Morris, "and there was no break in the wire, then he walked out through the front door."

"The first two that escaped didn't do that," Pike protested.

Carl stamped the floor in frustration. "Let me talk to Herder!"

Valdez struck the wall with his fist, nearly hitting the fly-paper. "We're wasting time."

"What for, Walthers?" demanded Morris.

"I know he'll tell me what we want to know."

Morris settled into Murnow's chair. "Why?"

"Haven't you fu—fouled up enough?" snorted Pike.

"Just bring him in. He's been cooling on the porch for an hour."

"He's real impressed with us," said Valdez. "He was asleep when I got here. Questioning him is a waste of time."

"Please," Beth said. "Carl knows what he's doing. When you spend all day talking with the prisoners you get to know them."

Her crush on him was visible to everyone in the room.

A trace of a smile flitted across Morris' face, and his anger softened. "'A cushy job,' they said. You'll just keep the shelves stocked. That's all a quartermaster does." He flicked his hand. "Bring him in," he said to Jones. "What have we got to lose?"

Valdez turned his face to the wall. Pike ground his teeth, his jaw muscles writhing like cats in a sack.

"Good evening, gentlemen," said Herder in German. He nervously twisted the cap in his hand.

"Sit," said Carl. "Do you know all these men?"

"Naturally. And the lady, too." He smiled at Beth. She nodded, then looked at Carl for an explanation.

"The last time we met," said Carl, "you said you were a political prisoner."

"No coffee this time?"

"We ran out of the truth serum to drug it."

Herder laughed. The others in the room stared at him, except for Valdez, who kept his back turned.

"My guess is," said Carl, "you'll want to talk today."

"Me?"

"You said red follows you. You were that kind of political prisoner." Carl made a cutting motion across his throat.

"It's possible," said Herder.

"So maybe you're a murderer, maybe you're a Communist. Maybe you're a murdering Communist. Whatever you were in prison for doesn't interest me unless you murdered Wieschensohn or the boy."

Herder checked the face of each person in the room. "So,

this is the game. You will accuse me of the murders and hang me so that you have someone to hang. How very National Socialist of you. Will you make a newsreel of my last breath?"

"Did you murder them?"

Valdez turned to listen more closely.

"You have already decided. Is this one of your Western movies? *The Ox-Bow Incident,* eh?"

Carl eased forward on his seat. "This isn't a lynching. You know what prison is like, eh, Jan? What do you think your friends are discussing right now? What do you think Läufer and Dorn and all those Nazis are thinking?" Herder lost a fraction of his usual insouciance. "Yes, friend, they wonder why I picked you."

"So? I wonder that myself."

"They know you are one of the penal battalion troops. It doesn't matter whether you were a political. Political is better for my purposes, but I saw you and you will suffice. They don't trust you. If we send you back, it won't matter what you say. The *Lagergestapo* will punish you."

"*Lagergestapo!*" snorted Herder. "What is this *Lagergestapo?*" He was trying to bluff, but he had lost his poker face.

Neither of them twitched a muscle. Carl felt lightheaded from the strain of it. It had not occurred to him until this moment that if Herder had been a murderer back in Germany, he might well be used for mopping up trouble. All that had flashed in Carl's confused mind as he had walked out through the fog was that Herder had said something about being a political and, therefore, probably had a reason to talk. Now Carl wasn't sure.

"Tell us what you know and we can protect you. Keep quiet and we shall send you back to the compound."

"I have always taken care of myself," said Herder. "Bastards and orphans learn to do that. And I am both."

Carl played his last trump. "Very well. And we shall let it be known that there was no tunnel."

"Who said there was a tunnel? The Americans. We let you believe it if you liked."

Carl turned to Jones and said in English, "Okay, take the guy back to the compound. Give him some cigarettes and act friendly."

"What did he say?" asked Pike.

Herder once again checked each face. This time he was nervous. Jones approached him. "Come on, buddy," he said.

"Wait," said Herder. "I need time to think."

"Time's up," said Carl.

"You must protect me."

"What are you to us?"

Despite the cold wait on the porch, Herder's upper lip had beaded with sweat. He was calculating desperately. His normal insouciance, however, came back as a grin lifted his entire face. "Ah, well," he said, "I turned in a partner once. These people aren't my partners. I hate them. If I am lucky, they will lose their war. If not, they will hang me. I am," he chuckled, "not the kind of criminal who is in fashion."

"There was no tunnel, was there?"

"Nooo!" Herder explained that the SS officers had become worried that discipline was eroding. The men saw that if they were being fed as they were, it was obvious that America had hardly been vexed by the war. An army, Napoleon said, marches on its stomach. Even with the censoring of newspapers, things got through. The man censoring the Erie paper, for example, left in the obituary of a man lost in action. He did not notice, however, that the man was said to have been lost two weeks earlier, near a Sicilian town which was supposed (according to the officers) to be far behind German lines. It therefore confirmed what they had heard from radio.

Later, when the Italians arrived, there were even more bits of information that indicated the camp Nazis were fabricating things. They said the Italians were not only liars, but might be Americans planted to weaken German fighting spirit. Everything was a vast manipulation to convert Germans to fight for the Allied cause, which was now desperate. All these assertions by the devout Nazis seemed more and more ridiculous to anyone with a clear head.

Another source of abrasion was the attitude of the SS men and regular Afrika Korps men towards the *Strafbataillon*. The penal corps had fought courageously, said Herder, but in a nearly impossible situation the Luftwaffe had strafed them to keep them advancing. This was a source of hilarity for the non-penals and a bitter memory for the penals.

The decision was that a greater discipline was to be enforced. A few men were beaten to remind them of their duty. Ude Wieschensohn was one of them. He wasn't badly hurt but he cracked up from the fear and began living like an animal. There were at least three other beatings, and, of course, an example was no good unless most people knew about it. Nobody had to say, "This man or that man was beaten by the *Lagergestapo*." Everyone knew. When a soldier staggered to roll call or pulled off his shirt to wash and bruises covered most of his torso, everyone knew what had happened.

Carl asked who did the beatings. Herder denied knowing. He suspected SS-sergeant Ansbach and a corporal named Budricz, who had broken a knuckle on the back of someone's head. Carl said he needed more names, but Herder insisted he didn't really know.

"Give us your best guesses, then."

"You've promised to protect me."

"Totally."

Herder shrugged and slowly offered ten names.

"Now," said Carl. "Tell me about Ülsmann."

"He was warned against consorting with you," said Herder. "He was warned against playing jazz. The beating got out of hand."

Carl was devastated. "They killed him because he was friendly with me?"

"Not especially," said Herder. "It was time for another example. In the evenings he'd leave the political discussions to listen to your singing or to the radio. When they warned him, he tried to laugh it off. The Nazis are very serious. Nothing is more dangerous than laughter."

"And they killed him for that?"

"They didn't mean to kill him. But it served their purposes. He was very, shall we say, absent."

Carl remembered how there was some attempt to cover up the escape of Gast and Rolsch, but none for poor Oswald. "I want to know who killed him."

"If I could tell you, I would. He did not deserve to die."

"He did not deserve a beating."

Herder shrugged. "Everyone gets a beating now and then."

"Where is the body?"

"I don't know."

"But it is inside the camp?"

Herder nodded. "How could it be taken out?"

Carl thought. The others, who had listened patiently, occasionally getting the drift of the conversation from a few words whispered by Valdez, leaned towards Carl.

"What'd he say?" asked Pike.

"Oswald was beaten. He died. There was no escape."

"Well, where is he?" asked Morris.

"I'd guess he was buried."

"The shovel!" said Pike.

"So then they killed Wieschensohn," said Valdez.

Carl reverted to German. "What do you know of Ude Wieschensohn's death?"

"Nothing. I would think he saw too much," said Herder.

"So do I. Have you ever seen anyone with a bayonet?"

Herder shook his head. "Things get stolen."

Carl had another thought. "What about Ülsmann's locker? Do you know of anyone taking Ülsmann's things? What about a musician's wing? With aluminum braid?"

"As was found in the boy's pocket?"

"You know about that?"

"Word gets around. Once he had no use for it, someone might steal it. The officers were angry about this. They did not think we should sell our patches and medallions. We would need them when the Waffen-SS liberated the camp. Läufer and Dorn are all waiting for Skorzeny to free them, just as he freed Mussolini."

Carl quickly summarized everything Herder had said.

Valdez exploded. "The Nazis have been allowed to operate freely, right here, while they were our prisoners!"

"What do you want?" said Pike. "We should tether them all to trees? Keep the camp quiet, said Tex."

"Well, it isn't quiet now," said Morris. "How do we know this guy is telling the truth?"

"They'd kill him," said Carl. "I promised him protection."

"Okay," said Morris. "I'll figure something. How's the fog out there?"

Beth cupped her hands and pressed close to the window. "I can see a flashlight on the tower."

"Maybe it's dissipating," said Morris.

"Let's go in and get some answers," said Valdez.

Morris held up his hand. "Private Jones, take this man outside. Give him a cigarette or something." He handed Jones a .45 automatic. "Pop him if he tries anything. And nobody comes near him."

Herder fidgeted at the sight of the pistol.

"Be calm," said Carl in German. "It's protection."

"One never knows," said Herder. "Nazis are everywhere."

"Not in this room," said Carl.

"Never be certain," Herder winked. "You were willing to throw away my life to get your answers. You have the heart of a Hamburg policeman."

Valdez started on his plans to roust the entire camp. Morris told him to shut up. "Gentlemen," he said, as if Beth weren't there, "there's a bigger problem here than which prisoner killed another. If they can keep their mouths shut, we may never find out. Two or three goons maybe did it. And the man who gave the order. Who will talk to us?"

"So we just say to hell with Oswald?" asked Beth.

Morris was flustered, probably because he hadn't expected to hear from the girl, or maybe because he wouldn't have expected her to say "hell." "That's not it," said Morris. "Who killed the boy? If the escaped man never escaped, he didn't play chicken hawk in the ravine." He glanced at Beth, then avoided her eyes.

The silence was colder than the fog.

"It could be somebody in the camp," said Pike finally.

"One of our guys," said Morris.

"Like Carl said," Pike added.

Carl shook his head. "I never said that. It could be one of the 4-Fs in town. I just don't think Oswald was the type."

"What is the type? A civvie with flat feet?" asked Morris, but no one had an answer. They didn't want to think about it.

"Maybe Oswald died the same way," said Beth. "Internal bleeding. A blow to the stomach."

"We'll, ah, have to find the body," said Carl awkwardly.

"Wouldn't there be another motive?" said Pike.

Morris leaned back in his chair. "What do you mean?"

"They killed him over jazz?"

"You're missing the point," said Valdez. "They killed him because he wouldn't go along. That's what's important. Wait'll you find out what's happening in Europe. It'll make you sick."

"Isn't that why you were transferred?" said Morris.

"What do you mean?" said Valdez. "All right. I wasn't taking it well. If half of what we heard was true—More should have been done. That's all I can say."

Pike clicked his tongue. "You can't kill everybody who won't play ball. Most of my men would be long dead."

"Most people do go along," said Morris. "It's human nature. They want to get ahead. You rough up a couple of malcontents and everybody else has an excuse to think they have no choice."

"Is there a point to this?" said Pike. "I want to check on my men."

"Do that," said Morris, "and everybody else get some sleep. We can't do anything until morning. Can you make it to your bunk?"

Carl nodded. "I'll help you," said Beth.

"I'll send somebody to the NCO barracks to escort you home, Miss Way," said Pike.

"Thank you, sergeant," she said.

Carl lurched to his feet. Beth took his good arm and they plunged into the fog, which had thickened again.

They walked in the gray silence, feeling their way along the gravel walkway, absorbed in thought.

"I'll never be able to sleep," he said. "I'm exhausted, but . . ."

"I wish we could go back."

"Back?"

"To the second just before you slipped."

"If the kiss hadn't been so nice, maybe I wouldn't have slipped," he said. "Maybe I was being punished."

"Silly," she said. She took a skip in front of him and blocked his path. "Maybe if you kissed me again, it will all go away."

"My nose is so swollen," he said, "I doubt we could get close enough."

"You still hurt?"

"After the doc popped the shoulder back in, I felt great. Anything would feel great after that—by comparison," he joked.

"Poor baby." She raised herself on tiptoes and kissed him on the forehead. Her lips made a small warm spot above his brow.

"I feel better already."

She grinned and they continued walking. "This terrible stuff won't go away," she mused.

"No," said Carl. The protective shell that had been kept around her was thin and cracking. She was hatching into realities everyone faced eventually, but that didn't make the shock any easier. He was sad for her. And guilty for having drawn her in. The worse thing, he thought, was that there might be no solution to who killed Oswald, let alone who killed the boy. That would be the worst thing for her to have to remember: that justice is rarer than perfect pitch. When that sunk in, you could never be the same.

"I just wish there was some way I could help," she said to the night.

"Stay away from this place," said Carl. "I was wrong to get you the job."

"The prisoners are nice. They cry a lot, you know. Real Italians do that. And they kiss their crosses. They give me little Marys they've carved, and rosary beads they've made out of scraps of wood."

The madonna on Natalie's dresser passed across Carl's mind. What did it mean? Was it merely guilt? If he'd been in the camp instead of chasing Natalie's tail could he have prevented Oswald's death?

"Well, you stay in town tomorrow," he said.

"Why?"

"Because I want you to. You've had enough trouble."

"You can't get me out of this now."

They seemed to have been walking a long time. They took several more steps in silence. "I tell you what," he said. "You check on something for me tomorrow, okay?"

"In town?"

"I can't go. You can call with what you find out."

She pouted.

"I'm not just trying to keep you away. It might be important."

The gravel crunched in front of them. Beth swung up the flashlight. Murnow emerged from the thinning fog. His eyelids were as puffy as a lizard's. "Walthers! You were confined to barracks!"

"Something came up, sir."

Murnow leaned forward, trying to focus on Carl's sling and bruised face. "What'd you do? Fall down?"

19.

He woke feeling as if each German had taken a punch at his body and each Italian a hard kick. He wanted to sleep, to fade into his cot like a ghost backing through a wall, but the sun was up and the habit of reveille had been mechanized into his body's clock. He lay still as possible but couldn't shake the illusion that his nose was pulsating, swelling up to twice its size, then deflating in successive heartbeats. It whistled when he tried to breath. Whoever had hit him must have a fist like a diesel piston. He came to the conclusion that they should check among the prisoners for Max Schmeling.

He hummed a few bars of "Tenderly" to hear how the sound resonated through his nose. Not good. We represent the Lollipop Guild, the Lollipop Guild, and welcome you to Munchkin Land. He could do the voices when MGM filmed the next Oz movie. He gingerly rolled onto his side and sat up. He'd live. His head swam. Ouch! Maybe he'd live. He stared at the sharp bones along the top of his feet and wiggled his toes. That didn't hurt, at least. He adjusted the knot of his sling, which he had slept in, then hefted himself up and padded to the mirror. His nose looked as awful as it felt. Around his eyes was a blue-black domino. Good morning, Sergeant Raccoon!

He hobbled to the infirmary, fortified himself with a trio of APC tablets, and waited for lunch by watching Sergeant Pike's MPs rousting compound C. Within an hour and a half, they had discovered a variety of contraband: three caches of greenbacks totalling seventeen dollars, four homemade knives, two kitchen knives, a homemade truncheon, and a five-pound bag of sugar. On Lieutenant Morris' suggestion Pike's men also looked for blood on sleeves and skinned knuckles. Nothing that looked like a bloodstain turned up and the three cases of skinned knuckles were obviously older than the punch to Carl's face. Since the German officers had access to the compound, they were inspected, too, but their hands were as impeccable as if they'd just been manicured.

It was Private Ronald Branden, a.k.a. "Ron the Con," who located Oswald Ülsmann's grave. Pike didn't like Branden, who had come to serve his country as Dahl had, at a judge's urging: march in boot camp, or march back and forth in a cell. Pike sent him with three other dogfaces to check under the barracks huts and on top of the brick support pylons that held them up. They found one of the kitchen knives under C-3 and a brown envelope with two dollars and some silver. Between C-7 and C-8, they paused for a smoke and Branden noticed the dirt in the alley was yellowish, with more rocks than in the area around it. When the killers had dug beneath C-8, they had dumped excess dirt there. Carl was on his way to noon mess when PFC Burgess hurried by on his way to Murnow's office.

"They found your clarinet guy," he said. "He's been playing with Jelly Roll Morton for a good while. You want a look?"

"Not before lunch." Timmy Firenzi and the police photograph of his father's body were enough stiffs for one lifetime. Gawking at Oswald wouldn't do the clarinettist any good.

O'Hurly joined Carl at the noncoms' table. "You missed breakfast. A superb rendition of shit-on-a-shingle." He held up a gray hunk of meat. "Only to be surpassed by this so-called sirloin."

"Sir Loin was one of the losers at the Kentucky Derby, wasn't he?" Carl returned.

O'Hurly laughed. The old joke was new to him. When his laughter subsided, he leaned close to say. "A lieutenant colonel's on the way. I figure Tex is hitting the trail, podnah."

"We'll just get another jackass," said Carl.

"Maybe they'll put Jack Morris in charge."

"That would make sense," said Carl dryly.

"You're right. It'll never happen."

O'Hurly chewed his meat. "It's tough, but it don't taste too bad, you know. Maybe the flatnose boys are feeling charitable."

"What do you mean?"

"That weasel Reese. When his people bid, suddenly there ain't no other bidders."

"Well, we get fed."

"And they get rich. It's a deal with the devil."

"Somebody's got to get rich," said Carl. "Murnow didn't get on you for last night, did he?"

"Naw." O'Hurly swallowed. "He forgot about you. Too worried about his ass. Consider the confinement order rescinded."

"I hurt so much, I don't care."

They ate in silence for some time. O'Hurly scanned the tables of the enlisted men. His chewing slowed and he placed his full fork down. "After lunch I'm taking a browse through the files," he whispered. "You want to help? Screw the regs. Maybe you'll see something I haven't."

"Has Elizabeth called?"

"No. You expecting her to?"

Carl nodded. "She's looking up somebody."

"Wait in the office with me." He peered back at the enlisted men. "If it's one of ours, I'll de-nut him with a ripsaw."

"A dull one," said Carl.

"The one they used to butcher this cow or horse or whatever the hell," said O'Hurly, prodding the steak.

With everyone distracted by the exhumation of Oswald, O'Hurly and Carl expected no interruptions. O'Hurly started at the back of the alphabet, Carl at the beginning. Carl frequently asked O'Hurly what some of the stranger acronyms referred to and tried to read between the lines. He soon developed a pounding headache. He was trying to spin a suggestive history out of air whenever he was poring over the file of someone he didn't know or didn't like. One of the soldiers had been returned from combat with hints of cowardice. Another had lost his corporal's stripes for spreading nasty rumors about a WAC. A few had flunked out as artillery men, pilots, or airplane mechanics. A couple were simply ne'er-do-wells who had been moved from assignment to assignment in a vain attempt to discover their appropriate niches. Carl eventually said it was pointless, these weren't the right kind of records to find something like that, but

O'Hurly, master of the files, insisted they had to keep plugging. He was certain he could conjure something out of the routine army paperwork. "Take this guy, Purcell," said O'Hurly. "He was reprimanded for 'ungentlemanly behavior' when he was laid up in the base hospital."

"So what does that mean? 'Ungentlemanly' isn't a reg, is it?"

"If it is I'll have to give up farting. Purcell was pinching nurse's asses."

"Is that what 'ungentlemanly behavior' means? Pinching asses?"

"Something like that. But nobody would bitch about it unless it was like, way too much."

"Or the nurse was a colonel's tootsie."

"Well, yeah," said O'Hurly. "What do you expect the file to say? 'Technical Sergeant Amos Foreskin, bunghole artist and bon vivant'? We've got some standards."

Carl's head throbbed. He wanted more APCs.

"Carl?" Elizabeth peered through the screen door.

"You made me jump," said O'Hurly.

"Did you find out anything?" asked Carl, slowly rising to his feet.

She got a good look at his face. "Poor baby!" she said.

"It only hurts when I laugh," said Carl. "What did you find out?"

She was crestfallen. "Really, nothing. Most people said if you wanted to buy souvenirs you should grab the first soldier you see and ask him, so I was about to give up. Then I went for a root beer and Mable mentioned that your friend Ansel Dahl sells a lot of things to a man named Clement Howard."

"Who's he?"

"An oddball."

"Yeah? Yeah?" said Carl eagerly.

"He lives in a big house on Robinson. He was gassed in World War I and he collects war things. His house was creepy. He keeps the blinds drawn and there are cats everywhere. But he showed me medals from the Spanish-American War. Two complete Civil War uniforms. Buttons and all kinds of stuff."

"What about the musician's wings?"

"He said he didn't have any white ones. Just red. He asked

me if I could get him any. He gave me his card and said he'd pay reasonable for any Italian stuff."

She handed Carl the card. It was yellowed but the engraving of his name was almost high enough to be read by the fingertips. "This looks good," said Carl.

"He won't sell anything unless he's got a duplicate and it isn't rare."

"But he might invite little boys in. Kids would go crazy over a collection like that. A kid might steal something, or he might give it to a kid to keep him quiet."

"Hallelujah!" said O'Hurly. "It wasn't somebody from the camp!"

"We'd better call the sheriff," said Carl.

"Wait," said Beth. O'Hurly was already dialing. "Wait!" she repeated.

O'Hurly pressed down on the cradle.

"What is it?" said Carl.

"He lives like Dracula," said Beth, "but he is the kindliest, sweetest little man. Maybe he's addled, you know, but he couldn't hurt a fly. You should see him with those cats."

"I hate cats," said O'Hurly, "and I don't trust people who like them."

"Beth," said Carl gently, "you never met this man before, right? He might have another side."

"Then you come talk to him. You'll see. How did you know Oswald didn't do it? Same way I did. You just knew. Well, this man couldn't do it."

"We can't take a chance," said O'Hurly.

"He's right," said Carl.

Elizabeth assertively took the phone from O'Hurly and replaced it. "He's an old man who collects things and feeds stray cats. That's all you know."

"Sheriff Bowers could find more," said O'Hurly.

"No," she said. "Someone might hurt him. He has coughing fits. He couldn't climb the ravine. You don't know that he ever had the wing. You don't know if he and Timmy ever met."

"She's right," said Carl. "When the word gets out that the German didn't do it, the town may be in a lynching mood."

"Yeah, but to lynch a dogface. Look," said O'Hurly, "it isn't our job. I say we dump it in the sheriff's lap."

"I've got a better idea," said Carl. "First, we'll ask Dahl if he sold him the wing. If he did, that should be enough to bring in the sheriff."

"What would that prove?" Beth protested.

"That Howard lied to you about having one. That maybe he had reason to hide the fact. You see?"

Beth bit her lower lip. "He didn't do it."

"What assignment did Dahl draw today?" Carl asked.

O'Hurly lifted a clipboard off the file cabinet. "His squad was off, but they probably got dragged into the roust."

"Okay. I'll head for the compound."

"I'll go with you," said Beth. Carl turned to say no, but knew there was no stopping her.

"It should be all right," he said. "The place is crawling with guards."

"You get back to me ASAP," O'Hurly called after them.

They arrived at the gate as a hearse pulled through. Carl and Beth lingered to watch it pass the tower and turn out towards the main road. Her eyes filled with tears, which she wiped away with her fingers. It would be impossible not to cherish someone like her. Maybe that's why his father had always worshipped his Mary, and why Musso was so protective of Elizabeth. No matter how obsessive or how much of a callous thug you might be, it was still possible to be touched by the right kind of woman.

"Private," he asked the guard, "have you seen Ansel Dahl?"

"Pike put him on the shovel detail. He should be out in a minute."

Inside the compound, a large group was still gathered about half-way down. A prisoner timidly stuck his head out the front door of his hut to see what was happening. A guard threatened him. On the ground in two rows were six prisoners who had been caught with contraband. "Let's wait under the tower," said Carl.

"Why don't we go in?" She hurried to catch up with him.

"I look like hell and I don't want to give them the satisfaction. I should think you'd had enough of that kennel."

"I'm not afraid," she said.

"I am," said Carl. He ducked under one of the cross bars that braced the tower legs. "He'll have to come out right there."

"Want some gum?" She held up a stick of Teaberry. "I'll share."

"Help yourself," he said, leaning back to sit on the second rung of the ladder.

"My pop won't let me chew at home. He says it makes me look like a cow."

"A cow? That's a laugh!"

She smiled folding the gum into her mouth. Even that offhand compliment, not really intended as one, had been soaked up like water on dry sand. He avoided her eyes. "It probably reminds him of tobacco chewers. Filthy habit."

"My grandpa Fastoli used to do it. He picked it up playing baseball for the Cleveland Americans."

Some soldiers left the compound. Dahl wasn't among them.

"You know," she said, "if you asked me out, I would accept."

Sitting on the rung had become uncomfortable, but he did not move. "I know."

"I haven't seen *This is the Army*, yet. And there's lots of places we could go dancing. There's the Rainbow Room in Erie. And there's the ferry to Canada. That could be a nice evening."

"I've had enough boat rides. And can you imagine me dancing?"

"You could take me to dinner then."

The rung seemed to be cutting his rear in two. "You're fresh for a girl," he said. He rose, faltering as he straightened. She gently took his arm.

"I wouldn't mind being kissed by you again," she said, close enough that he could smell the gum. She touched his cheek. He closed his eyes and exhaled as if being rinsed with warm bath water. When he opened them, all he saw was her violet eyes, drawing him in. Her lips, soft and moist, pressed against his until he let out a soft moan and yielded, tasting the Teaberry on her teeth and gums. His slung arm was caught between them and the back of his hand pressed into her breast as her fingers gripped his ears, pulling their mouths closer, directing the motion from side to side. His free hand hovered, then rested upon the strong curve of her hip, and ferociously pulled her closer as she clamped her thighs on his knee. When she broke for air, she pressed her head against his collar bone and he breathed the scent of her hair.

He was helpless. Her lips were the lotus blossoms that made you forget everything. Everything about her—taste, scent, the texture of her skin—intoxicated.

"No," he said.

"I squeezed you too hard."

He pushed against her hip. "No."

"What is wrong?"

"You shouldn't get mixed up with me. I've got nothing to offer."

"You've got you."

He didn't answer.

"You treat me like a kid. Why can't you treat me like a woman?"

He had no answer.

"Mr. Musso did threaten you, didn't you? A year ago he chased off an older man who had a crush on me."

"He should've," said Carl.

"I don't need protecting," she said loudly.

"I'm bad news. You're not my type," he said as bluntly as he could. It came out hesitantly, though, and his eyes shifted as he tried to appear callous. "Is that enough?"

"Your kiss says different."

"Hey," he said, "a kiss is just a kiss."

"If that's the way you want it." She had taken the stiff-upper-lip approach. He had expected more obvious hurt and he was prepared to deal with that. Her tough attitude, however, disoriented him. "Beth," he said, "you don't know me. The war's created this weird situation. If there were no war, you wouldn't be interested in me, not really. I'm a band singer. I go from town to town."

She crossed her arms.

"You'd end up hating me. Maybe someday I'll want to settle down, but not now. You're an angel, Beth. *I'm not good enough for you!*"

She faced him. Her violet eyes had gone as cold as the lake wind. "Ansel," was all she said.

At first it didn't register. When it did, a great emptiness filled him. How could he explain? Though he wanted her, he knew it wasn't right. If he could make her understand . . . But it was impossible. *He* didn't understand. "Let's get him," was all he managed, but she had already run ahead.

Dahl's fatigues were greased with clay. Chunks dropped from his trouser legs as he walked. "How ya doin', baby?" he said cheerfully.

"I've been waiting for you," said Beth.

"And me in my tux!"

Carl caught up. "We've got a question or two."

"Oh, darn, and I thought it was my lucky day. I'll meet you later. I gotta get this stink off of me."

"It won't wait," said Beth.

"Tony Birdsong and Ray Adams got sick. Tony twice."

"It was Oswald?" asked Carl.

"What was left, I think." He scratched the ground with his foot. "The Germans said so. You think it was somebody else?"

"No," said Carl. He remembered that when he was looking for Oswald, a German had said maybe he was "making fertilizer." They'd known already.

"The doc said he didn't go easy."

"What do you mean?" said Beth.

"I mean they used things to beat him. You name it. Rocks, boots," he made a kicking motion. "The doc figures the shovel was used on his head. They gave him a lotta pain, but he didn't feel it too long. After that it was just fungo flies, hitting him for practice. He was dead a long time before they stopped."

Beth shuddered.

"I didn't mean to—"

"I'm okay," she said.

"It was nasty," said Dahl. "I gotta go wash."

"We need to know some things, Ansel," said Carl.

"Did you buy a musician's wing from Oswald?" Beth asked.

"The shoulder thing? Like a patch?"

"Yes," said Carl.

Dahl's eyes tightened. "Like the one they found in the boy's pocket?"

"Exactly," said Carl.

"I might've. I bought a lot of stuff. I sold a lot of stuff," he leaned forward to whisper. "And if you accuse me of dealing in it, I'll deny everything."

"I don't care about that," said Carl. "Did you sell it to Clement Howard?"

"Who?"

"Ansel!" Beth said, as if dealing with a lying schoolboy.

"I know the man."

"So you took it to his house," stated Carl.

"I've never been to his house. At his furniture store."

Carl turned to Beth. "He sells used furniture on Main," she said. "Over a clothing store."

"Then he'd be in-between Timmy's Boy Scout meeting and the music store."

"Yes, but he's hardly ever there," she explained.

"That doesn't mean he wasn't there on the day—"

Dahl spread his brown palms. "Wait a minute. You trying to pin this on old man Howard? Nah!"

"Why not?"

"Oswald sold me one wing. How do you know that that's the one in Timmy's pocket?"

"Because Oswald put his initials on things. He scratched OU on the bell of his clarinet. He inked OU on the backside of his wing. I checked the one in the sheriff's office. It was initialed."

"Oh." Dahl thought a minute. "But he had two wings, right? He only wanted me to have the one. The other, he said, he wanted to keep."

"And he did," said Carl. "It was in his locker after his death. Has anybody tried to sell you that one?"

"No," said Dahl.

"You're telling us the truth?"

"I couldn't lie in front of a lady."

Carl shoved him. "Don't fool around with me."

"Whaddya want? I'm not lying."

"Then tell us what happened to the wing," demanded Beth.

"I don't want to say."

Beth and Carl glanced at each other.

"Are you nuts?" said Carl. "This could tell us who killed the boy."

"He didn't do it."

"Who, dammit?" Carl roared.

"I couldn't get away that day. I was supposed to meet the old man."

"Yeah?"

"So I knew Sergeant Lang was going to town."

"You gave it to Sergeant Lang?" Carl's heart skipped five beats. The chief cook. An American. A colored soldier. My God, they'd need a regiment to protect him. Carl leaped at Dahl, momentarily forgetting his arm was in a sling as he grabbed his collar. "You knew this and you didn't tell anyone?"

Dahl shoved Carl back, leaving a hand print on his shirt. "How did I know it was the same wing?"

"Jesus, Ansel, when the boy was found—"

"When the boy was found," said Dahl, "everybody knew the Heiney had done it. Get off my back! You think I enjoy digging up a rotten body? Leave me alone."

"Oh, no," said Carl. "You're coming with me. Now!"

"The hell I am."

"Stop it," Beth shouted. "Stop." She touched Dahl's shoulder. "Please."

He looked at her and turned sheep. "Lang's a big man," he finally said. "We could end up in tomorrow's soup."

20.

They found Lang in a folding chair behind the kitchens, smoking a cigar, staring at the ravine through spectacles hazed with grease and steam. Despite the coolness of the day he was in his undershirt, his massive chest almost bursting it. He hummed a tune Carl didn't recognize and didn't notice the three of them right away. He squinted up at Carl's stern face. "What is this, the coffee that bad this mornin'?" He noticed Beth. "How you doing, little girl? Them Italians have developed a mighty liking for you. They got nothing to say about you that isn't nice."

"Thank you," said Beth awkwardly.

"Believe them. They're good cooks. Good cooks don't flatter without good reason, no ma'am."

"We gotta know about the wing, Ralph," said Dahl.

"What you been doin', private? Rasslin' hogs?" Lang took several puffs on his cigar and blew a long stream of smoke from his nostrils, like a fire-breathing bull. As he stood, his dog tags jingled. "Wing?"

"The musician's wing," said Carl. "Ansel gave you a musician's wing to sell. It was the half-moon thing with silvery-colored braid."

"Oh, that."

"It was the one found in Timmy Firenzi's pocket."

"I thought it might be."

"You *thought?*"

Lang looked down into Carl's face and then at Dahl. "You sent me to town to sell those things and get you a pint."

"Yeah."

"I come back with the pint, didn't I? I didn't come back with no wing, did I?"

"Did you sell it to Clement Howard?" asked Beth.

"You know something," said Lang slowly, "when that kraut turns up dead this mornin', I had this little thought. 'Ralph,' says the thought, 'if they haven't got the kraut to hang for this, they'll just hunt up the nearest nigger.' But you know what? I said, 'Naw, that's all wrong. Mrs. Roosevelt she cares about how Negroes are treated. Things are changing. This is about as far north of Dothan as you can get in America and still be in America. Everything's jake.' Now here you come. You white boys disappoint me. You always tell us you're smarter than us."

"We're not accusing anybody," said Carl. "But you know what happened to that musician's wing. Whoever killed Timmy probably gave him that wing. Was it you?"

The fire in Lang's eyes was enough to burn his glasses clean. "You shut your mouth, or I'll shut it for you. You say something like that and niggers get strung up. How do you think the riot in Detroit started this June? I didn't join up to spend the war sneezing flour and dipping lard. I'm remembering the Massachusetts Fifty-fourth. I'm remembering the Three sixty-nine infantry, first to the Rhine in double-yoo one. But us niggers *still* ain't good enough to fight, are we? So we cook. We drive trucks. And mostly we get blamed. Don't matter for what. I ain't getting blamed for messing with that boy and if you hint around that me—or any of my squad—had anything to do with it, I'll get every last one of you. You, too, girlie."

"Hey, lay off of her!" said Dahl.

"We aren't here to lynch anybody," said Carl. "We just want to trace the wing."

"You heard what I said. It won't tell you nothing."

"Sergeant," said Carl, "how can you know that?"

"So now it's 'sergeant.'"

"Ralph," begged Dahl. "Don't get sore."

"Like I ain't got a reason?"

"The murder of a child?" asked Carl.

"The thing I sold ain't got nothing to do with it, I tell you. I had my suspicion at first. But it ain't the healthiest thing to go around turning in white folks. Anyhow, everybody said the kraut done it."

"But you knew different."

"Knew no such thing. I jes' keep my ears open at the mess. I didn't hear nobody say they thought the kraut didn't do it."

"Never mind that. We need to know what happened to the wing."

"Private Dahl gives me the things—"

"Three badges, an arm band, a regimental patch." Dahl was reconstructing the inventory.

"I go down the alley to the furniture store. He ain't in. I'm going to Robinson Street when some old cracker asks me where I'm going. Maybe the guy's curious, but maybe he wouldn't pester a white soldier, so I go back to Main. I'm real polite. I ask people if they'd like to buy some war souvenirs. I tell 'em they're from a Foreign Legion fellow who lost his leg."

"A good story helps the sale," said Dahl approvingly.

"Well, I sold the whole bunch."

"Who bought the wing?"

"Same guy who bought everything else. When I heard about the wing I thought about telling, but then I figure there's more than one of those in the German army. And then—"

"Yeah, Oswald got the blame."

"A day or so later, I got to run up to town to get Mr. Reese to do something about the sorry-ass potatoes he gave us. I'm kind of going back and forth, but I wander up to the sheriff's department. I didn't know where Private Dahl got the thing, you know. Anyhow I go in the sheriff's office and there's a woman there. I don't know whether she's a clerk or what. She says, 'What do you want, nigger?' So I lay it on and says, 'Why, missus, I was wonderin' if the sheriff man was busy, sho' 'nuff.' 'Can't you see those people are suffering?' she says. And I look in the sheriff's back room and I recognize the mother and her brother. That kind of throws me. 'Whatever your problem is, you'll have to come back.' Sho' nuff, says I, and I let it go."

"But, Ralph, when you heard this morning it wasn't Oswald—" said Beth.

"I was thinking on it. But a man in my position's got to be careful, don't he? I never seen any of you folks making social calls around this kitchen. When did you ever say anything to me other than 'Where's the catsup?' You come here thinking I done it, didn't you?"

They said nothing for a moment. "It occurred to us," said Carl.

"It might've 'occurred' to me, too. But it 'occurred' to you faster. Big buck nigger kills white boy."

"That's not fair!" said Carl.

Lang laughed loudly, his deep voice echoing in the ravine. "Naw, it ain't! But that's the way it is." He chomped hard on his cigar. "Now if you folks don't mind, I got to make sure those krauts ain't slipping red pepper in the stew."

"Wait," said Carl placing a hand on Lang's massive forearm. "You've got to tell us who you sold the wing to."

"Forget it."

"Who was he?" said Carl. "I'll have Pike on you. As far as we know—"

"Don't threaten me."

Carl dropped his hand. "The creep might have killed the boy."

Lang took off his spectacles and wiped them with the hem of his undershirt. His dog tags rattled. He leaned close. "It's white folks' business, understand? I ain't said nothing. You might go talk to the boy's uncle."

"The uncle? Louis Bassett?"

"I seen him in the sheriff's office. He couldn't've done it, now, could he? And if he did, nobody in this town's going to believe me." Lang hooked his spectacles back on his ears. They weren't any cleaner though the cooking splatters had been rubbed into concentric circles. "Good day, missy," he said, tipping his head to Beth. He plucked up his chair and went inside.

Carl let out a long, slow whistle.

"You believe him?" asked Dahl.

"Let me think." Pictures of Mrs. Firenzi and her brother had appeared in almost every edition of the local papers. Bassett wrote letters calling for justice. Even Fox Movietone had filmed the little round man for a newsreel. Lang was right to be cautious, but not only because it could blow up in Lang's face. The town might close ranks to defend Bassett, if it didn't get him killed. He was the kid's uncle, for Christ's sake! He must have passed the wing along. Lang had. Hell, Timmy could have taken it. There were a dozen simple explanations, not to mention the second missing wing, which could confuse things. Carl looked at Dahl and Beth, waiting eagerly, too eagerly. The three of them had hurried too quickly down a primrose path. They'd come out in a large, empty field. The musician's wing could lead anywhere or nowhere. They had been too eager to believe it was *the* clue. "I'm no cop," said Carl, giving up.

"We've got to call the sheriff," said Beth.

"What Lang knows probably doesn't mean anything," said Dahl. "But we've got to keep him out of it," said Carl.

"But why?" asked Beth.

"Because you can't get far enough north of Dothan. Because twenty-eight people were killed in the Detroit riot."

"This isn't Detroit," said Beth.

"How many Negroes in Erie might get beaten by suddenly courageous 4-Fs? Or in Cleveland? Or Pittsburgh? We've got to sit on this until we're sure."

"Why would people blame Ralph?" asked Beth.

"Because he's convenient."

Carl put his hand on Dahl's shoulder. "Can you keep your trap shut?"

Dahl nodded, then added, "S'pose Ralph did it?"

They were silent for several seconds, not daring to look at each other.

"Yeah, sure," said Dahl. "Mum's the word. Why not?"

"Get yourself cleaned up," said Carl. "And meet us at Murnow's. We'll get the sheriff."

Dahl flicked his thumb at the kitchen door as if hitchhiking. "Just tell me this, you think he's covering for one of his boys?"

"No. He can't trust the law."

"Hey, who can? You think my mom's DAR? But we're trusting him."

"So keep your lips zipped until the sheriff gets here."

Beth and Carl rushed along the gravel pathway to Murnow's office. O'Hurly was out and, oddly, the door was locked. Beth volunteered to go to the compound gate to find O'Hurly and Carl let her. She was treating him as if she barely knew him. Maybe he shouldn't have pushed her away. Maybe she could have changed him. A black airflow Chrysler was moving slowly towards Murnow's office. As Carl climbed down the porch steps one at a time, the car swung to Carl's right, then pulled sideways to the porch. A big man was driving, the thug who had questioned him in the Cleveland station. Reese popped open the back door. "Well," he said, "we were looking for you. Get in."

"I'm waiting for—"

"Get in," repeated Reese. He pulled a large revolver from his coat pocket and slid back against the opposite door. "We're taking a trip."

Carl glanced up at the tower and down towards the compound. No one was paying attention. "What's up?"

"Mr. Musso will explain."

"I can't leave without a pass."

Reese cocked the pistol.

The camp was full of armed soldiers, but a bullet would be faster than they would. He climbed onto the enormous back seat and pulled the door closed.

"What happened to you?" asked Reese. He plucked at the edge of the sling with his index finger.

"I lost a fight."

"Not your day, is it?" He lowered the hammer of the revolver slowly. "What're you waiting for, Charley?" The driver shifted gears and the Chrysler began to rumble towards the outer sentry box. "Make it good," Reese warned. He tucked the gun under his coat.

Carl didn't recognize the sentry. "Sergeant?" the private asked.

"We're giving him a lift," said Reese.

"See you later," the private offered.

"You bet," said Carl uncertainly.

The car headed for North East. "Can I say something?" said Carl.

"Relax," said Reese.

"They could shoot me for desertion," said Carl. "There's a war on."

"Mr. Musso wants to see you."

"They'll put out a search for me."

"Good for them."

"They'll know I left with you."

"Just giving you a ride is all I'll say. Charley and me dropped you off."

He said nothing for another mile. They entered town and turned left on Main. Carl noticed Mable sweeping the sidewalk in front of the drug store. The two priests who seemed to have been cemented to their bench in the park were still there. But the Andy Hardy cleanness of the town now seemed fraudulent. There were rocks here, too, and there were sorrows and cruelties and maybe degenerate uncles under them. "Is Musso in town?" Carl finally ventured.

"In the town he's always in."

It took a moment to sink in. "Cleveland? You're taking me to Cleveland?"

"Don't get excited. He just wants to talk to you."

"Oh, yeah, that's why you brought a gun."

"I like to make sure Mr. Musso gets what he wants. It makes all of our lives easier. That's the point in our brief sojourn on the planet, don't you think?"

"Making Musso happy?"

"Making our lives easier." Reese shook his head at Carl's stupidity.

"Listen," said Carl, sniffing to try to clear his nose, "Beth Way and I have a lead on who killed Timmy Firenzi."

"The kraut?"

"It wasn't a prisoner. I don't know what you know—"

"I know plenty. Ripped him up. Turns my stomach."

"Do you know about the wing?" The gangsters were silent as Carl explained, carefully leaving out Ralph Lang. Reese looked Carl in the face, his eyes widening.

"You think his own uncle—?"

"I was waiting for the sheriff. Maybe you call Musso and I come down to Cleveland tomorrow."

"He's tired of waiting for you. You mean the music teacher?"

"Maybe. He had the wing."

"I always heard jokes about funny uncles, but that was with girls. It's how a lotta dames get started." Reese patted Charley on the shoulder. "Pull over."

"Huh?" said the driver.

"I said pull over."

They slowed onto the gravel by a cemetery with an ornate iron fence. "Ernie said to hurry up," said Charley. "He's gonna be working the broad in a couple of hours."

The broad? thought Carl. Natalie?

Thoughtfully, Reese tapped the side of his nose with his index finger. "Let's go talk to the guy."

"What guy?"

"Louis Bassett."

"Why?"

"Don't you know? It was a kid. A Firenzi."

"I don't know no Firenzis," said Charley.

"We gotta show people we stand up for our own. Just because I set up business here don't mean I'm a real member of the community, but I don't wanna live where somebody gets away with something like that. I got kids, too."

"We'll do it tomorrow."

"We gotta show people we can take care of things. Turn around."

The big man turned and raised his hands. "But Ernie—"

"Have you got kids, Charley?" said Reese.

The driver's hands slowly dropped and his eyes narrowed. He shifted gears and they slipped back into town. When they cruised slowly by the front of the music store, the old man with hair like Toscanini was locking the front door. Reese prodded Carl with the pistol. "Ask him."

Carl rolled down the window. "Excuse me. You know where Lou Bassett is."

"Lou? He's sweeping out the back. Want me to get him?"

Carl looked at Reese, whose slight shake of his head told him what to say. "Nah, we'll see him later."

The old man bent down to look into the car, but before he could say, "No trouble!" they moved on. "Go on down to the alley," Reese said. "There's gotta be a back door."

"What are you going to do?" asked Carl.

"Have tea and crumpets," said Reese.

"You don't know for sure—"

"Shut up," said the driver.

The alley was empty except for a skinny mutt tearing with

both paws at an overturned trash can. "There!" said Reese. The little round man had just finished sweeping and was going back inside. The Chrysler rolled up to the open door. Reese checked the alley, as did Charley, and stepped out. Bassett turned, wiped his hands on his apron, and leaned out the back door.

"Can I help you gentlemen? The store's closed for the day." His voice was not what Carl expected. It was nasal, but lower. Carl had expected something more like Wimpy or Oliver Hardy. The driver walked around the front of the car, his eyes locked on Bassett's. "Gentlemen?" said Bassett, a quaver in his voice. Charley was now almost chin to forehead with him. He spread the tip of his fingers on Bassett's chest and shoved him backward.

"Get in there!" said Reese to Carl, poking the heavy revolver against the inside of his coat.

The spartan back room in which Bassett gave his lessons was done up like a parlor. A misshapen easy chair and sofa sat opposite an upright piano with sheet music scattered on it around a jar of hard candy. Next to the sofa, on the plain wooden floor, a dozen tin soldiers stood in a sheet metal service station with a sign that said Marx. Carl uneasily sidled into the corner. Reese kicked the door shut with his foot. Charley had backed Bassett against the piano, which whumped tonelessly as his hands and rump hit the keys. Reese stared at him for several seconds, then picked up a blue, wind-up airplane next to the service station.

"You like toys, Mr. Bassett?" asked Reese.

"They're here for the kids," he said, glancing up at Charley. "For the music lessons."

"I had a violin teacher. She never had no toys."

"I want the children to be comfortable." He tried to smile, but his scarred lip shook uncontrollably. "They'll like music better."

"Real noble of ya," said Charley.

"Listen, there's nothing to steal here," said Bassett. "We barely—"

Reese took his hand out of his gun pocket and grabbed the tail wings of the airplane. Coldly, he twisted them back and forth until the metal ripped and crushed. In a frenzy, he tore the plane in two, the raw metal cutting into his hand. Blood dripped from his fingers. Reese flung the scraps into the corner, barely missing Carl. Bassett's face was like a cartoon of the man in the moon, white, bug-eyed, glistening. Reese walked slowly towards him.

"You know why we're here."

Bassett froze, gaping in horror. Carl lowered his eyes. He wanted to be angry at the man, but instead was only sick.

"N-No," said Bassett.

"NO?! Whatta ya mean, no? No you don't know why we're here. Or no you didn't mess with the boy?"

"I didn't hurt Timmy!"

"Who said anything about Timmy?" said Reese. Charley grabbed Bassett by the collar and slapped him four, five, six times, until his face was a pink tapestry of finger marks. Bassett hunched over, trying to cover his face, whimpering like a tortured puppy.

"I don't hurt the children—I love them," Basset whined.

Charley exploded his fist into Bassett's stomach. The man collapsed onto the piano stool gasping for air, a long string of drool hanging from his mouth.

Reese tried to grab him by the hair, but there wasn't enough and his bloody hand slipped, leaving a red stain. "You know we know. How many besides Timmy? How many?"

"I don't hurt them. You can't say I hurt them. They like me. We're friends."

"And what about Timmy? Your own damned nephew!"

"Please!"

Carl's mouth was dry. He should run out the door and get the sheriff. But he was paralyzed by the memory of touching Timmy's hand in the leaves, of the tiny body that had seemed so heavy when he carried it out of the ravine.

"Hold him down," said Reese.

Charley fell on Bassett's back and clamped him to the piano bench with his arms. "I didn't hurt him!" said Bassett struggling.

Reese slowly circled the bench as Charley's bear hug seemed to squeeze the air and fight out of Bassett. The piano teacher's eyes pleaded with Carl, then closed. He stopped struggling and panted, sweat dripping from his face. "Please!" he whined.

Reese stepped behind him, reached around and unbuckled Bassett's pants.

"What are you doing?" demanded Carl.

"Getting even," said Reese, exposing the buttocks. He caressed the doughy flesh with his bloody palms. Bassett struggled like a pinned insect, then went limp.

Reese, grinning, picked up the broom from where it leaned against the wall.

"Jesus!" said Carl. "Don't!" Even Charley looked up with an astonished expression, though he did not relax his grip.

Reese lowered the broom end to within a few inches of Bassett's face. The piano teacher's eyes crossed as he looked at it. "Is this about right? Or is yours smaller? Okay, so it's a little thin. But the length will do the trick, don't you think?"

Carl stepped toward Charley, whose eyes blinked wildly for a moment, but then assumed the heavy-lidded expression of a bored factory worker.

Reese smiled at Carl. "So, you wanna do the honors?"

"We can't do that."

"Oh no?" Reese shook his head and Carl felt strangely humiliated. Reese slowly circled the piano stool and lowered the end of the broom. "Whatta ya think? Slow? Slow is better, don'tcha think?"

For an eternal second, everything was part of a motionless tableau. Then Reese barely touched the inside of Bassett's thigh.

"NO!" screamed Bassett. "NO! I DIDN'T MEAN TO HURT HIM! I DIDN'T! IT NEVER HAPPENED BEFORE. HE JUST GRABBED HIS STOMACH AND—"

"*Before?!*" Reese poked the broom at Bassett's quivering ass. His knees buckled but Charley held him tight.

"Nothing happened to them. Nothing . . ." Bassett broke down, blubbering.

"Who?" demanded Reese, his eyes like hot coals.

"That's enough," said Carl weakly. "We don't need to know."

Reese glanced at Carl, then abruptly swung the broom back like a baseball bat and broke it across Bassett's rear.

The broken end bounced up and landed on the piano keys, bringing down the cover with a loud thump. The resonance of the piano strings slowly faded.

Carl held onto the sofa back to keep from falling. Charley let the piano teacher go. Bassett slid off the bench and collapsed into a heap, vainly trying to cover his nakedness with his hands. There was a strong smell of urine and Charley checked his trousers as he stepped back from Bassett's puddle.

Reese bent over and held the broken end of the broom in his face, the end sharp enough to do surgery. "See that? It's broke. But I could still use it." Bassett whimpered. "Or I could get a new one, eh? It seems to me the only thing to save you is talk to Sheriff Bowers, eh? You got an hour. Are you listening to me?" Bassett nodded. "The word's goin' out. I'll see to it. Bowers is the only way to go, or Charley and I'll be back."

He patted Bassett on the cheek. "You take care, eh, Louis? I'll see you in the papers." Reese stood and examined the cut on his hand. "Let's get outta here," he said.

Carl was shaking and there was no air coming through his open nose so he gulped at the fetid air of the lesson room. He could not bring his feet to move until Charley bumped him while picking up the tin soldiers.

"Ya won't need these," he said. "I got a coupla boys that would like them, if ya don't mind."

Bassett rolled into an even tighter ball of fear.

21.

Carl was in a trance as they passed through town and into the open country. Every few miles a big barn appeared on each side of the road, but mostly there were vineyards or the dirt rows where vegetables had grown all summer. If they were lying about Cleveland, were taking him for "a ride," dumping him in a field would be logical. Especially a harvested one. It might be months before he was found. But Reese settled back as if expecting a long trip. The car was moving along at a cautious speed, as if the three of them were sightseeing. They passed a sign, "ERIE, 15 MILES," then a billboard for the Shorewood Hotel.

"This isn't a good time in my life to go AWOL," Carl said numbly. "I'm already in trouble."

"You should have saved your fighting for the enemy."

"Guess so," said Carl. "It isn't my forte." He was tired of the white lie he had used to explain his nose. There'd been no purpose in it in the first place.

"Need guts," Charley said. "You looked like you was gonna shit yourself. I can't picture you duking it out with somebody."

"I just wanted him caught. What you were doing—"

"Brought out the truth didn't it? He'll get fried now and everything's even."

"Is it?" mused Carl. "You enjoyed that, Reese."

Reese shrugged. "Call it righteous indignation."

Maybe the world was divided into devils who could enjoy things like that and angels who were incapable of it. What did that make Carl? He was certainly no angel. Maybe there were devils and angels and the bones they fought over. Nazis and Mafiosi and child molesters pitted against children and saints, with most people somewhere in the middle. Oswald had gotten in the crossfire. Maybe Carl, too. "Aren't you going to let me know what this is about?"

"Just relax. Ain't no broom waiting for you at the end of this ride."

"At the *end!*" Charley laughed uproariously. Reese giggled and patted the seat.

"A good one! A good one!" said Reese. "What's the matter, no sense of humor?'

"If anything happens to me, the sentry can ID both of you. So can Bassett."

"Alibis are cheaper than toenails. What've you done to Mr. Musso to be nervous for?"

"Nothing. Who says I did something to him? What've I done that you should kidnap me with a cannon?"

"Kidnap's a harsh word. I'm just following orders, being a good soldier. You ought to understand that. Maybe if you did, you'd get along better."

Carl searched his mind for some explanation as they entered a small town called Wesleyville just outside of Erie. They dawdled behind a horsedrawn hay wagon and Reese told him to lock his door. What did Reese think? He could snap open the door with his sore arm, and make a run for it before Reese could pull the trigger? Carl hadn't done anything but go along with Musso from the beginning. What could he be in trouble for? He hadn't found anything out about Natalie and Georgy Mack, but that wasn't his fault. Maybe this whole fandance was to scare him into doing more. That made some sense. It was clear they knew how to scare someone, but good.

Maybe Musso thought Carl was fooling with Elizabeth? Someone had blabbed about his kissing her. Who knew that? He'd kissed her in the ravine when they found the boy. Musso couldn't know about under the tower. Unless Beth herself told him. The woman scorned? Not her. She was hurt maybe, but too gentle for revenge. By the time they reached Erie and were passing between the factories humming with war production, Carl was convinced this was all just Reese being over-dramatic. Carl was guilty of nothing, even if this treatment made him feel guilty. There was no reason to worry. It was something dumb.

He repeated this over and over to himself as they passed through the town of Fairview, then Girard, and drew closer to the Ohio border. But his mouth was as dry as crushed Saltines. The only stop they made was at a Flying A station across the Ohio border. Carl's stomach was growling and his shoulder beginning to act up. He shifted as the attendant cleaned the front windshield, provoking Reese to say, "Take it easy," out of the corner of his mouth.

"Get the big guy to buy me some aspirin."

"What for?"

"Because I need some. APC tablets would be better."

"You'll be all right."

Charley paid, pulling a wad of gas rationing coupons out of his pocket that could only have been counterfeited or stolen. In a movie, this would be the moment in which the hero jumps the bad guy and wrenches the revolver out of his hand in the nick of time to plug the driver. But single-handed wasn't supposed to mean one-handed. And why? Nothing was wrong. Reese was over-reacting. He had to be.

The Chrysler moved steadily, monotonously, towards the lowering sun. They passed through other small towns. Ashtabula. Geneva. Painesville. Mentor. Reese said nothing. He offered Carl a stick of Black Jack gum, appropriately enough, but otherwise simply watched the scenery. Carl closed his eyes several times and pretended to sleep. The motion of the car, however, nauseated him. That was odd. The ship across the Atlantic had never made him sick. Neither the train rides nor the bus rides when he travelled with Buzz Bixby had bothered him. The cod and tea on the British ship and the greasy spoon dining on the singing trips weren't exactly bromides for the stomach, either. It was the Bassett thing. He had to stop thinking about it. He smoked his next-to-last Philip Morris, then saved his last. He'd smoke it later. There would definitely be a later time in which to smoke it. For sure.

As they neared the outskirts of Cleveland, the sun was directly in front of them, as if it were going to settle in the road. Charley took it full in the face, but was totally unperturbed, even when an Army truck burst out of the light and startled Reese by blowing its horn. The big guy would drive into a brick wall without noticing, Carl thought. It was very hard to picture him with children who liked tin soldiers.

They had just passed Euclid, Ohio, when the driver pulled off the road into a small gravel area. "It'll be dark before we get there," said Reese. "Damn!"

"What do you want me to do about it?" said Charley. "No drawing attention he said."

"I know." Reese poked Carl's shin with his foot. "Get out."

"Is this where you 'rub me out'?" He tried to say it like a joke.

"I figure you need a piss. I know I do. Motor's been squeezing my kidneys for the last fifty. Get out."

Charley peered in all directions. There were no vehicles on the road. A small light came on in a house far down towards the lake. He eased himself up beside a tree, fumbled and waited patiently. "Hurry up," said Reese, shifting from foot to foot.

"Don't bug me." There was a pattering sound as Charley's shoulders sagged in relaxation.

"Hurry up," muttered Reese under his breath. The driver shook himself and strolled back. Reese scurried to the same tree and frantically undid his fly.

"What about you?" said the driver.

"Over there?" asked Carl, pointing to a different tree.

Charley shrugged.

Carl stood for a long time, his penis in his hand, unable to relax. Reese cussed. The wind had changed and he had hit his own leg and shoe. He came back towards the car shaking his foot like W. C. Fields with a molasses pie stuck to his shoe. Carl waited for one of them to come up behind him and put the gun against the back of his head.

"Hurry up," said Reese. "You gotta piss, piss!" Charley cleared his throat and spat. Carl tried to concentrate on the image of running water, but the distant light winked.

"What the hell's keeping you?" Reese barked.

"It's tough with one hand."

"Well, don't expect me to help," Reese said.

Charley guffawed.

Carl spun behind the tree and charged into the brush. The ground dropped and he stumbled. He managed to keep his feet, crashing through the dying weeds.

"Hey!" roared Charley.

"Son of a bitch," yelled Reese.

Carl zigged, then zagged. You never hear the shot that gets you, he thought, and tried to run bent to the height of the weeds.

"Come back here!" said Reese. "Musso will be pissed off!"

The ground dropped further and became mucky. His shoes filled with water and slopped as he ran. He could hear Charley thundering through the dry weeds.

"To the left," shouted Reese. Carl changed direction again. The ground was rising. He heard them splashing. He could put more distance between them. He could reach the little house. He glanced back. They couldn't be in shape. They—

He tumbled into space. The weeds disappeared, the ground dissolved, and he had rolled into a ball, his knees blocking the sky. The earth rematerialized into an enormous fist and thudded into the small of his back, flattening him like a wad of bread dough. There was less a sensation of pain, than of head-to-toe numbness. Gotta get up, gotta run, he told himself, but it was only an abstraction. It was one of those awful childhood dreams in which the boogie man is coming with dripping claws and your legs won't move. I am paralyzed, he thought matter-of-factly. This is what it feels like to be dead. He had just noticed the first star of twilight directly above him, when the faces of Reese and Charley blocked it.

"Stupid prick!" said Reese. "What are you trying to do? I oughtta—"

Carl's eyes rolled, but he didn't pass out. Charley grabbed him by both arms and jerked him upright. Carl's shoulder drove a knife into the middle of his spine and he cried out. The pain tingled in his fingers and toes.

"Don't hurt the prick," said Reese. "Stupid bastard. My shoes are ruined!"

"What'd you do that for?" the driver said. Carl looked up at him, but his face was shadowed by his hat. They dragged him like a rag doll up over the log that tripped him. It wasn't a very big log, he noticed. It shouldn't have decked him like that.

The coldness of the water in the ditch put the feeling back in his feet, though he still staggered. When they reached the top of the incline, they leaned him against the tree and listened for approaching vehicles. Nothing but frogs. Reese yanked him by his sling towards the rear of the Chrysler. Carl weakly groped for the door handle, but Reese jerked him past it.

"Open the trunk," he ordered.

"Huh?" grunted Charley.

"The trunk!"

"He could suffocate in there."

"It's what? Twenty miles? Son of a bitch ruined my shoes!"

The trunk was hot and dark as a womb. A loose wrench bounced against his shins, and the smell of oil was as thick as syrup. He put his head on something scratchy and heavy as a horse blanket, and he tried to make out the other contents of the trunk. All he found was the jack and a screwdriver. Phillips, from the feel of the point. Later, a box of tire patches with the coarse lid for roughing up the inner tube bounced against his face. He had hoped to feel a lug wrench. That would part Reese's hair very nicely.

On the other hand, whatever was going on, Musso didn't want Carl killed. They'd had plenty of chances for that. If Carl suffocated, Musso would make them pay for that. If monoxide was leaking into the compartment, he wondered, how long did he have? Thirty minutes? An hour? He had once heard a rumor that wartime gasoline was dirtier than it had been before the war. Maybe it would kill you faster. But he didn't smell exhaust, so he assumed the compartment was tight. Too tight? An airflow Chrysler trunk held how much breathable air? Airflow! To suffocate in an airflow Chrysler would sum up his entire life.

He had another idea. Wasn't there some way to open the trunk from the inside? He felt screw heads and a lump that must have been the lock. He tried to picture it by using his fingertips. He used the screwdriver and could get nothing to turn. He pried and poked. He lost his place again and again. When they turned, he slid. When they stopped, he banged against the trunk wall. When they accelerated the box of tire patches appeared out of nowhere to slap him in the face.

When they stopped, he listened for the sounds of people on the street. He heard a trolley, the grinding of gears, and distant laughing. It would be dark by now. Lights would be dimmed. Few people would be out in midweek night, even in downtown Cleveland. It wasn't worth taking a chance kicking and yelling unless he was reasonably sure someone would hear, so he concentrated on fiddling the lock.

The brakes creaked to a stop and the engine quietened. He quickly hid the screwdriver in his sling.

Cold air rushed in. Carl squinted. Reese and Charley had stood back when they popped the trunk, anticipating any move with the jack handle or other weapon. Dim light revealed Reese holding his gun.

"Don't try nothing," said Charley.

Carl struggled to sit up. "Who, me? The Carolina Crooner? I'm just here to please."

Charley yanked him out. His legs wobbled like a marionette's but he stayed upright. They were in an alley. The buildings looked industrial, but old, as if built to make sabers for Sheridan's cavalry.

"Take him in," said Reese.

Charley shoved Carl towards a heavy door with large bolt heads and iron strapping. He rapped. Carl listened to the big man's breathing for several seconds, then a speakeasy slit opened at eye height.

"Got 'im," said the driver.

The door opened and yellow light poured out. "About damn time," said the man inside. "What the hell you do to him?"

"He tried to run away," said Reese, coming up behind them.

"You didn't have to break his arm."

"That was before we got him."

Carl recognized the man who opened the door. It was Musso's older bodyguard. They led him under a single, dim light bulb past a sink and towards a stage curtain. They were in Swing Land, Carl realized. He had drunk out of that rusty sink. Natalie had kissed him on the ear right where the body-guard pushed him past the dusty curtain ropes. A push broom leaning against an electrical box made him shudder.

Three incandescent lights formed a row of circles on the stage floor. Midstage, Natalie was tied to a chair in the center of one circle. Her legs were splayed unnaturally and her head lolled forward. Her blouse had been torn off and circular burns glistened on her shoulders and above the lacy edging of her brassiere. She was pale, paler than Timmy Firenzi when Carl had carried him out of the ravine.

"What took you so damn long?" barked Musso.

"We done a good deed," said Reese. "You'll be real pleased."

"What'd you do, save a kitten in a tree?" Musso chortled. He was a shadowy hulk a step out of the light. His hat covered his eyes but his fat jowls glistened. In one hand, he rested a bottle of Chianti on his massive thigh. In the other, he held a cane. Pluto, thought Carl, Lord of Hades, fat on the eating of souls.

"You pig!" he grimly muttered.

"*Buona sera,* Mr. Carlson. This place bring back memories?"

"Why did you kill her?"

The bodyguard covered Carl's face with his hand and shoved him back. Carl lurched, lost his balance, and fell on his rear.

"Don't hurt him," said Musso. "Not yet."

Carl sat up, but did not try to stand. He glanced back at Reese, who was handing the big revolver to the driver.

"What is this?" said Carl. "She wouldn't tell me anything."

"A tough broad," said Musso. "She's took a lot more than most men could." He *hmmphed.* "Took a lot more than I could. A lousy business. Lousy."

"But she talked?"

Musso took a swig from the bottle and wiped his mouth on his sleeve. "Suppose she did. That would fry your ass, wouldn't it?"

"I don't know what she accused me of, but it's a lie. I don't know anything about the Greek's disappearance. Honest."

Carl rose to his knees. "You've got to believe me. I did everything you said."

"You ain't bad!" growled Musso. His malignant chuckle vibrated from the catwalks and faded into the auditorium. The tables and chairs were all covered with sheets, a strange audience of misshapen ghosts. "You could've been an actor."

"Honest to God, Mr. Musso, I don't—"

Something slapped him on the side of his head. When he looked down at the floorboards, there was a white shoe. It was clean and new and was woven of reeds, like a Panama hat. He glared in the direction of the hood who had thrown it.

"That's yours, ain't it?" said Musso. "Very nice. Very stylish."

"What are you talking about?" said Carl.

"Put it on," said Musso.

"What?"

The hood slapped him on the back of the head. "You heard him!"

He glanced over his shoulder at Reese and Charley. Reese had a smile like he had when tormenting Bassett. Charley calmly picked his teeth.

Carl picked up the shoe. With his good hand he unlaced his GI shoe and slid it off. He fumbled with the white shoe, then forced his toe in. It took some wiggling with his index finger to jam his heel into it. "There," he said. "Is this some kind of torture? It's at least a size too small."

The hood turned to Musso's shadow with some confusion. Musso made a gesture with his cane. The hood knelt and squeezed the toe of the shoe.

"You got these in a wing-tip?" asked Carl.

"Shaddup." The hood raised his hand. "They don't fit!"

"Why should they?" said Carl.

"I told you—!" The hood backhanded him. The slap echoed across the hooded tables. Carl tasted blood from his reopened nose.

"Get the pants," said Musso. "She goofed on the shoes, that's all."

The bodyguard moved behind the curtain and returned with a pair of white linen trousers. He flung them in Carl's face. A small bloodstain from his face marked the cloth. "Put'em on."

Carl tugged the pants off his neck. "Sure." He pointed at his slung arm. "But it'll be a little—"

"Help him," barked Musso.

Hands knocked Carl back and clawed at his belt. They yanked down his pants like college boys humiliating a freshman. The memory of Bassett on the piano bench broke him into a cold sweat, but they jammed his legs into the expensive trousers and pulled them over his hips. Someone buttoned the waist. They were tight, but they seemed to fit. The goons then jerked Carl to his feet. He stood with a slight list with only one shoe on. The pants strained at his waist, then suddenly, as if from the fat man in the *Smilin' Jack* comic strip, the waist button popped off in a high arc. The pants slowly sank around his ankles in a heap.

The tough guys were astonished by this and looked to their boss. Musso stood, ruminating. He limped toward Natalie and lifted her head with his cane. When it dropped back, she faced directly into the light above. It rolled limply to one side and settled there. Her gold cross glittered in a short swing across her cleavage. "Okay, so the cunt got your sizes wrong, what does that prove?"

"What are you talking about?" begged Carl. "These are Georgy Mack's clothes." Air tickled the hairs on the insides of his thighs. He looked stupid: swollen nose, bloody lip. The sling. The mud stains from the ditch. He dropped his eyes to the heap around his ankle. No way. These weren't Georgy Mack's. He was a much larger man than Carl. He was only a few inches taller, but he had a chest like an oil drum and fists like sandbags. Natalie might have mistaken these for Carl's size, but would never have bought them for Georgy Mack. Whoever bought them had spent a bundle, too, and now look at them.

It was at that very moment the meaning of Natalie's madonna became clear. He now understood. Not all of it. Not the whys or the hows, but definitely the whos.

"What?" demanded Musso.

"Huh?" said Carl.

"You were gonna say something."

The memory of the quivering Bassett silenced him. "Nothing."

Musso shook with anger. "I can read it all over your face."

"I'm not your guy, Ernie," pleaded Carl. "These clothes were in Natalie's closet. I saw them. But I never had anything to do with them. She's running with somebody else."

"So you didn't go shopping with her," growled Musso. "She just got the numbers wrong." He smiled. "She was that kind of dame. She always got the numbers wrong."

The hoods laughed with him.

The laughter angered Carl. He had been ready to tell them what the madonna had told him, but he had seen too much. Natalie was dead and he was as good as dead. Going along with madmen was no less dangerous than defying them. Oswald had cooperated with the enemies of the "jungle music" that gave him pleasure. They put him in their bands and he thought he would not be tainted by their evil. But four thousand miles away in a land in which he should have been safe, the brutal secret masters of the compound beat him into hamburger, simply to make a point. And Carl, well, these guys were just another Gestapo. He'd gotten tangled crawling on his belly to ingratiate himself to another nest of spiders.

Natalie hadn't talked. Carl wouldn't talk. They'd find out soon enough. The piece of information he now knew wouldn't buy his life in any case. He wanted to die with a thin sliver of dignity. He wanted to die without anyone owning him. Like Oswald. Like Natalie. Maybe even like his father. It might be all the meaning he could squeeze from his life.

"Now if you'll tell us where the money is," said Musso. "The night will go much easier."

"Money? What money?"

"It's going to be that way, is it?"

"Ernie, you've got to believe me. I don't know about any money."

"It's real simple. Time was running out. We were going to have to pay Sal all over again. Then Precious tells me about the shoe size and I go bingo! Natalie's one bad bitch. She gets Georgy to whack the Greek, then she falls for you, or maybe just uses you to whack Georgy. Just try and tell me that ain't so."

"It isn't." The madonna, Carl urged himself, tell him about the madonna. Maybe there's a chance you could live!

Something wouldn't let him. Musso waddled back to his seat in the shadows. He took another swig of the Chianti and set the bottle on the floor. He reached into his vest pocket and took out a cigar. The hood scurried over and struck a wooden match on his fingernail. Musso puffed until the coal grew to the size of a red hot pinball.

"I don't know about any money, Mr. Musso. Honest to God! I don't know!" The echo coming back over the covered tables startled him. The ghosts were swaying, he thought.

Musso handed the cigar to his bodyguard. A considerate employer: Let the hired help have the fun. "Precious told us about you two. Like a couple of rabbits. But no Georgy Mack. No sign of Georgy Mack. He's a jealous man. You didn't flush him out. At least not for us."

"You set me up as a decoy."

Musso shrugged. The hood puffed to keep the cigar hot. "But then the clothes. Precious tells us that Natalie's talking about honeymoon cruises. She's not naming names, so we figured she meant Georgy. That's what you wanted us to think. That's why she played this charade of pretending that she's converting to the Church. You both had figured that Precious was on my payroll."

"How would I know about Precious? I only saw her two times in my life."

"If Precious hadn't accidentally mentioned the shoe sizes, we still wouldn't know. Georgy used to brag about his size tens. Big feet, big prick, he used to say."

"But the shoes don't fit me," said Carl.

"She guessed wrong." Musso sat silent for several seconds, as if in deep contemplation.

"Now, boss?" asked the hood. Cold nausea rose in Carl's throat.

"Ya know," said Musso, "you're not such a bad kid. Ya got led around by your *cogliones*. She gets Georgy to snatch Michael and open the vaults. Then you and Natalie bump him and get ready to scoot with the two hundred grand. The things we do for love. You're not the one I blame, but I gotta job to do here."

"Keep saying it and it still won't be true."

"Wake her up," said Musso.

The hood crossed to Natalie and drew hard on his cigar. "The face?"

"Someplace tender," he said.

"She's alive?" Carl moved forward, but Charley clamped his upper arm. He slipped on the trousers around his ankles and tumbled to the stage floor, looking up in time to see Musso's bodyguard hike her skirt over her knees. The hood then pressed the cigar tip hard into the soft flesh inside her thighs. "*NOOOOO!*" Carl bellowed.

For a moment there was only a curl of smoke as the stocking burned, then her entire body snapped as if in an electric chair. Her scream drowned out Carl and annihilated all sound. Her head convulsed from side to side and her chair nearly fell. When the hood straightened, she heaved up a slimy yellowish liquid that oozed down her throat and breastbone.

"You gonna talk, honey," said the hood. He slapped her. "Huh? Huh?"

"Fuck you," she panted.

"You see?" said Musso. "Tough bitch." His voice held amazed admiration. He took another belt of his wine. His sweaty face glistened. "But I figure she wouldn't want anything to happen to her pretty boy."

Natalie's head bobbed as she tried to focus.

"Turn the head so she can see better," said Musso. "Get the Carolina Crooner a chair. He's gonna sing for us and we want her to get a good view."

Natalie shook her head but was too drained to speak. The chair clattered behind Carl and the Charley hefted him to its seat. The bodyguard approached with the rope, his eyes glowing as hot as the cigar.

"Mr. Musso," ventured Reese.

"What now?"

"I'd like to get my train if you don't mind."

Musso chortled. "You're looking a little green."

"It's—I got an early appointment. The Navy's coming to inspect the cannery and—"

Charley looped curtain ropes over Carl's chest. "It'd be easier to talk," he whispered matter-of-factly. He tied Carl's free arm behind him, but merely bound the other against his chest. The screwdriver Carl had taken from the Chrysler's trunk pressed against his ribs. He'd never had a chance to use it, and likely never would.

"I don't know anything," said Carl. "Make him understand."

"Then why'd you run?"

Carl looked down at his bare, white legs. There was plenty of room for burning, once they got tired of his face.

"Go on," Musso said to Reese. "You don't wanna miss the last train, do ya?" He held out an envelope for him.

"Thank you, Mr. Musso. Thank you." He scurried behind the curtain.

"I don't trust that guy," said the bodyguard.

"Don't worry about him," said Musso. "He's bringing in more than the numbers."

"He's got a thing about hurting women," said Charley.

"He's a real gentleman," muttered Carl.

Musso studied Carl for several seconds. "I'll give you a minute, Carl, and then the games must begin."

Carl thought about what he knew. Viscerally, he didn't want to give Musso a fucking thing. He didn't know what was going on with the money, but he did know what the Virgin had said. At least he thought he did. Could he trade it for his life? He might. But it would mean Natalie's life for sure. This was what "going along" meant. It was something like the difference between *Übermenschen* and ordinary men. Ordinary men went along. "Supermen" did not. That's where the Nazis were wrong. Most of them reveled in being part of the gang. When the gang did something, they approved. When the Führer warned against jazz and Mendelssohn and expressionist painters, they fell over themselves agreeing and thinking their acquiescence meant they were supermen, too. But you couldn't be above the crowd by joining a crowd. When one hand washes the other, it becomes its slave.

The clatter of Reese closing the door broke off his thought.

"I'll tell you what you want to know," said Carl.

Musso leaned his great body into the edge of the light. "I knew you'd come to your senses."

"But first I want you to let her go."

Musso shifted around and adjusted his doughnut cushion. "Boy, I don't think the situation is clear to you. You think this is some Bulldog Drummond thing where you can ask for something like that? Negotiate? Stall for the cops? This is the real thing. Ain't no cops on the way. It's just business. Sally Mack wants his money. He wants the head of who whacked his brother. You and her. And my bosses want their money back, so's they can turn it over to Sally. This is a serious situation. There's gotta be blood. Now you can be begging me to die, or bang you can die. But either way you gotta die."

Quod erat demonstrandum. Musso made his case like my father, thought Carl. Point by point. You always wanted to please him, but you couldn't, could you? He was as determined not to approve of you as you were to get his approval. "I don't know a fucking thing," said Carl.

Musso nodded. The hood moved forward, gleefully smiling. He hovered the glowing cigar over Carl's eyes. Carl stretched back until he could feel all the tendons straining in his neck, but he couldn't close his eyes at the glowing flame. Quickly the hood pressed it into his thigh. There was a sizzle and Carl screamed, almost choking on the force of his own voice. The hood stepped back and put the cigar in his mouth. It had nearly gone out. The rank smell of singed hair filled Carl's gasping, until he tasted his own burned flesh.

Musso waited patiently until Carl regained some of his composure. Natalie watched him wide-eyed, struggling to keep her head upright. When their eyes met, he tried to look calm. She might tell the bastard, Carl thought, but he'd never. Name, rank, serial number—that's all. Her head dropped as if in shame, though probably from exhaustion. She might not be able to speak. "So, are we gaining any sense, Mr. Carlson?" said Musso. When Musso failed to deliver the missing two hundred thousand to his bosses, he was one dead whale, Carl thought. That was consolation. "Fuck yourself," said Carl. "I'll meet you in hell."

The bodyguard puffed the cigar to reheat it. Musso was distracted by the curtain billowing.

"Prick didn't close the door," said Charley. "I'll get it."

"It's cold out there," said Musso, taking another drink.

"Don't want Carl here to get pneumonia," said the bodyguard, his yellow teeth shining.

"Give him a matching one," Musso said flatly.

The hood bent over, teased the cigar around Carl's face like a magician about to palm a silver dollar.

"What the—?!" The driver's voice was cut off by the rapid burp of a machine gun. The bodyguard dropped the cigar and fumbled for his shoulder holster as the stage curtain danced from the bullets ripping through. A bulge appeared in it and the hood leveled his pistol. Charley ballooned the curtain back, then dropped dead through it.

Musso slipped in the puddle made where his Chianti had crashed to the floor. He balanced Colt automatics that he had drawn from each armpit. "Who's there?"

The question echoed. Musso sidled to his right even farther from the pool of light. Carl felt heat in his crotch. The cigar had landed on the chair seat directly in front of his genitals. He twitched the chair to knock it off.

"Cut it out," said the bodyguard, crouching and watching for any movement under the curtain.

"Who's there?" repeated Musso. "Have we got a quarrel? Are you with Sally Mack? Everything's about to be settled." He was easing deeper upstage, while Carl's torturer crept toward the end of the curtain.

The cigar rolled left half an inch, then right. It singed the hem of his boxer shorts. He shifted the chair again and the cigar rolled across and into his thigh. He jumped up with a grunt, lifting the chair. The cigar hopped into the linen pants around his ankles as the chair came down hard on the stage.

The bodyguard whipped his gun at Carl. "I thought I—"

The machine gun rattled again. The hood tumbled back, colliding with Carl, and crashing them both to the floor. The curtain danced as Musso fired from the dark at the back of the stage. The machine gun was now silent. Carl opened his eyes. The bodyguard lay across him, arms spread, his gaping mouth whistling, but his eyes blank. Carl wiggled, his shoulder throbbing. The chair had blown all its joints when they had fallen. He kicked at the cigar until it popped off the linen trousers and rolled upstage.

"Hey, fat boy!" shouted a voice.

Musso fired again. Carl squirmed and got out from under the crook. The machine gun had sliced open his torturer's midsection. Carl struggled out of the ropes and yanked the linen trousers off his feet. The screwdriver clattered to the floor. Still lying on his side, he plucked it up and strained to see under the curtain.

"'Zat you Georgy?" snarled Musso.

There was no answer. Carl looked around for the bodyguard's pistol. Nowhere. It must have been flung off the stage. He then looked back at Natalie and knew she was too far and he was too messed up to do anything for her. He decided to make for the edge. If he slithered down onto the dance floor, he could take his chances among the tables, maybe they wouldn't even know he was there. He tucked the screwdriver into his sling and pulled himself along with his good arm, smearing the tough guy's blood across the floor.

"Come get me, fatso!" yelled the voice.

"You're the one who come after me, ain't you?" Musso growled. "So try it." Musso's eyes shifted from side to side, the guns floating in front of him. He lowered himself and waddled behind the curtain. The machine gun pinged shots off scaffolding and pitted the back wall. The silence when it finished was as palpable as the iron taste in Carl's mouth, as the cloud of dust rolling downstage from the pocked wall.

"Dumb fucker," said the voice. The curtain was flung back and Michael Papanoumou, "the Greek," stepped onto the stage, his Thompson smoking. Except for a small track of blood creasing his left cheekbone, he was as elegant as if he had stepped off the pages of *Vanity Fair*.

Carl raised his hand slowly. He was sticky with his torturer's blood. "You hit?" asked the Greek.

He shook his head. The Greek quickly checked out the rest of the room and strode to Natalie. She had raised her head and was smiling.

"I knew ya'd come," she gasped. He knelt and she rested her head on his shoulder.

"We're gonna be together now, baby. By Wednesday we'll be in Vera Cruz, in a month in Buenos Aires. We're home free."

"Ya told me ya'd protect me."

"I'm sorry, baby. I thought we had another couple days. Musso panicked. But we got it now. They won't find these guys until tomorrow. By then—" He kissed her on the forehead. He worked the ropes loose and she flung her arms around his neck, trying to sob, but not having enough tears for it.

"I took care of Precious," he said. "That's how I found you. All we got to do is take care of the crooner."

Natalie was confused, but the Greek stood and aimed his Tommy at Carl. "Hey, I'm sorry. It's nothing personal."

"It never is," said Carl.

"You look like you seen a ghost, buddy."

"I knew you were alive."

The Greek winced. "Don't lie to me."

"I knew. Natalie didn't convert to Catholic, she converted to Greek Orthodox. Precious didn't know the difference or didn't tell Musso right. You say madonna to a Roman Catholic and he doesn't picture an icon."

The thought of how that little detail could have destroyed his plan plainly shocked the Greek. He put on a brave face. "The day my mother died she made me promise to go back to my roots, to marry Orthodox. I'd been dating Musso's niece Gina Fastoli and mama was afraid I'd marry her." He considered it for a moment. "Well, Musso didn't figure it out and it didn't do you a lot of good, did it?"

"That's me. The ten o'clock scholar. Those weren't Georgy's men who grabbed you, killed Harriet, and beat Natalie. They were your men. It was Georgy's balls mailed to Musso, not yours."

"I hope Musso gave them a nice funeral. They're all that's left of Mr. Macchianti, the son of a bitch."

"Don't you care," Carl asked Natalie, "that they killed your friend? Don't you care about the beating?"

"It was my idea," she said.

"The whole thing?"

"Just the beating," said Papanoumou. "Would you take that kind of beating for a couple hundred grand? You might want to, but could you? This is a hell of a woman. Harriet recognized one of the guys. We really wanted her as a witness."

"Couldn't help it," said Natalie.

"Big stakes," said the Greek. "A life on easy street."

"The money?"

"Buy at the sound of drums. You know that old saying? War is the mother lode. But our boys had a little territorial dispute with Sally's. Government contracts. This camp of yours, all the camps and forts, they need a lot of wood, coal, groceries, you name it. Only it's a lot easier to skim money off the government than the numbers racket."

"You're stealing from the war effort. Guys could die from what you do."

"It wasn't my arrangement. You think I liked these creeps? They'd have me running errands until I got caught in the crossfire."

"You had Musso under your thumb."

"For a while. But Musso's just the third cup on the tentacle. I was the fourth. There were a helluva lot more near the octopus's mouth and, brother, it's a big damned octopus. It was time to take the woman I love and get out."

"I don't understand," said Carl. "Why wouldn't Musso just tear into Natalie right away?"

"They were waiting for Georgy. Just an ordinary case of eye for an eye. Plus they knew I'd had Sal's share on me the night I was grabbed. They figured Georgy would bolt if they grabbed her. Georgy's never been the sentimental type. Sal was ready to start shooting, but the big bosses gave the Cleveland guys thirty days to prove Georgy had heisted the money."

"I still would have expected Musso to go after Natalie."

"And he'd have had to answer to the bosses who told him to wait for Georgy to show. I know these people. They think they're smart. They're not. The only goof was my timing was a little off," said the Greek.

"You were just in the nick, here," said Natalie.

"Can you walk?" he asked her. She nodded. "The good life's just beginning, baby. Go on out to the car? I'll put Carl here out of his misery."

So this is it, Carl thought. He was astonished at his own calmness.

"No," said Natalie.

"Nat, we gotta. No loose ends. He knows too much."

"He won't talk. He could've told Musso about the icon. He didn't."

"Nat, how do we know he didn't just say that? What proof have we got he knew anything before I walked in here."

"I knew," said Carl.

"It was too damn late to do you any good, now wasn't it? Or you'd have used it. You'd sell your mother to be a big star. You said that yourself."

"I know he would," Natalie said sadly.

Carl raised himself to his feet. "Thanks."

"Besides which," said the Greek calmly, "he fucked you, Nat. I can't let a guy get away with that."

"You told me it was the right thing. It confused them."

"I know." He shrugged. "What can I say? I can't leave somebody around who's had you. It's not manly."

"You've got a lot of guys to kill, then," said Carl.

Natalie could barely spit out the words. "Get it over with!"

"I love you, too," said Carl.

The Greek raised the barrel to Carl's head. "Don't move," he said. "It'll be quicker."

Natalie shrieked and grasped the Greek's arm. Musso was lurching through an opening in the curtain, his feet shuffling, his hands limp. Blood dribbled from the bullet holes in his belly and pattered to the floor. One of his Colts hung from his fat trigger finger like a grotesque ring.

He shuffled forward until the light was centered on him. He looked at the Greek, then his eyes rolled back and he dropped.

"The Mummy," chuckled Papanoumou.

Carl fumbled in his sling for the screwdriver. As the Greek turned, he leaped forward and drove it under his arm. Natalie clawed at Carl, but the shaft went in to the handle. The Greek spun towards him. The Tommy's magazine clipped Carl in the face and knocked him backwards. He flopped over the body of his torturer as the Thompson fired. With blank eyes, his free hand clutching for the screwdriver, the

Greek was jolted by the blazing gun into a grotesque pirou-ette, firing into the ghostly tables, raking the stage, obliterat-ing lights, and striking sparks off the catwalks.

The firing ceased. When Carl raised his head, the Greek had crumpled to the floor. Natalie lay beside him, wounds in her neck and hands.

Carl crawled up beside her. Her chin had been smashed by a bullet. He touched the neck she had smothered him against. There was no passion in it any more. When he stood he slipped in the Greek's and Natalie's mingled blood. They would never get to Buenos Aires but they were together at last.

"How romantic," he said. He listened to the unearthly si-lence of the covered tables and chairs, then snatched up his pants as shell casings skittered away from his feet.

Part III
Per Una Selva Oscura

During the break, as Carl carried his plate from item to item on the buffet, he heard several of the bride's friends at a table behind him.

"Did you try these mushrooms, man? They're great!"

"You ate almost the whole bowl."

"Munchie attack!"

"No, man, they're just great!"

"Hey, man! Hey! Maybe they're magic mushrooms! Wouldn't that be cool?" The table erupted in laughter, a sustained, knee-slapping giggling that few people paid any attention to any more. He passed the ice sculpture—carved into a dove carrying a peace sign—skipped the baked beans, spaetzle, and au gratin potatoes, and joined the bottleneck at the steamship round.

"Flashy tux," said a bald man.

"Thank you," said Carl. He reminded himself to take off the red lamé jacket while eating. "I try to keep up with the times."

"You're really doing an excellent job," bubbled a woman with a bouffant hairdo. "Do you take requests?"

"Everything but 'shut up and quit singing.'"

The man laughed an explosive "ha!" The woman narrowed her eyes, then grinned as the joke finally registered. She leaned forward unsteadily and put her hand on Carl's arm. She seemed to be sniffing at the Hai Karate after-shave he had splashed in his armpits. "Could you sing, 'The Moon Hits Your Eyes'?"

"'The Moon Hits Your Eyes'!" said the man. "That's not the name of it. The Dean Martin thing."

"'That's Amore,'" said Carl.

"Huh?"

"'That's Amore.' The name of the song." He bowed his head. "It would be my pleasure, beautiful lady."

She wiggled her head and made a cooing sound.

"Did you ever notice," Carl asked the husband, "how champagne brings out the roses in a lady's cheeks?"

"Uh, yes," said the man uncertainly. He pointed with his salad plate. "It's your turn."

"Oh!" said Carl. "Give me the burnt end," he told the carver. "I can't do rare." He butted the heel of his silverware to the cummerbund that brightly emphasized his round gut. "Gives me indigestion."

"Yes, sir."

Carl escaped before the woman invited him to sit with her. He'd ended up married after less auspicious beginnings. In the last few years the nastiness of marriage was no longer considered stylish, and he was glad for it, though people were just as foolish. Not wanting to say they liked rutting, they tended to use fad philosophies or ancient Oriental religions as an excuse to screw their brains out with whoever was convenient. McDonald's sex: hot and fast and located on every corner. On one of those corners somewhere from Tucumcari to Katmandu was Debbie, his daughter from his first lousy marriage, now seventeen—no, eighteen—and "looking for America" with two geeks who called themselves "Free" and "Siva-child." He knew this only because his ex-wife, Lane, had written him a letter blaming him for it. He hadn't seen her or Debbie since 1967, when he'd sung in a resort hotel in the Poconos. Ain't it funny how time slips away.

Situating the heaped plate on one of the speaker towers, Carl licked mayonnaise from the potato salad off his thumb and carefully hung his jacket over an extra music stand. He picked up his "fake book" and flipped to "That's Amore" to check himself on the words. He knew he knew them. Checking was just a habit. You could forget the newer songs in midverse no matter how many times you had sung them. Or checked them, for that matter. But the old ones—Cole Porter, Johnny Mercer, George and Ira—the memory ink they were written in was indelible. He stuffed a fat strawberry in his mouth and spontaneously raised his hand as he conducted his mind through the song. He wanted that same lilt Dean Martin got on *Ah, che bella!* That was all the magic of that tune, as far as he was concerned.

The guitarist, Jimmy Payne, pulled up a chair while Carl's fingers hovered. In his mid-thirties, Jimmy spent most of his time selling American Motors cars, though some months he earned more playing weddings and anniversary dinners. He was thinking about switching to Volkswagens, but thought they were a passing fad. "I got a couple of requests," said Payne. He pulled one of their business cards from his pocket. "The Walter Carl Trio" it said in green lettering, *"with the song stylings of Walter Carl."* Sprightly quarter notes danced around the name and phone number. Jimmy turned it over. "'Lucy from the Sky with Diamonds.' That's a quote, by the way: *from.* 'Big, Bad Leroy Brown,' 'Ebb Tide,' and—" he squinted to read the last. "Oh! 'Lovers and Other Strangers.'"

"Again?" asked Carl.

"It's a wedding. Tipped me twenty."

"Okay, as many times as they want. Does 'Ebb Tide' seem like a wedding song to you?"

"Better than 'Breaking Up is Hard to Do' at the last one."

"How about 'Please Release Me' at the one last winter?"

"I still think the bride had a bun in the oven."

"She had a big one outside the oven for sure. Did we get tips on the Beatles stuff?"

"Five each." Jimmy pointed at a white-haired couple. The woman had bound her forehead with a bandanna like Cochise's. The great chief, however, wouldn't have had a paisley headband. The rest of her was covered with blue bell-bottoms and a drover shirt that revealed every lax sinew of her sagging boobs. The man wore a lime-colored Nehru jacket, love beads, and a wreath of papier maché flowers on his head. Most of the petals had broken off and the wire base was beginning to look more like a crown of thorns.

"There's a hep cat if I ever saw one," he said dryly. "Nobody acts their age any more."

"Did you see when he was dancing with the bride? He put his hand on her butt."

"Nice work if you can get it. At least nobody has asked for 'Okie from Muskogee.'"

"The night is young," said Jimmy.

"Somewhere there's music," said Carl. "How high the moon?" He popped a cocktail wiener in his mouth.

"Mr. Carl?" The father of the bride gingerly leaned around the high-top of the drum set.

"Yes, sir?"

"I want to apologize for the shenanigans."

"They're just having a good time," said Carl. He used a napkin to wipe some of the sweat trickling from his muttonchops.

"They slip out to their van and smoke, if you know what I mean. My brother thinks I ought to throw them out."

"It would just make a scene."

"You're a good sport. The world is nuts today."

"The generation gap, you know. Hey, it's your daughter's wedding," said Carl. "Enjoy!"

The man nodded, bowing almost like an oriental, and backed away.

The guitarist watched him leave, then leaned close to Carl. "He does know we get paid the other half tonight?"

"Sure, sure."

"We ought to get it all up front." He glanced back at the hippies. "Trouble with those VW vans is that ten of the suckers will share one. If you could sell one to each . . . ."

Carl took a forkful of macaroni. "You know, Jimmy, if we played for divorces, we could double our income. Growth industry."

"I'll hire us for mine. If I don't kill her first. Ever hear of some jerk-off named Alan Watts? She reads him to me at night. I'm trying to watch 'Ironside' and she's reading me that stuff at the top of her lungs."

"Where's Leon?" said Carl, looking for the drummer. "We've got to get back to work."

"Let's start with 'Lucy' and get that over with."

"It'll keep. The world is nuts," said Carl. "It's always been nuts. I'm going to the bar. You tune up and stuff."

He put on his red lamé jacket, shot his cuffs, straightened his bow tie, then plunged into the crowd attacking the bar. The father of the bride was going to pay for this open bar with his entire estate when he got the bill.

A young white man with an afro, obviously stoned out of his gourd, pulled at Carl's sleeve. "Say, you're goood! You're better than Frank Sinatra." Beer sloshed out of the pitcher he was holding.

"Thanks," said Carl dancing back. He raised his hand trying to get the bartender's attention.

"No, I mean it. You're better than Vic Damone. Than Robert Goulet."

"Thanks." Whatta card! thought Carl.

The kid flashed a peace sign. "Than Jack Jones. I mean it, brother. Love!"

"Love," said Carl. The kid wandered off. At the rate he was sloshing, he wouldn't get two ounces of beer to his table. "Rum and Coke," he shouted. "Light on the rum!"

They started with 'Proud Mary,' which always got people up and dancing. The rest of the guests leaned close and tried to talk, or went back for seconds or thirds. In the back of the room the photographer took pictures of the bride, groom, and the rest of the wedding party. One of the hippies climbed up to dance on his table and no one seemed to mind. It was a wedding reception like a thousand others and as long as Carl wasn't too bad, they'd walk away thinking what a good time they'd had without ever thinking of the band again. He did several of the requests and for the first time noticed a woman in a pageboy hairdo and black glasses closely watching the trio from the edge of the dance floor. Usually this meant the set was about to be interrupted so that the cake could be cut or the bride could fling her bouquet, but the woman did not attempt to get Carl's attention. He smiled in her direction and moved into "Ebb Tide."

Two songs later, she was dancing with a tall man who neither looked in her eyes nor held her close. Her dark hair was streaked with gray and her plain blue suit contrasted with some of the flashy outfits other women were wearing. When the tall man turned her so that she faced the podium, Carl caught her staring. The bride's aunt, thought Carl. There was always a bride's aunt, slightly over the hill, sometimes divorced, usually unmarried, who regularly prowled the wedding looking for a one night stand. As the song ended, she politely separated from the man, who immediately bent over a seated woman and asked her to dance. These guys were always at weddings, too. Their role in life seemed to be to dance with every woman in the place, just to make sure the wives could nag at their husbands for not dancing. "Frank Sinatra, ladies and gentlemen," Carl announced. He snapped his fingers and they went into "Chicago," with what Carl thought was the funniest line in song, about the man who danced with his wife. One of the hippies began a mocking imitation of either Carl or Frank Sinatra, it wasn't clear which. Fuck you, thought Carl as he jovially smiled. The staring woman had gotten lost in the crowd.

The set ended when the father of the bride asked for the microphone and announced the cutting of the cake. Everyone rushed to the back of the room and Carl sagged to a seat. His rum and Coke had gone watery, but it felt cool and wet going down.

"Do you know me?" a timid voice said.

He looked up at the woman in the blue suit. You wouldn't be the bride's aunt, would you? "Wait a minute, you're, ah . . ."

"You don't remember."

"You're right. When I say 'wait a minute,' you're supposed to jump in with your name and save me the embarrassment. Let's try again. Wait a minute, you're, ah . . ."

"Elizabeth," she said quickly.

It didn't register immediately. He was inventorying all the weddings and bar mitzvahs he had sung. He was thinking of all the sloppy drunks he had picked up while singing in hotel bars and cocktail lounges.

She took off her glasses and he saw those violet eyes. He felt as if he'd been slapped and knocked his glass against the table top trying to set it down.

"Look out," she said, mopping the tablecloth with a napkin, and stooping to the floor. "There." She peered up at him and he was paralyzed. "I wasn't sure it was you at first," she said. "I kept thinking Walter Carl sounded familiar, but didn't know why. How long have you used that name?"

"My third wife, believe it or not, was a numerologist," he said numbly, automatically. "She cogitated my old name and calculated it was why I wasn't getting bookings."

"That's hilarious!" said Beth, touching his knee.

"You bet. She claimed to foresee all kinds of things. She didn't foresee how lousy our marriage would be, though. Six months total!"

"I'm sorry."

A lump was growing in his throat.

"I guess I look a lot different after all these years."

He was choking up and didn't know why. "You—you'll always be the same. Jesus! It sounds like a line."

She pressed harder against his knee and raised herself with a grunt. He abruptly shot to his feet and flung his arms around her. "Beth!" he said. "Beth!" He closed his eyes to hold back the tears and breathed the strong perfume behind her ear. "What are you doing here in Baltimore? I can't believe it."

"The groom is a distant cousin. My father was the uncle of—Well, never mind. How have you been?"

He turned to Jimmy Payne. "It's Elizabeth! The last time I saw her there was a war on."

"There's a war on now," she said.

"Thirty years!"

"Hi, Elizabeth," said Payne. "He talks about the Thirty Years War like it was yesterday."

"Screw you, Payne. That's you: Payne in the ass. Did you ever see anybody with eyes like these? Like Elizabeth Taylor's."

"Yours are nicer," said Payne. "Liz hasn't aged well. I tossed her to my pal Eddie Fisher, you know. Broke her heart. Then I fixed her up with Richie, but she still pines for me."

Beth smiled. She still had those full, girlish lips. Carl lifted her hands. "Let me look at you. You haven't changed a bit!"

"Liar! I almost missed the whole thing," she said. "There was a jam-up on the highway from Philadelphia."

"Is that where you live?" She nodded. "I sang up there two months ago. At the Carlton Arms. Walter Carl at the Carlton."

"The Carolina Crooner!" she giggled, pleased to have remembered.

It was Elizabeth, he kept saying to himself. Back on this sorry earth. "Sit down," he said. "You've got to tell me everything."

"Well," she said, straightening her back like a prim guest on an interview show, "I'm married and have five children—"

"Five? You? You can't have kids!"

"Three boys and two girls."

He slapped his forehead. "It's incredible. You!"

"My husband is an auditor. He goes around to different companies and, well, audits!"

"He does well?"

She nodded.

"I knew you'd get a good one."

"No husband is perfect," she said.

"But you're happy?"

"We've stuck it out." She bit her lip.

"And you've only been married once?"

She nodded. "There's only been one man in my life."

"You know how bizarre that is?" He laughed. "For a while I thought I was going to catch Mickey Rooney. But I couldn't afford the alimony, so I quit getting married."

She giggled, then covered her nose with the tips of her fingers. "I'm sorry," she said, "That isn't really funny, you know."

"I always thought of you as the marrying kind. Isn't it funny how we used to think there were two kinds of women? Jesus, I'm so happy you're happy." He squeezed her hands. "It, like, I don't know, gives me hope. After thirty years I still wonder what happened to you."

"And I, you."

They were silent for several seconds, her hands sheltered under his.

"So catch me up," he finally said.

"There's nothing much to say. I teach Italian part-time at Bucks Community College, Temple, and some other places."

"You're a professor?"

"Strictly part-time."

"My father was a professor, did you know that?"

"Really?"

"Yeah. William and Mary."

"You're still a wonderful singer."

"Thanks, but I'm losing range. The new songs, if you can sing them at all, aren't really songs as much as screams."

"You are as good as you were in the ravine."

"You didn't lie when I knew you. I'm just a scarred and wounded old bull elephant." He patted his cummerbund. "But you're still as beautiful." Her face and body had filled out and her skin had lost its translucency, but he could still see her in this matronly shell, exactly as she was in 1943, in her saddle oxfords and long black hair. For a change, he wasn't just saying it. To him, she *was* just as beautiful.

She blushed and again they fell silent. Memories were spilling from the back of their minds. All the junk in Fibber McGee's closet was crashing to the floor. Her hand trembled and he somehow knew she was remembering the same thing as he, the discovery of Timmy Firenzi's body. Sadness weighed down on him like a heavy blanket as he remembered Natalie, then the feel of Beth's lips came back as it had on so many nights just before he fell asleep. He'd kissed her—what?—twice? and yet he'd kissed her a thousand times, each time as breathlessly as the first. Did he want her to know how many times he had relived those moments? He wasn't sure. He had elevated her to such a sublime place in his consciousness, he thought he might no longer know who the real woman had been.

"I shouldn't have been so stupid," he said cheerfully. "I should have hunted you down, married you, and chucked this nutso racket."

"You know you'd never have been happy doing anything else."

He laughed. "This is happy? But it's what I do. You are what you do." One night in Miami, just after the gig in Havana had been canceled and his second wife had left him, he had no hint where his next meal was coming from. He crawled into a bottle with a determination that before dawn, he would kill himself. The sons of suicides were always aware of it as an option and it had often come into his mind, but this time he was serious. He had come to the conclusion that his father had killed himself because they had taken away what he did. As silly as it might be to rant about Nietzsche's *Birth of Tragedy,* it was no sillier, Carl had finally accepted, than being a nickel-and-dime Frank Sinatra. You do what you do and if something takes it away from you, there's no point. You no longer exist. The gun merely made his father's living death official, as the toylike .22 lying on the patio table would make his own death official. But one drink followed another. The sun came up. The untouched gunmetal glistened with dew. Why hadn't he carried it out? Inertia?

Sometimes he told himself it was because he knew there was always some place in which he could sing, that being a star didn't matter. That happened or didn't—making music was what counted. At other times, as in this moment of touching the back of Elizabeth's hand, he was sure it had something to do with his knowing that she still existed somewhere out there. He didn't understand it exactly. It was crazy. To use the word "love" for this feeling made it seem like it was something other than it was. No word captured it. It was spiritual, maybe. No, that word had been cheapened, too. It was just that if there were angels in the universe, you had to go on living, and though he knew it was totally irrational, Elizabeth had always been his angel.

He cleared his throat. "I was going pretty good until rock-and-roll came along. I even managed to get out an album. But I keep busy."

"Our kind of music will come back, don't you think?"

There was a whoop at the back of the room as the groom smashed a huge wad of icing into the bride's mouth. "They're always saying that the Big Bands will be back, but look who *they* are! The people saying it get more decrepit every day. Like me!" Carl laughed. "Who cares, anyway? *I* still listen to it."

"And me, too. When I'm unhappy, I used to dust off my seventy-eights and listen to them in the dark. Now I do it a lot when the kids are out on dates or I'm otherwise alone. But *you* still sing the old songs. You've had a career. I always thought you'd be a star. Maybe that's why I had a terrible crush on you. I knew you'd never give up. Think of all the people who gave up."

Think of all who died, he told himself. Téd Clough. Mack Mintner. Natalie. "My chance to be a big star has long gone. I'm just a kind of bullheaded dinosaur who keeps from starving by selling appliances and used cars. I was even the dreaded encyclopedia salesman for a while. You try to keep up with the times but they run away, if they don't run you over." He flipped his hand. "Ah! Some of the new songs aren't too bad."

"You know what I think," she said cheerfully. "I think you could still succeed if you thought better of yourself."

He spread his hands. "You mean this isn't success?"

"Stop kidding, Carl," she said like a mother correcting an adolescent. "People still are interested in jazz."

"I'm not a real jazz singer, never have been." He thought of his father again. The words "jazz singer" always made him think of the reconciliation at the end of the movie, a reconciliation that never happened for him. "Even jazz has gone weird these days. After be-bop, who gets it? It's just luck, being in the right place at the right time. That's what makes a star, luck and hype."

"Don't forget talent," she said.

He didn't want to argue the point. Once, he had thought he had the future by the balls. Then, poof, Pearl Harbor. He had treaded a lot of water trying to get back to that place, but the rip tide carried him further and further away. Now it was no longer in sight. He'd tried all sorts of insane things to get noticed. There was an album, and that appearance on "Musical Merry-Go-Round" with Jack Kilty in 1948. Most people never got that far in the business. Been down so long, looks like up to me.

The last night at Swing Land came back. He winced remembering what the screwdriver had felt like as it popped the skin between Michael Papanoumou's ribs and squished into his lungs. Why hadn't they found Carl's fingerprints? Maybe they got rubbed off as the Greek spun around. Maybe nobody in the police really bothered to reconstruct how the carnage had occurred. Why waste time and money when gangsters killed gangsters? Maybe Musso's bosses located their money and subdued the investigation. The papers speculated that Natalie had killed the Greek and that the battle was a dispute over the protection rackets. There was no mention of government contracts. The story quickly died. There seemed to be larger issues in 1943 than whatever a bunch of dead crooks had been fighting over.

Carl had returned to Camp Wayne and waited for the

other shoe to drop. When he'd left Swing Land, he had stepped over or around six bodies: the Greek, Natalie, Musso, Reese (whom the Greek had strangled), and the two muscle men. He assumed someone found Reese's Chrysler abandoned near the El Dorado nightclub where Carl had dumped it for a cab, but the papers never mentioned it. Private Ed Muskin, the sentry who saw Carl leave with Reese, could have linked Carl with Reese and Carl had expected him to, with all the headlines about the "Cuyahoga nightclub massacre," but all he said one day at mess was "Good thing Mr. Reese wasn't popped while he was taking you to town!" Carl had answered "Amen, brother!" and let that sleeping dog lie. Only the dead knew he had returned to Swing Land.

He was a bloody mess when he got back to Camp Wayne. His story was that he had gone AWOL to confront Louis Bassett. No one believed it at all. No one had seen him anywhere near the music shop or Bassett's home. Murnow's conclusion was that Carl had gone AWOL to get drunk in Erie or to visit a brothel, and had then gotten into some kind of fight. He lost his stripes. Murnow had started the proceedings and there was no stopping them after that, though being a private again made no difference to Carl. The investigating lieutenant colonel had little interest in Carl's unauthorized leave, but viewed it as only a symptom of a disease called Tex Murnow. Murnow had been given a discreet discharge and retired to Arizona.

Beth studied him as if trying to read his mind. "I was always sorry I left Camp Wayne."

"I guess I kind of hurt your feelings. Or at least I've flattered myself that I did."

"I learned a lot in the SPARs, though. I never really was sorry about that, but I always felt like I had run away."

"I've never heard the women's Coast Guard likened to the French Foreign Legion."

"I think it wasn't just you, though. Timmy and the clarinet player—"

"Oswald Ülsmann."

"And then Ansel and I finding Louis Bassett hanging from the transom was just too much. There's so much death in wartime, but these seemed so senseless. The whole camp was tainted with it."

"I'm glad Bassett left a note," said Carl. "At least we can be sure about the boy."

"When I saw him hanging there, his tongue bulging out—" she shivered. "I cried, Carl. I felt sorry for him."

"You have a good heart. Too good. You always did."

"Don't get me wrong," she added. "I hated him. I still hate him. Now that I have children if I knew somebody like him I think I could pull the trigger. He was pathetic and I felt sorry for him, but there wasn't anything he didn't deserve."

"No, I guess not. The guys who killed Oswald deserved the same."

"But they never got it, did they?"

"Not that I ever heard," said Carl. "It kind of makes you feel like you've misplaced something. Like you can't find the car keys to the universe." Nothing had worked out in a very satisfying way. The last time he had seen Elizabeth she testified at the trial of Helmut Ansbach for murdering Ude Wieschensohn with the stolen bayonet. She had looked even more beautiful in her Coast Guard uniform than she had at Camp Wayne. After the verdict Carl had promised to write, then rushed off to meet a train. Despite contradictory testimony, Ansbach was sentenced to hang, probably because Oswald's second musician's wing was found in his locker. The theory was that Ansbach had killed Ude because he knew that Ansbach had killed Oswald. It was only a theory, though, and a thin one. Whoever killed Oswald hadn't acted alone. One columnist argued that if Ansbach hadn't been so obviously and obnoxiously a Nazi who knew more than he was saying, he would never have been convicted. The word on Dachau and Buchenwald had gotten out and Ansbach could never have been acquitted, regardless of the lack of evidence. Later, when it was clear Ansbach would never reveal who was in the conspiracy with him, President Truman, on the advice of General Marshall, commuted his sentence during the two days between Hiroshima and Nagasaki. He served less than a decade of his life sentence. No one had ever been certain whether he had wielded the bayonet, though most people thought he had done it on orders of Albert Dorn, along with the beating of Oswald. Once the war was over, most people wanted to forget about it. There were new enemies in the world and the Nazis had been their enemies, too. The immense secret life of the prisoners pretty much remained secret. "Loose threads," said Carl. "Valdez said we should have hanged them all and let God sort it out. As you get older you either accept loose threads or you go nuts."

"But you lose something if you think somebody gets away with it," she said. "I believe in God, do you?"

"I'd like to. Hell, anyway. One separate devil for each guy who took a hit at Oswald, and one for each guy who knew something about it and wouldn't talk. That's a lot of devils. I hope, with every ounce of my crummy soul, they wake up every night of their miserable existences in a cold sweat and die in incredible pain." He tilted his head to one side. "But, unfortunately, I don't really believe it."

"You're a cynic, Carl Walthers."

"Hey! I'm a realist!" They laughed and he squeezed her hands again.

She turned thoughtful again. "I just had to get away. It was hard living with my pop after Mr. Musso was killed, too. So much death." There was a tone of apology in her voice which he didn't understand. He had distanced himself from her, not vice versa.

"Ernie Mussolini!" said Carl. "I haven't thought of him for years. I went to the movies once with Lane, my first wife. The picture was *A Touch of Evil,* and when Orson Welles waddles up on the screen, I started laughing. I thought maybe Welles had somehow known Musso and decided to imitate him. Then there was Charlton Heston in that Mexican makeup— I just couldn't stop laughing and the manager threw me out of the theater. Lane was really mad." Carl shook his head. "Whew!"

"He was good to my pop. Maybe he was mixed up in some things, but I light a candle for him every time I go to mass. We were related by marriage, you know."

"I didn't remember that."

"Through the Fastolis. Actually, the bride is related, too."

Carl nodded. They were talking but didn't seem to be saying anything. Was it always this way when meeting someone you haven't seen for years? He had always thought it would be different with her.

"Isn't it amazing how resilient we are when we are young?" she asked. "Only afterwards do I understand how all that stuff affected me. As it happened, I didn't know how dark a time it was for me or why I really all of a sudden talked to the recruiters for the SPARs and the WACs and the WAVEs."

"The place wasn't the same without you."

"And you! You always wanted out, should have been out, and then you volunteer!"

"Dumb move," he said. After he was busted to private, he had transferred to a regiment training for the invasion of mainland Japan. Maybe he was trying to make up for never really doing anything for the war. He never answered her letters. He had kept them for fifteen years, then somehow lost them at the confusing time of his second divorce. "I've never complained about the atom bomb," he said. "It saved my butt. Pardon my French."

At the back of the room, the groom was slowly peeling the garter from his new wife. He said something and the audience roared.

"One of the nice things about being young is that you can run away," she said. "When you have kids . . . ."

"Some people run away anyway," he said, thinking of himself.

"To tell the truth, I'm in a kind of dark spot now."

"Is that why your husband isn't here?"

She nodded, biting her lower lip. "He's met his Beatrice Portinari. *Nel mezzo del cammin di nostra vita, Mi ritrouvai per una selva oscura.*"

"Dante?"

"You learned Italian?"

"I recognized Beatrice from a quiz show."

"It means, 'In the middle of my life, I found myself in a dark wood.' That's me these days."

"I wondered why you showed up here in the dark woods." He leaned forward and touched both of her forearms. "But since you arrived, its getting a little lighter. I think you've always been my Beatrice."

She smiled at him, as if she thought he was just being kind. She was still innocent in her way, he thought.

The bride and groom left the reception on their way to what they thought was a new life. People renewed their assault on the bar. Jimmy Payne picked up his guitar. "Tell me about it later, okay? We can share intelligence about the dark woods. Promise me you won't leave," Carl demanded.

"I just got here."

"Afterwards, we'll talk all night, okay?"

She thought for a moment, eyes lowered shyly. Artemis, chaste goddess of the moon. "You're so slick, Carl Walthers, I don't know if I could trust you."

"You're the only person, ever, who could trust me. You make me good in spite of myself." He spread his palms. "Hey, I said talk. Why would I want to mess up a perfect relationship?"

She smiled wanly and bit her lower lip. "I'd like that. We'll get to know each other again."

He winked at her and thought, I've always known you.

"We'll talk about now. If we sit around doing 'those were the days' I'll cry."

"You betcha," he said. He stepped up to the mike.

"We've got three requests," said Payne, handing him a card.

"Forget them," said Carl. "Bill Haley and Elvis Presley and the Who, What, When, and Where can blow themselves." He flicked the card at the audience. It fluttered to the dance floor.

"First," he said, "'And the Angels Sing.'"

Payne looked at the drummer; Leon looked at Payne. "Are you drunk again, Walter?"

"What if I am? It's the Walter Carl Trio, isn't it? Well?" They shrugged and began. Carl looked straight at Elizabeth and raised his mike. He sang it slowly, elegantly. His voice was as fluid as it had ever been. She blushed and then trickles of tears moved down her cheeks. He closed his eyes to keep from choking up.

It was suddenly 1941. The hippies didn't exist. The bride and groom were not yet born. The "War to End All Wars" had lived up to its name and Korea and Vietnam were obscure blobs on maps. Jimmy Payne and his guitar were gone.

Buzz Bixby was conducting and Mack Mintner was waiting for his solo when Carl finished his first verse. Carl would do the silky slide and Mack would groove right in. He had a lot of songs he had been waiting to sing for Elizabeth. For a while, he would be the Carolina Crooner. Maybe he could be a star, just for her. For a while, he would be young and unscarred, there would be angels in the universe, and the world would still have hope.